SLA`

M000313199

THE PROMISE

During the dark days of the American Civil War
with death and danger ever-present,
'the promise' might be all people had to cling to.

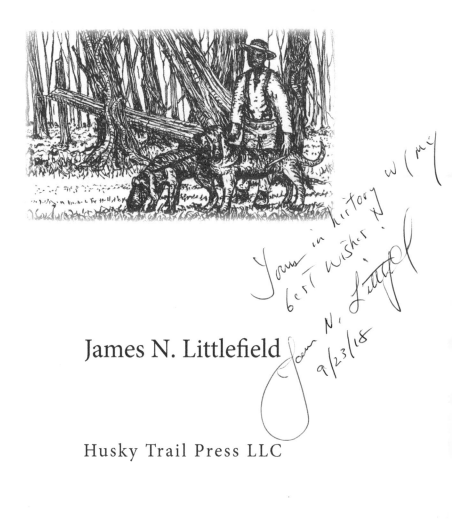

James N. Littlefield

Yours in history w/ (my best wishes!
James N. Littlefield
9/23/18

Husky Trail Press LLC

ISBN 978-1-935258-49-0

Illustrations by Stephen Marks-Hamilton
Edited by Marcus M. Worthington
Cover Design & Illustration by Gabriella Geida

Husky Trail Press LLC
7 Hurlbutt Road, #I
Gales Ferry, CT 06335
www.HuskyTrailPress.com
info@huskytrailpress.com

DEDICATION

This book is dedicated to our late bloodhound, "Molly." It was research into her historic pedigree that initiated the story of Coswell and Cynthia Tims. The empty leather tracking harness that still hangs by our front door reminds us that the journey she started must be completed without her.

"Miss Molly" (b.2004- d.2014)

"Iffen I was ever to find myself up yonder, standin' before them pearly gates and my ol' hound dog was the first to come runnin my way with tail all a-waggin' in joyful greetin', I would think no less of that exalted institution."

Coswell Tims echoing the sentiments of southern humorist, Bill Arp

CONTENTS

PART III Home Again

INTRODUCTION

August 12, 2014
Milledgeville, Georgia

As Raymond Richards walked slowly across the open field he peered intently into the small computer screen before him. That screen would hopefully provide the clues he sought...the information the City of Milledgeville had hired him to find. The Memory Hill Cemetery Association and the city government were both tired of the complaints and the often emotional outbursts of plot owners attempting to bury their loved ones, only to find that space occupied by an earlier, unidentified party. Between the lawsuits and the finger-pointing, folks had simply had enough. Mr. Richards and his ground penetrating radar were expensive, but everyone knew something needed to be done.

The machine was a curious affair, vaguely resembling a lawn mower or maybe even more accurately, a three-wheeled golf cart. As Richards pushed this contraption slowly over the relatively flat ground, the sensing pan housed at the bottom and squeezed between the machine's three wheels, barely skimmed the ground as it sent off information to the screen above. To the uninitiated eye it just looked like a series of wavy lines, but to a man with Richard's experience it told the story of what lay hidden beneath the grass. Ray Richards was very intent, carefully studying those lines and was more than likely oblivious to the sizable crowd that had gathered around, content to observe this early morning activity in the normally quiet confines of Memory Hill.

"Ahhh," Mr. Richards suddenly announced, more to himself than anyone else. "We have something here!" Several bystanders approached the vehicle which had now come to a complete stop near a somewhat isolated tombstone from the distant past.

"What have you found, Mr. Richards?" Barbara Bumgardner asked as she stepped from the crowd to engage the now excited researcher. Barbara Bumgardner was a relative newcomer to the Cemetery Association, but had really sunk her teeth into this long-standing problem of unknown bodies turning up in awkward places on cemetery grounds.

"We have a body, I am sure of it," Richards replied. "See the way these lines differ from those around them? Definitely a void and more than likely what is left of a coffin. I wouldn't be surprised if there were some human remains still there as well. But you wouldn't expect them to be so close

to this tombstone here, now would you?" Richards asked, almost rhetorically. "Why they are practically touching, for crying out loud," he added,
lowering his voice somewhat as he continued to gaze into the screen before
him.

"I am told this plot has always presented a puzzle of sorts," Mrs.
Bumgardner responded as both heads, seemingly on cue, refocused their
attention from the GPR screen to an old, somewhat pitted tombstone.
Somehow that white sandstone slab had managed to maintain an erect and
dignified posture despite both time and elements. It was unadorned with a
simple, short declaration carved into its soft center.

COSWELL ELIAS TIMS
1805-1873

"Now Mr. Tims' mother and father are buried over there," the middle-
aged woman offered, pointing to several other graves that lay off in the shade
of a large Magnolia tree which graced one of many well-manicured pathways
that wound their way through the scenic old burial ground. "I have learned
his brother, Jesse and Jesse's wife are buried there too, right next to the
mother and father and yet this gentleman is seemingly far off by himself. We
have our suspicions…quite strange, people have always thought."

"Get the shovels, boys," let's see what we've got here," interjected the
commanding voice of Milledgeville mayor John Chaney. Often gruff and
given to argumentation, this portly, middle-aged man had, for the longest
time, been reluctant to spend city funds on any investigation of this sort.
However, the unrelenting pressure from many quarters to do so finally
convinced him there was no longer any way to dodge the issue. Various
members of the Cemetery Association, Barbara Bumgardner included, had
been frequent visitors to his office and the letter writing in the local papers
had become more and more intense. Proponents for an investigation had
grown markedly and the wily, long-time politician accurately assessed that
the tide had definitely turned against him.

"I believe it is against state law to exhume a body without an archaeologist present," Bob Bumgardner shouted from the crowd, his knowledge
of such things having improved markedly since his wife's interest in the
matter. "Nonsense," was Chaney's curt reply. "This is what you folks
wanted and this is what you are gonna get and the less cost to the city the
better, I figure. Now let's get crackin' boys and put your backs into it."

Two black city workers complied with the boss man's demands and
began digging into the red clay soil. After a short time they were rewarded

with what remained of a crude wooden grave box. "O.K, pull that damn thing out of there," the mayor ordered. Mr. Bumgardner again registered a protest, but it fell upon deaf ears. "Those archaeology people will be here later in the afternoon to tell us what we need to know. Keep going, Mr. Richards, we want to make sure the city gets all they can for their money," he added. The machine sprang to life once more in its slow but steady quest for yet other hidden surprises that might lie buried and unrecorded in this traditionally white section of the city's famed forty acre burial ground.

Activity continued throughout the day and two archaeologists from Atlanta did show up as expected later in the afternoon. They dutifully began to examine what remained of a total of three unmarked coffins Richards had discovered and were subsequently unearthed by town crews. Many of the curiosity-seekers began to leave with the intense heat of the day, but several prominent members of the Cemetery Association elected to stay on.

Not surprisingly, Eugena McBride, Edie Crandall and Mattie Collins, dedicated friends and patrons of the cemetery, made the decision to remain and were engaged in animated conversation with Barbara and husband, Robert Bumgardner, specifically regarding the first of the three coffins exhumed that morning. The two archaeologists had spoken very little as they had examined that coffin and its contents, occasionally taking pictures and jotting down notes in their journals. After a while one of the researches paused momentarily to wipe the sweat from her forehead which gave Mrs. Bumgardner an opportunity to inquire into their findings.

"One thing we can tell you for sure, Ma'am. This is definitely the body of a woman," the older of the two female archaeologists announced as both investigators rose from their knees to put the partially decayed lid back in place. "About 5'4" tall, I would speculate. Had some years on her…most likely died of natural causes, no signs of anything to suggest otherwise. A wedding ring but no other jewelry or fancy trappings…poor folks more than likely. One thing I can say and I think my associate here would concur, this woman was definitely buried sometime AFTER this particular tombstone was put in place," she offered, as she wiped her hands quickly on her shirt before gently placing one hand on the white tombstone of Coswell Tims. "Hard to believe this was any random burial though, being so close and all. Very curious…yes, very curious, indeed," the archaeologist concluded.

The local newspaper, "The Union Recorder," ran a rather lengthy story complete with pictures of the "goin's-on" in Memory Hill. Actually, the whole town took much more than a passing interest in the activities there…some for legal reasons, some political or historic, some just out of plain curiosity. Rosa Billings, however, had her own reasons for following the story so closely.

Rosa Billings had never married, but always had a strong sense of family. Pictures on the wall of her modest one-story home on the south side of town attested to the high regard she held for those family members who had passed, as well as long dead heroes she had chosen to single out and recognize. Martin Luther King Jr.'s picture occupied a prominent place as did an image of a local Milledgeville minister from the 19th century by the name of Wilkes Flagg. Formerly a slave to Dr. Tomlinson Fort, the handsome and talented Wilkes earned both his freedom and the respect of the entire population of the City of Milledgeville during his lifetime.

Rosa caught herself glancing up at the pictures on the wall after finishing the latest article in the newspaper about the Memory Hill escapades. Returning her attention to the paper once more, she noted the highlighted section of the investigation and the speculation surrounding the mystery of the first coffin she had made with the same pen used earlier to complete the crossword puzzle she did each day with such great care and pride. Rosa Billings was conflicted, unsure of her next move. She placed the newspaper on the floor next to her chair and lit a cigarette. "Maybe I should call someone," she caught herself saying out loud. "I know who that woman was!"

Barbara and Bob Bumgardner found themselves carrying on substantial correspondence with other locals in the wake of the discovery of numerous "unauthorized" bodies that had found their way into the light once more; courtesy of Ray Richards and his amazing ground penetrating machine. All of them would most likely remain unnamed and unclaimed, they thought, soon to be reburied in a less-coveted area of the grave yard. Both knew that would then allow well-paying or well-connected families to use the now cleared and highly prized burial space for the deposit of any newly deceased loved ones. Problem solved, that is, unless one of the fifteen bodies uncovered by Mr. Richards over the past week had a specific name or story attached to it, or could be proved to have been legitimately buried there.

The phone rang in the Bumgardner home and Barbara stopped working on the computer long enough to answer it. The name on Caller ID did not seem familiar, but she decided to take a chance and answer it anyway. "Good morning, you have reached the Bumgardner's," she answered. "What can we do for you?"

There was a short pause, maybe just long enough for Rosa Billings to collect her thoughts and expel the smoke inhaled from her recently lit cigarette. "Mrs. Bumgardner?" Another short pause followed. "Ma'am... my name is Rosa Billings. I have often read your name in the paper in regards to the Memory Hill Cemetery. I know you folks are trying to clear up that mess over there with those old bodies that seem to always keep popping up. I'd like to talk to you about one of them in particular... actually; the one that turned up on the first day... you remember, the one they said was a woman?"

Barbara Bumgardner barely noticed that she had left home with neither hat nor raincoat to counter the slight chill and the substantial drizzle the morning had to offer. Getting into her car, she also became aware that she had absent-mindedly failed to turn off the computer in her haste to meet with the recent caller. Both she and her husband had developed a real attach-ment to that cemetery and its history since they moved into town a few years earlier and their newfound passion would be served even if it was now at a moment's notice. Rosa Billings' revelation that the caller was in possession of an old diary that she felt would shed light on one of the recently displaced residents of Memory Hill caused this cemeterian to drive a little faster than normal through the streets of Georgia's antebellum capital.

Barbara took very little note of the house or the neighborhood as she pulled into a dirt driveway in the black section of town. Knocking at the door, she was greeted with an inviting smile from a warm and engaging elderly woman and soon saw with her own eyes the document Ms. Billings had alluded to over the phone. After exchanging a few pleasantries, Barbara complied with her host's request to read out-loud the first entry. It was dated July 5, 1883.

"I takes pen in hand so's not to disremember that which might soon be forgot. My name be Penia Fitzsimons Tims, proud wife of Sanford Tims and truth to tell, my life ain't been no bed of roses, but with the Good Lord's help and a fair amount of doin, it has proved out to be this side of tolerable."

"Penia Fitzsimons Tims or "Little Peney," as she was called, was my great-grandmother," Rosa related. "She lived during slavery time and had a most interesting life. You are welcome to read the entire diary, but I think what you may be more interested in is what I have marked here closer towards the end."

The elderly woman's hands, although somewhat twisted at the knuckles, regained the manuscript and began methodically skimming through the well-worn pages as she continued to speak.

"My great-grandmother had a sister by the name of Cynthia. She was older and by all accounts an extremely striking and handsome woman. She was married to the love of her life, a man by the name of Coswell Elias Tims who just happens to currently reside under that tombstone that is sorta off by itself in the cemetery, you know, the one that has caused such a recent

commotion. From what Great-Gramma Peney says in her diary, the two of them were very much in love despite their color difference... and the fact that he was a slave catcher of all things. Why, my goodness, a less likely couple would you ever expect to see. Like my great-grandmother, her sister was a quadroon or 'high yeller,' as they used to say in the old days, but I guess they were able to keep quiet on the matter and lived happily here in Milledgeville right under the noses of white townsfolk for many years. My great-grand-father, Sanford Tims, he was their slave, although that was really in name only. When he got to marrying my great-grandma, they all lived together till after the war when that little secret of theirs finally leaked out and the Ku Klux paid them a little visit one night. It was at that very time that Mr. Coswell Tims lost his life trying to defend all that he had come to love in this world. The house was burned to the ground and Cynthia, Sanford and Great-Gramma Peney had to remove themselves to the south side of town where many black folks lived after freedom come. After all, we weren't about to be welcomed with open arms into most white neighborhoods. Guess the family went through some hard times after that."

Rosa finally stopped shuffling through the pages, presenting the diary to Barb Bumgardner once more for examination. "This entry is a number of years after the slavecatcher had passed," she added.

Barbara put her glasses back on and resumed reading the somewhat faded, but still legible manuscript as Rosa Billings lit another cigarette.

"My sister always said she wanted to be buried right next to that ol slave catcher and it seemed like there weren't nary a time when we'd go off to town in the wagon for supplies and gone by that graveyard when she didn't start in frettin and fussin bout ol Coswell lyin over there all by his lonesome. It broke her heart, it did. Again and again Cynthia made Sanford and me promise that when she passed on we would bury her right next to her man, maybe even touchin if such a thing was possible. With my sister's death early this mornin, it will soon be time to deliver on that promise."

"Now look at his short entry here," Ms. Billings said as she pointed to a spot further down on that same page. Mrs. Bumgardner continued reading.

"We buried my sister, Cynthia, today in Memory Hill. A sad day for us all but we made sure her fondest wish was honored. May both of em now rest in peace."

"What do you think, Mrs. Bumgardner?" Rosa Billings interjected.

"I think there's much more here than anyone presently knows," Mrs. Bumgardner replied as she closed the diary and, cradling it tightly in her arms, began to stare quietly out of Rosa Billings' large picture window.

"Oh...one other thing," Ms. Billings interrupted. I should also tell you this fella, Coswell Tims also kept a journal of sorts during much of his lifetime and that very thing came to light back in 2008, I think it was, when an old building down on South Liberty Street was being torn down. A fella from up north took the manuscript and had it published in a book called "The Slave Catcher's Woman." Tells all about how Coswell and Cynthia hooked up and how they come to live here. Many of the same folks Great Gramma Peney talks about in this diary are in that book as well. You might want to get yourself a copy before you wrestle with what I just passed your way."

"I will, Ms. Billings. I surely will," Barbara Bumgardner replied as she gently patted the old woman's arm before turning to leave. She went without saying another word, completely lost in her thoughts.

PART I

Home Ground

"It ain't empires, or politics, or principalities, or nations that are the most important in this here life. It's the simple family fireside, that's what it is."

Bill Arp

Chapter 1

MASTERS OF HOUNDS

Bob and Barbara Bumgardner were admittedly "hooked" on the recently evolving story of Coswell and Cynthia Tims, much, but not all, found in the book suggested by Ms. Billings. But perhaps even a greater acquisition was a complete copy of the original Tims' manuscript which they were able to secure locally from the Mary Vinson Library. It was more far-reaching and continued on for a number of years after the original book had concluded.

It seemed as if that was all the two of them talked about lately. Whenever Bob returned home from his part-time job at nearby Robins Air Force base, the first topic of conversation when he walked through the door was either about slavecatcher, Coswell Tims, or his woman, Cynthia, or Sanford, their slave, the hound dogs, or maybe even the cruel slave master, James Walker, whose evil presence shadowed many of the pages. Maybe it was because the story actually happened in the same place the two of them had stumbled upon after Bob's retirement from active duty in the Air Force, or maybe it was because the Tims family in the book was multi-racial as they were, or maybe it was simply because the Bumgardner's were now at a point in their lives where they could devote more time to understanding life and that always seemed to include a healthy dose of historic investigation. Whatever the reason or reasons, both were committed to seeing this story through to the final chapter.

"Bob," his wife asked impatiently as they sat quietly together on the sofa of their small apartment. "Aren't you almost done with that Coswell Tims book? I finished it days ago."

"Just finished the part about Walker's demise, Darling. I'm glad that s.o.b. got what he richly deserved. Now Coswell and his dog are headed back home with high hopes that his wife has not been permanently blinded."

"Well, I hate to play the part of spoiler here, but I'm going to tell you it all ends well. What is a little unnerving about the book is that it ends just before the Civil War begins. There seems to be an undercurrent of uneasiness about their vulnerable position. Read that to me at the end, Bob, where Coswell is speaking…yes that's it right there," she said as she pointed out the paragraph in question.

Bob began, doing his level best to offer a little bit of a southern accent neither had adequately acquired, but both felt the need to try out from time to time. "I reckon life had seen fit to grant us a little reprieve and we was all startin to nestle in once more, glad after what we had been through to still be alive and fortunate nough to be back together in the relative comforts of our home. Despite recent injuries that had surely left their mark, we was all more than a might grateful for the many blessins that had come our way. There was no doubt many dangers still lurked bout Briarwood what with the constant worry over our little secret leakin out and the changin political climate that saw the risin threat of civil war, but we hoped with Walker's death to have maybe gained some much needed space to take in a welcome breath or two."

"Oh, Bob, I'm so anxious to get started with the rest of the story that's found in this manuscript. What is really terrific about it is that it continues on through the war years so you can see how everything worked out or didn't. Now this is just where we need to start," she said, with a rising sense of urgency in her voice as she drew attention to a place she had marked in the text. "Let's begin this journey together, right now…just you and me. What do you say?"

Needing no further encouragement, Bob Bumgardner closed the unfinished book and laid it down on the end table with one page left unread. Husband and wife huddled together over the old manuscript which continued a story of long ago. That manuscript lay comfortably close to the diary recently acquired from Rosa Billings, almost as if their reunion had been preordained. Both researchers knew that together those two documents *could offer much to the story of Coswell and Cynthia Tims during a most contentious time in America's past. Having read the book about the slave catcher's experiences, the first entry in the larger manuscript caught the Bumgardner's somewhat by surprise.*

COSWELL TIM'S DIARY RESUMES

Entry: October 23, 1860

It was murder, that's what it was. It was foul and it was vicious. Blood was everywhere to be found. That sacred wonderment of human life had carelessly and recklessly been splattered about the room and covered the better part of the stone basement floor. I was alone at the time with no eyes but my own to bear witness. My stomach began to twist some, but I was powerless to turn away and continued to stare mindlessly at what was left of the bloodied human remains that lay at my feet. I suspected it to be the body of a single individual, but it was hard to tell as it lay in so many pieces, all carved up for the occasion. I reckon the butcher who done this felt he weren't finished after all the cuttin, as he had then begun to carefully collect and pile the pieces one atop the other in a neat stack, with the larger ones at the bottom and the smaller ones closer to the top. The victim's much damaged skull had been chosen to crown his efforts. I got it in my mind that the perpetrator must have wanted any and all who might come by later on to know that he took great pride in his work. It was easy to see where the larger segments of the victim's body had been dragged back to the pile for collection as they had left a bloodied trail on the floor. I never saw the like of such a thing in all my born days.

I stood there for I don't know how long, but all did not remain quiet and serene. Strange things began to happen. Items in the room just sort of began to slowly move about for no reason t'all. Furniture began to slide back in place; objects that had fallen to the floor in all the ruckus somehow resumed their former places of occupancy. Even the grisly pile before me started to reassemble, little by little, until the once dead and disfigured victim was able to rise up and stand once more. He would slowly pass me by, sayin nary a word as he withdrew from the kitchen and returned to the hallway where I somehow knew he had earlier come. He mindlessly closed the door behind hisself as he went, but not before I took careful notice of the nice clean white uniform he was sportin. I knew Doc Green always insisted his attendants dress appropriately if they were to work here at the asylum, but I would have to say this attendant did not look so spotless and tidy just minutes before.

All the blood on the floor had somehow strangely disappeared and everythin in the room now seemed back to the way it must have been before this calamity had ever taken place. I commenced to survey the whole of it one last time to see if all was now in proper order, but as I did, I got the strangest feelin that even though the attendant was gone from the room, I was not the only one who remained inside. My eyes went here and then over to there, until a partially visible form to the right of me caught my eye. Upon further review I determined it to be the figure of a man, a man who had taken to crouchin next to a large cabinet I could see contained many of the institution's dishes and pans. He was dressed in a hospital gown of sorts, had a shiny object in one hand and part of a broken chain fastened round one of his ankles. As he crept a little further into his hidey-place, the ankle chain made a slight clinkin sound as it dragged along the floor. I could sense the attendant out in the hallway took notice of that and started to turn back to investigate. I hoped he would change his mind before it was too late. Did he know what waited for him inside?

I wanted to warn the poor fella, but found myself struck dumb with the puckerin string in my throat pulled so tight I could not utter a single sound. "Don't open that door!" I wanted to shout, but those words only existed in my mind. I saw the doorknob turn and heard the door creak open. "Who's in here?" the asylum attendant asked.

I guess that's when I come to realize that I had me a front row seat to a grisly murder that was about to be played out yet again and I didn't have to wait very long for the next performance to begin.

A heavy meat ax, sharp and large, gleamed in the night lamp light and began to strike out repeatedly at the startled and hapless attendant. I heard him gasp for breath as the naked arm that held that wicked thing rose up and then fell, time and time again, As it did, it made the most sickenin sound as it come in contact with human flesh. I knew that sound and properly recollected it from my past. Years ago when me and Jesse was just little ankle-biters, we'd steal into ol' man O'Donnell's pumpkin patch on occasion and kick in his rotten pumpkins with our bare feet. That was that same wet, thumpin sound I just heard, for sure.

It must have been that very sound that caused me to wake with a start. That's when the bedcovers flew to the floor, freein me from this nightmare. I found myself all up in a sweat of perspiration and started to shake slightly with the cool night air. Cynthia lay quietly beside me and I was surprised she did not wake up as that woman is generally the noticer of even the smallest of things. But for some reason that night she slept on soundly despite all the commotion. I was wide awake and knew there would be no sleep for me the rest of the night. That was not necessarily a bad thing as it would give me some time to straighten certain things out in my head.

When you boil it all down, I guess I got Jesse to blame for this nighttime fantasy. After all, it was him who come by early that evenin with the latest news of an escape down at the Milledgeville Lunatic Asylum. That's how all that crazy stuff got into my head to begin with. I began to review yesterday with that in mind.

Early on there really weren't nothin unusual about it, in fact, it was a day like most days, that is, til Jesse dropped by after supper and started in with the latest news. Cynthia, she'd been workin in the house and Sanford had spent the better part of the day out tendin the garden. As for me, I was down by the small creek that runs through our property (we got ourselves twenty acres all tole up) and seein to the stick fence the three of us built sometime back that would keep the neighbors' dogs from killin our sheep. We don't have many, but that animal is quite helpless less they have friends in high places that can do for em. I swear if I see a dog anywhere near that pen in the days to come, I'll shoot the damn thing and if Lem Purdy's dogs kill one more of our little flock, I figure I may just shoot him as well.

Jesse's arrival weren't expected, but livin just a mile shy of our place and bein as though he is my business partner and all, we do spend a great deal of time in each other's company and frequent visits were not unusual. Now my brother lives alone as his wife Becky died of the pox many years back and even though he's never gotten over that loss, the excitement of the trail does give him other things to think on. I admit to lovin my brother with all that's in me as he has demonstrated time and time again that he always had my backside and the family's best interests at heart. Over the years Cynthia and Sanford have come to trust in the man as well. He could be a little cranky at times and maybe a bit too direct to suit certain folks' taste, but he has proved hisself to be a good man and has earned the respect of many over our neighbors and friends and that's bout as good as it gets.

With no knock at the door expected or supplied, Brother Jesse, last night strolled right into the middle of the room, appearin before us like some kind of phantom. The three of us was just gettin ourselves up from the table and young Sanford got hisself quite a start with Jesse's sudden arrival. Cynthia was quick to offer some leftover vittles and I offered him a welcome pat on the back.

"Just ate," was Jesse's reply, "but I do have some news we can all chew on a bit. Just talked to Doc Green down at the madhouse and, oh my, is that man all fired up. Seems as though one of them luniacks of his took to his heels and needs findin right quick. Now you know how the doc is with them folks...why, he cares for em like they was real people, like they was really worth somethin. He described this one, however, as 'very dangerous,' armed with a heavy meat clever and said we would be gettin paid whether we brought him back alive or wrapped around the backside of our horse. Now he never says that as a general rule, so I'm figurin this one is not cut from the usual cloth. He ain't no mindless individual like most of em who wander off the property cause they don't have the brains God give a goose. The doc said the man killed one of his best attendants fore he ran and left quite a mess in the process. Doc Green says you and me need to get out on the trail straightaway fore others outside the institution suffer a similar fate. What do you think about all that, Coswell?"

I knew Cynthia had heard every word Jesse said as she had them ears of hers pitched in just right for the occasion. Jesse even told me some of the more gory details in a lowered voice so's she might be spared the worst of it, but I swear that woman of mine could hear a leaf drop on a bale of cotton. The two of us did agree to leave at first light rather than attempt any dark night chase, even though it certainly made no nevermind to our fetchhounds. Such a chase could prove dangerous to a handler with a crazy fugitive crouched somewhere in the darkness fixin to strike out with a sharp metal object.

No sooner had Jesse's horse slipped off into the night, when Cynthia quick turned her back to me and stormed off in the opposite direction. Our home soon took on the look and feel of a morgue, or maybe it would be more fair to say one of them monasteries where residents had swore themselves to personal vows of silence.

Little changed with the arrival of the new day as Cynthia continued on with her quiet ways, busyin herself up with meaningless tasks at hand. But I took a vow of my own to end all this nonsense and stole up behind the woman, quiet as a greased wagon runnin in sand. I figured to spring my little trap by wrappin both my arms round her in a big-ol friendly bear hug and maybe squeezin her tight in a playful sort of manner. But darn my bristles, when I begin to put that plan of mine into motion, why, she spun out of my grasp quick as a cat, with both hands reachin out in the direction of my throat! The fact that she done that and the speed at which it was done took me completely by surprise, but her mood soon softened and those claws of hers did begin to retract. Cynthia's warm hands on my face slowly took to strokin at my chin as our eyes met. I knew there was some conversation to be had just around the corner.

I took Cynthia's small hands in my own, noticin that despite some roughness round the edges that hard work and time had supplied, they was still most as beautiful in shape and color as they was when I first come to hold em in that small upstairs bedroom down in New Orleans. Later, when I had the opportunity to further improve on the situation by marryin this same woman, I was able to add a ring to one of her beautiful fingers. I found myself twirlin that same gold band round and round for all it was worth, maybe stallin for time I was, as I thought bout what I might say that could ease her troubled mind.

"Now Darlin," I began in as confident a manner as I could muster. "It's been some ten years or so since I put this ring on this pretty finger of yours and you know I love you and would never tell you a boldfaced lie. I know how worried you are bout this here trackin job, but I ain't gonna let nothin happen to this husband of yours and that's a fact. I believe our marriage contract calls for both you and me to sign on for the duration and ain't it also a fact that both our rings say "FOREVER" on em? Now that's a sizable slice of time, don't you think?" (I guess I do need to say that us both havin gold weddin bands was Cynthia's idea, as I don't believe I know any other fella that has such a thing. I don't wear mine as a general rule, but I do respect what it means to my wife and count it as one of my most prized possessions. Someday when I am dead and buried, I hope that ring finds its way back to one of my fingers, to rest there for all eternity.)

Her blue-green eyes sparkled with concern. "But what if you don't come back?" were the first words from out of her mouth. "You know there ain't no guarantees in this life. I don't want your head to swell none, but I figure things wouldn't be worth much without Coswell Tims' boots muddyin up my floor on a daily basis. This trackin business is a fool's errand for sure and is gonna get you killed fore all's said and done. I've said it many times before and I'll say it to you once again…you and your brother need to think bout another line of work."

"Now Cynthia, we've had this here conversation so many times, more times than you and I have fingers and toes to count on, but you know how successful this family trackin business has been over the years. Why it puts food on our table, don't it? It's legal and necessary to boot. Folks round here do have a right to want all to be quiet and serene so's they can go on bout their business, don't they? Now I know this new job ain't the same as most, but frettin bout things that ain't yet happened is a real fool's errand for sure and don't profit anyone that I can see. Most of the stuff that people worry about don't never come to pass anyway," I concluded.

"Oh Coswell, it's that place down there, don't you see? It's the Devil's own mess of broth, that's what it is. We both can hear the awful screams and terrifyin sounds that come from that place, specially when the moon's full-up and the nights are still. Why it makes the flesh on a body like to crawl. Every one of em is crazy as a loon and that's why they're all kept under tight lock and key. And now one of the worst of em is out on the loose and armed with a meat ax in his hand, no less. Lordy, Lordy!"

"Darlin, I'll swear an oath right here and now that me and Jesse will go cautious if that makes you feel any better. I don't take to that place any more than you do, but we have to think this here is just like any other trackin job. What kind of reputation would my brother and me have if we told folks there was some people we was afraid to track? You know our bloodhounds are the best there is, they'll find that fella, sweetheart, you mark my words, and the Tims' boys stand to make a handsome profit for the effort, too. Don't you worry. We'll be fine. This here is just the cost of doin business," I concluded, puttin an arm round her shoulders only to let it glide gently down her back till it come to rest at her waist where I could finally get a good purchase and draw this woman in close.

Cynthia relented, or at least for the moment, droppin her head slightly with my last few words. She looked up at me again with a questionin stare, but I smiled back, recognizin her for the fine woman she truly was, a woman with more than a little sand in her gizzard and more pluck than was common, male or female. Her life had certainly been no bed of roses, but the fact that she stood tall on the perpendicular after all was said and done, give clear evidence of a woman whose inside beauty was more than a match for what was generously offered on the outside for all to take notice and admire. I felt the need to say one last time as a further guarantee that "even if it was to somehow rain red-hot railroad spikes and boilin tar," I would find a way to return to her side. A slight smile come to her beautiful face with that somewhat exaggerated statement and I kissed both her hands quick-like, pausin one last time to spin that gold band she wore so proudly on her left. Without another word, I turned away and headed off to the barn to see if our negro, Sanford, had readied up the hounds. I knew Jesse would be along straightaway and we would soon get on with the task at hand, the task of fetchin and returnin a madman by the name of Benton Wells to his rightful place of confinement at the Georgia State Lunatic Asylum or die tryin. ("Hopefully him, not us," I could not help think to myself.)

Ruminatin on what might lie ahead, I did have to admit that this weren't the kind of work me and Jesse would choose out-of-hand, but sometimes it was downright necessary as my brother and me had always been quick to advertise ourselves in the *Southern Recorder* newspaper as "Masters of Hounds" and as such would be willin to track anyone, anywhere, anytime. We did not want this to be an empty promise that the Tims Boys could not deliver on.

Now it is a certain-sure fact that trackin slaves runnin off the plantation had always been more profitable and even proved to be the mainstay of our family business, but this here emergency weren't somethin that could be conveniently ignored, after all, the safety of the entire community was at stake. Jesse, Sanford, me, the hounds and all our past experience, I hoped, would be more than a match for a single escaped maniac who we were told was minus one eye and missin his full measure of wits and sense. Of course, I also knew that wishin don't necessarily make a thing so, any more than Cynthia's worryin could prevent somethin from happenin in the first place. As Sanford and I readied up the hounds for whatever lay ahead, I tried to set aside any and all dark thoughts I might have begun to conjure up on the matter.

I found Jesse was thinkin long them very same lines when he finally arrived at our place. He had added a young and eager friend to our little band, a young man by the name of James Rufus Kelly. James Rufus was only maybe seventeen years of age at the time, but he was a great shot with the pistol he always wore at his side and had showed hisself to be smart and absolutely fearless when he had come out on the trail with us before. Losin his daddy as early as he did, I knew the boy was lonely and required a little direction and I agreed with Jesse's assessment that we might be in need of another helpin hand with this new assignment, although Sanford quietly showed hisself to be a little less than enthusiastic bout the addition. The four of us soon set out with two of our finest hounds. Jesse and me sat our horses while the younger two walked and talked to each other, each with a large trackin dog right by their side.

It was a bright fall day and the countryside was all gussied-up for the occasion, seemingly takin no notice or interest in human affairs. We passed no others on the way and it didn't take no time at all fore we come upon that dreaded institution. I could not help but recall Cynthia's earlier concerns despite my efforts to make light of em. Truth to tell here, we had only traveled maybe two or three miles down the road from our home, but one look at that imposin buildin before us made me feel like we'd almost been transported to a distant world, one much more dark and sinister than the one we had left behind.

After ringin the bell, the four of us stood outside the wooden palisade waitin for an attendant to unlock and open the gate. It was then I began to examine the place more closely. Two brick buildins side by each crowded most of the area inside the stockade fence. No inmates could presently be seen out in the early mornin mist, but dark smoke belched from chimneys high atop each of the structures. Cynthia would probably say these were "the fires of hell," but I knew they simply suggested a warm environment for the unfortunates housed inside. Live oak trees planted on the asylum grounds offered a hauntin look as their thick branches eerily twisted their way up towards the heavens. I had the sudden strange thought in my mind that if the inmates themselves was to come out here in this very yard, why they too might reach out with twisted minds and arms, wringin their hands and beseechin God above: "Why me, Lord, why me?"

My mamma, Hattie Tims, was a very wise woman and used to say bout any and all unfortunates… "There but by the grace of God goes you and me, Coswell, and don't you never forget that." And I never did. Jesse, however, was not of similar mind.

Ushered inside at last, two asylum employees led our little party to the basement where Benton Wells had done his dastardly work. We were escorted to the kitchen area and all soon stood solemnly before the remains of attendant Clayton Fowler. There was blood everywhere, more blood than I ever saw splattered about in any one single place. Out of the corner of my eye, I spied our negro, Sanford, turn away slightly, maybe so's to avoid bein overcome by the whole of it. I guess I would have like to have done much the same, cept'n in Jesse's and my line of work it was necessary to get a proper look-see at the place the crime had occurred, as well as get some idea what the man responsible was capable of. Only then could handler and hound have a fair chance of success on the trail ahead. Fowler lay all in pieces and I could see a single savage blow to the head with a sharp and obviously heavy instrument had split his skull most in two. That fact alone testified to this lunatic's great strength and resolve. This would certainly be no easy trackin job. I could feel goose flesh begin to rise up on both my arms.

We could all see it was a gruesome and savage attack, but I figured that weren't the reason for them chili bumps snappin to full attention. It was bad enough that I had to bear witness to this same carnage last night in a dream, but I also knew most of that my brother had supplied with his earlier visit. But there was somethin else that was much more bothersome. I knew for a fact Jesse never told me bout the pieces of human flesh bein piled up so nice and neat by the killer. I would have never forgotten such a thing and yet there it was in my dream last night. And to make matters worse… here we were in the full light of day and I'll be hogtied if I ain't lookin at those same pieces of human flesh clearly stacked for the occasion. Now how was that possible? How did I know before actually seein such a thing that that was the case? I shook my head back and forth and started wonderin if maybe Cynthia weren't the only one in the Tims family with strange and unaccounted for premonitions.

Chapter 2

DEVIL'S OWN MESS OF BROTH

COSWELL TIM'S DIARY RESUMES

Now this so-called "Georgia Lunatic Asylum" or "madhouse" that Cynthia was all in a pucker over, had been built some twenty years back round the same time me and Jesse got ourselves into the bloodhound trackin business (forty-one, if my memory serves me correct on this.) It was intended to house several hundred inmates from the State of Georgia who qualified as insane…lunatics, idiots, people with fits and others of same mind. Up till that time, such folks was simply put up in their homes or if they become too unruly, they was put in jail to be farmed out locally as enslaved labor. I guess it ain't no wonder that many counties objected to the idea of buildin this here place as they were reluctant to give up any free work force that might happen their way (despite the problems some of em might cause.) There were many other citizens (Jesse included) who felt these "crazies" were not deservin of any special treatment as they was thought to be "tools of the devil" and served no purpose in proper society other than to further burden good people with their financial support. "They should simply be done away with," it was often said. Nevertheless and notwithstandin, the asylum did eventually get built on forty acres of farmland in Midway, just a couple of miles south of where my wife Cynthia, me and Sanford had built our first and only home, a small farmhouse settin proudly on the outskirts of town.

I must admit the asylum grew to be quite a majestic affair, made of brick with wooden shingle roofs, the whole of it eventually built in the shape of a large "U". The entrance was constructed so's to face the Georgia capitol of Milledgeville with the backside lookin out over the banks of the Oconee River. They were tall buildins, for sure, with some twenty-three rooms on each of the four floors. Each of em emptied out into an airy passageway that run the whole length of the buildin. Glass windows on the outside walls had cast iron fixed window sashes. Women inmates was housed on the third and fourth floors with men on the first and second.

It was in the basement where this foul deed had been committed, but that was also where the whole institution sprang to life. It was there that a large iron stove with a system of pipes and chimneys carried warm air to all the floors. It was there where the kitchen was located, the place where all the food was prepared and sent to the dinin rooms of each floor with the help of a "dumb waiter." (I would have to say this was the most curious contraption I ever saw. It was operated by a series of pulleys that moved a tray up and down inside an open shaft. Quite clever, I thought.) Also, there were several storage rooms down there and a place to clean laundry and linens. Slaves and others who served as attendants also resided in this very busy and vital area of the institution.

"Somehow he got loose, got to the kitchen and managed to get his hands on a heavy meat cleaver what did all the damage," Will Farrell offered up behind me as I still continued to survey the devilment that had befallen the poor attendant, still lyin quietly in a pool of his own blood.

Mr. William Farrell, despite bein only thirty or so years of age at the time, had been steward on the place for several years now and admitted he had seen "a hell of a lot" durin his time here, but added that he never saw the like of this. "I knew the fella what did this was dangerous the day we brought him in," Farrell offered. "He was a wild man. He had great physical strength and had a crazed look in his eye...and I mean 'eye,' cause the man had but one to his name."

"Yuz mean dere wuz but one eye pokin out de middle ob hes

hed like sum boogerman?" Sanford asked excitedly, temporary forgettin his less than equal station in the current conversation.

Farrell looked over at the negro and then back at me. "I don't see why you let a nigger work alongside you in this trackin business of yours. Don't set a good example for others of his kind as far as I can see."

"Well, Mr. Farrell," I replied. "Sanford here is real handy with the hounds and he's taken a shine to trackin as well. My brother Jesse and me figures Sanford instinctively seems to be able to track his own kind and seein as how slave trackin makes up a good part of our business, he has proved quite valuable. He knows their mind, you might say. It may be that sometimes he does forget hisself some, but I guess what we are a-lookin at here is nough to make a man of any color- black, white, spotted or otherwise, maybe do just that."

"You may be right, Mr. Tims. I guess he ain't hurt the reputation of your trackin business none, leastways, not yet. And who's this young fella over here?" Farrell said, pointin in the direction of our young white assistant.

"My name is James Rufus Kelly, sir. Hopin to gain some experience and just help out where I can," the young Irishman announced sorta like a proud little bandy rooster.

"You know how to use that thing hangin at your side, son?" the steward asked.

"I think I can give a pretty good account of myself if the situation demands it," young Kelly responded confidently. Jesse and me always got a kick out of how quick the boy was on his feet and with his words.

Satisfied that the two younger members of our team were reasonably competent, Farrell turned back to Jesse and me and continued the conversation. "You fellas are always the first ones get called in whenever we have a runaway and ain't it a fact that you get your thirty dollar bounty right quick too, am I right?" Not waiting for an answer Farrell added... "Usually it ain't this bad though," as he stroked his chin and continued to look down at the mutilated corpse. Will Farrell had informed us before that the victim was a man by the name of Clayton Fowler, but now added that he had three brothers who all worked along with him as attendants here at the asylum. "Oh, they're gonna let out quite a howl when his blood-kin find out bout this," Farrell added softly, still continuin to stroke thoughtfully at his chin.

"Massa Tims," Sanford interrupted. "What bout dat eye?" I could see Sanford curiosity had gotten the better of him and he weren't lettin go of this investigation till he was in possession of a few more of the gory details. To soften his request up I offered that same question to the asylum steward.

"I do believe Dr. Green would be the one to talk on that subject," he replied. "As you know he is well aware of all the patients' histories and I will tell ya he is some upset over this recent turn of events. He was just here a few minutes ago and said he would be back straight-away, but I will tell you this. This one-eyed man refused to wear a patch over his missin eye and the flesh around it was all ragged and uneven, creatin shadows and darkness in that area of his face. But in the center of it all and in the right light, there was a clear openin, a hole where a body could actually see right inside the man's head where all his craziness come from in the first place. It was fright-enin thing to behold, but you just couldn't help but be drawn into it whenever you looked his way. After a spell patients and staff simply had to turn their heads in another direction out of sheer revulsion and disgust."

I looked over at Sanford and could see he was conjurin up a picture in his mind of a one-eyed monster. "I guess this fella ain't gonna win no beauty contests now is he Sanford?" I suggested. The negro met my remark with a timid smile.

Dr. Thomas F. Green soon entered the room with two similarly clad, white-jacketed attendants. I had him figured for a good man (leastways he didn't sell them snake oil recipes like the old super-intendent had done), but he did have the habit of usin a lot of them fancy college words which often made him hard to understand. I thought him to be of a good Christian nature who come by his work in honest fashion. Sometimes, however, it was my observation that the man let his heart overtop his head which could become a problem for both the institution and those livin nearby. More than once, residents of his institution had taken their leave, takin advantage of the good doctor's trust. Just slightly over five feet in height and slender of body, the man greeted me warmly.

"Well, Mr. Tims…I see we meet again and over some not-so-pleasant circumstances. I don't envy you and your brother tracking down the likes of Benton Wells, but I hope you get him real soon before he does too much damage out there," Dr. Green offered as we commenced to shakin hands.

"That's what we get paid to do, Doc," I replied. "Our dogs don't give a hoot in hell's holler who they be followin long as their noses get the proper exercise. Me and Jesse always go cautious and our young boys are no fools neither," I added, as I brushed back the front of my coat to reveal the worn handle of a Colt revolver that was always holstered backward on my left side. I have found over the years that little gesture went a long way to reassure folks that the Tims boys were all business.

"Well I guess there's a good reason why you fellas have been in this occupation as long as you have. Now, as to the man in question. It is generally my custom, as you know, to personally release a manacled patient when they arrive here at the hospital. A matter of trust don't you know. But Benton Wells was a different story. He was a fanatically religious fellow who had terrible delusions and had once even attempted to hang his own wife in God's name out behind his home. Tried to kill his own children in fact, said he read about such a thing in the Good Book. His family and neighbors finally got to the point where they were so afraid of him that they built a log hut on the premises and confined the man with iron handcuffs and chained his ankles together, anchoring them to a ring bolt on the floor. He was continually whipped and beaten, starved, had cold water thrown on him for several months, the usual things people do to try to help the deranged, but nothing seemed to work. They finally were forced to load the man up in a cart and bring him here to us." Dr. Green paused momentary to collect his thoughts.

"He came stapled to the floor of that wooden cart under the guard of two men, with his feet very much swollen from the chaining and with one eye out which previously in one of his furious and disruptive fits, he had torn from its socket and thrown it to the ground quoting scripture by saying 'If thy eye offends thee, pluck it out!' And so, unlike most others, Benton Wells entered our asylum with a need to be further restrained as we attempted to treat his condition."

"Lord-a-mighty, Doc. What could you expect to do with such a man?" Jesse inquired. "Sounds to me like the fella ain't worth a curse...no different than a mad dog what needs shootin straightaway for he takes a notion in his head to tear some good citizen all to pieces!"

"Well, that's just the point, Mr. Tims. Many of our patients do things that are out of their control and we must find the reasons for those behaviors. Just as my predecessors said, we assume certain sacred duties and responsibilities here at the asylum and must perform them conscientiously so as to gain the approval of our Maker who will be strict to mark injustice or oppression to the unfortunate, helpless or suffering fellow human beings. In order to start that process, however, we did feel it necessary to temporarily chain him in a room down here in the basement. We put him in a straitjacket and after several days of puking him with nauseates, giving him cathartics, digitalis, anodyne and frequent cold baths as well as bleeding him copiously, we did finally succeed in weakening his frenzy and tranquilizing him. He had, in fact, become quite rational and affable of late and we removed the straitjacket, but kept him chained to the floor for his and our protection. He began to converse rationally with our attendants on the state of the weather, prices of cotton, news or politics, but the topic of religion was absolutely forbidden. Things were going well, but I just inspected the room where he was kept and it appears he was able to tear the iron staple from the stone floor with the aid of a metal tool he had fashioned up. He must have been planning this for some time. Maybe our Mr. Fowler here had the misfortune to discover him in the kitchen just at the same time Mr. Wells had begun to enjoy his new-found freedom," Dr. Green concluded as he took in a well needed breath of air.

"Wow, Doc, that there's quite a story. Anythin else you think we need to know bout this man fore we head out on his trail?"

"Just that he may be headed for Macon as that is where his family lives and with that 'vengeance is mine, sayeth the Lord' mentality, why they could be in for a pretty rough time if he decides to return and repay them for sending him our way."

After thankin the doc for the information, Green and his two attendants quickly exited the room to return to Wells' former place of confinement in search of a scent item I requested which was necessary to begin the chase. Jesse and James Rufus left quietly at the same time to tend to the hounds out in the asylum yard. Sanford and me reexamined the scene of the crime once more fore startin to walk down the darkened corridor and up a flight of stairs to the front entrance.

It was just then that I noticed somethin that had been scrawled up on the wall many years ago. It was printed in large letters, some more faded than others. An earlier inmate must have had hisself a fine sense of humor when he scratched out the followin message. *"They said I was crazy, I said they were crazy, but I was outvoted."* I had to laugh as I pointed it out to Sanford. With no one around but the two of us, there was no need to keep secret the fact that the young negro was more than familiar with his letters. (That sort of thing did have a way of makin white folks a might jumpy.) Sanford give out with that big smile of his as he read it for hisself, revealin those familiar pearly white teeth with that endearin gap found right there twinxt the middle two.

Before we exited the buildin, Sanford pointed out yet another message he spied that someone had scribbled on the wall. This one read: *"Before you lock us up, take a good look at who brought us in."* I had to think on this for a spell. "Sanford, do you remember Ida Todd?"

"I members her, Massa Tims," he replied. "Ain't she de one dat worked down at de grocery stow on Warren St. wid her husband fer many yers?"

"That's the very woman. She was sent here by that man cause he said she went insane. She had lost $8,000 dollars in a business deal as I recall and he reported she then began to lose her mind. She started dressin poorly, wouldn't eat her vittles and took to silent weepin as I recall. He reported she gradually become violent and started dancin round like St. Vitus hisself, throwin her arms and hands about in a frenzied manner. She was tossed into this place for ten years solely on the husband's say-so, but when he up and died, folks found out there really weren't nothin wrong with the woman in the first place, only that her husband was angry at the money she'd lost and wanted the woman's share of what remained. It was all very sad …a 'miscarry of justice' one might say."

Sanford nodded his head with my recollection. A few minutes later the two of us finally reached the entrance to the buildin and Sanford opened the heavy oversized doors so that "Massa Tims" could step out into the bright light of day. It took us a while to get our eyes adjusted, but we soon saw my brother currently on one knee with an arm round a large, muscular bloodhound bearin both the name and rank of Colonel. The dog's half- brother, Echo, sat rite alongside him as usual. James Rufus held his leather lead in hand. I began to pass along some of the information gained from the earlier conversation and also told them what we had seen scribbled up on the walls of the institution.

Suddenly, the asylum doors was flung open and three men come runnin from the brick enclosure like the whole of it had caught on fire. "Mr. Tims, we're goin with you!" the lead man yelled out, as James Fowler led brothers Henry and John out the door. Almost out of breath, the elder brother was tremblin like an ol quiver bug with excitement when he finally regained his tongue. "We just found out that son-of-a-bitch, Benton Wells, done killed our brother and he is gonna pay in like kind. We are gonna kill him and cut him up into little pieces and feed him to the hogs, we are, and save the good people of Georgia the cost of a grave box!"

"You ain't doin nothin of the kind and that's a fact!" Jesse Tims countered forcefully as he rose up to his full height of some six feet on the perpendicular. Jesse was a tall one, that's for sure. He was lean and strong to boot despite his years, but the best thing I can say bout this man I be knowin all my life is that he could always be counted on by friends, family and his younger brother to do right by em under even the most difficult of circumstances.

"We don't need no one messin up the trail and all you folks are gonna do is get in harm's way. We don't need no lynch mob to slow us down and make things more difficult than they already is. And as for that cuttin up thing you got planned, well, that will be for the law to decide. The Tims Boys are law-bidin citizens for sure. Now you get yourselves back inside that there buildin, do your jobs and if we do our jobs right and proper, maybe we will have somethin for y'all fore too much time has passed," Jesse concluded forcefully.

The Fowler brothers hesitated momentarily, but Doc Green's arrival on the scene definitely turned the tide in our favor. "You heard what the man said, now didn't you boys?" Doc Green interjected after joinin our growin little party out in front lawn of the asylum. "If you want to keep your jobs here at the institution and collect that dollar a day with room and board added in, you will do as Mr. Tims suggests. Don't cost us a thing to use slaves as attendants, so you can all be replaced economically and right quick too." (I guess the doc figured to hold the trump card here as the Fowler brothers most likely were in desperate need of employment, but I knew it had been in all the papers that Doc Green had begun to hire more and more white staff due to the resentment some of the crazy white inmates felt towards their black caregivers.)

"But Doc, he's our brother," James Fowler weakly uttered as he pleaded his case one last time.

"And the Tims brothers are going to bring back the man who did this to him. You mark my words now," the doctor shouted out as the disgruntled Fowlers reluctantly turned and slowly began to trudge back into the madhouse to resume their custodial duties.

With the Fowlers gone, Dr. Green turned to me. "Now, Mr. Tims, as to the scent item you requested for your hounds here. How do you think they'll fancy this little token from our Mr. Wells?" he asked as he handed me a slightly yellowed pillowcase he had retrieved from the murderer's bed.

"That will do right fine, Doc," I said, as I carefully took the item in hand. "I reckon this will put their noses directly on that man's backside. Now Jesse, if you wouldn't mind fetchin the dog's harnesses off the horses, we can all get to work here!"

Now it has been our experience that a bloodhound trackin dog will seldom fail to deliver up a fugitive if the proper scent item is introduced. Sittin patiently while I quickly fastened up the buckles on both sides of the leather harness and lastly attachin a 20′ leather lead to the ring atop it all, I finished up Echo bout the same time Sanford readied up the Colonel. While still sittin quietly, both dogs got a healthy sniff of that dirty pillowcase with instructions to "FIND!" and, with that, the two began sniffin the ground round the institution till they come upon a scent that matched the one they had been given. The Colonel reacted first as was expected, and he laid his head back and let out with a long, sorrowful, bloodhound bay. True to his name and nature, Echo, he copied and did exactly the same. Assured now of the proper route the fugitive had taken, the two large bloodhounds began to pull Sanford and James Rufus off in a direction only the dogs understood.

The Tims Boys and their assistants were back on the trail once more with all senses of man and beast keen and alert. We sought a large, one-eyed and barefoot man by the name of Benton J. Wells. He was reported to be dressed in a white, flowin nightshirt. We knew he was armed and we knew he was dangerous. We had no trouble picturin in our mind's eye the sharp meat ax he clutched in his hands. The scent hounds, however, had their own picture of the runner, one they had stored up their noses for safe keepin. There weren't a two-legged or four-legged critter among us that day that didn't believe it was only a matter of time before we'd have the individual in question square in our sights.

Chapter 3

STRONG VINEGAR IN THEM WORDS

COSWELL TIM'S DIARY RESUMES

We had no way of knowin at the time that the asylum inmate, either by accident or design, had already stumbled well into the confines of the Milledgeville city limits. *The Southern Recorder* and the *Federal Union* newspapers that were both quick to carry the sensationalized account of the story later on revealed that his hasty escape soon brought him to a low-lyin swampy and mosquito-ridden area near the west end of Franklin Street, not two blocks south of the governor's mansion. Over the years that spot proved to be the perfect location for a bordello, as any complaints against such an establishment had to come from neighbors and the fact was there weren't many to be had in such an unpleasant environment. Phoebe Brown and Mary Baily bought it for almost nothin years back and run an establishment there for quite some time. Now that just happened to be the very point in time when me and Jesse was sproutin tail feathers and beginnin to crow. Mamma and Daddy warned us to stay out of places like that and I can see lookin back the wisdom of such advice, but I guess I have to admit at that youthful time we was drawed same like hogs to the trough.

I remember the ladies sayin they had few real expenses with their business, mostly just intense labor, but I do recall Phoebe complainin to Jesse and me one day that she had to pay a yearly $10.00 license fee just to sell liquor on the premises and said that would require her to service ten extra customers just to break even. She considered raisin her fee to two dollars a poke, but then thought poorly on the idea as it would make her less competitive with other such establishments in town. She decided that it was only fair then that Mary contribute her share…five men apiece, she said, as they was partners in the business and needed to divide things up equal-like, right down the middle. More important was concern over a $300.00 security deposit that was required by the city in order to guarantee "an orderly house." Fortunately for the girls, however, the town fathers provided that in the best interest of the state legislature and others who might be in need of certain services while visitin Georgia's fine state capitol. (I do believe those town fathers who made that gift possible were in due time properly rewarded for their generosity.)

Phoebe and Mary retired from the business some time back as their female charms began to fade, but a new crop of whores had taken up residence on that same piece of property with Polly Wade leadin a small but determined group of three or four young white women who had took up the trade. Jesse and me heard they was doin quite well for theirselves, but then it had been several decades since we had visited such an establishment and had no personal knowledge on the matter.

Now it was generally the case, not only in Milledgeville but throughout the south, that there was to be strict segregation when it come to whorehouses, after all, societies do need to maintain their lofty moral standards. But I reckon Polly got it in that pretty weedmonkey head of hers that she could make money by caterin to certain white men's taste with a little "chocolate delight" to be had on the premises if a customer was so inclined. I guess that fancy girl "Rachael" they hired was quite a looker and proved very popular with many white patrons who frequented the place, but the fact of the matter was that she didn't look so good after Benton Wells finished with her. No siree! In his demented state of mind he must have figured to be doin the Good Lord's work by keepin the races a respectable and healthy distance apart. My guess was and still is that this frightenin one-eyed man with a gapin hole where his right eye should have been and a meat cleaver raised high above his head in righteous anger must have been bout the last thing this young black woman was to see on this earth, that is, if her eyes was full-open at the time she peered out over the shoulder of the man currently mounted atop her. I reckon this customer just figured to have his ashes hauled for a dollar and be on his merry way, but the truth was he would never leave that room, leastways not in one piece. It took the ladies of the house a considerable amount of time after hearin bloodcurlin screams fore they got up the courage to enter that room and when they did, I'll be dogged if they didn't find two bodies chopped up so fine it was hard to tell white pieces from black. There weren't no trace of the man who done this, but as for the scent of that man, well, now that's a different bucket of possums altogether.

ﻪ   ﻪ   ﻪ

Our dogs moved fast, but were under control as James Rufus and Sanford, each with hound in hand, navigated the invisible trail that lay before us. Bloodhounds, excited masters of the unseen, do need to be kept restrained or they would quick disappear from view in the dense undergrowth and swampy terrain where handlers would soon fall behind. Jesse and me sat atop our mounts somewhat to the rear of our little group, followin behind with the intention of overseein the whole affair.

Benton Wells' large, shoeless footprints could occasionally be spotted whenever the ground got soft, givin testimony to the madman's hurried flight. Doc Green had told us he weren't wearin nothin more than a single thin night shirt, so exceptin for the heavy instrument he elected to carry along, the escaped fugitive was definitely travelin light. All of us was quiet and deep in concentration as we continued along the trail. The dogs made no noise, in fact, our hounds rarely took to barkin or howlin while they was goin bout their trackin business less it was when they first picked up the scent or at the very end when they was all anxioused-up bout finally meetin the runner in question. Dogs other than proper-bred bloodhounds often yap and holler in the extreme which is not only a waste of time, but does little more than serve as a warnin to the fugitive that current efforts need improvin.

It was a surprise to all of us when The Colonel suddenly stopped, sniffed the air, growled and barked twice. Both them dogs then began to pull their handlers towards an openin in the trees just a short distance ahead where we come upon a seldom-used dirt road. An empty farm wagon stood all by its lonesome in the middle of that road.

I heard Jesse cock his rifle as I drew my Colt from its holster. James Rufus, he did likewise, but Sanford, of course, needed to rely solely on the three of us as the law allowed the negro, free or enslaved, no firearms. (On our property and out of sight of others that was a different story.) As we approached the wagon we all took notice of a dead horse which was still harnessed and lyin horribly mutilated in the shafts and traces. Both dogs began to move about in an agitated manner, nostrils all a-twitchin, in an effort to better understand the situation. The two-legged contingent took to relyin on our eyes to accomplish that same task.

A quick read of the footprints told the story. The wagon had been travelin in one direction; a barefoot maniac had not long ago walked slowly in the other. Maybe there was a nod of the head as they passed, but a quick strike with the meat clever suddenly had disabled the horse, makin any passengers aboard fair game for the scantily-clad pedestrian. Tracks revealed that two people, one male and one female, had jumped from the wagon seat in a race for their lives. Maybe thirty feet up the road evidence clearly indicated that any such efforts had fallen well short of success.

The man had been killed first. His body lay face-down with his shirt soaked in blood just above where his suspenders crossed in the middle of his back. An old wide-brimmed farmer's hat lay next to his gray head. I turned him over. It was old man Jenkins, a man my daddy had done business with in the past. A woman lay up the road apiece, and I knew that had to be his wife, Dorothy May. Sure enough…she lay face -up with her eyes still wide open, an expression of horror fixed upon her care-worn face. From the bruises on her neck it appeared as if she had been strangled. You could see where the meat clever had been driven into the ground next to her head. For some reason known only to her demented killer, an alternative means of dispatch had been chosen. Followin the footprints it was obvious Benton Wells had then returned to the wagon to finish off the horse, cuttin the poor thing nearly all to pieces.

Common decency cried out for us to do somethin with the bodies, but common sense dictated that we needed to move even faster if we were to prevent a similar thing from happenin again. Sorry that we could not tend to things proper-like at the time, we redoubled our efforts and pushed on in hurried pursuit of the killer.

Wells' scent soon brought the dogs and our little band to a marshy area. Wary of moccasins and other such slithery critters, we began to trudge our way through the whole of it, finally emergin from the swamp covered in mud and wore out in the extreme. Except for the muck, both dogs, looked to be fit as a fiddle. I reckon there is good reason these muscular critters not only have thick pads on the bottoms of their feet, but oversized webbed toes as well. The Colonel (and Echo to a lesser degree) had successfully followed the scent of a determined and quick-footed fugitive these last three miles or so through some pretty rugged country.

When we come upon Polly Wade's bawdyhouse, Jesse and me dismounted and prepared to go inside while the boys kept the hounds outside ready to resume the chase at a moment's notice. More than a few folks was gathered round in the aftermath of this ghastly murder.

Sheriff John Strother was takin stock of the situation and was interviewin a number of people when me and Jesse come through the door. A quick look into the bedroom confirmed in my mind that Benton J. Wells had paid an earlier visit to the establishment and had left his tell-tale signature.

"Coswell," Sheriff Strother announced as he abruptly left the person he was conversin with and headed in my direction, hand outstretched. "We figured you'd be comin up the trail fore too long. My God, what a ruckus this was! Never seed the like of it. The women are mighty upset, I'll tell ya, and the whole town is in an uproar. This fella is crazier than a bedbug and we got to get him straightaway fore this kind of thing happens again."

"Well, I would agree with that assessment, Sheriff, so Jesse and me won't be wastin much time here. I can't imagine Benton Wells took his leave by the front door. Did our fugitive jump out one of them back windows?"

"I believe that to be a fact."

"Then we will bring the dogs round and get back to work," I replied.

"Oh, Coswell, one more thing fore you head out. That tracker, Lem Purdy and his worthless brother and cousins brought their dogs in and lit out after Wells. Said he was goin to do the town a 'public service.' Hope they ain't messed up the trail too much for you fellas. I told him I thought you and Jesse were most likely the ones to be officially called in, but he kinda scoffed and mumbled somethin under his breath I couldn't quite make out."

"I ain't surprised them fellas were able to find their way to this here establishment as I hear tell they are all good, steady payin customers, but their dogs are a sorry lot, maybe only fit for killin my helpless sheep out in the back pasture. Now you know I hates to discredit a man, Sheriff, but I swear there ain't a one of them Purdy's who could find the ground if they was to topple over backwards."

"That may be true, but they did get them three niggers that run off the Lamar place awhile back," the Sheriff offered.

"That's a fact, John," Jesse added in, "but as I remember, when that gold was found up in Lumpkin County way back in '28 and started our 'Georgia Gold Rush,' ain't it true that Frank Logan and his slave just plain stumbled upon the find? No, sometimes things turn out good or bad with nothin more than luck to account. I suppose the Purdy's could find Wells, but I wouldn't bet my life savings on it."

I give a little smile with Jesse's assessment, but we needed to get back to work if we were to make any headway here. Benton Wells had taken to the woods and had stayed away from the general population after fleein the asylum. The unfortunate timin of the couple in the wagon and stumblin upon the bordello notwithstandin, I figured things could have gone much worse if more innocent folks had crossed his path. We hoped that fortunate set of circumstances might continue for the time needed to catch this man and either return him to his proper place of incarceration or dispose of him altogether.

Sanford and the Colonel continued to lead the way, with Sanford and James Rufus switchin dogs after a few more miles to give the lead man a rest. Echo did not pull as hard as his older half-brother.

It didn't take long for our little party to realize Wells was definitely headed southwest towards Macon just as the asylum superintendent had speculated he might. His family was sure goin to be in for a rough time if we didn't find him first. Of course them Purdy boys had definitely muddied up the trail some along the way. There was plenty of evidence of the escaped lunatic, with canines and humans in hot and hurried pursuit. Sanford scoffed at the careless and unprofessional manner in which the fugitive was bein tracked. "Massa Tims," I heard him yell up to Jesse and me… "De dogs, dey's all loose en goin ebery which-away. Don' know ifen they's eber gonna find what dey's a-lookin fer." I saw Jesse nod his head in full agreement with Sanford's expert assessment.

Now I need to say straight-out that a good bloodhound what's trained up right don't go piddle-diddlin round when it comes to the mixin of footprints and such. If they have a good scent item to begin the chase with, why, they'll sort through any confusion and set their minds on the proper direction they need to go. Bloodhounds are unlike any other dog in that they are born and bred for the trail. If you take em young when they're about seven weeks old (that keeps em from bein "litter bound") and train em to track, first with their eyes and then with their nose, these here blooded hounds might just be makin money and be on a human trail fore the year is out. Sniffin is what they do best (bloodhounds have even been called "a nose walkin on four feet") and there ain't a part of this critter that don't testify to that very fact. Wrinkled skin holds scent, large noses gather scent, long ears sweep scent towards that nose and even the critter's long and large body with a neck that effortlessly allows the head to drop and be close to the ground for hours on end, suggests the dogs' general disposition. They love the trail, they really do. It's actually like a game to em and when they finally find the fugitive in question these critters often want a little appreciation for their work. They bear the runner no grudge and the trouble is they often want some acknowledgement from the very folks they catch. I will guarantee there is no way we are gonna let the Colonel or our Echo put their paws up on the asylum escapee's shoulders and offer up a blood-hound tongue full on the face like they might want to do, not with that asylum inmate armed and dangerous.

I have found that time passes quickly on the trail. We traversed some pretty thick piney woods, only to then come upon low-growin bushes that grow profusely in the soil of central Georgia. Numerous brooks or branches, as they are commonly called, did offer up an obstacle or two. We was constantly on the lookout for snakes in the swampy areas, particularly moccasins, as they were many and deadly and don't give no fair warnin like the rattlesnakes we often encounter.

The sky had turned overcast over the last few hours, offerin up the threat of rain. As a result the fugitive's scent would soon be drawed down to the ground more so than was common. It would be a good day for trackin, to be sure, and the dogs was now pickin up the pace as they moved quietly through the underbrush. I spied a catbrier that caught on the Colonel's red coat, but that wrinkly skin of his was purposely designed not to tear and it harmlessly lost its grip. I found my mind momentarily movin away from the asylum murderer, as thoughts of how much I had always loved the thrill of trackin and bein in these beautiful woodlands come to my mind.

No one spoke and the dogs made little noise, at least for now. As my mind wondered, I thought back to when I first took to trackin. Why I weren't nothin more than a little shirttail boy, maybe ten or eleven years old, I was. Jesse helped at first, but it weren't long before this younger brother of his had woodland secrets all his own. Tracks on the ground soon come to have real meanin for me as I found they could tell the story of a wild and untamed way of life that was hidden from the eyes of most people. I know for a fact this made the youngest member of the Tims family feel real special.

I'll wager that few folks know that squirrels, chipmunks and muskrats have four toes in front and five in back where most other critters have five and five. I figure there would be few folks who would know how to track a possum, even though that's bout as easy a trackin job as there is. Possums are a five and five critter, but the front feet go out every which-a-way formin a star-like imprint on the ground. The back ones, they look almost like human hands, long thumb and all. Sometimes you can see traces of their rat-like tails left on the ground as they mosey along. I seen possums play dead when dogs attacked, with the dogs becomin so confused over the unusual turn of events they would lose interest. I witnessed a possum one day get bit by a good-sized rattlesnake and the snake couldn't believe any white, rat-faced critter paid his bite no nevermind. Each creature in the woods has its own secrets and it takes a skinned eye and maybe a keen ear if a man wants to join in.

Because I was able to unwrap so many mysteries of the trail, there was more than a few critters I brought home for supper in my younger days. Many were the grateful hugs my mamma would provide and welcome pats on the back my daddy would give me for a job well done. (There weren't nothin more delicious in the Tims' house than roast possum, taters and collards.) Even when I got my first trackin dog, I never forgot the lessons I learned all by my lonesome out in them woods when I was no more than half a leg high. Great memories, they were.

We had been on the trail several hours when somethin happened that rarely occurs when trackin with more than one dog. The two animals had a difference of opinion. Colonel, he wanted to go one way, but Echo remained firm in his belief that the correct trail lay off in a different direction. We had never seen this, especially with Echo who generally imitated the larger dog's behavior (after all, that's how he got his name.) He was so insistent, however, that me and Jesse decided to split up our little band. We agreed I would follow Sanford and Echo, while Jesse would trail behind the Colonel and James Rufus. We were pretty sure this was Echo's lame attempt for the first time to assert hisself to no good end, but bein unsure of that at the time; we agreed to divide our forces.

After maybe another half hour or so, seemingly out of nowhere, a pistol shot rung out, interruptin the silence of the deep woods. Sanford, he pulled the leather lead up tight and I could only imagine James Rufus doin likewise iffen he had heard the same thing. I motioned Sanford to stop all movement and be quiet as I cocked my ear to give a listen. Have you ever noticed that when folks catch an unusual sound, they will always stop and do that very thing? They will study on it awhile and make every attempt to listen even more intently for a repeat, but if there ain't none to be had, they will generally disregard the noise altogether as if they never heard it in the first place. Never could understand the reason that was so. Maybe folks just don't trust somethin out of the ordinary less there be some further evidence to support it. We have found in our line of work that not actin on that first sound could have dangerous consequences.

Nevertheless and notwithstandin, a second shot set the whole matter to rest. This one was accompanied by the faint sound at some distance of dogs barkin and people yellin. Here things had been so quiet and serene for so long a time and now commotion and chaos promised a lively replacement. Wells had to be at the center of it all, we figured, with Echo maybe havin made the right call after all. Our little group redoubled our efforts to reach the source of the distur-bance. I figured Jesse most like as not, had to be close by and would soon join us.

Before a stutterin man could manage a whistle, we come upon a rock outcroppin that had been formed up on one of several small hills. Settin atop my horse, I was rewarded with a pretty fair view of a good-sized cave entrance which appeared to be at the center of all the confusion. I got the notion in my head that Benton Wells must have taken refuge inside that enclosure with his pursuers doin their level best to dislodge him from the premises. The pursuers were most certain the Purdy Boys... Lem Purdy, his brother, and several of his cousins, now comin into full view outside the enclosure. I could see that pistols was drawn and bein waved about in a confused and agitated manner. There was lots of yellin as well.

"Looks like we're in time for the party," I yelled over to Sanford, as I spurred the horse forward, movin quickly past both the dog and his youthful handler.

As I pulled my mount up hard after a short dash to the cave entrance, I let my presence be known to the man in charge. "Lem, would you be standin in need of a little assistance here?" I yelled out as I dismounted.

I could tell he was surprised, maybe even shocked, at my sudden appearance. "Well, yea, I reckon we would, Coswell," he said somewhat reluctantly as he looked my way briefly, only to glance back worried-like at the cave entrance. "Things went from bad to worse monstrously fast here, I'll tell ya. That fella in the cave is possessed of the devil mightily. We tried gettin him outer there, but two dead dogs and one dead Purdy just ain't produced the desired results."

"Now, Lem, I know he ain't armed with nothin more than a kitchen utensil, but in a close quarters with darkness his ally, my feelin is that he's too dangerous to confront directly and may need to be smoked out." Just as I uttered those words, Sanford and Echo reached us and I suggested that Sanford quick fetch some lucifers from the saddlebags so's we could begin the necessary operations.

As Sanford collected fire starters, he also grabbed some bindin rope which had earlier been throwed over the saddle horn when we had held out some hope of bringin the fugitive back to the institution alive. (I felt that possibility was dimmin mightily.) Where was Jesse and James Rufus, I thought to myself? They could really be of use now.

With no instructions from me, Sanford started in gatherin up some dead piney boughs that was lyin scattered about on the ground. I held tight to the dog's lead (I didn't want our dog rushin into the cave by hisself) but soon wrapped it round my arm so's to free up my hands in order to use my knife to cut the rope up into several small pieces. These would be used to tie several tight bundles of the loose sticks Sanford had collected. I saw Lem Purdy eyin Sanford closely as the negro even made a casualty of his own shirt, tearin up cloth strips to add to the bundles which was sure to increase the amount of smoke and flame offered up. It didn't take Sanford and me more than a few minutes time and we was in possession of a half-dozen or more first rate incendiaries.

"Massa Tims, I'se toss em here en dere," Sanford offered as he took the lucifers along with bundles of dead pine branches he carried in his hands or put under his arms, and cautiously headed off in the direction of the cave entrance. "I'se gonna toss sum fer inside en mebe leeb sum ob dems outside close de entrance where he jus mite be fool nough ter try en fetch em," he added softly. Lem Purdy and five of his family members watched in utter fascination, guns still drawn, as the bare-chested young negro efficiently went on bout his business.

Sanford crept up to the cave entrance, not knowin for sure the exact location of the dangerous occupant within. All present watched as he methodically lit and soon tossed them flamin piney knots into various areas of the dark hole, one by one. All waited to see what might happen next.

Maybe five or ten minutes passed by with little or no change, just smoke could be seen comin from the mouth of the cave. Eventually, we thought we detected some slight coughin noises, but then all went quiet once more. After a spell, however, we all definitely heard a snortin noise of some kind. It sounded like a mad bull or maybe a locomotive startin to get up the proper head of steam. And then... why then Benton Wells come out of that cave like he was shot out the mouth of a cannon!

Now a large figure attired in a dirty and bloodied nightshirt, flyin from out the darkness into the light with assault weapon raised high above his head, ain't exactly an image a body would be inclined to ever forget. I think it's fair to say that image skeered the lot of us nigh onto death. But that weren't the whole of it. From deep inside his throat, Wells issued forth a tormented scream that had to have come from the depths of hell itself. It didn't help matters none that the man wore a strange demonic grin upon his face as he rushed to daylight.

What looked to be a ghostly image appeared to gain speed and close the distance between him his now fleein pursuers. With his nightshirt wavin off behind, he swung the heavy instrument he held in his right hand wildly... underhanded, overhanded, cross handed and everythin in between. He managed to nick Jeb Purdy pretty good on the arm as he passed him by, but seemed intent on his cousin Lem. For some reason it seemed, Wells had fixed his sights square on Lem Purdy, maybe cause he instinctively knew it was him that was givin out all the orders. Overcome with fear, instead of usin the gun he held in hand, Lem Purdy also had turned tuck-tail and run for his dear life.

Sanford was back and off to the side of the cave entrance when all this excitement started, but the young black man again jumped into the thick of it and immediately began pursuit when Wells passed him by. Sanford caught up after a short dash and threw hisself at the madman's feet. I remember Daddy sayin that as a general rule it didn't profit a man to corner somethin meaner than hisself (there was no doubt in my mind Wells was the meaner of the two) but I also knew Sanford's good heart and best intentions might enlist some heavenly support and give him a fair chance against a very dangerous opponent.

Now Wells had certainly come on like the hammers of hell, but when Sanford got hold of his ankles, the man did drop like a stone. It reminded me of a dog years back who got brought up short. A neighbor of ours had a mischievous mutt that needed to be restrained outside his house so he tied a long rope round the critter's neck and fixed the other end to a sturdy stake that he drove deep into the ground. Well, that dog took off like a shot one day when another of his kind dared to invade his territory, but the poor thing run out of rope fore he run out of enthusiasm which caused his back legs to surpass the front ones at a high rate of speed. Needless to say the critter found hisself lyin stunned and flat on his back, wonderin what could possibly have gone wrong. It was one of the funniest things I ever saw. Same thing was with this Wells fella here but there was nobody laughin at this time.

The lunatic's nightshirt now lay in tatters by his feet after Sanford tackled him as the two had come crashin to the ground. Wells shook the black man loose like he weren't nothin but a swatted fly. He then went on about the business of retrievin the meat clever that had flown from his hands. Sanford knew what the outcome would be if the man was to be reunited with that instrument, so he gallantly pressed the attack, springin at him and grabbin the lunatic around the shoulders.

Wells seized Sanford's throat and started to choke the life out of him, but they both soon took to wallerin round on the ground so's it was difficult for anyone else to get a word or a bullet in edgewise. Just about that time Sanford done the cleverest thing. He jammed the thumb of his right hand directly into Benton J. Wells' one good eye! Now accordin to the asylum superintendent, it had been Wells himself who had eliminated the other eye in a fit of religious passion. Maybe now if he were thinkin clear on the matter, he might be forced to come to the conclusion that the Good Lord knew just what he was doin in the first place when he issued two eyes to each individual and that individual weren't gonna improve on the situation through his own efforts, despite any religious convictions to the contrary.

Wells let out a loud holler as he again throwed the pesky negro to the ground, shakin his head from side to side in an effort to clear his vison. He then feverishly began to grope blindly along the ground in an attempt to locate the deadly kitchen utensil. Eventually succeedin in that effort, the man stood up tall on the perpendicular and began to swear an oath, loud and clear it was, as he raised the meat ax in the air. "I will fight all the demons of hell if that is my lot, but through me God's will shall be done on this earth!" he proclaimed loudly.

I'll never forget that proclamation because it said a lot bought how most all men see themselves as heroes, despite behavior that might be to the contrary. Sanford lay before him on the ground, half mesmerized, eyes big as saucers, helplessly figurin he might be the first victim of that grand pronouncement. But as Wells lifted his arm to strike a fatal blow, three shots rung out in succession, all from three different quarters. I knew one was mine as the powder smoke from the barrel of my Colt rarely told a lie, but James Rufus had fired on the run and Jesse rifle shot from atop his horse had all successfully discharged, arrivin together at the intended target. The other half of our trackin party had shown up just in time. The body of former asylum inmate Benton J. Wells slumped lifeless to the ground.

The Colonel and Echo both come and give the body a little sniff with the rest of us joinin Sanford for a closer look. James Rufus was still breathin hard from his mad dash to the rescue, but Jesse quietly held his rifle in his hands as he stood next to me. My Colt was returned to its leather home at my side.

There was a few quick pats on the back all around for a job well done, but Sanford, he found hisself drawn to that carcass like a blowfly to a dead rat. You would have thought by this time he would have had enough of the likes of this Wells fella, but that eye of his still remained a thing of mystery and interest. Sanford turned Wells body over and took a good long look at the deep, fleshy cavern where the missin orb should have been. "Good Lord in Heaben…how could a man do dis ter hisself?" he asked.

"He must have figured he was doin right or he wouldn't have done it," I replied.

"The man was nuttier than a fruit cake and needed to be dispatched," Jesse offered. "Any thoughts he might have had in his head about bein a man of God was pure fluff and fancy, I'd say."

"Guess it don't really much matter, gentlemen," I added in. "Lookin at those three holes in the center of his chest just tells me that whatever he thought, he got hisself outvoted in the end. Rememberin the writin on the asylum wall, Sanford knew just what I meant by that remark and I saw him chuckle silently to hisself.

Now dogs and people had scattered greatly in the confusion and all had continued to keep a respectful distance from the activity. The Purdy dogs stayed back, occasionally barkin, but not willin to risk life and limb by goin too close to the kill until their masters made the first move. The Purdy Boys, although they outnumbered the dead man six to one, were much like their dogs and had also given the corpse a wide berth. All were slow to return.

Lem Purdy and his boys finally did join our triumpful little group. There weren't no doubt the man was tryin desperately to regain some of his lost dignity. "This young fella here ain't afraid of nothin and that's some nigger you got there, Coswell," came the words from a still shaken Lem Purdy. "I guess I owe both more than a passel, specially your boy here. When things quiet down some, Coswell, would you consider rentin Sanford out for a spell to help me and my family? I would make it well worth your while."

Now normally I would never have even considered such a thing as there was little I had observed over the years in Lem Purdy that I found favorable or trustworthy. I certainly would never begrudge a man his bald head, but maybe the fact that he never consented to wearin a hat even when out in the hot Georgia sun said somethin about his bluster and general inclination.

I also would never begrudge a man his low, heavy-set stature, but from that lowly position he always give folks the impression that he was in an all-fired hurry and seemed to want everyone to clear a path in front of him. Townsfolks knew he had more than his fair share of difficulties growin up, what with his father bein a tomato-nosed fella often higher that a Georgia pine. His mamma weren't the most stable of people neither as time and again she took to lockin herself in her bedroom, weepin mightily, so maybe there was a little play to be had in the wheel regardin their son. "Meanness just don't happen overnight," my mamma used to say, but I guess the main problem I always had with Lem was he was wound awful tight and always seemed to have a strong appetite to fight somethin or someone and folks, me included, generally chose to steer clear. Nevertheless and notwithstandin, I guess I did feel a need to consider his recent offer. There was Sanford's opinion on the matter that certainly needed to be added to the general mix. Cynthia and I knew Sanford was startin to look for a woman of his own and just might be wantin to save up some money if such an opportunity presented itself.

"I would take very good care of him," I remember Lem Purdy a-sayin to me as we placed Benton Wells' dead body over the back of Jesse's horse for the return trip to the asylum. There are some real advantages to hindsight, but as I look back, I should have been smart enough at the time to have been able to taste the strong vinegar in them words.

Chapter 4

TWO-FACED AND PROUD

"Well, that was fun, wasn't it?" Bob Bumgardner offered, as he and Barbara pulled into their driveway at the end of one very long day.

"Just creepy, if you ask me," was his wife's quick reply.

Barbara and Robert Bumgarnder were serious about the historical journey they had begun together and inspired by what they had read about Coswell and the Georgia Lunatic Asylum; they had decided to take a quick trip out to nearby Midway to see what remained of the place.

"You can certainly envision what it must have been like at the time. Quite majestic, actually. Didn't the security guard there tell us it was once the largest mental health facility of its kind in the world? Once housed as many as 13,000 patients, he claimed. Shame the whole thing is now going to wrack and ruin," Barbara stated, as she shut the car door and the couple ascended the few steps to their apartment landing.

"It was nice of that guy, what was his name, Horace?...to give us the 'cooks tour' of the buildings and grounds. I guess it pays to claim we are historians working on the history of the place. Not really a lie, I guess. Lots of derelict rooms and things abandoned and most of it in bad need of repair," Bob responded. "Some of the older buildings didn't even have roofs on them, for crying out loud. I don't know if it's even worth it to keep the security and maintenance people on the property. The place hasn't been used for any public health service in the last half dozen years or so I believe he said."

"Well, if I was a ghost that would be the perfect place I would want to haunt," Barbara added. "The morgue. The operating rooms. How about the cemetery, Bob? Didn't old Horace tell us that 25,000 inmates are buried out there? Can you imagine that? I'll bet Benton Wells was one of them. And all those nameless cast iron markers that look like popsicle sticks popping up out of the ground. Pretty spooky. I'm afraid we won't be going back to that place anytime soon, or at least I won't."

The conversation continued as they walked into their apartment and Bob took off his jacket. "Even when things were in full swing back in Coswell's day, you could see by the manuscript we are reading that Cynthia thought along the same lines as you. Didn't she say it was 'the Devil's own mess of broth' or something like that?"

"Yes, she did, but didn't you get a kick out of what Horace said about how parents in the south sometimes tried to discourage their children's' bad behavior by threatening to 'send em off to Milledgeville.' Everyone knew about the lunatic asylum located there. Sounds like a Hansel and Gretel story to me, but then this was no fairy tale and many of the horrors were real. I do like what that woman said who seemed to know so much about the history of the place. 'This institution has witnessed the heights of man's humanity and the depths of his degradation.' She said some doctor who once worked there told her that very thing. I think we are in agreement here. Let's forget about the Georgia Lunatic Asylum or the Central State Hospital or whatever it was last called. Tonight why don't you and I go back to the diary of Peney Tims that Ms. Billings loaned us," Barbara Bumgardner suggested. "Might be a welcome change of pace."

After a quick supper, the Bumgardner's did just that.

DIARY OF PENIA FITZSIMONS TIMS

"I takes pen in hand so's not to disremember that which otherwise might soon be forgot. My name be Penia Fitzsimons Tims, proud wife of Sanford Tims, and truth to tell here, my life ain't been no bed of roses, but with the Good Lord's help and a fair amount of doin on my part, I'll be, if it ain't proved out to be the better side of tolerable. My mamma always used to say that trouble as a general rule gets balanced off pretty good in this world if the body only has the strength to endure and over the years I have come to see the wisdom in those words. Much of the pain and sufferin I was asked to carry in my early days took a turn for the better when I chance met up with a man by the name of Sanford Tims. Bless his soul! He was good man who always done right by me in the years we had together. I always thought it odd that despite all a person's struggles in one direction so much of life can be charged up to nothin more than the wind shiftin and decidin to blow in another. Our meetin was the most fortunate of accidents."

Well, that story had its beginnin many years back when my ol Mistus, Julia Fitzsimons, took a notion in her head to leave our home in Huntsville, Alabama not long after her husband, Massa James Fitzsimons, passed on. After sellin the plantation and auctionin off most of the niggers, the small group of us what was left removed to Milledgeville, Georgia where the Mistus had herself a sister who was also a widow woman. Now I don't figure that Mistus of ours grieved all that much when Massa died cuz he was a rascal and was known to father a passel of chillin on the place, includin both me and my older sister, Cynthia. The Mistus hated him for that, not only cause he proved to be unfaithful, but cause she thought we maybe looked to rise above our station bein as white as we was of both skin and features.

Mamma, now, she was the fine lookin mulatter woman and had really struck the Massa's fancy many years previous. He called her his "house woman." Their daughter and my sister, Cynthia, why she was even whiter than the Mistus and certainly one of the most beautiful women there ever come to be. I was a few shades darker in color (more like Mamma) but was blessed (or cursed) with many of Massa's fine white features. The way Miss Julia would squint up that bespectacled face of hers whenever she laid eyes on us told the whole story. She hated us mightily, as if all three of us was personally responsible for all the evil that was to be found in the world. But like many a proper southern lady, the woman was powerless to do much bout it and generally kept dark on the subject, leastways in proper society. Course, things was different round the Great House as her anger spilled out with constant criticism, scoldins, beatins and other humiliations for those of us who found ourselves directly under her daily care and control. There was times as young'uns when she would take to whippin Cynthia and me mightily and would often make us kiss her whip when she got tuckered out. She would say that it was a pity that poor ol whip had to work so hard to set things right. I members sometime if she was specially angry the blood would run down our little legs onto the floor and she would say it was all our fault in the first place and make us clean up the mess we had caused. Mamma was forced to stand by and watch as she, like all nigger mammies and pappies on the plantation, was powerless to even protect their own offspring. Miss Julia liked to see Mamma squirm like that. After Massa died the first servants sold off was Mamma and my sister, Cynthia, leavin me alone to face the wrath of this vengeful and spiteful woman.

I reckon to have been maybe seventeen years of age at the time, but in many ways I felt myself equal to the task. When she left, Mamma had told me to "be strong, smart and trust in the Lord," them's the exact words she whispered in my ear fore she got up in the wagon and left with her new master, Mr. James Enoch from up Eatonton way. I have to say with a heavy heart that I ain't never set my eyes on her beautiful face or heard her soft voice since that day. Some nights I would lie in bed and strain mightily to think on every bit of that woman…her words and her face, but also the way she walk and the way she would touch me when I had a bad dream and woke up cryin. All this was gone forever cause it suit the white Mistus' fancy.

It weren't but a short time later when Cynthia, she too be taken from my sight. She got sold off to Massa James Walker to live with him on a farm up north in St. Louis, Missouri. I will always remember the last time we spoke. She held my hands in hers and said that I was her "special sister' and she seed many good things comin my way in the future if I only had the strength to endure. I could not have known it at the time, but one good thing was that someday she would come back into my life. I took heart in her words, but grieved heavy for the loss of the only two people in this world I truly loved and who loved me. I never thought it right that families could be separated in such a way. To my mind it went agin every law there was in nature.

But it may have been the Massa hisself, though he be lyin in the low grounds, who unknowingly give me the strength I needed to continue on. You see Massa fancied hisself a great scholar and give all his servants on the plantation ancient Greek and Roman names. He give me the name "Penia" and I remember he say that it was an old Greek name for "weaver of cunning," or somethin akin to that. Folks like to call me "Little Peney" and often did so with a wink and a smile as if they always thought I was up to somethin. I know I did live up to my namesake on more than one occasion. Like many slaves, we often took great delight in "puttin on the massa," as the sayin goes. It was really much like a game, but it could have serious consequences if you was to overstep or miscalculate.

Now it were agin the law for a slave to be caught even holdin a book in their black hands, let alone tryin to read it, yet I done fooled Massa and the Mistus when it come to this forbidden activity. Early on when I was given the task of watchin over their youngest son, Jonah, when he go off to get his lesson from Mrs. Jones (a northern lady who married Hezekiah Jones and made money as a private tutor) why I would look in and listen, quiet like, from outside the open doorway as the sons and daughters of many of the surroundin plantations all learned their letters. I would practice them same letters by blowin hard and deep on the glass window near the door and I would use the first finger on my right hand to form up letters of my own. I was always careful to make sure I wiped the glass clean when the lesson was over so's not to ever give myself away. Both Cynthia and Mamma wanted me to teach em what I'd learned, but they was always kept so busy with housework or Mamma too busy tendin Massa in his private quarters for much of that to have ever happened.

Another time I fooled Massa was when I was maybe fifteen years of age. Mamma told me that was a dangerous time on the plantation for a young black girl as she could begin to expect some changes to come into her life, specially if that young woman had the misfortune of bein pleasin to the eye. Conversations to be had with white men could soon become suggestive in tone, she said, and often times there would be great pressure applied to wear down the young woman and separate her from her innocence or any wished-for virtue. Despite the fact that niggers are property by law and can be used by those in charge as they see fit, many a white owner, their sons or overseers (I figure maybe it was to ease their conscience some) would make efforts to try and make the relationship appear like both parties was in on the deal. Little gifts would be given, small kind-nesses shown and the greatest temptation of all, perhaps a better life offered, but behind it all was the implied threat that if she was to give the white man the go-by, there sure was gonna be hell to pay. That's what happened to both Mamma and Cynthia with Massa Fitzsimons pickin Mamma out when she was but fourteen years of age to begin a life as his personal "house woman" servant.

Cynthia, of course, was his daughter from that sparkin so her predator had come from a different quarter, from high atop the pulpit, in fact. Reverend Samuel Perkins was responsible for tendin to the moral values of slaves on numerous plantations, the Fitzsimons place being one, and he straightaway took a fancy to my older sister when she was but twelve years of age. It's true she was quite advanced in body at the time, but he made the clerical decision that she needed a little "special counselin to further advance her spiritual well-bein." (That's what I members bein said, but truth to tell, the only well-bein he seem to be furtherin was his own.) If you think real hard on it, this peculiar institution of slavery don't just lower them folks in bondage, but has a way of lowerin all those around em as well. As I heard a well-educated white man once say: "The temptations definitely grow greater when absolute power is given one person over another. It is a rare individual indeed, who can escape or resist slavery's evil influence and the personal corruption that's sure to follow." Now I would certainly have to agree with that white man's opinion on the matter.

One day Massa Fitzgerald, he called me to his study for a 'serious matter,' he had said. He got right to the point and informed me of his intention to breed me with one of his big field hands by the name of Silas. I knew Massa had found out from one of the other house servants bout them soiled bed linens of mine, despite Mamma's best efforts to keep quiet on the subject.

"Now Peney," I member him sayin, "you is a woman now and that means you need do your part on this here place. The 'Good Book' says you should be multiplyin and replenishin accordin to scripture and I do believe you needs to start in straightaway in the procreation business. Silas, he's a stout fella and I believe he'll sire up some fine, stout children who will do right by our family, both black and white. Have your mamma bundle up your things and you go over to Silas' cabin tonight. You hear me, girl?"

I remembers droppin my head down to my chest with the news. All I could weakly utter was that I didn't want nothin to do with no field hand as that weren't right and proper for a house nigger, after all, we was higher-up folks and that needed to be taken into account.

"Now don't you pout like that," Massa told me, "and don't give me no sass or I will have you tied to that post out there and stripped down for a good whippin. Get on with you now and the next time I sees you girl, there better be with some swellin in that black belly of yours!"

With that announcement I was dismissed from his presence

and I run upstairs to the small bedroom under the staircase that Cynthia, Mamma and I shared. They both must have been goin bout house business at the time so I laid down all by my lonesome on the bed with tears just a-leakin out both my eyes. I was careful none of em reached the pillowcase or the sheets like those tell-tale stains had done that give away my recent womanhood. Massa he know everythin that go on round this place, I thought to myself, and I'd get a whippin for sure if he knew I was cryin over any decision he had made. Lordy, there sure was plenty of confusion swirlin round in that young head of mine, standin in need of advice from Mamma and my big sister, Cynthia. One thing I knew for certain... I knew I weren't no woman. Why my little titties was no bigger than crab apples and I didn't know nothin bout lyin down with a man or havin any chillins of my own. Good Lord in heaven what was a girl to do? What could I do? When the Massa speak, he speak what's to be done and everyone round here knows that it's a fact that a plantation master is like a little king and he would run his kingdom accordin to the way he was so inclined.

When Mamma finally come up to the room them same tears returned. After I told her of Massa's wishes she pressed her forehead to mine and say she thought if we put our two heads together she was sure we could think on somethin to do. She soon began to bundle up my things, but as she did she suggested when Silas come in from the fields and returned to the cabin, I should just tell him it weren't my time yet and maybe we could just pretend to live together the way Massa say. Mamma said she weren't sure this trick would work as "it's hard fer a man to go agin his basic nature," she told me. "Black or white, rich or poor, young or old, the Good Lord done put the notion in mens' heads to always want to waller round inside a woman. Don't know the reason for it but maybe that was so's to ensure there's always the proper number of people," she said. "A person can't pretend to know the ways of the Lord, Peney, but you see if you can reason with Silas first fore we try anythin else," she instructed.

Late in the afternoon I took all my worldly belongins and went over to the Silas's cabin in the quarters. I tidied things up and swept the dirt floor, makin all look quite tolerable for when Silas come home. I had even made a nice fire on the hearth by the time the big field hand finally made his appearance. I stood up to greet him as he hung his straw hat on a hook and took to lookin me over like I was a piece of meat hung up in the smoke house.

I figured to be the one who would start in doin the talkin. "Silas, has Massa talked to you bout you and me livin together in this here cabin?" I asked.

"Massa say you are my girl now and you are to take care of the cabin here, do the cookin and take care of ol Silas and do whatever he want. I would tell you right now I has a powerful need to lay with you so you get yourself over to that bed and get undressed so's we can get started."

"Are you crazy, nigger," I said in as forceful a manner as I could muster up. "I don't even knows who you be yet."

"Don't matter. I feel a powerful need to have you right at this very moment."

"Silas, can't you see I ain't no woman," I said, throwin back my shawl and showin off my flat chest, narrow hips and underdeveloped body. "I could not do right by a man such as you," I said in as flatterin a tone as I could muster.

"Massa's wishes be Massa's wishes. We can't go agin em," he replied, tryin to put a cap on the conversation as he continued to look me up and down.

I started in then tellin him of Mamma's plan, but found myself speakin much faster than was common.

He listened and looked at me hard for a spell, but didn't let me finish as he grabbed my arm and began draggin me off in the direction of the bed which was attached to side of the cabin with two ropes that hung down from the wall. Knowin Silas weren't havin no part of Mamma's plan, out of desperation I reached for the poker on the hearth as he dragged me along. As I grabs the thing, I steps back and swung it pretty good off in the direction of his nappy head and succeeded in dealin him a smashin lick. He let go of my arm and give me a shocked and angry look.

When his head clear somewhat he spoke. "Massa say you got to do this. You gonna get a whippin for sure when I tells him tomorrow mornin what you done," he said, as he grabbed his hat, looked at the poker I still held in my hand and, staggerin slightly, walked out the door.

"You just stay away from me, you hear!" I yelled, as he disappeared from my view.

Shortly after Silas left the cabin, I leave too and run back into the Great House. It was full dark at the time but I knew the way and didn't need no moonlight to guide me. I come in the back way and went upstairs to our room. None of the house servants saw me. Mamma say she was not surprised by the way Silas acted and said she had another plan cooked up to save her youngest daughter. Her plan showed her great love for me, as she had decided to offer herself to the field hand despite the fact that she did not like his crude nature and the fact that he was certainly beneath our station as house servants. Mamma told me she would secretly lie with Silas and see to all his worldly needs if he kept dark bout our arrangement.

I figured it to be maybe a month or two where Mamma would come over faithfully to the cabin late most nights and I would be excused to go outside so's she and Silas could be alone together. I could hear him puffin and groanin for hours at a time and admit in my curious youth to the temptation to want to spy in the open window to see all that was goin on. But in the back of my head was the story Massa told many years ago bout why the Negro race was cursed by God to be slaves in the first place. Noah's son, Ham, he said, did a terrible thing after the flood by lookin at his naked daddy while he lay fast asleep. For that sin he would be banished to the wilds of Africa where he was to start up the black race which the Bible said would be cursed forever. I figured if I saw my mamma like that, why, somethin bad would happen to me as well, so I never give in to the temptation to peek my head in.

After two months' time, Massa see there ain't no swellin in my belly and he say he gonna make other arrangements. Things went back to the way they was early on, but how we laugh over how we trick Massa, specially since Massa was often doin his bidness in the same place where the field nigger, Silas had been tendin his bidness just a short time earlier. Oh, how Massa would have howled had he knowed such a thing! I'm sure Silas would have been whipped dead for it, so all parties kept quiet and Massa never knew a single thing bout the plan we had all cooked up.

Yes, I would learn to dodge round pretty good over the years in the Fitzsimons house. It sure is true what is said down in the quarters that all niggers must have two faces…one for theirselves and their own kind (one real face) and then another to show to the white man. Always wear a mask and never give in to the temptation of bein honest with a white person, it was often said, as that moment of weakness could cost you plenty down the road. I was proud to have wove my clever and deceitful web many a time through the years with Massa and "Julia Devil" as we all come to call her. It give me a sense of power and made me feel good bout myself. I found this would certainly come in handy that one fall day in Milledgeville when I had to fool the Mistus one more time down at the general store when the shock of seein my sister Cynthia again almost give us both away.

Chapter 5

A BRUSH WITH DEATH

COSWELL TIM'S DIARY RESUMES

"Good mornin, Mr. Tims," the early mornin visitor offered as he stood on the porch of our small farmhouse on the outskirts of town. The sun was just peekin over the hill at the time and I was makin every attempt to get the sleep out of my eyes and adjust to the new light of day. A rather tall fella on the other side of the doorway spoke out once again.

"My name's Patrick Kane and I work over at the Jarratt place. We got us a runaway over there and have been unable to locate the negro in question. It's our blacksmith, Andrew. That boy took to his heels last night and Mr. Jarratt has a powerful need to see him returned as soon as possible," the overseer reported. "Valuable piece of property, he is Mr. Tims. Got treated real good over the years and was well trusted which is why it is so hard to understand why a nigger like that would run. Can you and your brother and maybe a couple of your hound dogs come over this mornin and give us a hand? Mr. Jarratt would be most beholdin."

I stepped barefoot out onto the piazza to get better acquainted with this fella and thought I'd toss in a comment of my own. "Don't matter how well-fed or well treated anythin is, Mr. Kane, if they find theirselves locked inside a cage they're gonna want to get out. It's a lot like when Jesse and me was young'uns and had us a pet raccoon. Now we treated him right fine, I mean to tell ya, but whenever we'd take to jigglin the door handle or opened the cage door just a scratch, why, I'd be lyin if I said that critter weren't always in high earnest to better his circumstance. I believe the same holds true with darkies. We have found over the years that even under the best conditions of confinement, if they feel they have a half a chance of gettin away, they'll run sure. I would even go so far as to say that very fact has kept my brother and me in this family business over these many years."

"Come now, Mr. Tims," Jarratt's overseer answered as he began to agitate some. "Don't you think most darkies are generally content with their lot in life? After all, their food, clothin, housin, and doctorin are all seen to by obligin and generous masters. Sure, there are few ornery ones that run or cause trouble, but then I've known some white folks I wouldn't turn my back on. Now wouldn't you agree with that?"

I guess maybe I rolled my eyes some with the last of these early mornin comments, all of which had been aimed in my general direction. I have seen first-hand over the years since we been in this slave catchin business, the strong desire enslaved people have to be free. Now it's true that most will not run, but then, I figure that might just testify to how smart they is. They know the deck is heavily stacked agin em. A black man or woman runnin in a white man's world don't generally amount to much more than fiddlesticks and frustration, but that don't mean black folk are content with their lives as property. If the odds improved or their situation was to go from bad to worse where they felt they had less to lose or more to gain, why they'd run and that's just a fact.

Not willin to take the time to point all this out to my uninvited guest, I interrupted the conversation with a loud request. "Sanford would you fetch my boots for me?"

"We're just wakin up round here, Mr. Kane. It will take a little time to get things all readied up." I noticed Kane had calmed down some and I couldn't see the need to restart that former conversation and breed a quarrel this early in the mornin.

Sanford promptly brought my boots from the house and I slipped em on one at a time, noticin with a certain amount of pleasure when I stood up that the height of the early mornin visitor had shrunk considerable.

"How is it that slave of yours never runs, Mr. Tims?" Kane inquired, obviously wishin to return to his former line of exchange.

"Well, both Cynthia and me treat Sanford real well. Why we even ask his opinion on some matters and allow him to help out with our trackin business. He knows his place, but I don't believe he feels that he's in a cage, kinda feels like a respected member of the family, I would say."

"Sounds dangerous to me. If this 'peculiar institution' of ours is to continue on, then the lines between black and white have to be carefully drawn, wouldn't you agree? You can't treat em like people and expect em to work like property. Why, the whole system as we know it would break down and come to perdition."

"Well, rest assured Mr. Kane, that ain't bout to happen anytime soon," I responded, as I strapped on my trusty sidearm. "My guess is that it would take a war or some other earth-shatterin event for that to ever be the case. No, this peculiar institution of ours is gonna be with us for many years to come, I figure."

"That's good news for you in your line of work and for us over at the plantation as well. Could you imagine who you could get to do the work if there were no darkies to be had? I'm afraid it would be the economic ruination of the entire nation. It scares hell out of me to think that Lincoln fella might get elected president in the upcomin election. Everyone knows the man's a ravin abolitionist. Why, I heard tell…"

"Mr. Kane, forgive me for sayin this, but you are startin to distress my ears on this fine sunny mornin. I have found that politics don't generally profit a man and I think tendin our own business and not lookin too far off in the distance might be in order. All I know right now is that we need to catch a nigger blacksmith that run off your place fore too much time has passed. Now I expect Jesse to arrive any minute as we had intended on trainin up one of our young catch hounds this mornin fore you come by with your request. We could be underway within the next half hour or so if all goes accordin to plan," I told the early mornin visitor.

The door to our house suddenly swung open and my wife, Cynthia, come out into the light of day. A welcome relief from the discussion, her presence always brought a smile to my face. "Coswell, are you and Sanford gonna work today on that fence that got tore down in the last storm?" she asked, as she started walkin over to where Kane and I stood on the porch.

"Oh, Mr. Kane… this is my wife, Cynthia," I offered by way of proper introduction.

"Pleased to make your acquaintance, Ma-am," Jarratt's overseer replied, as he took off his hat and bowed slightly. "I hate to take your husband and your servant away from any important work here, but we do have us a little problem over at the Jarratt place that requires a professional hand."

"I will get to that fence when I get back, Darlin," I interrupted. "Sanford's taken to readyin-up the horse and I'll tend to the dog. We'll start on the trail as soon as Jesse comes by."

"Just stop in the house fore you leave, Coswell. I have somethin important I need to talk to you about," she said, as she turned to go inside. Recognizin a possible slight, she turned back in the direction of our early mornin visitor and added with a nod of her head: "Nice to have made your acquaintance, Mr. Kane."

As Kane silently tipped his hat to the lady of the house, it went through my mind how different things might have been had all fifty-two cards been properly laid out upon the table. Respect for women was an avowed way of life in the south, but the woman, of course, had to be white in color in order for that to be the case. Nevertheless and notwithstandin, I have to say I wouldn't swap my Cynthia off for nobody.

With Patrick Kane mountin his horse and gallopin off to the Jarratt place, I went out back to the barn to ready-up the dog. I figured we only needed but one fetchhound for the job ahead. We had five of em at this particular point in time and they was all was glad to see ol Coswell when I reached the pen inside the barn. "Colonel," he sat up straight and tall, figurin he would be the likely one chosen for the task at hand, after all, he had done a pretty fair job chasin Benton Wells recently. "Echo," maybe even shared in even more of that glory, but I knew he did not like to work alone. "Duke," now he was lookin for a chance to redeem hisself after missin a runaway last week and Annabel, our only female, owned a reputation as a great tracker, but was somewhat timid as she sat off to the side some, givin me that coy look that says… "You might want to pick me, Coswell."

A small black and tan pup my wife had started callin "Wrinkles" was also among the brood, but looked more confused than ready. That dog didn't lack none for eagerness as I sensed he was takin stock of all that was around him. I paused long enough to give the young critter a little look-see even though both of us knew his time had not yet come. Cynthia was right to have named him what she had, I thought to myself. Why he sure had a fair amount of growin to do if he was ever goin to be able to fill in all that loose, wrinkly skin of his. I think it's fair to say that you could fit two and a half dogs inside the soft outer coverin of fuzz and fur. I did figure his curious nature might very well produce good results in the future. For some strange reason that pup reminded me a great deal of our young friend, James Rufus.

Hopefully makin a good business decision, I promptly announced: "Come on, Annabel. You and me is goin for a little stroll this fine mornin."

"Coswell, you in there?" come a voice from outside the barn.

"Right here, Jesse," I replied, as I continued to tend the hound just selected. Jesse stood in the open barn doorway lookin like he did most days. He was definitely not a self-conscious individual and really didn't give a damn what others thought of his appearance. His coat, for example, looked like he had used it for shotgun practice or like he just tore through a briar patch and was fortunate enough to have escaped with his life. Why there were more holes in that thing than there was cloth. I just smiled, but felt the need to mention that I thought our successful trackin business would allow for a new coat or two.

"This one suits me right fine, 'Little Brother,' and it's all broke in just the way I like. Why it would take years to get a new coat to be as comfortable as this here one," he concluded.

All high fashion aside, I began to pass along the latest news. "We got ourselves a little change of plans, Jesse. We need to head off to the Jarratt place to fetch his blacksmith, Andrew, who run off last night. Might just be a good day for us with his value high as it is. He ain't no ordinary field hand, mind you. This fella is highly prized on the place. Now if you'll consent to finishin up here with Annabel, I'll go offer my sweet good-byes to the lady of the house."

Comin inside, I was immediately set upon by my lovely wife. She surprised me when she reached out and grabbed at my arm. "Coswell, I had an awful dream last night and I just can't shake it. I want you to take extra care out on the trail today. I saw danger comin from strange and unexpected places. Why, it was as if the devil hisself rose up before ya to strike…all pretty cloudy in my mind now that I'm full awake, but the feelin it just ain't gone away."

"Don't tell me, Cynthia, you've taken to conjurin like them

women down in the quarters what wears the gopher dust in a bag round their necks and do all the prophesizen. I know you have some special abilities but, you know what, sweetheart…most every time I go out on the trail you say the same kind of thing. Maybe you think it's the worryin itself that keeps bad things from happenin."

"You know how you always say a person should listen to the voices in their head if they make an effort to speak up, now didn't you say that?"

"Well, yes I did. What exactly are those voices sayin to you?"

"They're sayin you better be 'watchin, lookin and listenin,' real careful like, if you want things to turn out favorable. You need to go extra cautious today, that's all I'm sayin. You hear me now, Mr. Tims?"

"Yes, and I thank you, Mrs. Tims for your great concern. I will take all this under proper advisement and keep a skinned eye and an open ear for trouble," I replied, as I reached out for my woman and drew her in tight, givin her a kiss full on the lips, one I knew she would remember hopefully long after I had disappeared from her mortal vision.

"Darlin," I whispered softly in her ear, "Don't you never forget this man of yours will love ya for good and always." With that heartfelt pronouncement, I released her from my lovin grasp and set my hat purposely upon my head. My wife said the exact same thing in reply by simply offerin up a little smile and a nod in return.

Three men, two horses and a single hound dog later, a small but determined group wound its way northwest in the direction of the Jarratt plantation. Sanford walked close beside the leashed hound with Jesse and I both mounted on our horses. We were in high earnest and all readied-up for the occasion, believin ourselves more than equal to the task at hand. We had done well over the years, we had, even though there are many folks who do not hold slave catchers in high esteem. Now I know that another person's opinion of me is really none of my business, but it does get under my skin sometimes, makin me bout as touchy as a sore-backed horse on the subject of green flies. What I really hate most is when someone starts in shakin their finger at me like it were a snake's tongue, tryin to put a respectable distance tween us so's to preserve their own lofty moral status. Mamma used to say folks that do that, they don't realize there are three of their own fingers pointin right back in their direction. Now that does say somethin, don't it? Those folks can keep their fingers, their snakes and their viperous opinions all to themselves, I come to figure.

Plantation master, William Jarratt, welcomed us most cordially when we reached the place and soon give Annabel a sniff of an old hat Andrew had wore down in his blacksmith shop. With that little ritual properly tended to, we were finally ready to head out across the plantation field and begin the chase.

Sanford was in the lead, takin up his position some 20′ behind a sniffin red hound. He held a long leather lead in his skilled black hand. Annabel was a good and considerate canine and would not pull any more than was necessary to continue on any path she has chosen. Sanford was a master houndsman who would gently guide the dog back on task if she temporarily become distracted. It sure was great for the Tims boys to have an experienced handler like Sanford, as it freed the two of us to ride and keep a watchful eye from our lofty position. A man in a tree, a negro with a stolen firearm, sudden movement in the brush, all were things we kept a proper watch for. But as Cynthia offered early on, sometimes danger can lurk in most unsuspectin places, maybe right under a man's nose, or feet to maybe be even more clear on the matter.

As we continued along the trail I thought back to that warnin. Now if I had a dollar for every one of my wife's forecasts of doom, I'd be a rich man indeed. But I knew those feelins of hers was well-intended and done out of love even if nothin generally come of em. For some reason that made me think of Cynthia and Sanford a few nights back tellin some tall tales of their own from time they spent down in the quarters. Cynthia, she started in first tellin an amusin story bout a slave by the name of "High John, The Conqueror," and how he lived on a terrible Mississippi planation down in the delta land.

The white folks there were so mean, she said, rattlesnakes refused to bite em for fear they would poisonin theirselves. It was a cold hard fact, she added, that rattlesnakes bit only niggers down in that neck of the woods. She said that with a face as straight as a poker. She went on to say that white people were so mean they would sometimes shoot a slave just to bet on which way he would fall…frontwards or backwards and then take to whippin the dead man's mamma if they lost the bet when he fell the wrong way. It sure was a tough place for a slave to live, but the good news was that "High John" always seemed to come out the top dog and always got the better of his master and other white folks by usin his wits and cunnin gainst their greed and evil ways. The slave community even fancied him a "conqueror" and said why he was "so big that he had to stoop down at night to let the moon pass him by." Cynthia did admit this accountin may have been one of them "Molly Bright" made-up stories, exaggerated more than a scratch, but it did prove the point that all people need to have messages of hope that they can believe in.

Sanford, hearin bout them rattlesnakes, couldn't seem to let go of that and jumped right in to the conversation when she finished, tellin a story of his own bout how it was them snakes come by their rattles in the first place. Sanford told us that it was a certain-sure fact that the rattlesnake originally had been given but one gift from the Creator and that was the gift of beautiful colors. Trouble was that them colors was a little short on the protection end of things and did very little to keep this handsome creature from bein stepped on and injured by those walkin about. Now this began to happen on such a regular basis back in them early days that he said the snakes all got together and sent off a petition to the Good Lord in search of a suitable remedy. After reviewin the petition, God (after lookin in the mirror at his own black skin) thought he had done a right fine job of colorin things up just right, but then decided it probably weren't no fun to be stepped on so much. Sanford said God agreed to then give the critters poison so's to better protect themselves, thinkin that this would solve the problem, but it just created another.

It weren't but a short time later when a host of other critters come forth with a petition of their own, claimin these snakes was now bitin and killin so many others that all lived in mortal terror. In His great wisdom, God finally decided to even things out with a general compromise. The snake could keep its poison, but was given rattles and had to offer up a fair warnin fore it struck. And so it has been this way ever since, Sanford concluded. But one thing our young Sanford forgot to include in his rather fanciful tale, was the fact that in late August rattlesnakes round Milledgeville, Georgia begin to shed that skin of theirs and in the process make less noise then agreed upon in the compromise. To get right to the heart of the matter and stop chasin the devil round the stump, our Sanford was bit by a seven foot rattlesnake in the back of his lower left leg on August 29, 1860 when we was out on the trail lookin for Jarratt's runaway and we thought for sure our boy was a-fixin for the heavens!

It just seemed to me like one moment Sanford was walkin along all business-like and then the next minute the same fella was lyin in heap on the red Georgia clay. There was a scream of pain to be had somewheres in the midst of all that, with Sanford lettin the leash drop from his hands as he fell to the ground, grabbin at his naked lower limb. He had just stepped over a dead log where a large rattlesnake had recently taken up residence, most likely tryin to rid hisself of his last and latest skin. Jesse quick shot the reptile in the head, but that did nothin to relieve poor Sanford. He was writhin round in pain and I quick come to his side and told him to lay as still as possible and I would tend things best I could. Jesse picked up the dead snake and tossed it off to the side, careful not to get too near the business end which still had the ability to do some damage. We all knew that a bite of this nature from this size and type of snake usually did not end well.

"Jesse, quick make a fire while I try my hand at doctorin here," I shouted out, as I took to removin my sidearm and slid the leather holster off the belt. Usin that belt I wrapped it tight round Sanford's upper leg, foldin it just right so's it would stay in place. Turnin my attention then to the bite itself, I took out my knife and cut back from each fang mark, openin the skin so's to better get inside. I sucked blood and venom from the wound best I could and give Jesse the knife with instructions to heat it red hot at the tip for what lay ahead. While he was doin that, I let the tourniquet go for a few seconds, allowin some of the poison to enter the negro's body. I remember readin an article in a newspaper some time back written by a doctor up Philadelphia way (I think his name was Dr. Mitchell) bout this very procedure and remembered him sayin to repeat this same process over and over again every twenty minutes or so for some two hours before removin the tourniquet altogether. That way there was less shock enterin the system at one time, he had said. I tightened up the tourniquet once more before I continued on.

"Jesse, is the knife ready yet?"

"Almost, Coswell. Let's give it a few more minutes."

This last part was tricky as the tip of the knife needed to follow the fang marks as deep into the wound as possible fore the hot knife itself was laid across the opened up flesh on the surface. I could smell that flesh burnin as I worked. Dead flesh weren't supposed to carry poison to the rest of the system if I remembered correctly. Sanford, he let out a fair-sized holler, but kept his leg as still as he possibly could.

As we was finishin up, Jesse come up with a right fine suggestion and that was to fetch us a wagon from a nearby farm as we both knew Sanford needed to lie as quiet as possible so the poison didn't get all stirred up again. Jesse said he believed we weren't too far from the old Tucker farm and he knew the widow woman who lived there and thought she might be accomodatin. Actually, down home in the southland it is generally the custom for slaves to be cared for by any white folk in the area if the need arises. If a negro was comin back from somewhere with a pass and it got too dark to continue, for example, he would be put up and fed by a neighbor at no charge. This was just common courtesy one slave owner would extend to another. Miss Nellie Tucker, along with a widow sister by the name of Miss Julia Fitzsimons who happened to be livin with her at the time, proved to be most helpful and very considerate neighbors durin this time of great need.

Chapter 6

A PAINFUL DECISION

DIARY OF PENIA FITZSIMONS TIMS

I have to say the first time I ever laid my eyes on Sanford Tims was a memorable one. A young black man was brought in to the farm one afternoon, bad snake-bit on his lower leg. His owners, two brothers that was in the slave catchin business, were very concerned bout his welfare (I first figured cause he must have been a smart nigger and one what made em a lot of money.) One brother was quite tall, but looked to be kinda rag-tag and scruffy. The younger one was quite a handsome fella, well-spoken and well-dressed, sure of himself, but not boastful proud. They brought their servant to the farm in a wagon as the poor thing had been bit nearby out in the woods. They knew it was important that he lay quiet in order to get well. Miss Julia's sister agreed to have him tended to and I was given the job of lookin after him. On the younger brother's instructions I was to keep warm, wet bandages soaked in wet ashes and vinegar on the whole of his leg and change em up whenever they cooled. They both seemed to really care about this servant of theirs who, I found, went by the name of Sanford. I did what they told me to do for the better part of two days, I did.

Now when he first got here I had to do other things as well. The younger brother, who seemed to know quite a bit bout medicine, but weren't no doctor, said Sanford needed to have some Kill Devil Whiskey inside his body and lots of it so Miss Nellie Tucker went into her private supply. I tried and tried to get the man to swaller the prescribed amount, but he couldn't tolerate it. He just tossed it back up. On the older slave owner's instructions I fetched a squeeze pump from the kitchen and squirted the whisky into his body from a different location, one not so pleasant. I guess you could say I learned more bout this Sanford Tims than I bargained for, but despite the closeness we shared, I don't think he said ten words to me the whole time he was in my care.

Them same two slave catchers come by to fetch him in their own wagon after a few days' time, but I never saw hide nor hair of either of em as Miss Nellie had me tendin to other things. It was obvious this Sanford was a fine lookin young man, black as night and well-built despite his recent misfortune, and I found the space tween his two front teeth tickled my fancy no end. I greatly regret never havin had a chance to say any proper farewells, but I did find out by listenin to the Mistus and her sister in conversation that the men who owned him were local slave catchers, Coswell and Jesse Tims, who also lived in Milledgeville and this servant of theirs helped em in their slave-catchin business. I know sometimes a person will turn agin their own kind if it profits em, but I didn't get that feelin here. Maybe I was just wishin this Sanford to be a good man. Secretly I hoped I might see him again, maybe sometime down the road if such a thing was possible for a person of my humble circumstance.

Well, I remember it to have been early September of that same year when an advertisement in the *Southern Recorder* from William Butler's general store happened to catch Miss Julia's eye. A recent shipment from Philadelphia had just come Butler's way up the Oconee River from Darien for the fall and winter fashions and he proudly announced the arrival of "choice broadcloths, blue, black or mixed casimeres, red, white or yellow flannels, Irish linens, silk striped vestings, black and pink cambric, silk flag handkerchiefs and hose made of cotton and wool," (or so said in the broadside.) Miss Julia, she got powerfully anxioused up as did her widow sister, Miss Nellie Tucker, when they both took to readin all bout these things.

Soon a plan was hatched for a trip to town with Miss Nellie's servant, Old Zeke, given orders to hitch the horses up to the wagon and make ready for the trip. I was instructed to go along as well, tucked in behind the three of em in the back of the wagon. My job was to fetch anythin these two fine ladies might decide to purchase while at the store. Of course I spy Miss Julia carryin that switchin stick of hers along with her reticule as Old Zeke took her arm to help her into the carriage. I took to wishin her faithful servant would just let go of ol Julia Devil if he had half the chance so she would fall flat to the ground and maybe break a bone or two in the process. If such a thing did happen, why I do believe my conscience would be as clear as the water in a high mountain stream.

A large sign "Butler's General Store" soon greeted us as we rounded Buffington Corner and Franklin St. give way to South Wayne. This was the first section of town to see business developed, I remember Miss Nellie sayin, as we all took notice of the green buildin with large gold letterin over the door, across the street from the town's Market House. This was my first trip into town in the year or so that we had come to reside in Milledgeville. Old Zeke, he hitched the horses up to the railin in front of the store and dutifully helped both women out of the vehicle so's their feet would gather the least amount of mud or animal waste possible. Animals, we noticed, ran rather freely throughout the town, with pigs bein the biggest offender. Most did have nose rings, however, to keep em from rootin under fences, but they was allowed by town officials to pick up loose garbage on the streets. I heard Miss Nellie tell her sister that there was a man specially appointed by the town fathers whose job it was to come round twice a week with a public cart to clean all the streets and alleys of "filth and other offensive matter," but I saw nary a trace of any such individual the day of our trip.

I was ordered to remain in the wagon as Old Zeke brought the two of em over to the store. He held the door open and bowed politely as the ladies disappeared inside. He followed behind em and I could soon see through the store window him standin with his hat in his hand. In short order I found myself lookin round from my raised position in the back seat of the market wagon. Folks, they was comin and goin as there looked to be a fair amount of store tradin goin on that day. I noticed men walkin, some arm and arm with their wives, women strollin slowly and havin lively conversation with other women often of the same age, and there was children, some attended and some unattended, playin freely about the street. Both white and black folk could be found in considerable numbers, but I reckon there to have been more whites than blacks on that particular day despite what I learned that Baldwin County could lay claim to an equal number of both. It was interestin to watch people go to and fro, seein the way they acted and treated one another. Negroes would bow and scrape as they give way to white folks on the sidewalks, men would tip their hats to the ladies they met. Children, black and white all mixed in together, were busy doin the same childish things that young'uns always do. A group of em off in the distance could be heard squealin with delight, maybe even louder than the small pig that continued to slip from their grasp.

As I looked up and down the street, I soon took notice of another farm wagon that come to a stop on the sandy street just a few buildins from where we was hitched. A man got out and helped his lady friend from her seat and they began to walk in my general direction. The man was dressed in a black sack coat and tan trousers, a green brocade vest and straw hat. He walked purposeful and his boots give a strong sound as they fell upon the wooden sidewalk. He had well-tended-to hair on his face and I could tell he wore a gun on his belt … maybe looked to be a law and order man, but I could see no badge. There was somethin quite familiar bout him.

The woman on his arm was dressed tolerably well, but not in refinement in a green day dress, black high-topped shoes and a tan colored, rather fancified hat with a feather wavin from the top for all to see. Her hair was all done up and tucked under that hat as was right and proper for the time and the woman carried herself with a certain dignity and grace that I not only found favorable, but quite familiar. Why they were bout as fine lookin a white couple that ever took to walkin the streets, I thought to myself. But as the woman turned her head slowly away from her man as their conversation appeared to have ended, it was right then and there I first caught sight of her face.

My mouth must have dropped straight down with my jaw scrappin the wagon floor as I recognized the woman. IT WAS CYNTHIA, MY GOD, IT WAS CYNTHIA! My long-lost sister who I had not seen in many years! She weren't in St. Louis after all with that slavin man she gone off with and she obviously weren't no slave neither, as that was as plain to see as the nose on your face. I most jumped from the wagon with joy to rush to her arms, but then thought better on the matter after further consideration. If Cynthia and her man-friend (who I now recognized as one of the Tims brothers who had brought Sanford to the farm) were to go inside the store which it looked like they was fixin to do, Miss Julia would certainly see Cynthia and recognize her for the white nigger wench her dead husband had sired and who had growed up under her control on the Fitzsimmons place. I figured that would not go well for my sister in her disguised condition and I knew I had to use my wits and do somethin right quick!

Just then Old Zeke come out of the store to say Miss Julia wants me to come and fetch the boxes and packages containin their recent purchases. I gets inside and heads over to the counter where everyone was a standin and I just hopes for the best. When I hears the creak of the door behind me, a quick glance over my shoulder tells me that the handsome couple had entered the store. As Mr. Butler begin to hand me the first rather heavy package, I give some quick thought as to what I should do and I decides straightaway to turn quick, playin like I lose my balance and in the process fall in the direction of the Mistus. I tumble hard into the old woman knockin her down to the floor. Both package and servant landed right atop her, compoundin the agony. I bounces up fresh as a daisy and starts in makin my apologies to everyone for my clumsiness, but I notice to my satisfaction that Miss Julia's eyes are closed shut and she ain't listenin or seein no one at this particular time. I turns my head to the side, just enough for my sister for the first time to see my face.

"Pe…" she started in, but quick as a flash reversed direction and let out with a "Po…poor woman, what has happened here?

"I was clumsy, Ma'am and should have knowed better," I replied, as I cast my eyes down to the floor in response to the beautiful white lady's inquiry.

Cynthia, she look away from me and look down at the old white woman who lay crumpled up on the floor. My sister's mouth fell open with a slight gasp and Cynthia put both hands up close to her lips. She knew who she was lookin at. Oh yes, she knew that ol Julia Devil whether them eyes of hers were shut closed or open wide and squintin away like she always done. Knowin she needed to leave immediately, I heard her say kinda low like, but loud enough so's all nearby could hear: "Coswell, I'm feelin a might faint seein this poor lady hurt so, would you please help me back to our wagon." With that, her man, without sayin a word, took her by the arm and the two of em returned to their market wagon without makin a single purchase.

Miss Julia, she finally come to on the floor and began to look around, maybe so's to make some sense out of this recent catastrophe. Mr. Butler and Old Zeke helped the woman to her feet and she began to slowly dust herself off. She give a disgusted look my way and I see them eyes of hers crinkle up in that ol familiar way. "Let's go home, sister," she said, adjustin her copper specs, all the while never takin her eyes from me. Oh, I knew for sure there was liable to be a heap of torment to be had fore, and if, I was ever to see my long-lost sister again.

Back at Miss Nellie's place instructions was given to her favorite servant to fetch some rawhide from inside the barn and accompany me out back to the whippin tree. I knew he did not want to be party to this, but I know he couldn't risk the same punishment hisself as that old body of his would most likely not live through it. My hands was soon tied high above my head, both of em with a leather strap and my feet was tied below. On Miss Julia Devil's instructions I had been stripped as naked as the day I come into the world. Old Zeke tried to look away for modesty's sake as he done it, but he dutifully continued to do his mistress' biddin. I was left alone for some time in this exposed condition, dreadin what was sure to come. Several of Miss Nellie's servants walked by, goin on bout their business, but not a one of em said a single word that reached my ear. I also took notice of some of Miss Nellie's white neighbors that happened by to watch the goins-on.

Now over the years I had been struck many times with the switch and knocked on the head with various things the Mistus could get her hands on. She once hit me in the back of the head with the butter churn dasher so hard that I passed out on the floor, but I had never before been whipped out in full view for all to see. I began to recall what field niggers had to say on the matter. They say there was two things they hated most sides the pain. One was when and if they was forcefully undressed for the occasion, takin away all modesty and demonstratin for all there to see that you owned nothin in this world, not even the ragged clothes that once covered your back.

The other thing they told me they hated was if the whippin made no sense and they felt in their mind they had done nothin wrong to deserve such a thing. Now iffen a nigger had stole somethin or had tried to run away they could at the very least make sense out of why there was punishment to be had. But often times the punishment was due to the master's orneriness, maybe excessive drinkin or some imaginary infraction that he or she thought needed a strong hand. In any case such a whippin would play tricks with a slave's mind and could make em question the reality of the world around them. Now I did know the reason why I was gonna be whipped…that made sense even if I weren't happy bout such a thing, but I certainly come to understand what the field workers meant bout bein shamed and naked, exposed for all the world to see. I could feel the hot mid-day sun on my back, my buttocks and the backs of my legs as I awaited the inevitable punishment I knew was soon headed my way.

After a spell Miss Julia Fitzsimons come out the door with her sister close behind. Followin after Miss Nellie come Jonathan Hunter, Miss Nellie's man in charge of things on the farm. He weren't really an overseer, like there would be on a large plantation. With less than twenty black folks on this here residence, this place would properly be called a "farm" and the owner disallowed the exalted label of "planter." But Massa Hunter was her right-hand farm man and in his right hand right now was a bullwhip all greased up special for this occasion.

"I want very little skin left on that black back of hers," Miss Julia ordered, as her man took up a position slightly to the side and to the rear of me. The thought went through my mind that her request sounded like some high payin customer orderin up a special cut of beef at a roadside tavern.

I set my mind to endure this punishment with little or no complaint, but the first blow with the full force of the bullwhip made me rethink that plan. The shock of it took me by complete surprise. It was absolute horror and agony, truth to tell, and both my eyes come to see stars. The sting and pain of the leather snappin hard across my back took no time t'all to travel quickly throughout every single part of my body. I did not know how I could possibly bear even one more blow, but havin no choice in the matter, my personal thoughts were of little consequence. I members after five or six of those same hard lashes, I started in screamin horrible and pleaded with the Mistus to please make him stop, but that made no nevermind. I then started to buck violently against my restraints, but again that was all to no good end. Nothin could save me. Merciful God in heaven, the pain was so great! I tried prayer, but that was not allowed and any petition to God or mercy found the whip to strike even harder. I remembered nothin more after maybe the twentieth stroke of that long strap of braided leather.

Old Zeke told me later that they give me near 100 lashes that day and I was lucky to have survived the ordeal. It took several days fore I could even move or stand. I had been placed in one of the two cabins down in the quarters and ordered tended to by the field hands who lived there. They were quite familiar with this sort of thing as punishment with the bullwhip was not uncommon. They knew my pain and sufferin and took right good care of me, they did.

Years later when I would lie in my husband Sanford's arms at night, we would often take to runnin our hands over each other's backs and the both of us could still feel the deep furrows in the skin from bein all tore up by the master's whip. It was a constant reminder of them terrible days before freedom come. But I would have to say that all I remember thinkin the whole time I was lyin face-down on that cabin floor after that whippin… "You did not kill me you damn bitch woman and I will live to someday dance on your grave and see my sister, Cynthia, once more!"

Chapter 7

A DEVIL'S BARGAIN

September 1, 2014
Milledgeville, GA

The two journals presented a unique opportunity that was not lost on the Bumgardner's. Not only did each one add its fair share of historic information, but coming from two different quarters they also offered a much wider perspective. It could also show how two different people could possibly view the same thing and yet have different ideas about it. Bob found himself taken with the voice of Coswell Tims and his almost Mark Twain-like country wisdom, despite his rather unsavory avocation. Bob's wife, Barbara, favored the voice of Penia Tims, or "Little Peney" as she was called, and thought the woman courageous and strong in the face of seemingly overwhelming obstacles. The story of Coswell Tims and his family continued to spring to life, courtesy of the two old manuscripts that had somehow, almost miraculously, managed to find their way into the 21st century.

COSWELL TIM'S DIARY RESUMES

"What we gonna do, Coswell?" Cynthia asked, as our wagon rattled along in pretty much the same ruts and furrows that had we had fashioned just an hour or so previous. A little store tradin was all we had in mind this day, but I reckon maybe we got a little more than we had bargained for.

Cynthia continued to talk excitedly. "I can't believe they be livin right under our noses over at the Tucker's Place not five miles from our doorstep and we never caught a single whiff off it. I reckon I do remember some of the ladies gossipin bout Miss Nellie takin in a widow sister and her servant, but who would have ever guessed that would have included my long-lost little Peney. Oh Peney! Why, Coswell, you and Jesse was over there just the other day tendin Sanford and never was any the wiser, but then neither of you would have recognized her if you saw her now would you? Maybe if you heard her name. I should have gone with you for sure…no…no… maybe good the way it all happened seein as Miss Julia would have recognized me straightaway. Oh, I'm just talkin up a storm now ain't I?"

I did not say a single word, knowin there was still more to come out.

"Peney, oh my poor little Peney," Cynthia repeated. "Why she just helped keep our little secret, didn't she, but good Lord in heaven, I'm afraid she is gonna pay a heavy price, knowin the devilment the Mistus is capable of. Julia Devil, oh how I hate that woman. By my reckonin that little sister of mine most like as not be gettin a pretty good cowhidin right about now for what she done down at the store. Oh, what's a body to do, Coswell?" Cynthia concluded.

Not really havin a plan formed up in my mind at the moment I was kinda dreadin the end of Cynthia's heartfelt lamentation here. Of course I could feel the pain of it, but what to do? "Well, there ain't a great deal we can do for her at the moment," I finally offered, "cept'n maybe study on it for a spell, digestin things best we can. I do know we both would like to turn this wagon round this very minute and go fetch your sister, but it don't pay to be too hasty. "Go slow and go sure", Daddy used to say. There's laws to consider and we don't need to fall into any trap ourselves. First we need to get home to Briarwood, Darlin, and tell our Sanford bout all that's happened.

With most of the swellin gone and him startin to get on his feet some, ain't he gonna be in for a surprise when he finds out the woman he has been talkin bout the last few days be your own blood kin. Why he's been offerin up some mighty high praise of late for that woman, callin her his 'angel of mercy' and such. He said he was so sorry after all she done for him that he never even come to catch her name. It's fair to say we are currently standin in need of a plan and I do believe with a little effort the three of us can do just that."

Arrivin home, Sanford slowly emerged from the house to tend the wagon, goin bout as fast a pace as his present condition would allow. He asked straightaway where all the packages was from our recent purchases and that's when we shared with him the fact that our store shoppin plans had taken a sudden and surprisin turn.

"Dis wobban, she be yer sister, Miss Cynthia?" Sanford questioned excitedly upon hearin the news of the mystery nurse. "Why Sanford know she be sent frum hebben above...take good care ob Sanford atter I's bit. Now she do dis fer her big sister, put her own self in de debil's path. Fine wobban. Fine wobben, deed! We can't let nothin bad happen ter her. We needs ter go fetch her rite quick, Massa Tims!"

"Hold on there, Sanford. We'll do somethin, but now just ain't the proper time," I added in. "We would need a good reason to go over to the Tucker place and check on things. Maybe tomorrow we could bring a little gift to Miss Nellie for her recent kindness and look round the premises while we're there. What do you think of that idea?"

"Coswell, I think we still have that good bottle of city whiskey in the backroom that Colonel McKinley give us in appreciation for that trackin job some time back. At the very least, makes sense we should pay the woman back in kind for what was used to treat young Sanford here," Cynthia suggested. Sanford nodded his head with full approval of our newly hatched plan.

"Then that's what we'll do. Me and Sanford will head out with that gift first thing in the mornin and see what comes of it. Maybe we can get a little sleep tonight. We'll all have plenty to do tomorrow, I'm sure of that," I concluded.

                                               *   *   *

The early mornin sun wasted no time heatin up the day as

Sanford and I set to readyin-up the horse and wagon for a return visit to the Tucker farm. As I made the effort to take my wide-brimmed straw hat from my head to wipe away a few beads of sweat that had taken up residence there, I looked up to see an unexpected visitor comin up the road in a trail of dust. Why I recognized Lem Purdy straightaway fore he ever come to within jawin distance. Damn, if that fella didn't always have a need to show off that bald head of his and I said the same to Sanford. The young fella replied that it was almost as if he was darin Mr. Sun to do his level best to lay him low.

I remember years ago tellin Lem a story I heard from a reliable source when this same subject come up for discussion. There was a famous Revolutionary War hero by the name Nathaniel Greene who come to Georgia with his lovely wife, Katie Littlefield Greene, after the American Revolution. Congress had seen fit to award the man a plantation in Savannah for his military contributions durin that conflict. Now here he was a smart man by all accounts and a great general as well, but somehow it seems this one sunny day back in the summer of 1786, the general just plain forgot to put a hat on his baldin head when he went outdoors. Got hisself Georgia sunstroke and died, he did, and that's after all the time he had spent on the field of battle and lived to tell about it. I remember Lem just laughed when I told this story and remarked that this fella was a Yankee from Rhode Island and, after all, he had no business bein down our way in the first place. "Folks should know enough to stay in their rightful place," he said that day and I remembered at the time I sorta suspicioned that remark to have included more than just some geographical consideration.

"Howdy, Lem, what brings you out bright and early this mornin?" I inquired, as Lem Purdy pulled in the reigns and drew up his horse. Sanford took his leave and departed for the barn, but not before tippin his ragged straw hat in the direction of "Massa Purdy."

"Mornin, Coswell. I heard tell that boy of yours got hisself snake bit and I come by to see how he was gettin on."

"Well, that is awful kind of you to ask. As you can see he's up and about, lucky to be alive. In fact, he's makin a little trip over to the Tucker place with me this mornin. They took right fine care of him over there and the Tims family wants to thank em all and return the favor," I replied.

"Why that nigger leads a charmed life, now don't he?" Lem Purdy responded. "He seems to come out smellin like a rose no matter what shit-pit he's throwed into and that may be just the reason I come by this mornin. You see the Purdy family got us two big trackin jobs and we sure could use that boy of yours straightaway to bring us a little good luck. I'll pay ya a real handsome wage to rent him out for a spell. You and the Missus could put that money right in your pockets without any of the normal fuss and bother that come with a bondsman. I'd be willin to ante up a hundred and fifty dollars for a single month's work which is better than some gets for a whole year and, of course, I would be responsible for food, doctor bills and any of the other normal expenses. What do you think bout that offer, Coswell?" Purdy concluded.

"I don't know, Lem. The boy's still a little wobbly and we do really need him round our place here. We never did get Mr. Jarratt's runaway so we will most likely have to tend to that soon. Maybe ol Sanford should stay right where he is," I concluded.

Wipin the sweat from top his head with his kerchief and puffin out his chest some from high atop his horse, Lem Purdy took to announcin: "I need to tell ya. We got that boy, Coswell…that black-smith of Jarratt's that run off. Our dogs chewed on him a bit, but I don't believe there's any permanent damage done, that is if he don't use his left arm for a spell. He'll know better than to run off again if the idea ever gets into that head of his, after all, these people need to know their place, now don't they? Jarratt paid us top dollar, too. Now I need that boy of yours, Coswell, for the two jobs that are comin our way."

"Tell you what I'll do. I'll sit down with my wife and Sanford tonight and we'll give you an answer in a day or so," I replied, as I continued to get things readied-up for the trip to the Tucker farm.

"Sounds fair to me. I'll be by in a couple of days," the early mornin visitor replied as he turned his horse and spurred his mount back to the nearby confines of the Purdy compound.

ॐ　ॐ　ॐ

Recallin an earlier plan the three of us had once concocted years back that allowed our escape from New Orleans and bondage for both my wife and Sanford, we had once more conspired to put our collective heads together to decide how best to proceed. Cynthia reminded Sanford and me that as a general rule it behooves folks to always work together as she said the Devil is always doin his darndest against each and every single one of us. Of course Cynthia could not be a party to any return to the Tucker farm as there would be no way to hide her identity from her former mistress. That would have made her sister's recent sacrifice all for nothin. No, this part of the plan would fall to Sanford and me.

With Sanford soon holdin reins in hand, I sat right up there with him on the same seat. Folks who might take notice would find that perfectly acceptable, but only because there was no other seat to be had in our old farm wagon to provide proper separation. Our loyal servant's suggestion was a good one, that he would wait in the wagon where slaves was bound to come by and strike up a conversation (negroes was always interested in the latest gossip and were quick to engage a visitor) while I would go into the house to visit with the two widow women and thank em most properly for their recent kindness. At the same time Sanford could ask some questions and nose about and maybe find what had become of his "angel of mercy." The first part of our plan went off without a hitch.

When I returned to the wagon after a cordial visit, I could tell Sanford was more than a might upset as he shook his head repeatedly, but remained silent. I had a bad feelin myself when Miss Julia told me the slave girl who had tended him had took down sick and was not well enough to come out to see me and accept my gratitude for her efforts. I suspected the worst. We left the farm with no words said twinxt the two of us till we reached the main road then Sanford then opened up like a flood gate.

"Massa Tims. Dat young woman, Peney, she be lyin down in a slave cabin all cut up. Look like dey done tore all de blood frum her body. Pore wobben, she lay shiberin, face down on de floor. She jus moan when Sanford talk ter her, but when I touch her hair, soft like she done me, I tole her I would cum back ter heps her, but don't know iffen she hears me or not. De ol nigger woman dat wuz tendin her say I'd better leave fore Mr. Jonathan Hunter cum by. I skedaddled, but Sanford he can't forget bout what he saw, Massa Tims."

Cynthia began to cry when Sanford retold that part of the story upon our arrival home. I decided another trip to the Tucker place was in order. This time it would be to make the Fitzsimmons widowwoman a substantial offer on a disobedient and unruly female slave by the name of Penia, an offer she would promptly refuse. "Not while I am livin," she had said.

DIARY OF PENIA FITZSIMONS TIMS

The Mistus sure was lookin poorly of late. I know she ain't been sleepin very well the past few days. Her hands was startin to tremble some and she was more than a might forgetful at times which weren't like her at all. She complained of a funny taste in her mouth and with blue lines visible along her gums and the blue-black edgin I began to notice on her teeth, she give off a most unhealthy look. Miss Nellie advised callin a doctor, but Miss Julia say she didn't want all the fuss and bother.

My life was different after that whippin, as I spent more time at hard labor out in the fields. Didn't really mind as I got away from the constant supervision and scoldin that come with bein a house servant. I still did sleep in the house after the day's work was done and, truth to tell, I thought considerable bout that slave, Sanford, in the dark hours of the night and even believe I remembered him sayin somethin bout comin to fetch me some day. I may have dreamed it but, oh, if that could only be true, I thought to myself. I began to think more and more bout him as time passed by.

A day or so later I happened to be in the kitchen talkin to Sadie, the cook. She had prepared food on the Tucker farm for many years, but recently had run afoul of Miss Julia and had been quite severely whipped on her say-so, but not as bad as was done me. Sadie, she tell me she never been whipped in her whole life and it certainly weren't right that Miss Julia had her whipped, seein as the woman weren't her legal owner. Sadie was mixin up batter for some late night biscuits when the two of us started in talkin bout the physical changes I had noticed recently with Miss Julia Devil.

A hard smile come over Sadie's face and her eyes took to squintin up some. "I'se gonna show you somethin, Little Peney, but you can't tell no one else," she said softly. Sadie put down the wood spoon and bowl and took my hand. She led me over to a seldom used closet where she pointed out an old mirror propped up agin the back wall. Turnin it round she asked me what I saw. I could see that some of the silver lead on the back side had been scraped off, most likely with a kitchen knife. "Miss Julia ain't got long now. She gonna get what she deserve," Sadie said, most hissin them words out between her clench teeth. "That woman goin to hell where she belong!" she forcefully added.

I knew what Sadie was doin would most likely result in a noose bein tied tight round her neck, so's I kept dark on this new information despite some personal misgivins I had on the matter. Two days later Miss Nellie found her sister, Miss Julia Fitzsimons, lyin dead in her bed.

Normally the well-known Doc Fort woulda been called in I was told, but due to his recent death (which seemed to be this side of a town tragedy) a young doc by the name of Dr. White was asked to come and examine the body. Sheriff Strother showed up bout that same time and I figured with the two of em bein there together, Sadie's time was short. I was glad I had an excuse as most of my recent time had been spent outside of the house. Lead poisinin took place over time Doc White had said, and this was not the first time a slave had sought revenge by addin lethal ingredients to their owner's food. It had never happened on the doc's own plantation, he said, but he could recite instances when that very thing had occurred elsewhere. All knew the family cook was fixin for the gallows.

Miss Julia's body was laid out on a coolin board, washed and made ready for the ground. After servants had prepared her all proper like as was the custom, folks on the farm, white and black, were allowed to file into the house to view the body. Oh, how the darkies on the place wailed and cried and said such fine things. Like most viewins and funerals to follow, servants said just what they knew white folks wanted to hear, but to each other they just smiled and said under their breath that she got just what she deserved. They whispered that she sure was gonna be surprised when she found out that there weren't no colored folks down in hell to fan and cool her off. No sir. Miss Julia Devil would have to fend for herself in the next world and see how she like them flames a-lickin away at those soft white feet!

Poor Sadie was missin from the funeral as she had taken up residence in Sheriff Strother's jail. Doc White, who owned some 65 slaves on a plantation of his own, was a good man by all accounts and not known to be vengeful by nature, but he needed to do his duty as it was perfectly obvious how this woman had died. His testimony put the noose round Sadie's neck for sure. As a criminal her body would become the property of the state and as such would most like as not find itself bein cut up and studied in that medical college over in Augusta. Black bodies made up the majority of those studies; I hear tell, with slave owners sometimes sellin off their dead negroes to get their last final ounce of value from their earthly remains. It is a very sad thing when you let your mind think on it and I don't mean to make light of it all, but I could not help but wonder at this time what was to become of me with my Mistus now lyin in the low grounds.

COSWELL TIM'S DIARY RESUMES

It did seem like Savannah was a faraway place for the auction of any local slaves to be held, but I reckon it did make sense. What with all the local chatter bout what a deranged darkey done to an elderly white widow woman over at the Tucker farm in Milledgeville, those in authority must have figured the further away the sale of any one of them farm hands was, the better might be any financial returns.

I guess this had to be one of the biggest slave auctions in the country's history with over 400 slaves up for sale at one time. Folks come from all round when they heard the news, why, there weren't a hotel room or other lodgin space to be had anywhere in the area. One of the slaves to be cried off in that auction was Penia Fitzsimons, sister of my beloved wife. Coswell and Cynthia Tims fully intended to be in attendance for that event and be among the large number of expected bidders.

"These here are the finest niggers for sale in the whole State of Georgia," Mr. Bryan, a well-known auctioneer, announced in a loud and clear voice the day of the sale. "Most ain't never been sold previous and have lived on one single plantation their whole lives. They are an industrious and loyal lot...a right fine investment for discriminatin investors who want to get the worth of their money."

Over two hundred bidders readied themselves with white inspection gloves and pen and paper for the sale of these human beasts of burden, each of em to be individually announced. The entire racetrack where the auction was to be held was all abuzz despite the light rain that began to fall over the festivities. That did nothin to deter eager buyers. Many of em, includin Cynthia and me, had taken advantage of the preview that had been offered the day before for early inspection. Many potential owners had examined mouths, hair, eyes, joints or any other parts of the body they felt might influence their value. Many had walked beside, felt of, and conversed with these bondsmen and women in an attempt to determine their fair market value. Some potential buyers brought doctors along with em to ensure the health of their purchase. Some buyers was so keen themselves that they could pinch up the skin on the back of a darkey's hand and determine their exact age based on the stay of the pucker. Many was interested in Little Peney, but the scars soon discovered on her back, caused many likely bidders to back off and look elsewhere for a more compliant servant. I thought that was right smart of Cynthia when she made her sister pull down her newly-supplied calico frock from off her shoulders and show all the folks in attendance the results of her obvious recent disobedience. Any embarrassment Peney may have felt over the white woman's demands, I'm certain-sure was more than balanced off by her knowledge that the same white woman who twirled her parasol around in such a high-handed manner was, in truth, her possible rescuer. When it was Peney's turn to finally walk up on the block, there was but three people includin the two in the Tims family who were interested in offerin up a bid.

"Three hundred dollars, three hundred dollars…do I hear four," came the rapid call of the auctioneer. "Four hundred!" I yelled out. Cynthia nervously again rotated her parasol in her hands with my bid as the auctioneer attempted to encourage still higher offers from others. "Five hundred dollars," come a voice from behind us and off somewhat to our left. It sounded somewhat familiar.

"Six hundred dollars," I shouted out in response.

"Seven hundred!" that same voice yelled back.

No other buyers but the two of us now remained in the potential sale. I raised myself up some in an effort to seek out my competitor. At first I could see no one, but slowly the crowd began to part some clearin a pathway for a low set man with a bald head. The voice and the face were more than familiar. It was none other than my neighbor, Lem Purdy, now hurriedly makin his way towards us. As the bid now stood at seven hundred dollars, the auctioneer repeated and pleaded for still more money for this "fine lookin little mulatter woman."

"Coswell, you seem to want this wench pretty bad," Purdy announced, still a fair distance away and tryin to have his voice heard over the din of the crowd. As he got closer, I heard him say… "You must really feel indebted to her for tendin your nigger the way she done. Tell you what I would be prepared to do. You rent me Sanford for our agreed upon price and I'll be more than willin to back off this here biddin."

"Seven hundred and fifty dollars!" I finally shouted out as the auctioneer's gavel fell to the table in front of him, signalin the end of this particular sale. I saw Cynthia bounce up on her toes and let her parasol drop slightly as she put both her hands together in gratitude, happy to have her lost sister back once more. I was happy for her and remember I had a big grin on my face as I turned to shake Lem's hand.

Despite the persistent drizzle this had been a bright sunshiny day for the Tims family. But that don't take the whole of it into account. A fella once told me that the brighter the light was, the darker the shadows could be. I guess I never thought too much about that til now. Here I was smilin like a sorry fool when I shook Lem Purdy's hand on the deal, not knowin at the time that I had placed the future happiness of our family into very dangerous hands.

Chapter 8

AND SO IT BEGINS

COSWELL TIM'S DIARY RESUMES

Early on when I was first learnin to navigate the family farm wagon, Daddy, he give me some sound advice on the matter. He said comin down a hill weren't near as easy as it might first seem and could even prove to be a man's undoin if he didn't take all the necessary precautions. If you didn't watch your speed and use that wagon brake at the side, he told me, why that wagon could pick up speed and threaten to overtake the very critters up front that had consented to do the pullin. If that ever come to be, he said, things could change from bad to worse in a flash and leave a man with nothin but a dim memory as to how good it all was back down the road apiece.

Now I have always felt change could be a good thing, leastways it's natural and should be expected. But it's often the case that nature has a way of tryin out new things just to see what works and what don't and a smart fella (just like a smart businessman) needs to sort through any new inventory that might come his way to see what could profit him or possibly bring about his ruination. The Tims' family faced just such a dilemma shortly after we purchased an attractive young slave woman down Savannah way and brought her home to Milledgeville to live with us as part of our family.

It all started out good after the sale with both Cynthia and Sanford more than a might excited bout this latest family addition. It was good-natured fun, it was, but both parties did set out after her like a hog and a hungry dog in a race for the vittles. Cynthia, now she got to her first and she and her sister spent the longest time all huddled in together, tryin to make sense out of all that had happened since their lives as slave women had tore em apart. It was plain to see they was tight as fiddle strings and shared a deep and abidin love. Sanford, he kinda respectfully bid his time, lurkin off to the side a bit, but you could see by takin stock of little things he said and done that he was plannin to mount a full-scale courtin operation and had big plans in his head for this little gal. He soon found Peney was of like mind and it weren't long for the two of em would invent excuses to go off and spend quiet time together. Cynthia and me knew they was soon weavin at the same loom and it weren't no surprise to either one of us when Sanford come forward one night and asked permission for him and Little Peney to be hitched up in marriage.

It had only been a day or so earlier when the two of em had gone off to pick blueberries (or at least so they said, as there weren't many berries in the basket upon their return) when Cynthia and me had ourselves a little conversation bout slave marriages. She told me that in the slave community many black males shied away from such a commitment cause they was afraid of possible separation down the road which was the master's legal right. That was a real concern and it has been my observation over the years that if the breakup of slave family was to profit an owner in some way, why that slave would have to be a real favorite to avoid that particular outcome. Oh, how those white masters would often go on and on bout how much they loved their black family and how they always knew what was best for em, of course that might just include separatin em at some point ....man from woman or mammies and pappies from their children. I have heard slave owners go so far as to claim that even if that were to happen (under "extreme circumstances," they might say) it really weren't that bad cause niggers don't have real adult feelins like white folk do and are basically quite childlike. They can be emotional after a sale, that's admitted, but they also point out they can soon be seen singin out in the fields, courtin a new lover and havin more babies. All this is proof, it is often said, that nigger love don't run that deep. Both Cynthia and me agreed that observations such as these are most likely not proof any natural inclination on the part of the negro, but if any of that is true, it really is just a means of survival forced on em by circumstance. It made perfect sense, we concluded, for those same owners to cling tight to such carefully crafted opinions, makin for a clear conscience and a good night's rest.

Cynthia told me that black males that did contemplate marriage often sought a woman outside of their own plantation. These "broad-wives," so called, were chosen because they was removed from a man's daily contact and any poor treatment visited on em by their masters was hidden from their view. Imagine how difficult it would be, Cynthia asked, to watch your wife belittled and abused right before your very eyes when as a husband you was powerless to do a single thing on her behalf? When my wife asked this question I could not help but think back to a time when Cynthia was kidnapped from our home by her former master and what I had to do to bring her back. It was hard times all around, but even harder to imagine how any man would deal with that when utterly helpless to do a single thing about it. Best to not witness such a thing in the first place, they must have reasoned. But slaves, after all, are people and people do fall in love and many in the slave community did want to be seriously joined up together and recognized as a married couple despite any and all of the uncertainty or misfortune that might be headed their way. I reckon the power of love can be that great, but it sure don't come easy under such circumstances that I can see. Our Sanford did have it better than most.

The weddin went off without a hitch. It was held at our home with the parson down at St. Stephens church officiatin the ceremony upon my request. There weren't no "jumpin the broom" which was often the case for field hands (Sanford told us he weren't too good at jumpin backwards anyways and was afraid to get off on the wrong foot by revealin his wife's superior capabilities) but a real service was in order with Father Judson M. Curtis tendin to all the proper white vows, Bible readins and such. Of course with both parties legally slaves, there weren't no official report placed anywhere into the town records. (Many plantations did keep such records, however.) As with any and all slave marriages it was just for show and really had no meanin, ceptin for those directly involved.

Sanford had a little money saved up which Cynthia and me kept for him in our bedroom, but he proudly announced to the whole family after the service was over his intention to add to that so's he and Little Peney could get a place all their own. Although any new buildins built on Tims' property for blacks would officially be listed as "slave quarters," this did not dampen their enthusiasm one scratch. The Purdy job soon to come was looked upon as a good thing as the money from that was thought to come just at the right time.

Now I would like to believe I would have never allowed this to happen if it was totally up to me what with my reservations bout the Purdys and Lem in particular, maybe lookin to Sanford and his bride's enthusiasm as an excuse for my cloudy judgment. Be that as it may, our Sanford would soon become the temporary property of Lemuel Purdy for the agreed upon rental price of one hundred and fifty dollars cash-money for one month's work, an arrangement we would all come to regret.

The Purdy place, it must be said, is over on the west side of town, a sorry and ramshackle affair with dilapidated cabins and outbuidins scattered bout the landscape and a fair amount of clutter to be had in the spaces in between. Old wagons lay in heaps, rubble lay strewn about, tools rustin where they was left last used... nothin really havin a proper place to call its own. I reckon there were five or six Purdy families a-livin there at the time, some married and some not, one less Purdy due to a recent encounter with Benton Wells' sharp meat cleaver. Heard tell it took no time at all for Jeb Purdy's widow to take up with one of the cousins for her children's sake and also for the betterment of her own circumstance. Not an uncommon occurrence at all down in our neck of the woods and I suspect elsewhere as well.

When Sanford first laid his eyes on the place after sayin all his proper farewells and remindin us he would return promptly in one month's time, he told us later (much later than planned) that his first impression of the Purdy property was that it was no wonder they was poor trackers. "Dey's folks most bad as beggar trash, I tells ya. De whole place dere in need ob sum proper tendin. De dogs, dey wuz dirtier den dere owners, but not by much. I neber seed such a site en all my born days. Seem like everythin on dat place done cum ter grief."

Sanford did say the Purdys greeted and treated him well at first, but he began to get an uneasy feelin the longer he stayed. An old, hairy-lipped woman waited supper on him which he thought unusual given his humble circumstance. He was the only negro on the place. It didn't take long for Lem to start in explainin the trackin jobs that they would soon undertake. Sanford said he felt better as he began to imagine his value in the four weeks to come, but on the second night before they were to set out on their first trackin assignment, he said he again become uneasy when Lem stated in tellin a familiar Milledgeville story that had his own special twist added to it.

The story harkened back to the fall of 1833 when the statehouse in Milledgeville caught on fire. It was around mid-day on November 16th with the legislature in full session when townspeople first noticed flames shootin from the roof of that famous medieval-lookin buildin. Both houses of the legislature emptied out and it seemed like all of Milledgeville was soon enlisted in the effort to save the structure from possible ruin. Valuable papers, money and furniture was brought out and laid on the grass as bucket brigades went to work. Legislators from around Georgia rolled up their sleeves and women and children manned the pails and fetched blankets from their homes. Slaves jumped in without any orders from their masters. But it was the action of one individual in particular that Lem Purdy wanted to single out in his retellin of the story. His name was "Big Sam" and he was the slave of John Marlor who just happened to be the architect and builder of the place.

Big Sam was soon to be found walkin along the roof edge of that tall building and tossin down burnin pine shingles to the ground below. "And the damn fool did it without a safety rope," Lem recounted. But he also added in somethin else. "It was in full view of the townsfolk in order to enlist sympathy for his enslaved condition." Sure enough, after the buildin was miraculously saved there was great support in callin this bondsman a real hero and takin steps to grant him his freedom. The state legislature even approved $1,800.00 to purchase Big Sam from his master, but it was Lem Purdy's daddy, Orville Purdy, who had the good sense to convince town folk this servant should now become a ward of the state and be given the task of performin maintenance work round the buildin he seemed to love so much. "No nigger should rise to any exalted position," he said his daddy had wisely counselled. When Big Sam was eventually given his freedom by the state some twenty years later, Lem said his daddy had passed away by that time and it fell to him as his son to try and talk some good sense into them state officials, but it was all to no good end. Over all protests, Big Sam did find hisself fully emancipated in 1852.

Sanford listened intently as this story unfolded and said he couldn't help notice the fire that still burned in Lem's belly over this long ago event. I guess Lem even went so far as to say his daddy was the real hero in the story, claimin to be the first one to spot the flames and then later watchin over the money that lay out on the ground without ever stealin a single dime. "Damn buck nigger got all the credit and what did Daddy get… nothin, and he was a white man for God's sake!" Lem concluded, as he shot a quick look over in Sanford's direction. Sanford told us that this story unsettled him some, not cause it weren't a thrillin tale mind ya, but because it was obvious the Purdys were findin other, more personal meanin in a story that might have future consequence for him, considerin the part he had played in Lem Purdy's recent rescue. Yes sir, Lem was the very spit and image of his daddy (even though that man was a little taller and did have the good sense to wear a hat) and Sanford began to think there might be somethin that run deeper than gratitude on Lem's mind now that he found hisself beholdin to a black man of inferior station.

Sanford told us many of the early suggestions made during his time there were met with compliance, even if the Purdys seemed a little reluctant at first to change. For example, when he pointed out to em that the vicious yellow dog they had by the name of "Buck" chewed up way too many of the runaways they chased to turn a profit, they agreed to have a harness made for the dog down at the saddle shop. That way they would not only have control over the beast, but control of the pack as well as Sanford had noticed that the other dogs looked to ol Buck and always followed his lead. Also, it did not profit slave catchers to all ride horses, Sanford offered, as a great deal of important information was lost to the handler and the dogs as they hurried along. Of course the Purdys all wanted to ride cause they each was bout as lazy as shingle makers, but they did eventually come to see the wisdom of Sanford's words with all but one comin down off their mounts to more closely examine what fugitives might have left behind.

Sanford said the first trackin job they went on he read the trail for em, pointin out foot imprints and how they told the story of a man or woman's weight, height and if they was walkin, runnin or sneakin round. He taught em how to look for broken branches, over-turned leaves and discarded items the runner had left along the way. He showed em how to tell if the fugitive was injured or gettin tired or confused and desperate or if he or she was confident and knew where they was goin. The first fugitive was captured in only four hours' time, Sanford said, and the Purdy clan was all very proud of their accomplishment with Lem promptly dividin up and sharin the early profits with his family.

The very next day they set out to track another bondsman who had killed a fellow slave on a nearby plantation. The owner was willin to pay dearly to get the murderer back as the dead negro was one of his favorites and maybe the most valued piece of property he owned on the place. Again Sanford proved adequate for the occasion as he was easily able to locate the slave in question. Sometimes black folks will turn on one of their own kind if that individual had violated one of their sacred livin arrangements. This black murderer had shown hisself to be a real danger to the slave community and with Sanford's insistence, they was willin to give him up.

Sanford said that by his account nine runaways was found and returned to their masters as his one month tenure there drew to a close. He was unsure as to the amount of money the Purdys had made, but guessed by his experience in the Tims family business that the amount was well over one thousand dollars, maybe even closer to two thousand. And of course the Purdys learned some valuable lessons that they did not know previous which would continue to profit em in the future. Sanford said he was lookin forward to goin back home in a couple days' time when one night Massa Purdy intro-duced him to a man who, he said, had just happened to drop by the place for a little friendly visit. His name was Starling Finney.

"I did not know who he wuz, but when I fust look into dis man's eyes, Massa Tims, I knew jus what he wuz," Sanford later told me. "Lordy, Lordy… I knows I wuz lookin into de cold, dead eyes ob de dreaded slave speculator."

It was April 12, 1861 when Lemuel Purdy showed up at our door with the news that Sanford had for some unknown reason, run off. We found out later, that day would be one our country would never forget as well. Shots had been fired over in South Carolina at

Ft. Sumter, the first shots of the War Between the States. Changes were comin our way for sure, and there weren't a single one of us in our family that believed those changes might be for the better. I knew that wagon brake my daddy told me about had let go comin down the hill and we was all in store for a mighty rough time fore things would ever, if ever, return to the way they once was.

Chapter 9

SANFORD IN CHAINS

COSWELL TIM'S DIARY RESUMES

I believe I can say with a fair degree of certainty that Starlin Finney would not have disagreed with the South's resolve to stand firm on its basic principle to protect and preserve our "peculiar institution." But that same man (whose evil presence would soon haunt our lives) must also have known deep down inside that any conflict comin our way as a result was bound to alter how he might go bout his business in the future. Folks that know anythin t'all bout the slavin institution, know that slave speculators over the years have generally enjoyed a right fine life. They are considered by many to be an important part of the nation's business establishment and do see themselves pursuin an honest American callin. They would offer that they are tryin their level best under difficult circumstances to provide for themselves and their families. They are frequently away from the comforts of home and loved ones and it weren't easy, they might add, to successfully read the supply and demands of the slave market, acquirin merchandize at a good price and then movin em along to a place and time where a respectable profit could be realized. Despised by some, dreaded by those in bondage, admired by many for their wealth, they would claim they only did what they thought necessary. I have heard it said more than once that it takes a very special man with a great deal of patience and energy to deal in negro speculation.

Unlike slave catchers who generally came from the lower levels of society, slave speculators are often found at or near the top end of the peckin order. Bank directors, judges, planters, politicians and others in positions of authority are often found among their number. Subscribin to this, perhaps the darkest side of slavery, and bein involved either directly or by hirin the job done, these slave traders are sometimes singled out or blamed for many of the worst travesties of the institution. I found it quite interestin that many of them same slave owners, who were so quick to point their finger off in the speculators direction, often become willin partners when money and human property was to change hands. I guess it's more common than not for folks to blame unpleasant things on others rather than take any blame themselves, but I have found over the years that if a person were to honestly find themselves the cause of a particular problem, that did have a certain built-in advantage. Why with only one person to blame, it makes the solution all the easier, now, don't it? The problem here, I reckon, is that with money jinglin so loud in their pockets, it must have made it near impossible for slave owners to be able to listen to any good reason why they should consider doin business in any new or more enlightened manner.

Not allowed to make direct eye contact with a white man due to his lowly station, Sanford said just a quick glance in the direction of slave speculator Starlin Finney at the Purdy place was all the convincin he needed to forecast the outcome of this encounter. He knew straightaway, he said, that the life he had once enjoyed at Briarwood would soon be a thing of the past. He said the man's venomous eyes had the look of a natural predator and held not one small trace of joy or human kindness. "Dem eyes wuz black as a nigga coal burner, Massa Tims. De wuz de eyes ob sum long dead kreature, one dat death's broom shuda swep from dis eart long time pass," I remember Sanford later testifyin quite forcefully.

Physically the slave speculator Starlin Finney was as big as a horse and powerful built. He had huge hands which moved about menacingly as he talked or twitched nervously when they occasionally hung by his side. When those hands of his shot out partway through the conversation, Sanford found hisself locked in Finney's vice-like grip. A quick attempt at freedom was fruitless. Finney slowly drew the young black man in towards hisself and speakin in a measured and hushed tone, confirmed Sanford's worst fears. "You now belong to me. Do you hear me, boy? You understand that and you need to know nothin else in this world."

DIARY OF PENIA FITZSIMONS TIMS

Oh, Lord in heaven, where is my man tonight? This very evenin Massa Purdy come by the place to give us the news that Sanford had run off. That be so much bullfeathers and Massa Tims told him as much. Purdy said Sanford was an arrogant nigger and he had suspicioned that he would run if he ever got the chance. We all knew better. There was sharp words to be had all round, but nothin really come of it. I thought my sister, Cynthia, was gonna rip the man's eyes from out his head. Massa Tims did say that if he found Purdy was in any way responsible, the price he would pay would be a heavy one. Purdy said a white man should not be blamed for the natural inclination of blacks and that Massa Tims with his lenient treatment of Sanford was most likely to blame for the situation in the first place. With no agreement to be had on the matter, Purdy soon stormed off in a huff.

It would be three years, three long years, fore the truth of the matter would see the light of day and that truth was that my Sanford had been illegally kidnapped and sold by Lemuel Purdy to Starling Finney, slave speculator from up Virginia way. Unbeknown to us at the time, a black coffle of human property was slowly makin its way south from Milledgeville to the rice and sugar cane fields of southern Louisiana.

Sanford later said he had a pretty fair idea of what lay ahead when another attempt to free hisself from Finney's grasp did nothin to alter the situation. With Ezra Purdy successfully blockin his exit, a scuffle had ensued where Sanford was quickly overcome and chains placed upon his wrists and ankles. As Finney deposited the keys securely inside his trouser pocket, he announced his immediate intentions to the two Purdys who stood at his side. "I'm afraid we are gonna have to knock some of the stuffin out of this boy fore we go any further. Let's buck him up, fellas."

Sanford later told me the two Purdys eagerly embraced the task at hand and tore at his clothes until they lay shredded in a heap on the floor. He was soon placed naked in a seated position, his knees doubled up under his chin. Lem Purdy then produced a stout stake which was inserted behind both his knees. Now completely helpless with his backside exposed to the whip, my Sanford could easily be turned from one side to the other as his captors desired.

The bullwhip that Finney always wore loosely wrapped around his shoulder now sprang to life and began to fall repeatedly on the flesh of one good man. The blows were delivered equal to both sides of his body with high purpose and resolve. I remember Sanford later tellin me he could not help but notice how the blood took to puddlin under wherever he sat. He could feel it sticky and wet beneath him as he was violently turned back and forth by the Purdy boys as he continued to endure a punishment that seemed to have no end. Finally, instructions was given to take Sanford "out of the buck" and wash him down with salt, red pepper and water. Again the Purdys were happy to respond and after the money changed hands, Sanford, still naked, was roughly tossed into the back of Finney's wagon, soon to join with thirty or so others who were also the negro speculator's personal property. Sanford told us later he was driven to a plantation owned by a man named Ben Tarver, a Methodist preacher who owned some sixty slaves over in Jones County, not ten miles from our Milledgeville home. Sanford said Tarver was a terrible-bad man who was given to braggin that he had the fastest cotton pickers in all of Georgia, most likely due to frequent contests held on the place as well as his relentless use of the bullwhip. The reputation the man enjoyed in the county was despite the fact that even his neighbors saw him as a barbaric slave master, he did have the redeemin quality of bein one mighty fine preacher.

For two weeks Sanford said Finney's coffle stayed on the Tarver place, with Finney goin off daily to town to dispose of some of his stock, only to purchase others who might better suit his future business needs. With hard work required in the mud of the Louisiana rice and sugar fields, strong males were the most desirable and many of the women and younguns Finney had purchased earlier back in Virginia or along the way were sold or traded off at this time. Light-skinned individuals were also disposed of as it was thought that the darker the skin, the heartier the worker. Those who did not leave with Finney for the local market (includin my Sanford) was set to work in Reverend Tarver's cotton fields. It was hard labor with little food or rest. Tarver did not believe it proper to feed his workers until noon day, Sanford said, and then not again until nine o'clock at night and even then it weren't much, just corn made into a cake, just enough to keep em up on their feet. But it was a business arrangement after all, with Tarver benefittin from the fact that he was providin a temporary home for the speculator's property while Finney completed last minute arrangements for the final and hopefully the most profitable part of his slave tradin operation.

Now there were neighbors who come by our house to express their condolences bout "the Tims servant that run off," many recountin how they had suffered similar indignities when ungrateful bondsmen over the years had taken to their heels. But that was short-lived, as talk of the recent war with the Yankees began to dominate any and all conversation. I have found over time that life don't wait for ones' own personal problems to be resolved for it continues upon its merry way.

Gunfire had been heard from one end of the state to the other with news of succession in January of this past year. Lights were placed in windows, cannons fired off and church bells rang out. Many a torch-lit parade was held throughout the state. Fiery speeches was heard on many a street corner with general excitement everywhere. When Massa Tims began the investigation of Sanford's disappearance, he said it seemed like folks were consumed with only one thing…standin up to the evil politicians in Washington City like the just elected Abraham Lincoln who were known to be backed by corrupt northern businessmen and crazed and unreasonable aboli-tionists. These folks were an ungodly lot, for sure, and it was a certainly a worthy cause the south had undertaken, it was thought. God was expected to always be on the side of the more religious and God-fearin south in the days to come. Truth to tell, the Tims family did have some mixed feelins on the matter.

Early attempts by Massa Tims and his brother to pick up the trail over at the Purdy place come to nothin, despite the use of "The Colonel," our best hound and a scent item I had provided. Massa Tims told Lem Purdy it was a might suspicious that there weren't no trail to be had, most as if someone had bundled up ol Sanford and carried him off the property. Searches of the surroundin countryside met with similar disappointment. Any slave auctions we got wind of in the area always brought out someone from the Tims family, hopin against fadin hope, to discover a clue as to Sanford's whereabouts.

One auction in Milledgeville we happened upon was held inside a small shed where a large white man with venomous eyes and huge hands was sellin off several small slave children to local buyers. One of our neighbors, Thomas Stevens, who had hisself a plantation over on the Clinton Road maybe eight miles from our home, bought three of em from this man at a good price as the seller appeared quite anxious to rid himself of his youthful stock. We knew nothin of the seller, havin never seen the man before, but many of us knew Stevens. He had a reputation as being as tight as a sausage skin, a real skinflint, and a great rogue as well, as he would often buy young slaves cheap and teach em to go out at night and steal corn from nearby plantations to be used in his still making whisky. The unidentified man holdin the auction had set up a primitive scale of sorts, using his saddle (which he knew the weight of) to be balanced off against human weight on the other end. By doing so he was able to sell the we'uns by the pound.

As we watched the proceedins along with maybe twenty other folks, we all knew those three children most like as not were cursed with a life of trial and tribulation. Recently taken from their mothers, the two boys and one quite frail girl would now most likely find themselves the object of Stevens' well-known temper. It was said that the new owner had the annoyin habit of always laughin and smilin regardless of his disposition at a particular moment. It was also said he laughed the loudest while in fits of passion, particularly when that involved punishment of his human property. The three young blacks (who we figured to be barely over the legal limit of ten years for children to be sold without their parents) were quickly hurried off after the sale, but unfortunately for us no adult male slaves made their appearance that day on the auction block. Surprisingly, Jesse and Massa Tims did talk to this seller afterwards about other slaves that he might have in his possession, but not there at the moment, indicating they would be willin to pay good money for a strong male in his prime. The man replied that he wished he had such an item in his inventory, but confessed to havin none at the moment. In fact, he said, he too was lookin for prime, "grade A" hands, eighteen to twenty-four years of age, dark of skin, hearty and intelligent.

I do remember Massa Tims tellin Cynthia afterwards that he found it hard to like the large, tall slave trader who ran the auction and said a fella would be wise to never turn his back on such a man. "Mark my words, Darlin, he's more slippery than any lawyer ever took a fee," I remember Massa Tims tellin my sister. He also added that he could never forget his face and that would (unbeknown to us at the time) prove valuable down the road. I firmly believe there is justice to be had in this world and I never lost sight of what Mamma used to say to Cynthia and me as young'uns..."weepin may endure the night, girls, but joy come in the mornin. Halleluiah and Amen to that!" Oh, Sanford. Will I ever see that beautiful face of yours again this side of heaven?

COSWELL TIM'S DIARY RESUMES

Now secession weren't somethin all Georgians took a likin to, but a pro Union person had bout as much chance of success for his point of view as a crippled mud turtle in a horse race. I guess the governor of Georgia, the honorable Joseph Emerson Brown, made his point well when he said it just weren't the big planters with lots of niggers that would lose out if slavery was to end. He reasoned that if the institution were no more and blacks was to be set free on southern soil, they would be granted equality with whites with the two races would be forever joined in together. Very few white folks in the south, rich or poor, could imagine any such thing. War with all its horrors would be preferable to that, it was thought. It would be a fair thing to say that most southern soldiers did not go to war to maintain slavery (as they never had any slaves of their own) but were willin to put their lives on the line to preserve their superior status over the black man, whatever form that might take.

Milledgeville, bein the capital, become the very place where Georgians would commit themselves to secession. Followin in South Carolina's footsteps, folks from round the state began streamin into town in droves for weeks and it seemed to be bustin at the seams as the event grew closer. A woman our family knew over in Macon by the name of Mrs. Mary Nesbit reported in their local paper that "ten railcars went off from here Tuesday and as many on Wednesday...all headed for Milledgeville."

The galleries and lobbies of the statehouse were soon set to overflowin when official secession papers was finally signed on January 19,1861.The Milledgeville Grays, Oconee Volunteers, the Baldwin Volunteers and other military groups soon was formed up, along with the First Georgia Regulars. It took no time at all for the entire state to become one vast recruitin camp with the drums of war echoin loudly from mountains to seaboard. Women, children and people of all ages got caught up in war fever. Oh, what a wonderful frolic folks thought this was all gonna be.

Through all the excitement, the Tims family continued to search for one of our own. With my brother and me both bein too old to join up or eventually be conscripted into the military, we continued on with our business affairs. It would be fair to say that we did have have mixed feelins bout things as we certainly did not want to see the south trampled on by outsiders, feelin the need to stand by our neighbors and the Great State of Georgia, but that slavery issue which seem to lie at the center of everythin sure had many tentacles that sprung from it, all in need of careful sortin.

Before war's end Sanford would thankfully return to us and tell the story of his abduction. Until that time we would search far and wide for our young friend, and prepare to endure the trials and tribulations of the military conflict that was sure to come our way.

Chapter 10

THE KELLY'S TAKE UP THE TRAIL

COSWELL TIM'S DIARY RESUMES

I have known more than a few Irishmen in my lifetime and have come to believe they all share certain common traits. As a general rule they seem to be a passionate lot, easily aroused and excitable. Sometimes they get a little too hot under the collar and have to be cooled off a bit, but I really like their toughness (you always want to have an Irishman or two on your side in a fight) and also their loyalty and the lengths they will go to for those they hold dear. I know the Kellys never forgot that time early on when Jesse and me went out on a stormy night with one of our hounds to find their little baby sister Elizabeth (she is 5 years younger than James Rufus.) The poor thing had wandered off into the woods and got herself good and lost. When I carried her back into the Kelly home, I remember there weren't a dry eye to be had anywhere on the premises. Plenty of bear-hugs to go round as well. I reckon it should have come as no surprise to find a couple of Kelly's standin there when I opened up our cabin door after a forceful thump or two.

Our Irish friends, James Rufus Kelly and his older brother George, had come by the house to announce their intention to conduct an exhaustive search of their own for young Sanford in the wake of several weeks' disappointments and dead ends. Both said they had their sights set on joinin the Confederate army as soon as possible so's they could "get into the fracas fore the dogs quit barkin," they said, but first felt they needed to help out their good friends, the Tims family. The Kelly's liked Sanford, despite his inferior social status, appreciatin both his competence in the trackin business and the fact that he was respectful of all his superiors. The Irish seemed to always be fightin to maintain or advance their fragile public status and the negro was often square in their sights as a potential adversary. I do know for a fact that if the Kelly clan knew Cynthia's and my little secret, our friendship might suffer some as a consequence.

The Kelly plan was for James Rufus, George and their other brother, Charles, to visit every plantation and farm, knockin on each door, one after another, to find clues to Sanford's disappearance. It was time-consumin to be sure, but seein as though the dogs proved ineffectual, eye-witnesses must be relied on. "Someone had to have seen somethin," young James Rufus announced hopefully.

We discussed the new plan at some length. Jesse and me had already looked and talked to many local people and some beyond who we thought might be able to offer up some information, but I admitted there was still plenty of ground to cover. As we sat round the table that night, we were all of like mind that Sanford must have been kidnapped, most likely by slave speculators who often do come through our area in the summer months or in the early fall of the year. That way they could buy what was needed to get a fair launch on the New Year's plantin cycle in the Deep South. The slaves needed for those markets could only be found within our own country as the federal government had seen fit to outlaw the importation of slaves, I believe, way back in 1808. I remember my daddy, Obadiah Tims, tellin me once that he remembered that time well and shared the opinion that was a right fine idea as too many blacks were comin into the country and that could upset the natural balance of things, he had said. "Folks need to make-do with those they already have and if they want more they should breed em like was done on the farm," I remember him sayin. It weren't no secret, however, that the increasin demand for manpower in the Deep South was currently bein supplied by the transfer of slaves from the upper south to the lower regions.

It was also no secret that there were three ways slaves might be makin that journey. They could be gathered up in the Chesapeake Bay area near Baltimore and Richmond, placed in special made up ships and sailed down to New Orleans, the greatest slave marketin port in the lower south. With some 50-150 slaves packed tightly into the confines of them vessels for the 20 to 25 days the voyage normally took, many slave speculators chose this route as there was "less wear and tear on their stock," they reported.

Rail car was another alternative, made more popular with time. There weren't a railroad runnin south that didn't offer a "nigger car" where 20-50 slaves could be properly accommodated, chained together and watched over careful by their owners so's not to inconvenience any payin white passengers. Shipment was fast, makin for quick turnover and again the stock was generally found to arrive in good workin order. Unlike the water route, the problem with this method was that rail tracks did not generally offer direct lines to their destinations and some walkin or other means of transportation often was necessary to fill the spaces in between.

We all knew that the most popular and cheapest method of movin slaves south was by means of a coffle, or just plain group foot walkin. A coffle could be as large as one hundred slaves, but that required more food and supplies to be brought along and more white security to be hired. A much more manageable numbers of thirty to fifty individuals was far more common. The average coffle of that size could generally make 25 miles a day if the weather was agreeable.

We all had seen coffles before and several different observations on the matter were shared. Jesse reported that he saw a coffle some time back that he figured was made up of maybe fifty slaves, with what looked to be the strongest men chained together in pairs and some of the women tied together with rope the size of a bed cord. He said the women carryin children were not chained, nor were the young children who were able to walk along on their own account. Some men, he said, were also unrestrained, he reasoned because of their tame and quiet nature. George Kelly chimed in and offered that he saw a huge coffle one time that was singin, dancin and laughin as they went merrily along. Little Peney, forgettin herself for the moment, said that might very well be the case, but it was all under the threat of "steppin lively" and all for show. Scowls from the Kelly quarter and one from sister Cynthia as well, put an end to any personal testimony our servant might have continued to freely offer.

Given Milledgeville's interior location and poor railroad

connections, it was agreed that a coffle was most likely Sanford's fate and there certainly would be a need for that group, however large or small, to rest and restock. As the Kelly's got up to leave, they said they would be headin out in the mornin to look for such places and persons and would return only when they had good news on Sanford's whereabouts. Our whole family was grateful, we told em, for the efforts on our behalf and we indicated we would continue to look for clues in our area as we went on about the family business.

DIARY OF PENIA FITZSIMONS TIMS

Why, I be bout as nervous as a long tailed cat in a room full of rockin chairs. My hands are shakin and I ain't slept a wink in the last few days. I almost said somethin the other night I shouldn't of when the Kelly brothers visited our home. I know they are only tryin to help, but I would say from personal knowledge there ain't no joy to be had in bein any part of any coffle and it ain't just the walkin part that's bothersome. The separation from familiar places and loved ones is hard to endure. The humiliation of bein driven to market like so much head of beef cattle, the insults that come your way from the drivers and onlookers, the confinement and lack of privacy when nature would make a call, obligin any white man who wanted a poke and, of course, how could a body ever forget the ever-present floppin paddle that always was on hand whenever coffles was formed up.

It was an evil thing, it was, the flop itself bein made of heavy leather maybe a foot and half in length and maybe bout as wide as a human hand. There is a wood handle to be had on it as well, maybe another foot or so long. It is a special tool that all coffles found necessary to carry along in order to keep things all quiet and serene. Whip marks on a slave that would soon go to market was bound to reduce the value considerable, so this instrument was especially prized as it broke no bones, drew no blood and any redness or swellin to be found on the skin would soon disappear. An infraction by one of the slaves (often times for not 'lookin bright' and sellable, like maybe puttin your head down and mopin) was usually dealt with in the followin manner. The rule-breaker was spread naked and face down with both hands and feet firmly secured to the ground and the floppin would begin with the paddle applied to the naked slave's backside for a period of about a half an hour. I believe that to be the average time for such punishment. "Flop, flop, flop" would go the paddle, with the pain just incredible and continual, I was told. It was somethin all niggers dreaded. I never been flopped myself and never really been a member of a coffle, but I've talked plenty to my black brothers and sisters who had the misfortune to experience such a thing. I thank the Good Lord that my circumstance have changed from them early days where this was a very real possibility for us all, but I have to believe the pain of not knowin what has happened to my man might hurt every bit as bad.

       ം   ം   ം

Good news! The three Kelley brothers just rode into our farm yard a short time ago and said they had information on Sanford's whereabouts. We all gathered excitedly on the front porch as they told of their efforts the last week or so. It seems as though they finally had the good fortune to have stumbled upon the Tarver Plantation over in Jones County and had talked to the owner, Ben Tarver, about some recent slave tradin activity he had witnessed and actually had been party to. He told the Kelly's that he was an honest man and wanted nothin whatsoever to do with any stolen property; after all, he was a Methodist minister in good standin. He admitted a coffle of slaves had come through maybe three or four weeks back and he had put em up, and one member definitely fit the description of our missin negro. He even said he remembered this one young bondsman in particular, dark of skin and smart as a hooty owl ("but quiet," he said) who, he noted, had a natural space between his two front teeth when asked to speak. ("He never smiled," he also reported.) Tarver said the coffle was composed of about 60 members and was headed south to the New Orleans slave market.

One other very important thing. He provided the name of the man who owned this business venture. His name, he said, was Starling Finney. Tarver described him as a big and powerful man from up Virginia way who came with quite a reputation in the slave speculatin business. Tarver said he believed Finney always dealt in legal slave tradin and said he was shocked to learn that some of his stock might be stolen from legal owners. I saw both legal owners of Sanford Tims look over at one another knowingly when the Kelly's passed that particular information our way. Coswell and my sister, Cynthia, realized they had not long ago had the misfortune of meetin that very same man Ben Tarver had just described.

COSWELL TIM'S DIARY RESUMES

After dischargin the news about Sanford, I guess the Kelly Boys just about stumbled over one another in an all-out race for the recruitin office. They figured and rightfully so, that the Tims family would take things from here. All three would join the Confederate Army of Northern Virginia, as part of the 14th Regiment, Georgia Volunteer Infantry and would see more than their fair share of fightin over the next couple of years. (A fella has to always be careful what he wishes for, now don't he?) They left behind a younger brother and three sisters to tend their mamma, Rebecca Kelly. She had been widowed for some time now. Folks stayin at home would also suffer as time passed by. The Tims family weren't no exception, but for now we knew we needed to use our wits and whatever resources were at our disposal to find Sanford and bring that boy back home.

It was most fortunate the Kelly's got that information from Tarver when they did, cause by the time they passed through the door of that recruitin office, they most likely were greeted with the news of the South's first great victory at a place called Manassas.

The word we got on the matter was that both armies had met for the first time in July near Washington City, with the Federals boastin to sweep the Rebels before em and drive em back to the City of Richmond. Led by a general named McDowell, they attacked the Confederate forces that dug themselves in on the other side of a small stream locals called Bull Run. I reckon things did not go as planned as Southern reinforcements come to their aid and the north panicked, takin to their heels. The battle was a rout, it was reported. In the local *Federal Union* newspaper there was a note that added: "On the day of the battle, carriages filled with spectators eager to see the Confederate defeat flocked from Washington to the battle site, but they were sadly disappointed as the South carried the day."

The news was generally met with great favor and many local folks felt confirmed in the belief that a single Johnny Reb could lick ten of them northern city boys. They pointed to the heroes of the battle, General Beauregard (the leader), General Johnson who was the one that brought in the reinforcements by rail car and a man by the name of Thomas Jackson who held his position so firmly during the battle, why they give him the everlastin name of "Stonewall" for his heroic efforts.

The town continued to be all abuzz with the news of that first battle between north and south. I guess the Federals are callin it the "Battle of Bull Run" and I know folks round here say with a snicker and a smile that's a right proper name for it as the North turned tuck-tail and accurately demonstrated what proper runnin form was all about in their haste to return to the safety of Washington City.

DIARY OF PENIA FITZSIMONS TIMS

Cynthia and Massa Tims had a long discussion tonight bought the proper way to go bout fetchin my Sanford. With the news the Kelly brothers done brought us, we all knew a trip to New Orleans was in order. Cynthia wanted to go and help her man, but Coswell felt it might be too dangerous and strenuous a journey.

"Maybe I should remind you, Mr. Tims, that I have made that journey before and was none the worse for wear, I might add," my sister offered. It was true that Cynthia had proven herself quite resourceful and capable as she and Sanford had earlier fled the clutches of their master, the cruel James Walker. Disguises and darin had proved the difference as both had successfully traveled the Old Federal Road all the way to their new home in central Georgia. "As I remember, Coswell, seems to me you trailed behind some while Sanford and I led the way," she added.

"All true, Darlin. It does almost seem like a miracle that our plan worked as well as it did. Everyone did what they had to do that's for sure. But this here…I don't know. To go back into that hornets' nest?"

Cynthia didn't waste no time respondin to his concerns. "I don't have no fond memories of New Orleans neither, but it has been ten years. Can't imagine anyone would recognize us after all the time that's passed, Coswell, specially with Walker dead. Why, I think you and I might just make a fetchin couple as we nose around down there," Cynthia offered.

"Which way you think might be best to go, Darlin? Remember that poor Sanford's been gone for most three weeks now and I think we need to speed up any rescue operation."

I sat quietly as the back and forth continued.

"Well, I heard tell the Federal Road is most all growed up now and only passable in certain places. As for goin down by steamer from Savannah, didn't you say that would take at least 25 days and that's if there's good sailin weather to be had. I would say railcar would be the quickest way for us to travel, even with rail lines only goin some of the way, here and there. With coaches and paddle boats in between I'd be willin to wager if we planned this thing right, we could be in New Orleans in a week's time," Cynthia offered.

I looked to my older sister and nodded my approval of her good sense plan. I saw smiles all around as I knew the rescue of my Sanford was about to begin.

PART II

The Search

"There are mountains off in the distance that may seem impass-able, but, by golly, when we eventually get there, ain't it true we always find a gap?"

Bill Arp

Chapter 11

ALL NICE AND PROPER LIKE

COSWELL TIM'S DIARY RESUMES

"Coswell, where you goin in such an all-fired hurry this mornin?" Cynthia asked as I finished up my breakfast, got myself up from the chair and grabbed for my hat that lay on a small table next to the front door.

"Got to go see Sheriff Strother, my dear. Important I do that fore we head south," I replied.

"You think the law is gonna help us get Sanford back?"

"No, I don't, Darlin, but that ain't the reason for the visit. Be home shortly and fill you in on all the details," I added, as I give my woman just a cur-tailed kiss on the cheek, knowin full-well she had herself a mess of unanswered questions in her head bout my sudden need to run to town and see John Strother. She knew me well enough to know I seldom did things without some thought and maybe even an announcement or two made beforehand.

But ridin into town give me some valuable time to review all that had passed through my head the night before. I just couldn't sleep for the life of me, even took to countin my sheep, but I would have to say in the shake of lamb's tail, an idea come to me that might just prove more valuable than sleep or sheep in the long run. We had been preparin for our upcomin journey to New Orleans to try and fetch Sanford and had thought of little else, but I come to realize last night that a few pieces were still not in place.

❧　　❧　　❧

"Howdy John," I announced after hitchin up my horse and comin through the door of a smallish brick buildin set back off Wilkinson Street. It was located in front of the large state penitentiary, but slightly behind the old court house. Those buildins have sat right there for as long as I can remember.

Sheriff Strother greeted me warmly as was usually the case. We had knowed each other and worked together many times since he come to be sheriff as a young man back in '49 I believe it was. What I really liked bout him sides being a friendly sort (less you was a lawbreaker) was that he was very thorough when it come to investigatin and he kept the best records of anyone in Milledgeville and I believe I that would even include the city clerk, Agnes Bell, whose job it was to keep account of all official goings-on.

"What brings you to town this mornin, Coswell?" he asked.

"Well, John, as you know our servant, Sanford, seems to have gone missin and I suspect foul play. I believe it to be a fact that he's been stolen by unscrupulous slave dealers and is currently bein taken to the New Orleans slave markets. Cynthia and me will be on our way there in a day or so to fetch him, but I feel the need to review the folks I already know in that city. Do you still have the records from when Walker contacted us bout those two darkies of his that run off and happened to get caught up in our pattyroller net that night, oh, maybe ten years back?"

The sheriff walked over to a large cabinet and promptly opened up both its front doors. "I'm sure I do, Coswell. That happened just after I took on this job. Yep…got it right here," he said, as he withdrew some paperwork from the file and laid it down in front of me.

"Just what I be needin, John. Do you suppose you could fetch me a piece of paper and a little somethin to write with?" I asked.

As he turned to respond to my request, I looked down at the two notes before me. The first one was written in the sheriff's own handwritin and was marked August 15, 1850. It indicated a telegram had been received notifyin him of Mr. Walker's intention to pay the fine and the upkeep for his two slaves Cordelia and Julius, along with travelin expenses and a 500.00 advance (with a promise of more to come) if someone could be found locally who would make the long trip to New Orleans with both slaves in tow. This note was accompanied by another one sent a week later by Walker hisself makin good on that promise. Walker's address was right there at the bottom of the note as I knew it would be, but truth to tell what I really sought was positioned just slightly below and to the right of that. Under the man's address was a signature. Both my eyes come to rest on "James T. Walker" scrawled big as life at the bottom of the note, the dead man's mark plain for any inquisitive person to see.

Handin me a small piece of paper, a pen and an open ink well, Sheriff Strother sat down on the other side of the desk, pushed his chair back and put his feet up on the desk top. He put his hands up behind his head. As I began to write we talked briefly about another gentleman I had met down there, a fella by the name of Long who owned a large and profitable slave trader yard. I told the sheriff I thought at least one of these two fellas must still be up on the topside of the earth as neither Long nor Walker were all that advanced in years when I had done business with em before. The Sheriff did not know nor did I offer the fact that Walker had been dead for most of that time largely due to the efforts of the individual who sat across the desk from him and was currently scribblin down this now worthless address.

Strother and I talked as I wrote, but lookin up frequently to continue our conversation had a way of stretchin out the task at hand. I needed that time to copy three important letters exactly as Walker had written em at the bottom of the note. Now most of the letters in his name weren't of much consequence. When Mr. Denison was teachin Jesse and me to write down at the Milledgeville Academy when we was young'uns, we was told as a general rule small letters were much the same for all folks as that made it easier to understand any message written or received. Them smaller letters was even all set off together on a consistent fifty-two degree slant so there weren't much variety there. But it was the capital letters, Mr. Denison said, where a person was allowed to show off any special talents or inclinations. Lookin at the signature before me, I noticed Walker favored long skinny capital letters with tight loops, rather hastily drawn. They indicated a man who was in a powerful hurry and not one who wanted to be remembered for any thoughtfulness, individual flourish or artistry. I copied all three capital letters from his first, middle and last name, exactly the way the man had written em on the letter. When I finished, I ended our conversation and thanked the good sheriff for all his trouble. I blew hard on what I had written and folded the paper in two, puttin it in my top shirt pocket. I walked out of the sheriff's office just as nice as you please with one more important piece I needed to illegally forge a bill of sale for our missin Sanford.

∾ ∾ ∾

"Cynthia, would you mind goin to the back room and fetch me the box under the bed that's got all our legal papers in it?" was the first thing I asked when returnin home. I knew Cynthia was somewhat befuzzled by all this, but brought the box out to me just the same without a single word. She stood silently by as I slowly began to pick my way through the contents.

"Here it is, Darlin...Peney's official bill of sale they give us down in Savannah," I shouted out. "Now, if we make a few changes here and there and practice this here signature that just came my way, why I do believe we'll be one step closer to where we need to be in this matter."

"Coswell have you taken leave of your senses? What in heaven's name you be talkin bout?"

"I got to thinkin late last night that we didn't have no legal way to get Sanford back as he had never been purchased from his legal master, James Walker. When it comes right down to it, I reckon I stole the boy, now didn't I? If I were to go down to New Orleans and demand to have our bondsman legally returned, why they would look at me like I was some sorry fool if I was minus all the proper papers. Now I ain't sayin this is all gonna get done legal-like, but it sure would be nice if it could happen that way. We need this bill of sale for Sanford, my dear, iffen the law is ever goin to have a chance to favor us," I concluded.

Cynthia nodded in silent agreement and continued to watch as I worked. Little Peney, she soon come into the room and asked what I was so all-fired busy doin. It took me all the better part of an hour to compose the following "legal" document.

"I, James Walker of St. Louis, Missouri, in receipt of seven hundred dollars on this day do sell, grant and convey, to Mr. Coswell Tims of Baldwin County, Georgia his heirs or assigns, one negro boy of dark color by the name of Sanford, said negro about thirteen years of age and found to be sound of body and sensible of mind … a slave for life. This legal agreement is entered into willingly by myself and Mr. Coswell Tims on this 28th day of August, 1850."

The agreement was signed by none other than James T. Walker (skinny letters, tight loops and all) and witnessed by two people, two sisters in fact, who offered to practice their forged signatures and barely adequate penmanship just for the occasion. As for me, I was quite proud of the job I had done with Walker's name. For all the evil the man had done us, the very least he could do was to sell his slave to us before he completely vanished from mortal vision.

"Do you think I should make out another one of these for "a fine lookin mulatter woman by the name of Cynthia?" I inquired after I finished readin the illegal bill of sale for Sanford and set it down on the table.

"What good would that do? You are my husband all legal-like and nothin can change that."

"Well, actually, if our little secret leaked out you would go back to bein a slave and I would more than likely end out a permanent guest down in Penitentiary Square. I might be wearin different color clothes than the ones I wore down there earlier this mornin. Why, the more I think on it, things could complicate up in a right fast hurry. Now it's illegal for white and black to marry as we know, but more like as not we would just be driven out of town, maybe have our house burnt to the ground or somethin akin to that. But if there was no bill of sale then you could be claimed by the county with your so-called husband now guilty of even the greater crime of slave stealin, kinda like it is here with Sanford. What do you say, Darlin?"

"I say such a document could prove our undoin if someone ever got their hands on it. Frightenin to think on, but I guess bein turned out as trash and no account by townfolk is better than you bein in prison and me standin on the sellin block. Write that document, Coswell, and let's hope and pray for the best and that nobody ever sees it but the two of us."

"Hopes and prayers are the stock and trade of mankind," I thought to myself as I dipped my pen back into the small, blue inkwell and continued writin. I also began to think on where we might hide such a document so's only the two high contractin parties here would ever know of its existence.

Chapter 12

TRIAL BY ORDEAL

November 10, 2014
Milledgeville, Georgia

Robert Bumgardner took his antique pen in hand and quickly scribbled down a short notation. He liked the way that pen felt when he held it. It was a much appreciated gift from his Air Force buddies upon his retirement and he knew it definitely had not come cheap. It was an old Waterman, complete with the antiquated eye-dropper. Bob knew it to be one of the first fountain pens ever made, dating back well over a hundred years. He correctly assessed that the gift was given not just out of friendship, but because the givers knew just how much history and historical things meant to their black comrade-in-arms. Although Bob never flew as his dad had once done for the Tuskegee Airmen in the Second World War, Bob always found himself the go-to-guy whenever a historic question popped up. Now here he was on the trail of a 19th century southern slave catcher and, by golly, he would do so armed with an appropriate article from the time. That story was getting more and more intense and both he and his wife, Barbara, readily admitted to being totally caught up in this saga that had come their way courtesy of not one, but two journals written over a century ago…one of them by Coswell Tims and the other by his sister-in-law Penia Fitzsimons Tims.

Primary documents such as these were highly prized, the "main course" for any serious researcher and these two amateur historians fully appreciated the privileged place they now enjoyed at the table.

The couple had just driven back once again from the home of Rosa Billings, the granddaughter of Penia Fitzsimons Tims where they had managed to retrieve a missing piece of information from the helpful relative. Some pages from Little Peney's diary had been found missing from the original manuscript Bob and Barbara Bumgardner had been examining, but luckily Rosa succeeded in supplying those missing entries, unsure why they had been removed in the first place. "Just too violent, would be my guess," was her answer. "Maybe Great Gramma Peney just couldn't bear this part of Sanford's painful story and had removed the pages. Interesting that she did not discard them altogether, though," she had added. In any event, the pages were found along with many old letters and keepsakes that had been stored in the same worn wooden box.

Bob continued to jot down some things he remembered Rosa saying during their visit as his wife examined once more the once missing piece of the diary. It remained undated.

"Dat man knowd jus what he be doin. We wuz all walkin, cep'n de smallest childs who rode up in de supply wagons. Finney en hes men, de rode de hosses. We wuz driben sum 25 or 30 mile a day by my rekonin, all ob us chained in pairs wib a larger chain holdin dem pairs togeder. Eben de womens wuz chained up and de weren't spared de paddle neder iffen de begans ter fall behind. We only stops at noonday fer de hoe-cakes en water en den agin at nitetime when we would be told ter gader sticks ter make a fire en eat de best meal of de day, offen time Johnny-cakes wid sum peas en bacon rind. Sometime we stop at de plantations where we wuz put up fer de nite. Uder times when we comes on ter de cities, we's put up in nigger jails called 'barracoon's.' Dese wuz large brick buildins wid housins jus fer niggers… womens and chilens on de second floor en mens on de fust. Dere wuz large wash tubs on both ob de floors en long tables fer eatin. De were de best places fer ter stay, but we did not stop by dees places most time. Most time we jus sleeps by de side ob de road, sometime in de porin rain. One thing sure…de furder down de road we gets, de better de feeds us, de less we wuz whipped en de less need der wuz fer ter tie us togeder cuz folks de stopped lookin back ober dere shoulder where de comes from. We wuz all lost fer sure en der wuz really no thinkin bowt escape at dis time. We wuz like walkin dead folk, I would tells ya, wid little or no hope fer any future time, despite how wonderful dey tels us it all gonna be where we's goin. We all knows it don't pay a black person ter put much stock in de white man's promise."

Bob Bumgarder stopped writing momentarily as the phone rang in the kitchen. He elected to answer it as his wife appeared way too wrapped up in her examination of the newly acquired information.

"Barb, it's for you," Bob Bumgardner announced, as he handed the phone over to his wife. "It's Edie with the latest from city hall."

Edie Crandall, along with Eugenia McBride and Mattie Collins, had been on the case since the very beginning, ever since those early bodies had come to light down in Memory Hill courtesy of Ray Richards and his high tech GPR. Just as feared, the bodies that had been unearthed were presenting a problem, particularly the remains of a certain woman who was found buried right next to the grave of Coswell Elias Tims.

"Hello, Barbara," Edie Crandall began. "Just like we suspected, the mayor is having a real fit over the specifics you two are providing in regards to the Rosa Billings' relative. He really does not know what to make of it. Most of the other remains have no ID whatsoever and I believe they will soon be conveniently shuffled off to a common grave elsewhere on the premises... definitely out of sight. Folks with money and power want real bad for their relatives to occupy a prime spot like where Cynthia's body was found. Bill Millar's family is really pressing hard to get old man Millar buried in that exact place. He claims he has a right to it as it is stated in an old family will. The mayor wants to inspect that journal you have in your possession to check its authenticity. I saw him today and he said he would like you to come down to city hall tomorrow so he can take a good look at it. If you do that, Barbara, I wouldn't leave it with him. As we all know, sometime with city government, 'inconvenient facts' can quickly disappear with no explanation to follow."

"Well, I definitely will go down to see Chaney tomorrow morning," came the reply on the other end of the line. "And 'no,' I would not leave Peney's diary with John Chaney. No way! Just too much temptation there. He does need to see the document, however, if we are going to make the case for a reburial of Cynthia Tims in that same area. Why don't I drop by your house tomorrow and we can go downtown together.

"Sounds good to me, if nine o'clock is a good time for both of us."

"That's fine...I will see you then," Barbara concluded, as she handed the phone back to her husband. "This diary of Peney's is a potential political lightning rod, Bob. Chaney wants to see it tomorrow, but Edie and I are going to watch over it like a hawk. Would you please turn on the tape recorder and play back what Ms. Billings had to say about Sanford before I read that in the journal for myself?"

Bob complied, now glad that he had taken his wife's advice and brought *that small, hand-held thing along for the ride. Amazing, he thought, how often taking a woman's suggestion turned out to be the right thing to do. After a click and a short pause the story of Sanford's abduction continued through the voice of his great-granddaughter.*

"My great grandfather told of several other events that happened along the way to Louisiana, one which specifically involved his kidnapper, the slave speculator, Starlin Finney. He told of a woman of means by the name of Mrs. Atkinson whose job it was to accompany the coffle in an effort "to keep up all proper appearances for the sake of society," it was said. She had her own black attendant, a young woman of smart appearance and Great Grandpa Sanford said each night they stopped, the mistress would take one of her horses and ride off to a nearby farmhouse to sleep the night away in greater comfort than was possible out on the trail. The beautiful servant girl was always left behind to sleep on the leaves with the rest of the slaves, the reason bein that the mistress did not want to pay extra for the servant's lodgin. The mistress would, however, always faithfully rejoin the group early the next mornin and all would continue the next day on the journey south. Finney, he took notice of all this and desirin the young girl for his own selfish ends, plotted one mornin to leave a little earlier than was usual and by a different route than had been planned previous. As a result, it took a great deal of time for slave and mistress to reunite and in the meantime, Finney, why he forced the girl up into the supply wagon (after throwin the black children out) and brutally proceeded to ill-use her. When finished, he invited his companions to do likewise. This continued on for several hours, Sanford told the family, and the womenfolk in the coffle spent much time talkin and cryin over the event. All agreed and said what a great and powerful shame it was. "But de Lord he see dat for hisself en he write down in his book jus what happen," Sanford had added hopefully at the end of the story. (He forgot to tell us at the time, but remembered later on that the young slave girl drowned herself two days later "leabin behind de few clothes her owners once gib her rite dare on dat muddy bank where her footprints disappeared into dat deep dark wadder."

"Did Sanford ever try to tell anybody that he had been kidnapped illegally and was the property of Mr. Coswell Tims of Milledgeville, Georgia?" Bob had suddenly interrupted.

"No," was the quick reply. "It would have done no good with Finney as he knew many of the particulars and didn't give a lick. Sanford said he never really come in contact with other whites in authority who might have had the power to do somethin, til they got themselves to New Orleans proper and by then it was too late. Sides, my great grandfather had been warned

many times over by others in the coffle to NEVER, under any circumstances reveal such truth as awful, terrible things could come of it. A story bout a slave named John Glasgow, passed along by one slave in the coffle, went a long ways to convince him his mouth should remain closed-shut on that subject."

"John Glasgow was a British citizen and a free black man who had landed in Savannah a few years before Sanford's abduction. He came aboard an English ship, piloted by an English captain. They were to take on a shipment of rice to bring back to England and Glasgow was temporarily imprisoned by law as are all black sailors or passengers while their ships are at anchor in southern ports. No liberty was allowed as it was felt potential troublemakers or at least not fit examples for the local bondsmen to observe would result. Unfortunately for John Glasgow, the voyage was delayed longer than intended and a great deal of money was spent by the captain renting out local slaves to help with the work of fillin the ship's hold. After being told of a substantial additional charge for the black seaman's upkeep in the local jail, the captain saw fit to abandon his black crewman in order to save himself a few dollars. After all 'he was only a nigger,' the captain had reasoned. A wife and two young children back in England never heard a thing from their beloved husband and father again, it was said."

"But that weren't even the worst of it," Rosa Billings added excitedly as she continued on with the story. Evidently Glasgow was sold to a man, Thomas Stevens of Baldwin County, Georgia for the sum of $350.00. Master Stevens soon come to dislike "de arrogant look on dat new slave's face en de haughty way he carried hisself which very much resembled dat of a FREE man," Sanford said, and vowed to "whip de nigger pride rite out ob him." This he did and with a vengeance. When Glasgow tried in desperation to reveal the truth of the matter to his new master, Stevens flew into an even greater rage and threatened the new slave with (to use Sanford's exact words) "de horrors ob de picket."

"Bob…shut that thing off for a minute. Here it is in Sanford's own words about this thing called 'the picket.'" Barbara excitedly began to read out-loud from the diary page.

"De picket, oh Lordy, de picket…it be most horrible! Dat's what happens ter John Glasgow en should nebber happen ter no man…white, black or any color in between. What dey dun is dey took him off to a gallows where der be two poles en a crosspiece ter be found. Weren't no noose hangin from de middle, but der wuz sum pulleys en rope dare en his wrists wuz hung from em. One foot wuz drawed up en tied, toes downward, ter de knee. De oder foot wuz left free ter dangle in de air. He were ter hang dere some-

wheres tween heben en eart, but Massa Stevens, he done drove an oaken stake into de ground wid a sharp end a-sticken up in de air. John Glasgow he wuz stretched, turned, whipped en twirled bout, til he wuz sic en dizzy en jus needed ter rest dat foot on some'n solid. When he come ter rest it upon dat sharp stick, I wuz told dat's when all de fun begin, as dat's de bery time when dey took ter spunnin him round by his bent knee so dat de sharp stake it go deep into de foot, most clear down ter de bone, but de man holdin de pulley rope he pulls on it so's it don't go so deep ter stop all de merriment. Dem utter slaves tell me dat de screams could be herd fer mile round. Make Sanford's skin crawl ter eben think on it to dis day. John Glasgow wuz neber de same man en he neber able ter walk rite again after de picket."

"When we arrive in dat city of New Orleans after some five weeks walkin by my rekonin, we wuz brought ter a large trader yard owned by a man name Massa Freeman. De yard itself wuz square in shape en surrounded by buildins on all sides. It wuz rite dare en de center ob de city on de busy street cross from de St. Charles Hotel.

"De buildins round de yard wuz fer all de people who come dare...eder fer niggers, viewin folks, or dem dat buys. Sides the large area en de center where der were a central platforms ter be had fer de large auctions wid many peoples in attendance, de buildins round dis area wuz fer special things. Some wuz fer private lookin, some wuz fer small auctions, special floors wuz fer ter punish dose dey thought deservin (de floppin room, fer example), large eatin halls fer de slaves, oder rooms fer de buyers en still oders fer dem what brings en de 'stock.' Dare wuz eben one buildin special fer de trainin en exercisin ob slaves. Any rooms in dese buildins what did face de streets wuz hebily barred wid iron."

"Dare wuz maybe 500 slaves dare at de time en one wuz a mullater by de name ob Robert. He wuz put in charge ob all de niggers. He wuz called 'de steward' and often time he play de violin when de slaves dance fer ter get de proper exercise."

"All slaves wuz giben new clothes. Womens wuz giben calico dresses en head kerchiefs en men wuz giben pants en shirts (usually white), along wid a coat, a hat en shoes. We wuz all dressed up fer de circus. Meals wid plenty ob bread, bacon, coffee, vegetables en fruit wuz offered ter fatten all us up fer de sale. Mens wuz separated from de womens at dis time en de womens were den separated from dare chillens. Dem groups dey wuz lader sorted by size like stock en de general store. All wuz reminded by Robert ter look bright en happy. Dem individuals dat did not do dis wuz dragged ter de floggin room by Massa Freeman en his partner fer a proper floppin. All wuz gloom en despair. I waited my turn en den knew I would soon be

sold off, most likely into de swamps en bayous ob de back country. I come to figure maybe I neber come back from dare, but I wuz hopin fer a miracle. I wuz a-hopin en a-prayin Massa Tims en my fambly would somehow come en fetch ol Sanford."

"My God," Barbara Bumgardner announced, as she placed the torn out pages of the manuscript down on the table before her. "Can you even imagine such a thing?"

Chapter 13

HELP IS ON THE WAY

COSWELL TIM'S DIARY RESUMES

In no time Cynthia and me lit out, Jesse and Little Peney takin us down to the rail station in our old market wagon. I guess we must have looked quite a sight, all smarted up as fine as we was for the trip, a-settin up there on them rickety seats with Jesse drivin and Peney on her knees in the back for any nosey onlooker to catch sight of. My brother had consented to stay at our house and take on any business at hand and Peney, why she would tend that house while we was gone. We hoped if all went well to return within one months' time with Sanford right by our side. "The Good Lord willin and the creek don't rise," as my grandmamma used to say.

I did not disremember the bill of sale I drawed up for the occasion, along with clothes and a few things to eat which we had throwed into Cynthia's travelin trunk. I sure was glad I had that shoulder holster made up down in the leather shop, one quite similar to Walker's, but without the sheath alongside to carry that evil lookin, bone-handled dagger that had once been held to my wife's throat. Darn my bristles if that knife weren't the same one that Walker had plunged deep into my side that day long ago. I still got the scar and from time to time Mother Nature sees fit to remind me of that sorry event, specially on rainy or overcast days.

Now this holster carried my favorite .36 caliber Colt and saved all the discomfort of a sidearm worn on the hip. I could definitely see why Walker had chosen just such a contraption for his visit to Milledgeville ten years back. I also couldn't help wonder if the man had been buried with that empty holster after they fished his dead body out of the Tennessee River, just south of Chattanooga. No need to ponder that at this time, I reckon, but goin back to a time and place where much of this happened just jarred loose a flood of bad memories.

I was also glad Cynthia was armed. As a slave she was never allowed anywhere near a firearm, but as my wife, I wanted her to know how to protect herself. She had proven quite capable with a rifle and even with my ol 36, but I admit she didn't at first care much for the gift I made her of a small derringer pistol. She said she couldn't hit the broad side of a barn with the blessed thing, but I said if she could hit somethin that was just a few feet in front of her, it might more than serve her needs. "Let the danger come to you," I had advised. The woman wore it well, inside a cloth travelin pouch which was tied round her waist inside her dress. A hand could easily slip into that garment from either side and grab on to that little gift should the need ever arise.

After sayin our heart-felt farewells at the rail station, Cynthia and me boarded the train (so- called, cause an early observer once saw all the rail cars hitched up together, sayin they saw a whole "train" of em, one right after the other, and, I'll be hornswoggled if that name weren't here to stay.)

The route we had planned out on paper would be an odd one for sure, almost circular in nature, it was, but necessary if strictly usin railcar was our intention. In order to get to New Orleans (which is southwest of Milledgeville) we would have to first travel north, turnin west up on the Tennessee border and then travelin most all the way to Arkansas fore we would finally turn south and go through Mississippi to reach our New Orleans destination.

We began this epic little journey with a short trip to Gordon, some seventeen miles away. That little line runs on to Macon where the longer Macon and Western Railroad would bring us to Atlanta. I got to thinkin when Cynthia and me took our seats in the "Ladies Car," how it was early on when folks first thought this steam contraption mounted on wheels and runnin on rails would be the death of any adventurous passenger…either because it was goin so fast they could not take in a needed breath, or would shake em so violently they would cease to be conscious. Well, of course them things never did happen, despite the fact that the machine did reach speeds of 20 miles an hour or so which was twice as fast as any coach, or even now more modern ones where a good train on a good track could reach speeds of an incredible 40 miles in a single hour's time. Quite a machine, this steam locomotive.

Cynthia had never been on a train before, but took to it straightaway. She had spoke to Mrs. Abigale Anderson who tended the general store on South Wayne a number of times recently and the woman give her a great deal of information on rail travel and proper railcar deportment. Cynthia reminded me how lucky I was to be by her side cause train companies look protectively towards womenfolk and children, she said, and as a result provided them with the safest and most accommodatin travel conditions. Their car was always located well away from the engine where the greatest danger lay. Mrs. Anderson said that "the closer to the engine, the less valuable the passenger." As a result, the "Ladies Car," so called, was further away from all smoke, soot and possible danger of explosion than most all other cars on the train.

I have to admit that my Cynthia did make a fetchin picture in her blue travelin dress with matchin wide-brimmed hat. I always loved them black high-topped shoes she often wore for special occasions. Despite the fact that she had never even set a single foot on an iron horse in her life, she looked for all to see like a woman who was comfortable in her surroundins, comfortable with the finest car on the train, one with carpets, upholstered seats and inlaid wood furnishins and topped off with a "ladies compartment," which boasted both washstands and dressin tables. "Why, if you weren't with me, Mr. Tims," Cynthia offered, "you'd be saddled up close to the engine in the smokin car with all the noise and confusion. Mrs. Anderson done told me, excuse me, I must remember where I am, 'passed along the sentiment that if a man was lucky enough to be improved upon by the presence of a woman, only then do the railroad people believe him civilized enough to enter this particular car.'"

I nodded my thankfulness, reached over and planted a kiss upon that cheek of hers, as I could not help but smile over her little reminder. I guess it was true that the slave catcher's woman had civilized me considerable in the ten years or so we have been together. She may have surrendered to me back in New Orleans, but I guess it's more than fair to say that it's me who is now the prisoner.

With our trunk stored safely in the windowless baggage car (which was behind the wood and water car called the "tender") we stretched out in our adjustable low back seats and looked forward to our next stop in Atlanta. It was there where the rail line joined up with the famous Western and Atlantic Railroad that would take us out of Georgia, just over the Tennessee border to Chattanooga. Most folks in Georgia knew that 138 mile line real well as its great cost of over four million dollars and its twisted nature often made it the butt of many a joke. The line did serve the state well, but become our undoin when the Yankees captured it durin the war. I guess it's true that there ain't one single thing a person can name that ain't really a mixed blessin if one were to look on it more closely.

When we reached Chattanooga, a black porter advised us it was time to remove ourselves from the train as we would soon be changin lines. Baggage would be unloaded only to be reloaded again and in the meantime we could do any freshenin up or takin in food that a body might require. The Charleston-Memphis Railroad required an eight cents a mile fee for a single person to continue on over the next three hundred miles or so, almost to the end of that line. I counted out just a little less than eighty dollars for the two of us at that depot. My billfold was considerable lighter when I put it back inside my coat. No wonder there was so much money to be had in the rail line business, I thought to myself. Folks was willin to pay for the convenience of it all, specially if one was fortunate enough to ride with the ladies in this fine rail carriage.

When it come right down to it, I reckon the rail lines pretty much reflected what was thought bout folks in general. I noticed that redtails weren't allowed inside the trains, although I did come to see two or three of them savages ridin along on the rail car platform durin our journey. My guess is that was allowed despite the fact that I figured them to not to be payin customers. They would have to share space with men who chose to relieve themselves from time to time off them same platforms as the train sped merrily along. Negroes, Chinese and other non-whites was allowed on board, but they were strictly confined to the baggage car. Some of the trains we rode in had a special "negro car" where groups of slaves could be locked up when bein moved from place to place. Non-English white folks was allowed in the smokin car only, but was generally snubbed by their white superiors. Women, who were not white and white of the highest order, were not given any special treatment. Only Cynthia's group (oh, how I chuckled over that) had the use of this fine and distinguished place on the modern iron horse.

We did have us a little ruckus one evenin when a fella from the smokin car found his way (staggered, I should say) into our little sanctuary. Bein as he was without a woman or child, he was immediately asked to leave by the rail person in charge. He paid the fella no nevermind t'all and even started in cussin up a storm and carryin on somethin frightful, doin it all as loud as he could and right in front of the womenfolk. There weren't no doubt the man was higher than the hair on a scared cat's back and just couldn't hold on to his liquor. I felt the need to stand up.

"Excuse me, young fella. I do believe you have entered a place you don't belong," I stated as calmly as I could. "Now why don't you head back to where you come from so all can be quiet and serene."

"And who do you think you are to be making such a request?" he shot back, slurrin his words some.

"My name is Coswell Tims, sir, and I believe I speak for my wife and all these fine ladies here," I said, as I put my hands on my hips, brushin my coat back some in the process, just enough to reveal the firearm that hung from my left shoulder. As a result, I found without addin a single word more to the conversation, an agreement had definitely been reached as the gentleman willingly turned hisself around and troubled us no more.

As the miles rolled by we took to lookin out the windows at the Tennessee, Alabama and Mississippi countryside. Not too much different than Georgia, we both agreed. Lots of trees, fields and a sprinklin in of towns here and there. I was told the glass windows we looked out of were a welcome improvement over the open windows of just a few years previous. One woman passenger told us she was burnt pretty good and her dress completely ruined from the sparks that was throwed from the engine on a journey she had made just three years back. "It's a sinnin shame that a body had to hold their parasol over their heads to keep off the sparks. It just weren't a comfortable or safe way to travel," she willingly offered.

The view outside the windows did provide interest, but both Cynthia and me often took to imaginin young Sanford face on the glass before us and shared as much. What must our young man be goin through at this time, we wondered? He had been gone most a month now and we both figured if he went by coffle as suspected, he would have arrived in New Orleans just about a week ago after a journey of some three weeks walkin. It may have even taken em longer if the weather had been bad for any length of time or if Finney had stopped to make more sales, so we hoped that when we arrived it might be possible that he had only been there a few days.

Our journey by railcar, although by no means a direct one, would take us maybe four or five days to complete if all went accordin to plan, that is if the rail lines actually run all the way to New Orleans as Mrs. Anderson had assured Cynthia it did. Doin some ready cipherin over the whole of it, that would mean that Sanford would have only been in New Orleans for maybe a week or maybe even less when Cynthia and me made our arrival. Hopefully that would allow enough time for us to catch sight of, or still get information on, our missin bondsman. We knew it was much like it is with our hound dogs, the colder the scent, the harder the trail would be.

Reachin Memphis, we again were displaced along with our trunk and found us a new home headin south on the Mississippi Central Railroad. Now this was the first time in our journey we was actually headin south towards the port city of New Orleans. Before this we had been headed either north or in a westward direction.

There was one last change of lines to be made at Canton, Mississippi where the New Orleans, Jackson and Great Northern Railroad promised to take us the last 206 miles to the rail station in New Orleans proper. This last little piece of the journey come at the cost of $96.00 for the two of us. I guess I gulped a little with the fee, but with all the swamps and difficulties the buildin of this section of road had recently required, I guess them railroad folks wanted to get their money back as soon as was possible. When we finally stepped off the train in New Orleans at the rail station on the corner of Calliope and Magnolia Streets, we both could brag on the fact that we had managed to make it all the way from Milledgeville, Georgia to New Orleans, Louisiana, entirely by rail car, a feat that would have been impossible just a couple of years before. Cynthia and me both agreed the worst thing about the whole affair was the many stops along the way (24 on the last leg of the journey alone) with only fifteen minutes allowed to eat or tend to any personal business as a general thing. Folks would get awfully anxioused up over that and we was no exception. When we did stop for wood and water to make the necessary steam, only then would those stops be a little longer and much more agreeable. All in all, though, it had been a good journey, but we knew our search for Sanford had really only just begun.

I figured the best place to start would be the trader yard down by the wharf, the one owned by Major Long. I knew that place well as I had done business with the man before when I come to the city to return Walker's two slaves. We had no way of knowin if Starlin Finney did business with him like Walker done, but at the very least we might come away with some information that could prove useful in our search.

A distinguished lookin couple by the name of Cynthia and Coswell Tims soon stepped to the New Orleans streets, arm and arm, and began to walk down towards the wharf and in the direction of the slave trader yard. We both looked to take in all the fine sights. The buildins were huge and stately, dwarfin us mightily. We walked for maybe twenty minutes or so, commentin on this and that, when, as we come to the river, suddenly I felt my Cynthia go almost completely limp in the knees. Why at first I thought she had tripped over somethin and figured it to be a mighty good thing that I had proper hold of her arm so's to prevent a serious fall. "Are you alright?" I asked.

I could see she had gone pale in color as well as she struggled to speak. "Coswell, do you see what I'm seein?" she asked, as she pointed her finger in the direction of the dock.

I give a look and saw the thing, ridin quietly in the waters of the harbor. It was a steamboat, faded white in color and somewhat rundown. Its familiar stern paddlewheels, double smokestacks and pilot house perched high atop its three decks had not changed one bit in the last ten years. On its side was printed in large black letters the name of the vessel. "*Enterprise*," it stated boldly.

It was hard to continue on as both us felt a sudden urge to turn around and head back to the safety of our room at the St. Charles. That ship was a most unpleasant reminder of our past. That boat was where Cynthia had been confined as a slave when she awaited the journey to St. Louis with her new master, James Walker. His desire to possess her had allowed her admittance to the second deck, whereas most of her kind was resigned to the lower deck of the boat. But even those private quarters, she knew very well, could do little to protect her from the dangers of her enslaved condition.

It was also on that ship where I had met Walker for the first time and where he give me the money for returnin his two slaves. I did not like the man when I first met him. I guess it's true what my daddy used to say… "Some things, son, you can tell just by lookin." (And there weren't a single thing he did or said at a later time that would ever cause me to change my mind.)

Although it did discomfort us powerfully, we decided to overcome any misgivins we might have on the matter and continue on rather than return to our hotel room. In another few minutes we reached our destination as the sign above the door clearly spelled out the name of the man we sought. That storefront weren't much different than that of any other business on this busy street next to the Mississippi River and I remembered from an earlier time what made it unique was the trader yard itself which was located behind the main office buildin. The yard was quite large as I recall, surrounded by maybe a 12' high wooden fence.

As we entered his office, that same Major Long who I had done business with years ago as a Georgia slave catcher, I spied still sittin at his desk in much the same way as I had remembered him. His favorite whip lay within easy reach right there on the table. I expected as much.

"Major Long, so good to see you again after so many years," I announced, as I moved towards him with my hand outstretched in greetin. "I do not know if you still remember me…Coswell Tims? And this here is my lovely wife," I said, as I pointed and made a slow nod off in Cynthia's direction. "I believe the last time we talked I was doin some work for a gentleman by the name of Walker."

"Oh, yes, Mr. Tims, I do remember you quite well. You were the slavecatcher from Georgia who returned Walker's slaves and as I recall, chased down a few others who ran off while you were here. Have you been well, sir?" was his hearty reply.

"I have indeed, Major Long. I must tell you that fortune has seen fit to smile on us some as our farm up in Georgia has done right well and we continue to add a bondsman or two each and every year so's to help run the place. I am now here, not as a slavecatcher returnin two-legged property for money, but as a potential buyer," I stated.

"Why, Mr. Tims, you mean to say the State of Georgia cannot supply you with your needs in this area? You come all this way for a couple of niggers?"

"Actually, my wife and I decided we would combine business with pleasure in this case, sir. She always wanted to visit this fine city of yours, specially after all the nice things I had to say on it and folks are well aware some of the stoutest stock in the south come right through this city bound for the rice and sugar plantations, now ain't that a fact? We are lookin right now for a buck nigger, maybe 20-25 years old, dark in color so's he can keep up with the work and hearty and strong of body. Want him to be bright as a steel trap, too, we do. You have anythin like that available at this time, Major Long?"

"Well, no I don't, to be honest with you, Mr. Tims. You might be better served by Theophilus Freeman. He and his partner, Mr. Burch, have a place right across from the St. Charles Hotel. It's a large place, much larger than mine, with room enough for five hundred darkies. I do believe that Mr. Williams, Mr. Redford and Mr. Finney, three of the largest slave speculators in the entire south, just brought in their groups this past week and I feel certain many would fit the description you just gave. I would try them before I went anywhere else," Long advised.

Cynthia suddenly interrupted. "Major Long...Do you ever do business with Starling Finney?" Not waitin for an answer, she added: "We have heard he has had great success in the business and has a most delightful reputation. It' so easy to get cheated in negro speculation, don't you agree?" she concluded, as she took to fannin herself due to the ever risin heat of the room. She had took me by surprise when she mentioned that name and with such familiarity, but I was glad the question had been asked nonetheless.

"No, Mrs. Tims. Finney only does business with Freeman and has done so for as long as I can remember. In fact, you and your husband better get on over there before much time has passed if you want to get yourself a decent pick. Those three traders bring in the best stock and they are generally the first to be sold off," Long concluded.

"We will do just that, but one last thing, Major Long, if we may. The two of us will be in the city for a week or so and would like to look up Mr. Walker. We noticed the *Enterprise* is currently docked down at the wharf and figured he just might be in the city," I asked.

"Well, Mr. and Mrs. Tims, I am sorry to report quite a sad story, yes, quite a sad story, indeed. You see, Mr. Walker left here to go north on a business trip many years ago and never returned. Been quite some time now. Nobody knows whatever become of the man... disappeared without a trace, you might say. We believe he went somewhere up in your neck of the woods. Took two of his servants with him, but they both turned up missin as well. Must have been some devilment at hand, for sure. James Walker was legally presumed and declared dead a few years back and his estate up in St. Louis finally settled. One of his sons, a fella by the name of Thomas Walker now runs the place. That is his steamboat you saw down at the dock as he is currently here on business. In all honesty he is probably my most important client and a good man of business I would have to say."

"Well, thank you kindly, Major Long, you have been most helpful," I concluded, as I shook hands with the slave trader as Cynthia and me began to take our leave. As the two of us walked back to the St. Charles, she leaned in close to me so's to almost whisper in my ear. "Coswell, you suppose that Thomas Walker fella be white in color?"

"Not one chance in a thousand," was my quick response.

Chapter 14

PREMEDITATED, ON PURPOSE

COSWELL TIM'S DIARY RESUMES

We stepped out of Long's office onto the cobblestone street and again headed back up the wharf intendin to return to the room we had secured at the St. Charles Hotel. Cynthia did find it necessary to pause briefly as we again passed by the steamship *Enterprise*, but the ship remained completely silent, harmlessly tethered to the dock. This time my woman's knees did not buckle like before, but she did report the oddest feelin that had come over her. She said she now felt for sure she was bein watched. I asked her to look all around as it was gettin late in the day and there were few people out on the street and none of em appeared to be payin us the least bit of attention. I told her that I thought maybe her mind might be playin a trick or two on her, sorta like it was when I would go out on the trail and she would offer up all them strange premonitions of hers.

"And what happened the last time I got one of those so-called strange premonitions bout the snake bitin our Sanford? What about that? Now, I ain't foolin, Coswell, I can feel eyes on me for sure and just look how the hair has taken to standin up straight on the back of my arm."

Well, I did admit the hairs was standin at full attention like soldiers on muster day, but I suggested to her that only proved the "scare, not the stare." Now I thought that to be downright clever, but Cynthia did not find the remark the least bit amusin and I felt the need to immediately apologize for makin light of her discomfort. I did offer to take one last real good look around on her behalf, but seein nothin out of the general run, told her I just had to trust my eyes on the matter and reported all was well. Of course navigatin a city has its own perils that are different than those out on the trail, so I suppose there could be places a person might hold up and not be seen by someone unfamiliar with the territory. Was it possible that a man could be standin at that very moment in the pilot house of the *Enterprise* with one of them long spyglasses in hand, one eye fixed intently upon my beautiful wife? Was it possible that individual knew the identity of the person he was lookin at? Was it also possible that same man would soon pay us an uncomfortable visit with regrettable consequences? I guess we shouldn't ought to dismiss any such possibilities as "most anythin can be possible between hell and breakfast time," as Daddy often said.

Unaware of any dangers at hand, we returned to our current place of residence where we had checked in earlier in the day and walked under the vast pillars of the St. Charles Hotel and up the stairs to our room on the second floor. Gone was the same huge staircase that once fronted this grand buildin. Gone also was the famous dome that had once been perched on its top. Much had changed since the fire and since our earlier visit back in the spring of 1850.

It had then been our plan to "hide" from Walker in the grandest of style as Sanford, Cynthia and me had plotted our escape from just that place. I'm sure at the time we thought our efforts was much more likely to come crashin down than it was for this huge, one-acre, landmark to do so, but that turned out not to be the case. Almost one year from the time we hightailed it north to Milledgeville, a fire broke out just beneath the eaves of the old north wing roof and spread rapidly. The firemen did not have hoses long enough to put the fire out and it continued to spread. As the desk clerk told me when I inquired about the changes in the buildin, he related the followin account of the disaster. "I saw the whole thing with my own two eyes and it haunts me to this day," the man reported. "It was a scene of great confusion. Boarders were busy packing up, husbands were looking for their wives, wives were wringing their hands in agony as the winds shifted southward, the flames increased in intensity and the dome came crashing down. Soon the pride of our city had become a mass of ruin. It was a miracle with 800 people here at the time that no one was killed," he emotionally recalled.

Because the St. Charles was so important to the city of New Orleans, I guess there was no time wasted in rebuildin it as the new one was completed in just two years' time. It sure was a beautiful place and like the one before soon enjoyed the reputation as the "Grandest Hotel in the South." Now, this may have not been the sentimental nuptial journey the two of us had hoped for when we signed on, but it certainly provided a welcome refuge after that little episode on the wharf, nonetheless.

As I closed our room door behind us, Cynthia spoke up with the courage gained from our new-found privacy. "Well, Coswell, I can't really account for that feelin that come over me back there, but it sure was a powerful one, I would tell ya that."

"My feelin is that you have a powerful fear that someone might recognize you from before. Those were hard times for you, I know, but I don't think there is really anyone down here who still remembers either of us and think how we have changed over the years. No, Darlin, I believe we will be just fine and be able to go on bout our business," I assured her.

We continued to talk as we began to change our clothes and tidy up some before goin to supper in one of the hotel's many dinin halls. "I guess we did get us some useful information today," Cynthia added.

"We now have us a name and tomorrow we will meet this 'Mr. Freeman' and see what he knows of our Sanford. Also, we come by some interestin things bout Walker, now didn't we? Ain't it a hoot that one of his mullater children inherited all of his earthy goods up in St. Louis after treatin all the colored folks he sired up on his place so bad all these years? I wonder what kind of man this son of his turned out to be?"

"Sometime negroes that own slaves are just as ornery as white folks, but it is true that sometimes they're good people who just keep their own family as slaves so's to keep up proper appearances. They get on with em right fine when the white folks ain't poking their noses in. Hard to tell for sure, I reckon," Cynthia said, as she collapsed into a comfortable chair next to the bed.

I followed her example and both of us, half dressed, stretched out, exhausted from travelin on the rail car and weary from all we had gone through this first day. We fell asleep almost immediately. The two of us did miss out on any fine supper that was to be had. But we thankfully also missed out on any worry that might have been in our heads on what the comin day might bring along with it.

    ~o ~o ~o

When I first shook the hand of Theophilus Freeman, I was taken by his cordiality. He doffed his hat to Cynthia upon introductions and willingly offered his services to the two of us. He did say he was surprised to see a woman on the premises as that was a very rare occurrence, "especially a woman of such beauty and grace," he had said. "It has been my observation over the many years I have been in this business that the trader yard and all it entails generally offends the sensibilities of the fairer sex."

"I assure you, Mr. Freeman," replied Cynthia, "I am well equipped to deal with the realities of such a necessary place and look forward to your help and guidance." I was not the least bit surprised by Cynthia's bold and confident response.

We repeated our desire as we had done with Long, to possibly purchase a slave from his current inventory and gave as close a description as we could of our missin bondsman…bright, strong, young and dark of color. Freeman said he felt we had come to the right place. He suggested we should feel free to walk about while he tended to some last-minute duties as the mornin viewin session was to start promptly at ten o'clock. Bein as we were comin up upon that very hour, we quickly parted company and Cynthia and me began a little personal look-see of the premises.

It certainly was a large place, located directly across from the St. Charles it was. All brick on the outside, I would say it took up a whole city block with what appeared to be many rooms or buildins that sprung from the open yard in the center. Only a few people could be seen, some white and some black, but our guess was that most of the merchandise for sale was bein readied-up and bein strongly encouraged to "look bright and step lively," as Little Peney had once accurately, if not discreetly, shared with us.

We soon wandered into the gamin room where a number of men was busy playin cards, but they quickly laid em down on the table as they glanced at their pocket watches which indicated it was gettin mighty close to that special hour. We followed em out to one the nearby viewin rooms and soon found ourselves in the company of maybe twenty blacks and perhaps half that number of white folks. Potential buyers had struck up conversations with those offered for sale and we did find that many a slave began conversations with certain buyers they thought might treat em well. Most slaves I have known over the years are quite skilled at readin the looks, gestures and words of those white folks they might be forced to serve. After all, the stakes were mighty high and their very lives depended upon it. White masters and mistresses on the other hand, were generally very poor at understandin the motives and nature of their black property.

Numerous trader yard employees stood ready to offer their assistance, perhaps addin information on a slave for sale or help with negotiations that might follow. Sanford was nowhere to be found. We visited several other viewin rooms, but not the private ones where we was told more intimate examinations were currently bein conducted. Our hopes was startin to fade.

Catchin sight of Mr. Freeman who seemed to be everywhere and anywhere and moved quick on his feet for a man of rather advanced age, we made an attempt to catch his attention. "Excuse me, sir. We understand the notable Mr. Finney has recently brought in a likely group. Mr. Long tells us they are a hardy lot. Are any of them about, sir?" I inquired.

"They came in a little less than a week ago and sales have been very brisk since then," the slave dealer responded. "Go to viewin room #14 across the yard and you will see what remains of the lot."

With that we hurried over to where we was directed and saw maybe a half-dozen negroes sittin at a common table. They all stood up in respect as we entered the room. Several began to engage us in conversation as it was my guess they were told they would pay a heavy penalty if there was to be any long delay in their sale. Sanford was not among them, but I did find me one of their number who appeared both bright and well dispositioned, despite the smallpox scars that marred his face and body and his somewhat stooped carriage.

"What is your name, boy?" I inquired.

"My name be William, sir," he replied.

"How long have you been here, William?" Cynthia asked.

"Maybe bout a week now, Mistus," he said with a slight bow.

I leaned in a little more closely to the slave and he stepped back slightly, unsure of my intent. Lowerin my voice some I made him the followin offer. "William, I will give you a solid gold piece if you can supply me with the information I want to know. I am lookin for a slave by the name of Sanford who came in with your group." I then proceeded to give the best description I could, right down to the space between his two front teeth. A glimmer of recognition come over his face with mention of that last little detail. His answer had me and Cynthia hangin on every word that came from out his mouth.

"I knows him, Massa. He be dat slave Benjamin. He sold on de bery fust day we comes here to a sugar farmer down en de bayou. I don't members hes name zakly, but he wuz frigtenin en his appearance en manner. Not like yuz folks. I would work hard en be loyal to yus iffen yuz wuz ta buys me," William offered.

"We cannot entertain such a thing at this time, William. Now here is that gold piece I promised you. Do you remember anythin else about this slave named Benjamin?" I asked.

"Benjamin, he wuz smart, but say he had a secret dat needed to be kep hid. Wuz he your slave, Massa?" William asked rather boldly.

Surprised at the extent of this slave's understandin, I felt the need to answer honestly. "Yes, he was and we want him back real bad," I indicated, as Cynthia nodded in agreement.

I closed William's hand around the gold coin and put a finger to my lips in partin. The slave took my meanin and nodded back in agreement. It had been settled by all parties involved that we would stay dark bout the conversation that had just taken place.

Cynthia and me withdrew from the viewin room and had us a little private conversation on our way to yet another. It was agreed that we would wait til the first viewin session was over at one o'clock to put any further plans into motion.

We continued to wander into a number of other such rooms and saw many a heart wrenchin sight. A slave woman cryin desperately to be sold along with her child which was soon torn from her arms, an old black man, a "used up nigger" on his knees pleadin for a master, any master, to care for him in his declinin years. We talked to a white man, a first time buyer who was filled with self-doubt and fear of disappointin his young wife and family. He engaged us in conversation and admitted the newness of it was very overpowerin. "I just want my wife to be happy," he had said. "I need to spare her the drudgery of washing, cleaning, cooking and child raising that would make her old before her time. I love her so very much and only want what is best for my family," he had offered passionately. We both expressed sympathy for his plight, and told him how it was buyin our first servant. Cynthia made up an incredible story which I agreed with completely. When he left to go on about his task at hand, Cynthia whispered to me that in his confession of love for his wife he may have left out one little detail. He forgot to say how ownin a slave would benefit his public status. "Once you got a nigger of your own," she said, "why then you were really SOMEBODY in the white community," she said.

The buyin session ended at one o'clock sharp and that saw Coswell and Cynthia Tims again on their way to Mr. Freeman's office. He was already there a-settin at his desk and writin feverously in a large ledger book of some kind as we entered.

"Sorry to interrupt, Mr. Freeman, but may we have a brief word?" I asked. As we took the seats offered us, I continued on. "We were unable to find what we was lookin for this mornin after a great deal of effort. We even went over to where Finney's stock had been delivered. Not much left, I'm afraid. I can't help but think one of em would have been a perfect fit. Did they sell for a great deal of money, Mr. Freeman?"

Finney began to thumb back through the pages of the book that lay before him. "As a matter of fact, Mr. Tims, they sold for top dollar," he offered, without sharin any of the details.

"Well, sir, I figure we may be out of luck this season. We will continue to look for a spell, but I fear we may go home empty-handed."

Risin from his chair with arm extended, Theophilus Freeman wished us well and said he was sorry he could not accommodate us.

"We will continue to look around this afternoon," Cynthia inter-jected. And so we did…right there in the man's personal office and with him absent from the premises at the time. It was a bold plan, but desperate folks will do desperate things, now ain't that a fact?

When we spotted Freeman fully engaged in conversation with some eager buyers, Cynthia turned to me and quietly announced that time had come to commence operations.

We reached the man's office in short order and looked around considerable before tryin the unlocked door. My wife slipped in first and I followed behind after one more look in all directions. The two of us went in kinda slow, most like folks would do if they were goin up to an old log that they thought they seed a snake run under. Don't think that really served much of a purpose, but it didn't hurt any to speak of. Cynthia immediately went over to the desk and seized the ledger Freeman had recently consulted. She began to thumb through the thing, turnin it slightly to catch the light comin through a nearby window.

"You need to hurry, Darlin," I reminded her. "Freeman could take a notion in his head to come back at any time."

"Here it is near the end, Coswell. I recognize the name 'Benjamin,'" Cynthia excitedly announced. "You read what it says and let's hope we can remember all the particulars."

I read aloud from the followin document.

SEPTEMBER 6, 1861

SLAVE BENJAMIN...SOLD TO LUCIAN A. BIENVENU

OF LAFOURCHE PARISH, LOUISIANA

FOR THE SUM OF $1,800.00...CASH MONEY PAID IN FULL

WARRANTED SOUND BUT NOT GUARANTEED

ತ	ತ	ತ

Later, back in our room we patted ourselves on the back for a job well done. "Lucien Bienvenu of Lafourche Parish, Louisiana," we repeated to ourselves until we could finally write it down. The two of us had escaped bein suspicioned and was lucky to have not been spotted either enterin or leavin Theophilus Freeman's private office. I felt so good about it that I couldn't help but sit myself down in that same comfortable chair I had fallen asleep in last night and put my feet up on the bed. I asked my wife and partner in crime if she wouldn't mind fetchin my pipe and some of my best smokin tobacco I had stored in our trunk. She obliged and I filled the pipe and lit it off, leanin back as far as that chair would allow.

"Now what you think you're doin, Coswell? You're a-fixin to break the furniture and dirty up that nice bedspread with your boots?"

"Don't worry, Darlin...I'm just feelin the need to do a little 'puttin,' that's all."

"What do you mean, 'puttin'? I never heard of that."

"Well, I'll tell ya, Cynthia. 'Puttin' is when you relax your body all over and take to puttin your feet up on somethin real comfortable like I'm doin here. You see that puts your body at rest so's then you can put your mind into motion. Works like a charm if serious thinkin is what a person has in mind. My daddy used to do it and he'd take to 'puttin' whenever he had somethin real powerful that required his full attention."

"Well, what important thing you be 'puttin' on, Mr. Tims?"

"Well, right now I'm thinkin that you would make a right fine preacher's wife, my dear. We know that certain parsons may have their demons, but they are certainly more respected in polite society than any ol broke-down slavecatcher like the one you got hitched to. Yes, indeed. The more I think on it the more I figure it's time you and me got ourselves into the soul savin business and I have me a pretty fair idea who just might be the first lost soul in need of rescue."

"Would that be our lost servant, Sanford, who currently resides with a fella by the name of Lucien Bienvenu down in Lafourche Parish, Louisiana?" Cynthia responded.

"Halleluiah and amen to that, sister," I said, as I took a puff on my favorite smokin pipe and began to seriously contemplate the mission that lay before us.

Chapter 15

UP IN POWDER SMOKE

COSWELL TIM'S DIARY RESUMES

The last time I found myself alone on the early mornin streets of New Orleans it was more than ten years previous and I was on my way to do some serious store tradin, lookin to buy some new clothes to disguise both Cynthia and Sanford so's they could flee the city and, hopefully, their bonded condition. This time it was to get me some proper clothin that might better suggest my recent callin to the ministry. Now I know them folks are supposed to be respectable, but I have seen many of em over the years and took to watchin em up close and I have to admit they made me bout as doubtin a Thomas as there ever was. I even wondered where some of them barnyard preachers got their papers from as there was so much devilment to be found among em.

Cynthia had quite a tale of her own to tell on the subject. She was young and he weren't. He should have knowed better, but he didn't. It was done premeditated and on purpose and I don't expect it was easy for a child at the tender age of twelve to lose her innocence through no fault of her own. That experience did wither her youth some, but she is now thirty-four years of age and no longer at the mercy of the Christians. She also has me by her side, but has proved herself over the years to be a formidable person in her own right. I left that woman I love all curled up and sleepin in our room just as innocent as you please, our plans for today already worked up earlier the night before.

As I tried to set my sights on the mornin tasks at hand, I could not help but think back to the wee hours of the mornin when that same woman and I come to find ourselves all tangled up tight in each other's embrace. It was the first time since we been in this fair city that we had been together in such a manner. What with the travel and all the worry that sort of activity had temporarily been placed on hold. But it is a necessary thing as we all know and it broke out like measles in a fit of passion, worthy of both high contractin parties. When it all come to completion, there weren't a single word that needed sayin twinxt the two of us.

Now I have found this sparkin thing to be difficult for a fella to fully understand. It is a true wonderment, for sure, and as such does deserve its fair share of examination, don't it? Now as I see it, the whole thing must have been planned up yonder way back in the beginnin as a way of bringin people of different persuasions, male and female, together so's to ensure the survival of the human race. It was made to be so enjoyable that it would be hard to ignore by either party. But the one thing that remains a puzzlement to me to this very day is the timin of any such event. Now I cannot pinpoint the reason for Cynthia's sudden passion, but I wish I could as I might be able to make some predictions that would come in handy in the future. Was it cause the two of us was back in the same place where our lovin relationship had its start? Was it because she was proud of me for my part in our newly developed plan? Maybe she was feelin good about herself and her part in all this and that confidence made her more agreeable. Could it have been that she felt some responsibility or guilt in the matter cause this necessary activity had been delayed for so long? My goodness, maybe it all boils down to the position of the moon last night, or maybe some clock set to tickin inside that head of hers, or perhaps a combination of things that could only be sorted out by the greatest of minds and only then with the greatest of difficulty. There must be a reason why doors on necessaries have two very different images carved on em. Some of them buildins have suns while others have moons as we all know. A man knows well enough to enter the one with the sun on the door as that image suits him well, out in the daylight and easy for all to see. A woman, now she uses the outhouse with the crescent moon carved into the door and silently tends her business. I figure that little moon-door buildin is just right for the sisterhood…dark and mysterious as they all are, beautiful (both occupants and buildin with maybe a few fragrant lilies a-growin nearby) but when all is said and done, impossible to understand in the full light of day. As I pondered this for a spell, I thought on somethin Jesse had said to me one day while we was out on the trail. I remember I was goin on and on bout the wonders of the bloodhound trackin dog when Jesse offered his opinion on the matter. He told me that a fella don't need to be worryin bout any complicated process when all that's necessary was to just sit back and appreciate the results. I reckon that to be an example of the wisdom an older brother might bestow upon a younger one and with that in mind, I figured to conclude my thinkin on this love makin business, at least for the time bein.

With all these thoughts runnin through my head, I guess it weren't no wonder I absent-mindedly walked right by the city hall which was on the same street as the St. Charles. Really made no nevermind as I could just as easily take care of the map business I had planned on doin there upon my return from the shops down on Canal Street. That's where I found them disguises ten years back and figured I just might be able to do the same thing yet again.

It weren't long fore I had in my possession a long black overcoat and one of them wide-brimmed, round-topped hats (black, of course) that preacher men seem to favor. Managed to get me a Bible as well and with my store tradin at an end, I started to mosey back to St. Charles Avenue to finish the day's tasks. I must admit I felt a little funny when I slipped into an alleyway to exchange my old hat and coat for the new. Found myself afterwards walkin a little different when I held that Bible close to my chest for all to see. A package containin my old clothes hung from my other arm.

As I strolled along, I admitted to missin my shoulder holster some. I had taken that lethal contraption off yesterday when we went to the trader yard (you don't carry a gun into a prison, now do you?) and earlier today I left it once again, this time storin it away in Cynthia's trunk as I considered the peaceful nature of my new religious callin. But Cynthia, she had remained armed durin all this time, as that small derringer I give her was completely hidden from view and she admitted it did give her a feelin of security, despite some misgivings about her ability to ever hit any intended target.

છે   છે   છે

Cynthia later said the knock at the door had startled her. The man standin there when she opened it, she said, looked vaguely familiar, but his smile and kind words of welcome gave reassurance that he was what he said he was, a hotel official makin sure all good-payin customers was satisfied with their accommodations. Once inside, however, she said she began to have herself second thoughts on the matter.

He was a tall man, dressed in a dignified manner and had a way about him that suggested he was more used to given orders than takin em from any hotel manager. Things started out well, what with the friendly smiles and all. Sittin down across from one another at the table near the largest window in the room, he continued to welcome Mrs. Tims and her missin husband to the city and the hotel (he seemed to know that missin part in advance) but soon asked if the fine couple had done any walkin about the area to see all the fine sights. Before Cynthia could offer up a reply, he asked her specifically if she had occasion to visit the wharf to see the fine ships currently docked there.

"What would be so interesting about those ships?" Mrs. Tims inquired.

"Well, one of em happens to be mine," came a louder than expected answer. "That is, I happen to be the captain of the steamship *Enterprise* and have been for some time. I worked for a man named Walker awhile back. So sad about his disappearance, don't you think? Reynolds is the name, ma'am, Captain Reynolds, if you will. If you don't remember me, I sure do remember you!" he stated menacingly.

"Captain Reynolds, I do believe you are mistaken. My husband and I are in the city for the first time in an effort to secure a bondsman for our farm. I assure you we have never been here before."

"That's a lie and you know it," he responded quickly with ever-risin anger in his voice. That husband of yours is that Georgia cracker that Walker hired years ago. Saw the two of you together on the wharf the other day. Maybe fancier clothes, but I recognized the two of you straightaway and knew you were up to no good. You, madam, are the slave girl, Cynthia, am I correct?"

Cynthia told me the pause after that question made any further protests useless. "I am that girl," she calmly replied. "What do you plan to do with your new-found information, sir?"

"It depends on what kind of arrangement you and I can agree to."

"What kind of arrangement would you be interested in, Captain Reynolds?"

"One that involves you and I on a much more intimate basis. I assure you the captain's quarters are quite lavish and comfortable and would suit a grand lady of your resurrected stature."

"Why you do flatter me, sir, given my humble origins. My husband will be gone most of the mornin. Would you like to start in with some early negotiations that might just end with such an agreement?" Cynthia responded suggestively.

He answered with actions, not words. Reynolds come slow outta his chair, with a slight squint of the eye and a hasty pass of the tongue over the upper lip. That was matched by a suggestive smile from across the table. Cynthia slowly rose from her chair. She warmly offered the man her left hand, extendin it to the slave ship captain, but as she done that, her right hand busily sought an openin on the other side of her dress.

  ∿ ∿ ∿

I did finally manage to arrive at the city hall, a beautifully built stone buildin officially christened "Gallier Hall." We needed a map of the area for our plan to go forward and I believed this to be the best place to secure such a thing. A smallish fella with large copper spectacles come out of nowhere almost immediately and sort of took this visitin preacher under his wing. He began to explain the lay of the land, so to speak, (I figured he might just be anglin to get hisself into heaven for all his great efforts on my behalf.) He told me that the Good Lord sure had seen fit to bless me as a railroad called the "Opelousas" had been completed just a couple of years back and that would take me all the way to the place I needed to go. He went on to say that railroad had been almost a decade in the makin as swamps and bayous had to be crossed, fill brought in to raise up roadbeds, and bridges built over open water. Lots of German and Irish immigrants had been hired, he added, to supplement local slave labor. What with the diseases many would die from and the tremendous cost, this fella claimed the whole achievement was a downright miracle and "a marvel of modern engineering." He willingly provided me with a map of the whole area and pinpointed Terrebonne Station deep in the Lafourche Parish district where he felt my intended mission to bring Christianity to the heathen folks on the plantations might best be set into motion. "May God always go with you, Reverend," he offered as we parted.

"And may He be with you as well, sir," I offered in return.

Now I might have felt a small tinge of guilt over hijackin the clothin and callin of a man of God, but I tried to weigh that against the evil that had come our way. Sanford had cruelly been snatched up, we figured driven like an animal to a faraway place and forced to labor in the unhealthy cane fields of Louisiana under the direction and control of some crazed Frenchman by the name of Bienvenu. We would get our Sanford back legally or illegally, I figured, and with or without the full blessin of The Almighty.

As I turned my key in the lock of our hotel room door, the door creaked open and the strangest sight greeted my eyes. My wife sat there quietly on the fancy sofa right in the center of the room, diligently tendin to some sewin task. Such was the nature of her concentration that she did not even look up or make any effort to rush and greet me as was her habit. Somethin was not right here. "Cynthia?" I inquired. "What's wrong?" Before she could answer I added another question to an ever inceasin list. "Is that powder smoke I smell?"

My wife finally spoke up, but still did not for one minute take her eyes off the task at hand. "Look behind the other sofa, Coswell, and you might just get an idea of the goins on here this mornin," my wife replied in a low voice, as she finally put the finishin touches on her mended dress. She placed her needle and thread down on the table next to where she sat. She finally stood up and made her way over to me for the first time, sayin nothin bout my magical transformation into the fine parson who currently stood before her. I glanced over towards the other sofa as she had instructed. She nodded her head in that same direction and I walked over to give things a proper inspection. There lay the body of a quite tall man. There was no doubt the fella was dead as a stone hammer as he lay completely still and his is eyes was full open and fixed on the ceilin above. There was a large red stain that had formed-up right in the center of the dead man's chest.

"What on earth happened here, Darlin?"

"Do you remember him?" Cynthia asked.

I examined the corpse carefully, even gettin down on one knee for an even closer examination. "Can't say as I do," I replied.

"Well, that right there is Captain Reynolds of the good ship *Enterprise*. When I told you the other day bout that feelin I had bout bein watched, well it was him that was doin the watchin. You should never question me, Coswell, bout such things when I feel em as strong as I do. Anyways, he told me that he saw me with his spyglass and recognized me straightaway. Said he knew I was that nigger wench that Walker was so all- fired fond of despite the years that have passed. Also said he recognized you as that slave catcher from up Georgia way that Walker had hired to return his lost property. He said he always suspected one or both of us might be involved in his disappearance and said he remembered just what Walker had told him the very last time he saw him when he left his ship with two black servants fixin to take a train up our way. 'They can run, Captain Reynolds, but they can't hide forever,' were the man's last words to me and that man never returned, now, did he?'" As Cynthia spoke I could tell Reynolds words (and maybe the pistol shot) still echoed in her ears.

After a short pause, Cynthia continued on with her story. "After sharin all his suspicions with me, the man made a most improper proposition and started in my direction. I let him come on and quietly slipped a hand into the side of my dress, lookin for the little pouch that held that fine gift you give me some time back. I have to admit you was right on that one, Coswell. It more than did the job. Course it did put a fair-sized hole in one of my favorite dresses, now, didn't it?" she added almost apologetically.

"Might have muffled the noise some, sweetheart. Did anyone come to investigate?"

"I don't believe anyone heard a thing."

I put my arms round her for the first time since I come into the room and felt a slight tremble come to her after all the bravery she had displayed this day. "You are an incredible woman," I whispered softly in her ear.

"And you...why you are all dressed up for the occasion now, aint ya?" she said as she pushed herself away to now look me over more closely. "Maybe as a minister you got yourself one of them premonitions in your head that you'd be presidin over a dead man's funeral today."

I could not help but laugh and she did as well, but then all turned serious again as we both began to wonder bout how we might now dispose of the dead body we had in our possession. "Maybe if the two of us think on it for a spell, we can come up with a proper answer," I offered.

Cynthia went over to Reynolds corpse and respectfully (or maybe it was just cause she did not want to look at it) covered it over with a blanket that had been stored inside our trunk. We began discussin the proper way to proceed and decided even though there was a back way out of the hotel, all the streets was too crowded most of the time for any attempt to leave with the body and hope to not be noticed. There was certainly no way we could hide the corpse in the room and leave it here with our name boldly printed on the hotel register. After several other ideas was tossed around and dismissed, the two of us come to the same conclusion at almost exactly the same moment in time. "THE TRUNK!" we both shouted out.

As that same trunk was loaded into the wagon early the next mornin, I instructed the two black hotel workers to "mind themselves and be careful as the Mrs. and I had some very important and fragile things inside." I had secured a rented wagon from the same livery I had used years back. They did not remember me, but then what with a different name and callin, I guess its no fault of theirs. I recognized none of the people at the livery either, figurin maybe the workforce had changed a great deal over time.

Cynthia and me was helped up into the wagon by the hotel servants as we made ready for our journey to Boutte Station, some twenty-two miles away. It was there we would catch the Opelousas Rail Line which would take us on to Thibodeaux where Bienvenue had his sugar plantation. Now we could have ridden the rail line the whole way from the city, but that would not have satisfied the issue of the dead body in the bottom of the trunk. I just could not imagine Cynthia and me tossin Reynolds body from the train in full view of the passengers as we rode merrily along, but I could see in my mind's eye the two of us stoppin by the side of a deserted back-country road in a small wagon and droppin off some vittles into one of the many dark swamps that comprised much of the low-lyin landscape. In fact, we did just that very thing a little later in the day and when them sharp-toothed critters who called them places home come to the dinner table at such a high rate of speed, it give both of us great encouragement that Reynolds remains would soon be of little concern. "Breakfast is served," I think I even said as we rolled Reynolds' body into the water. It took no time at all for the eager reptilian congregation to partake of the good parson's communion offerin.

Leavin the wagon at Boutte Station later in the day with instructions to have it returned to the livery as soon as possible, we found our now much lighter trunk stored securely in the baggage car of the train. We felt we was finally gettin close to our Sanford now, but unfortunately at this time we was ignorant of a number of things. We was unaware that Bienvenu had already been alerted by that slave dealer, Freeman. We did not know that the negro, William, (minus his gold coin) lay near death in the slave pen from a horrible beatin. Most important of all we did not know that Sanford would soon be spirited away from the plantation we intended to visit in a carefully concocted plan to convince Cynthia and me to abandon any intentions we had of rescuin our stolen bondsman. All of these things was unknown to us at the time, but would not remain so forever.

Chapter 16

"DE FLAMES OB HELL WUZ A-LICKIN AT MY FEET"

It had been an interesting meeting to say the least. Edie Crandall and Barbara Bumgardner had brought the diary of Penia Fitzsimmons Tims along with them to City Hall for the mayor's review. Rosa Billings had earlier approved the meeting and the inspection of her prize family diary on the condition that it not remain in the mayor's possession. The women had assured her the document could be entrusted to their safekeeping, but she was reminded that it was absolutely necessary that it be inspected if there was any future chance to advance their cause.

John Chaney was polite to say the least. The ladies were wary, but both sides got on "tolerable" as the old saying goes. Some key sections were read out-loud and other pages photographed within full view of all assembled. Much was discussed. Chaney reassured the women he just wanted to get all the facts straight before going forward with any plan for the reburial of the woman who had been removed from her Memory Hill resting place next to the grave of Coswell Tims and now temporarily resided down at the Johnson Funeral Home on West Jefferson.

"Oh, Bob," Barbara Bumgardner announced. "I just know Chaney is up to something. I know he is a pretty popular mayor, but it just seems like he talks out of both sides of his mouth. I always get the feeling that he has some deep inner feelings that he hides with all his fancy words. Do you ever *notice how he looks at the two of us when we run into him in town? It isn't what he says. He's always very polite, but I get the feeling a white woman and a black man together makes him uncomfortable."*

"Now I wouldn't let that bother me too much, Barb. Ever since we moved here we always see 'the look.' And have you noticed the same people look at you differently when you are by yourself as opposed to when we're together? No, we're outsiders. Good ol' southern hospitality and manners dictate they must be polite, but old habits die hard. The good news is that there are many folks we have met here that seem to genuinely like and accept us and even embrace this interracial story we have stumbled upon."

"Oh...and that reminds me. Rosa Billings dropped by today with a section she said had been torn from Penia Tims diary. She found it along with some other old papers and thought it should be included with the original manuscript, but was not sure where it belonged," Mr. Bumgardner concluded, as he handed Barbara Little Peney's rather distasteful accounting of her husband's ordeal.

⇛ ⇛ ⇛

"I was a-prayin fer a miracle, Peney, but de Good Lord, he stood silent on de madder. A man by de name ob Bienvenu, he buys me, long wid sebral uders. We wuz chained en handcuffed en marched out of de trader yard, passed rite by de gran en glorus St. Charles, out ob de city en into de surroundin countryside. We hab us a long journey but Massa Lucian he say we been well-fed en spoiled in de pens en now it be time ter pay de fiddler. We knows what dat mean. Lucien Bienvenu wuz tall en hab a rounded face wid hair de color ob a red rooster. He had whiskers sproutin out dat face en he wave his hands in de air all de time when he be talkin. He speak funny, too. Guess it be called 'Cajun' or 'Creole' or sumthin like dat. Sometime we don't eben know what he be talkin bout en we afraid when we gets to de plantation dat goin to be big problem fer us. Bad nough tryin ter understand de white man as it is, widout him talkin bout what we can't make heads or tails ob."

My husband continued to tell his sad but incredible story. How he was marched with the other slaves across the swampy bayou country of southern Louisiana. How he finally found hisself at the Cyprus Grove Plantation, the home of a new owner, Lucien Bienvenu, one of the biggest sugar growers in all of Lafourche County. There is where Sanford told me he realized he had become "one ob dem dat labors en de obens ob hell."

COSWELL TIM'S DIARY RESUMES

The Cyprus Grove Plantation was certainly a fetchin sight. It was right on the main waterway, Bayou Lafourche, and I suppose if you saw the plantation from the river you would think all was right and proper with the world, what with the scenic waterway and the well-maintained levees that held all in place. But if one was to actually stand before the plantation house itself (also beautiful and well-maintained) which was set back maybe two hundred or so yards from the river, one might get the feelin that the land, despite bein lush and green, had dipped considerable and could be engulfed at a moment's notice if them levees was to ever break loose. That might be why maybe twenty or so black workers could be spotted at the very moment we arrived, workin busy like so many pissants on a rotted stump, out there on those embankments while Cynthia and me was busy makin all the proper business introductions.

"Mr. Bienvenu," I began, as a large man stood before me with hands full on his hips and a questionin look upon his face. "My name is Reverend Richard Granger and this here is my wife, Dorothy. We are down here meetin with many of the plantation owners in regards to offerin a Christian message to your workforce. Slaves who get the spirit are generally more compliant and are less trouble, we have found over the years. They become better and more productive workers and that's a fact. Would you be interested in such a service, sir?"

A short pause followed, but the plantation master soon let out with a rapid and lively response. "Reshard Gron-jay, you say? What kin of name is dat?"

"Well, it's English, sir. Never gave it too much thought. Bienvenu is French, right?

"Well dat it be. Many fok round here speak like me. We live here in da bayou many years, no? Now bowt dat ting you ask. We are for da most part sugar planters and don't have no time for religion or much else for dat matter. We had a minister he come by dis place maybe two year pas, but he weren't here fer da long time. Don't tink da climate agreed with him much, you hear? But I don't see a reason why we can't go inside, get us out of dis heat and maybe tawk sum on dis matter," he concluded.

I looked over at Cynthia as we followed the man into his luxurious home. I think we both felt that we could understand him better if only he did not talk so fast. Lucian Bienvenu did prove to be a gracious host, however, willingly sharin information with us about his sugar operation and the world he had inherited from his father. "You know Jim Bowie, dat fella dat die over in Texas sum time back, yes? Why he owned da plantation wid his two broders right next door to dis place. It was and still be called 'Acadia.'"

Bienvenu went on to tell us his "fahter knew all tree of dem Bowies damn well." He added that they had themselves quite a slave tradin business with a pirate named Jean Lafitte who supplied not only the Bowie family needs, but the labor requirements of many of the planters and other people who had started movin into the towns and villages along the river. What was most advantageous bout this place, he said, was that the bayou forked off from the busy Mississippi River up in the north and wasn't but 60 miles from New Orleans to the southeast, so despite it seemingly bein out of the way and off by itself, Bayou Lafourche and the plantations that dotted it really were "right dare in da middle of tings." We told him we had taken a train from New Orleans all the way up to nearby Terrebonne Station where the horse and buggy we had rented allowed us to complete our journey to his seemingly distant and remote doorstep.

He acknowledged our trip with a nod of his head. I produced from my carryin case the map of the area I had obtained from Gallier Hall back in New Orleans. I unfolded this rather large affair and asked him if he would be so kind to also suggest other plantations that my wife and I might visit. We told him that even if he did not require our services, there assuredly would be others who would jump at the chance. I again pointed out that we had experienced great success in the past Christianizing the negro.

A well-dressed servant poured us a much-needed drink, but before that liquid ever touched our lips and the sugar master had sufficient time to respond to my request, another servant dressed in much the same manner, come rushin into the room. "Massa Lucien, Massa Lucien, de slave, Benjamin, he done take ter his heels again!" I could feel my heart leap most into my throat with the mention of that name and I knew my wife shared that same reaction. I was afraid to look over in her direction.

"Damn dat nigger, he has been noting but trouble since da day

I bought him, heh? No wonder dey tell me he was 'sound but not guaranteed.' If he was guaranteed, my money be returned, no? Well, he can't run too far as I just see him out near da mill fore you fine people reach my door." I very much regret I must leave dis moment to tend to business. I…"

"Mr. Bienvenu," I quickly interrupted. "I can assure you this is just the kind of behavior that can be avoided with a slave whose got hisself religion. Could my wife and I accompany you and help find this unruly fella?"

"You come. She stay. We go," was his quick reply.

Bienvenu grabbed his shotgun and ordered one of servants to look after the preacher's wife as he felt the chase would be too strenuous for a woman "of her delicate nature," he had said. The drinks was left sittin upon the table along with our map as we quickly exited the plantation home and began our trek out across the half-grown cane fields that almost completely dominated the landscape. I could not fail to note the beautiful flower gardens that surrounded the Big House. So many fine-lookin tropical flowers that I had never seen before. I guess it's true what many say… these here sugar plan-tations, why they suggest paradise itself.

We passed by the mill, the centerpiece of the sugar cane operation. It was quiet at the moment, a far cry, I was told, from when the rollers and presses were in full operatin capacity durin the late fall grindin season. I guess that's when the paradise look of the place give way to grief and tribulation for all concerned. A tall smokestack presided over the whole affair, a large brick buidin with narrow windows and an oversized arched front door which seemed to beckon the sugar carts and their sweet contents inside. Bein a trackin man I noticed straightaway the well-worn ruts in the soft ground from many such wagons that had made that trip in the past.

Several more negroes joined us on the way, some with dogs that they said had been given the slave Benjamin's scent. All were anxioused up in the extreme and wanted out on the trail. The dogs were set loose. It's a good thing they barked up a storm or we would have lost em right quick. We all followed a good distance behind. Only the plantation master, Lucien Bienvenu, carried a firearm.

We had probably walked all of two miles when the fields began to give way to a ribbon of woodlands and a few large Cyprus trees began to appear with dark moss hangin low off their branches. I figured we had entered a forest of sorts, but that thought quickly faded as low-lyin marshes and swamps began to offer a gloomier and more sinister replacement. I began to fear for our Sanford's safety, seein as he had stumbled upon such a dreadful place.

"Here, Massa, lookie here," one of the handlers yelled. We quickly gathered round on the bank of a dreary and menacin swamp as a bloody shirt was held in the air for all to bear witness. "Dis be Benjamin's, fer sure," he announced, with the dogs yappin their agreement. Also pointed out to us was the presence of several swamp gators of monstrous size swimmin quietly about, much larger than the ones we had offered a meal to recently. "My God," I could hear myself utter. "What a horrible way to die."

"Dat boy cost me good money, no?" the sugar master bellowed loudly in seemin frustration. "I spend most two tousand dollar for him and da grindin season ain't even yet begun. Damn my luck, heh?"

I tried as best I could to continue to play the part of a minister on a mission, puttin aside any personal feelins I had for our unfortunate friend. When she heard the news Cynthia knew she had to do much the same. What we did not know at the time was that Lucien Bienvenu had staged a much better performance than ours, one worthy of a Shakespearian theater actor and his audience of two had fallen for the whole of it, hook, line and sinker. We truly believed Sanford to be dead and our mission now at an end, and it was only with heavy hearts that we attempted to finish playin out our parts. Bienvenu probably had hisself a fine laugh later on, however, at our rather abrupt exit and our unintentional but definitely dwindlin interest in Christianizing his workforce. Those drinks remained right there on the table alongside a map of the area which we had absent-mindedly forgotten to take with us. Our quest was at an end. It was time to return home empty handed and share with Sanford's wife the tragic news.

But as I suppose any good minister might say, it must always be kept in mind that sometimes hope and miracles do happen in this world and it would come to pass that Sanford's voice would someday reach our ears once more and it weren't from the grave neither. Why, that boy would one day even thank Cynthia and me for bein so absentminded as to leave a perfectly good map behind for his use. It would become his North Star and guide, lightin his way from bondage. The Good Lord must have special fondness in his heart for fools and even though me and Cynthia had been foolish and fooled

mightily, we would stand to be rewarded cause our Sanford, that boy
had resources all his own.

∾   ∾   ∾

"Coswell, how we gonna get home now?" Cynthia asked after
hearin the latest news at Terrebonne Station. We had given little
thought about the war when we had left Milledgeville on our noble
quest to liberate our abducted bondsman. The South was winnin the
early battles and we were shocked to learn that New Orleans had just
fallen to Federal gunboats. Evidently the Union Navy had avoided
the two forts that guarded the entrance to the Mississippi, even findin
a way to negotiate the chains, rafts and booms that had been placed
there as obstacles. We was told a man named Butler had been put in
charge of the captured city and he was a "beast, for sure," they said,
as he had seized the property of disloyal residents and had begun
to destroy farms and farm machinery in an attempt to weaken the
South's ability to feed itself. He would eventually even break down
some of the levees in Bayou Lafourche and burn sugar plantations
to the ground (including Bienvenu's) to further that same end. More
importantly he began to encourage slaves to run off the plantations
so production would fall and residents would starve. Beast Butler
also took a great interest in the railroads, includin the one we had
planned to use to return to the city which was now under military
control. We saw no Union soldiers on board durin our trip, but we
did see many a blue uniform when we reached the city itself.

"We are gonna have to think on this a spell," I answered. "We
need to talk to someone who knows more about this current situation
than you and I. Maybe Major Long would have an idea or two. He's
a pretty knowledgeable and resourceful man, besides bein bout the
only fella we really know here."

∾   ∾   ∾

Major Long was the only one in his office when we arrived
(dressed once more as Mr. and Mrs. Tims) and the trader yard stood
silent. "I can't believe this all happened, I really can't," was Long's
first response. "Why Jeff Davis and his boys up in Richmond have to
be this side of fools, irresponsible indeed, to not have better defended

us. Here we are, not only the greatest city and port of the Confederacy, but damn if New Orleans doesn't offer control of the entire Mississippi. Disgraceful, that's what it is, just disgraceful," Long asserted.

"We would certainly agree with that, Major Long," I offered. "This does not bode well for our secessionist efforts. A blockade could strangle us and if the whole Mississippi is taken that would allow them to squeeze us from many sides. What has happened so far?"

"General Butler is taking our slaves and calling them 'contraband.' Says we are using them for the war effort and therefore they can legally be seized. Niggers are starting to run off as the word is spreading."

"Can you imagine what that will mean for your business and mine, let alone the economy of the entire south? All we can do is weather the storm here and hope our armies are successful on the battlefield. Now, Major Long, my wife and I need to return to Georgia fore things tighten up any more. Do you have any suggestions, sir?" I asked.

"The railroad is already in their hands, at least the parts around here. There is also spring flooding and many delays. I would not go back the way you came. Perhaps by sea to Savannah," he offered.

"Could you make such a journey possible, Major Long? We would certainly be willin to pay for that service and for any connections you may have."

"I know a captain....young fella, bright and unafraid. He's got a schooner that he says can "outrace the wind" and he told me he sees the Federal blockade as an opportunity for both patriotism and good business. I believe he is still in the city. Let me give you his address," Long said, as he scribbled the man's name along with other information on a piece of paper and handed it our way.

"You two are fine people and I'm so very sorry we were unable to accommodate your wish for a suitable bondsman. Maybe this will help make it up to you. Oh, and one other thing. We have all been on the lookout for our Captain Reynolds of the steamship *Enterprise*. He has been missing a number of days. If he was here he might have been the one to transport you and the wife upriver so you could catch the railroad further north where it's still free from Union control. I hope nothing nefarious has befallen the poor man," Long concluded.

"Maybe Captain Reynolds is on a social visit, perhaps renewin old acquaintances. Probably just down in the local dodgery, havin hisself a snort or two. Maybe stumbled onto some female companionship. You know how those ship captains are, Major Long."

"Don't think that's the case here, Mr. Tims. Reynolds is a good, God-fearing and responsible man."

"Well, if that's true I hope he turns up in one piece. One thing we don't need as the war heats up is a shortage of those stalwart kind of fellas," I concluded. Cynthia nodded her agreement, but with a little sparkle in her eye fore the two of us offered a courteous bow in Long's direction and thanked him one last time for the contact he had provided. We knew we could be swallowed up in this thing unlessen we removed ourselves as soon as possible. The Tims family needed to make fair weather for themselves and get home to the safety of Milledgeville, Georgia and do that as soon as it was humanly possible.

Chapter 17

HOMEWARD BOUND

COSWELL TIM'S DIARY RESUMES

"Reverend Granger, I do have room for you and the Missus on board, but I'm afraid it's gonna cost you a pretty penny," schooner captain Matthew Latham announced after a quick introduction. I had switched clothes so as to possibly improve on any negotiations that might be needed. Any discussions to be had by our captain and Major Long in the future bout a couple of potential slave buyers and a fleein minister and his wife would amount to little more than closin the barn door after the horse got out. Cynthia and me had had enough of the fair city of New Orleans to last us two lifetimes.

The blockade runner *Defiant* stood ready to leave on the evenin tide, her hold empty except for maybe a half dozen early passengers or so, who, like Richard Granger and his wife, Dorothy, needed to get somewheres in a right fast hurry with hopefully a minimum amount of interference from Union gunboats. As we commenced negotiations I hoped my pastoral persuasion might enlist a certain amount of sympathy or respect as our funds had sure become mighty low of late. If we could not book passage for maybe four hundred dollars, I figured we just might have to swim home.

"It will be six hundred dollars for the two of you," Latham stated bluntly.

I gulped quietly. "Four hundred," was my counter offer.

"For four hundred dollars you can stand at the dock and wave good-by when we leave," the captain replied. Obviously my position as a minister had little influence on this young, but tough man of business.

"Now four hundred's a fair price and I expect it will be honored. Along with that I will bring aboard the blessins of the Almighty to ensure our safe journey."

"Well, that sure is mighty nice of you Reverend, but I think I'll pass on that offer."

"You do so at your own peril, Captain Latham. Oh, by the way, are all your passengers aware that your ship carried Yellow Fever when it last came into port?"

"That's a thunderin lie. There weren't no yellow jack aboard my ship, I tell you!"

"Why, it just so happened that I was recently at the deathbed of one of your latest payin customers and he was cussin you up a storm for what he said were 'unhealthy conditions aboard your vessel.' Said you should have flown the yellow flag and submitted to a proper quarantine when in port. He definitely held you accountable, Captain Latham, before the poor fella passed away. No, I'm afraid I am going to have to tell everyone tonight just what this dyin man shared with his pastor, after all, they do have a right to know."

"There weren't no yellow jack aboard and you know it, Reverend Granger. But you win. I don't have time to scrub the ship down or wait out any lengthy quarantine. Four hundred it is. You and the Missus better be on the wharf by six o'clock, you hear?" the resigned captain responded in an attempt to possibly regain some small measure of his earlier footin.

"The Good Lord does work in mysterious ways, does he not, sir? I have no doubt He will keep your ship free of disease and bless our efforts to successfully run the Yankee blockade," I said, figurin to properly cap the climax on our recent business arrangement.

The captain grumbled some under his breath as Cynthia and me took our leave and walked from his office on the dock, down Canal Street to a small café we had discovered earlier for some quick vittles. We had ourselves about two hours' time fore we needed to be back at the dock and ready to depart, that is if things all went accordin to plan. Cynthia, she felt the need on the way to inform me I should be downright ashamed of myself for lyin and usin the Lord's name in vain in such a roguish manner.

"Well, He does work in mysterious and wondrous ways, Darlin, wouldn't you agree?" I offered up as my last and only defense.

ॐ   ॐ   ॐ

We had us a good little meal and hoped it would stay right where it was when the ship began to toss and turn. There were perhaps a dozen or so folks all tole up when we returned to dockside and I think I saw Cynthia roll her eyes some when I offered to say a little prayer on behalf of all the passengers for a safe and successful voyage. (I have been told that "behind every great man there is always a woman rollin her eyes.")

There weren't no Union soldiers at the dock and the captain told us we didn't have to worry till we passed by several well-manned places down river just before we entered the open sea. Ships came and went freely from the harbor, he said, but headin out from shore (or comin in from the same) might merit some Federal snoopin.

The sleek four-masted schooner made sail and began its journey down river. The breeze was slight, but adequate for the occasion and all the passengers crowded up on deck to see what they could see. Beautiful plantation homes abounded, some showin damage from recent skirmishes. Negroes were observed workin on various tasks along the banks and a few miles south of New Orleans the captain drew our attention to the plantation home of Confederate States Attorney General, Judah Benjamin. The captain said this talented Jewish official had successfully escaped and had recently took up residence in Raleigh. Flocks of geese, pelicans and swans could be seen and heard wendin their way over our heads.

It took some time before we approached the once-proud Ft. Jackson, but once we did we began to see the wreckage of boats and fire rafts from the earlier set-to between blue and gray. We carefully navigated around the remains of one large burned-out steamer that sat in the mud on the port side of our ship and we all wondered about how it met its end as we silently passed it by. It was fast comin on dark and the captain said we was right on schedule, but did advise us to begin to clear the decks and go below as there might soon be a need to "operate in an rather evasive manner" when we left the mouth of the river and entered the great waters beyond.

We sailed on for several hours more with the evenin now as black as a coal cellar. The captain told us that blockade runnin captains generally chose to depart or arrive at a blockaded position durin the darker two or three nights of the month which tended to be those that preceded the occurrence of the new moon. (Jesse and me weren't no strangers to the changes of the moon due to the type of business we was in.)

There weren't no great excitement to speak of or "evasive measures" that needed to be taken durin this time, however, much to our delight. I guess it's like one woman passenger said to Cynthia… "My goodness, after all, the night is so dark and the sea is so wide, ain't it?" With the small number of Yankee ships that had been assigned to the blockade and the many miles each was to cover, all knew the odds did favor our little vessel.

Captain Lathan shared with us the next day that if our luck held, why we could be in Savannah in two to three weeks' time. He figured to sail along at about 10 knots, coverin maybe two to three hundred miles a day if the wind held and the Yankees did not present a problem. The miles between New Orleans and Savannah were one thing, he claimed, but the journey needed to also include a stopover in Bermuda along the way where he said our hold would be filled with supplies necessary for the war effort. That would add a fair amount of time to our journey. All passengers give out with a loud cheer for the man's confidence and patriotism. The first of those qualities I never doubted, but the other I would certainly begin to challenge in relatively short order.

Most folks spent the next days out on deck as that seemed to offer a remedy for the rockin of the vessel and the tendency towards sea sickness which many seemed inclined. At night we all slept on feather mattresses that lay flat on the lower deck floor, a chamber pot off to the side of each and every one. I would say it was a pretty intimate settin for the lot of us and I noticed Cynthia was reluctant to tend to necessities within view (although darkened) or hearin distance of the others. There was a plantation owner and his daughter, a grocer and his wife, a widow with her young female servant and numerous others who composed our little party of refugees. We spent a great deal of time in conversation, we did, mostly bout the war and the south's chances in the conflict. I was asked on numerous occasions to assure the others that God was certainly on the side of the more righteous and God-fearin southland.

We reached the English island of Bermuda in due course, about what was expected. Before the war I was told it weren't much more than a collection of sleepy little villages, but I would have to say things was all hustle and bustle when our little ship come to call. Large crafts from numerous nations crowded the docks and the warehouses were bustin at the seams with products soon to be loaded and moved elsewhere. I even overheard one person callin this place "the offshore confederacy." I did take special notice of some of the large, modern, steam-powered blockade runners that were there in port. Many were said to be made in England and they were gray in color and low to the water so's not to be easily spotted. Smoke stacks were low and swept back with only one lonely crow's nest providin a necessary lookout from the decks. Most were long, over 200 feet in length I'd say, but had a shallow draft. All had their paddlewheels on their sides. They were fast and could provide instant fortunes for their owners if they were successful. It was pointed out to us that one trip could most like as not pay for not only the cargo, but the entire cost of buildin the ship as well. Our modest cargo was brought aboard by a hard-workin, but small team of darkies, takin the better part of a day to complete. While that was happenin, our captain plotted our course for the last leg of the journey to Savannah. So far, so good, but as my grandpappy would always be quick to remind us…"there's been a heap of whisky spilt twinxt the counter and the mouth even if it ain't got but the last two feet to travel." With that warnin full in my mind, we set sail early in the evenin with our supplies firmly stored below and all hands assembled on deck.

My first impression upon gettin underway was that the schooner has slowed some, what with the heavy load that had been added. One of the passengers told me all could be jettisoned in a heartbeat if it became necessary to increase our speed and outrun any fast-approachin Yankee ship. When I passed that information along to my wife later in the day, she whispered to me that that very thing had once been the case with human cargo that left Africa for the United States. "It's an old story, Coswell, but a true one told and passed down through my family over the years. If a slave ship was runnin out of supplies or was spotted with its illegal cargo, the first thing tossed over the side were the Africans they carried. Such was just one more tragedy of what folks call 'The Middle Passage,'" she had said.

It was around midday when captain, crew and passengers were above decks, when I decided I might sneak a quick little looksee at what had been brought aboard back in Bermuda. I snuck quietly down the narrow wooden steps and reached the bottom of the hold proper where many casks and wooden crates offered themselves for investigation. Some of em were clearly marked on the outside and needed no guesswork and many of the boxes and crates that were unmarked were open with their contents easily identified. I expected to see (and did) hogsheads of salt and barrels marked "gunpowder." I was surprised to see one large crate marked "Samuel Colt, Hartford, Ct." and peekin inside discovered many Colt revolvers, similar to one I owned that was up in Cynthia's trunk. There was a price list included and I could see this northerner weren't the least bit adverse to sellin weapons to his avowed adversary. Crates of blankets and army shoes lay alongside. Medicines, includin quinine used in the treatment of malaria, were right there as well, as were canned meats, cut nails and paper, all necessary items. But what I found most interestin because they made up the bulk of the cargo was those things unnecessary for the war effort. Tea, coffee, wine, tobacco, pipes, soap, fine cheeses, candles, cigars and liquors lay there in abundance. Maybe even more revealin were the large containers of ladies clothin, perfumes and silks, boots and expensive shoes, wire frames for hooped skirts and bonnet frames among other things, hardly necessities intended for our stalwart boys up on the front lines.

"Excuse me, Reverend," a sudden voice loudly announced behind me. "You certainly are a curious fella for a minister. Maybe you missed your calling and should have gone to work for those Pinkerton boys up north. What do you think you are doing down here in my hold?" Captain Latham inquired.

"Well, captain, I do admit to bein smitten with a certain curiosity, especially seein as I was informed by one of your passengers that many blockade runners possibly like yourself often take full advantage of wartime shortages and do a little profiteerin in order to line their own pockets. That bein the case the war effort would be seriously undermined, wouldn't you agree?" I asked in response.

"This is all no business of yours, Reverend."

"Well, I guess it is my business as I am a loyal son of the south and also a man who is concerned about the souls of the Lord's flock, people like yourself, Captain Latham."

"God helps those who help themselves."

"That has been said by every recruitin agent who ever took up the devil's cause," I countered, quite proud of my new-found spirituality.

"When this war is over and God only knows who will win, I figure I owe it to myself and my family to make sure we will continue to survive in proper fashion. If I have to be a little selfish to do that, so be it. I'm only doing what I feel is necessary. You see that hogshead of salt over there? Sells for $7.00 in Bermuda, but that same hogshead brings over a thousand dollars when it safely arrives in Savannah or Charleston."

"What you're doin is wrong, Captain, and as a minister of God I fear I can no longer guarantee the Lord's blessins upon your efforts," I concluded (rather indignantly, considerin the rather shaky ground I personally stood on with my recently high-jacked profession.)

"My skill and my skill alone will bring us through and that will be with or without help from the heavens above, Reverend Granger, you can be assured of that. Now if you would, sir, please join your wife and fellow passengers on the upper deck, and I would also thank you to quit poking around in my cargo and into my personal affairs."

&ent; &ent; &ent;

The Captain's skill and his knowledge of the situation we found ourselves in, I do have to admit was quite remarkable and worthy of praise, my own included. He knew that Savannah had been blockaded round the same time as New Orleans by the Union Navy, but unlike the larger city to the south, it had not been invaded and occupied. Ft. Pulaski had been intended to defend the Savannah River (the city is actually quite some ways upriver) but it had fallen when the Federals appropriated one of the many nearby islands and placed their newfangled rifle cannons in an advantageous position. Captain Latham knew which islands the Union controlled at the mouth of the river and was aware of occasional gunboat forays up the river the north had attempted from time to time. He also knew the channel, its depth and any friendly shore batteries that might aid his cause. We headed for the river proper in the dead of the night, unseen, or at least for the moment.

"There will be no talking and no lights, not a single one," the captain ordered. "We need to pass through these islands undetected if we expect to have a chance of making it." We were all told to go below with only the captain and crew remainin above deck.

We were all anxioused up in the extreme as we silently moved along. No one spoke and all below was in darkness. I held Cynthia's hand in mine and we all hoped for the best. I'm sure many heartfelt prayers were sent aloft at this particular time.

It was only a short while later when all aboard the vessel heard a terrifyin scrape and grindin sound and we knew we were now, for the first time, in some kind of trouble. We had definitely hit somethin, but it was hard to imagine we had run aground on mud or rock shoals seein as though our captain had so expertly guided us this far. Turns out that what we had struck and stuck hard on was a recently sunken Confederate gunboat that Captain Latham would have had no advanced knowledge of. The schooner *Defiant* had been stopped dead in her tracks just as we were about to enter the Savannah River.

The captain come below deck and breakin his rule of silence, explained the situation and his plan to set all aright. The large sails on the ship had been brought down and he requested all the able-bodied aboard to assist the crew in dislodgin the ship, first by means of winch and anchor and, if that was unsuccessful, by attemptin to use the ship's numerous rowboats to pull her free. If that was also unsuccessful, cargo would have to be jettisoned as there was no time to wait for an advantageous tide. If our ship was still stuck when the mornin sun made its appearance, the captain assured us we had a good chance of bein spotted and blown into the smallest of splinters, compliments of the Union Navy.

We tried to see to all he requested and do it as silently as possible. One rowboat was lowered and the ship's large anchor was rowed out a ways and set in the mud. An attempt was then made by several of us to turn the capstan in an effort to draw the ship towards it and pull it off the wreck. When this failed, cloth was placed on the oarlocks of the ship's three remainin rowboats to muffle the sound and they was all lowered into the water, one at a time. We pulled mightily on them oars, I'll tell ya, rowers from all four of the small boats makin every effort possible to stifle any grunts or groans that might give us away.

When we finally felt the *Defiant* move ever so slightly, we redoubled our efforts and in short order the schooner was set free of the wreck. The captain had again proved his competence and his plan had definitely altered the situation mightily. Maybe this talented young man was correct in his confident boast and brag. Maybe he needed nothin more than his exceptional nautical talents to succeed. All rowboats was returned to the ship and secured, the sails were hoisted once more and our trustworthy craft recommenced her journey up the Savannah River on an incomin tide. As a minister such as myself might well say…"delivery was thought to be close at hand."

But any "delivery" experienced that night would be limited to but a few lucky souls and come at a high price. I must admit that much that happened that night is still somewhat jumbled up in my mind. What I do remember is that there was no moon, only a few stars that lit up the sky. I did worry a little bout that, but the sound of the creakin riggin as we continued to sail along worried me much more. From my trackin business I knew how well sound could carry over a large body of water. Everyone on deck, be they passengers or crew, was as still as a statue and as quiet as the grave. Cynthia and me at the time stood at the port side of the vessel, facin the largest stretch of open water. Our hands gripped the railins tightly as we both gazed silently out into the blackness. Things was quiet, almost too quiet.

But that would change in a flash as out of the dark of night a devil's tongue of fire and flame shot forth from the shore and lit up the sky. It was followed by the splash of heavy cannon shot hittin the water not a stone's throw from where we were. Many of the passengers and crew, includin Cynthia and me, could feel the spray on our faces and let out a collective gasp that testified to what we had all just witnessed. All feared mightily for what might happen next.

Again the skies lit up and again another shot was fired from across the water. This time it hit the *Defiant* somewhere in the bow section of the vessel. It struck with such force that many of us was tossed to the deck like so much wheat chaff blowin about in a windy gale. Cynthia and I still clung desperately to the railin, but many of the others now found themselves pitched about or scramblin over the bodies of others, most of em screamin and hollerin in all the confusion. In their haste some even jumped overboard into the watery blackness below. "What do we do, Coswell?" Cynthia shouted. I grabbed her hand and we run for all we was worth towards the stern end of the now-damaged vessel.

Another burst of fire from the Yankee shore battery had us suspectin the worst. Them Yankee scoundrels was zeroin in on us for sure and they had us dead in their sights. This time their cannon shot caught Captain Latham's craft square amidships and everythin there was of it seemed to evaporate into the night. Don't know whether that was the result of enemy cannon fire or perhaps the gunpowder we carried below may have added to the catastrophe, but I would tell anyone foolish enough to pull up a chair and listen, the sound was deafenin and the force and power of that explosion was never to be forgotten.

I found myself tumblin through the air, arms and legs flappin like a barnyard chicken. When I hit the river I took in my fair share of water before spitten and sputterin restored the balance. It was still dark, but pieces of the ship were ablaze everywhere, offering themselves as torches, lightin up the devastation. I could see no one in particular, but did hear a few people screamin in pain and callin out for help.

"Cynthia, Cynthia," I remember yellin desperately to the heavens and anyone else who might be within hearin distance. I give no thought whatsoever as to how lucky I was to be alive. All my thoughts were fastened on to my wife. I knew from many years' experience that she was a resourceful and quite capable woman, but I also knew she never learned the fine art of swimmin as slaves were purposely denied that skill. Masters figured that such a thing might possibly aid their bondsman's escape. If she was still alive, her resources this time, I reckoned, might not be adequate for the occasion. Where was my Cynthia, for God sake?

Burnin debris was floatin about. Them Yankees even fired off a few more shots for good measure before they decided their target was no longer worth the effort. I splashed about, again callin for my wife, tryin my best to rise up in the water for a better look. I did spot what first appeared to be a human form clingin to a loose piece of wreckage. It was about twenty yards from where I was at and I set out towards it for all I was worth. However, I found my wool minister's coat was makin that attempt most difficult. Kickin hard with my feet, I was able to remove the offendin article of clothin without sinkin to the bottom.

When I did reach my destination, I found it to be human, but it was the body of a dead man. When I turned him face up towards me, I could see it was the young and self-assured shipmaster, Captain Latham, and to his credit, he must have been alive when he reached and grabbed on to the floatin debris he still clung to. How he managed to do that with half his face missin remains a puzzlement to me to this day. I let his remains slide beneath the surface of the water, but not before the image of escaped lunatic inmate, Benton Wells, flashed through my brain. He too was facially disfigured, although it was of his own doin, as I recall. One thing sure…both were now dead and gone, swept from this earth by death's steady broom.

I was becomin more and more fearful that I would never see my wife again. We had promised each other "forever" but maybe that someday we thought to be so far in the future might just be now, perhaps this very night. "Cynthia, Cynthia," I yelled. If she answered back, I did not hear.

I continued to search around the wreckage. There was not much there that gave me any encouragement. The callin out of others had ended and many of the fires had begun to go out. I continued to bump into floatin bodies and wood from the vessel, a cask or two bobbed in the water, but I was beginnin to think I might be the only one who had survived this calamity. But then I heard a voice.

I soon saw a man standin in the bow of a small skiff. He was callin out to any possible survivors. "Over here," I yelled. Two men pulled me aboard and I immediately asked if others had been found. They said I was the first one livin they had pulled from the water, but the other skiff, they believed, had picked up several survivors. I told em that my wife was out there somewhere in the darkness.

"Maybe we'll find her," was my rescuer's only words. We looked for some time and did find several dead folks, pullin aboard the bodies before headin in towards shore. The other boat was already there on the bank. I jumped out of our skiff as soon as we reached shore and ran towards it. Three people inside sat shivering in the middle of the boat, partially covered with blankets. "Oh, Coswell," one said as I peered over the side. "I knew you would never leave me."

"I promised I wouldn't, didn't I?" I answered back, admittedly shaken by the whole turn of events. Despite this horrible tragedy and the terrible loss of life that come with it, I couldn't help but figure myself to be the luckiest man in the whole entire world.

We were fortunate to have been picked up by a group of local men who kept watch at night for blockade runners or others who might have run afoul of federal artillery. They passed us along to some church people about five miles upriver. Even though they had little themselves, they offered the four recent survivors enough to sustain life. They dried our clothes best they could the next day and then give each of us a little sack of cracklin bread and an old whiskey bottle full of water as we gratefully departed. They wished us well.

We were told the railway from Savannah was miles ahead, but we was put on the right road and instructed to keep walkin til we hit the rail lines and then head west til we come upon the rail depot. It was a long walk, but by the end of the followin day we had not only reached the tracks, but had arrived at the station just before dark. We had no money in our pockets and looked to be just about what we was, a rag-tag band of refugees. Folks took pity on us. The ticket master generously said we could hop on the next train, but only if there was extra room. He said he would not allow us to take the place of payin customers or allow us to interfere with any military exercises.

When the train did arrive, we found a good portion of it was occupied by soldiers and war equipment. There was only a handful of civilian passengers to be found on board, with maybe another half dozen added at our stop (not countin us.) We passed the time away talkin to the boys, many with a great deal of battle experience. All wanted to hear bout how things was gettin-on back home. We tried best we could to talk only bout the good things that were happenin, but, of course, that did put a limit on the conversation. Cynthia said they all looked so ragged and tired and we could not help but feel bad for the lot of em.

We traveled northwest to Gordon for what seemed like endless hours. The other two survivors (a man and a woman, but not related) were both from Gordon so when we arrived, at least half the refuges had made it safely home. Cynthia and me continued to walk north the last seventeen miles or so, but the good news was that we were in familiar territory and knew just where we was headed. I ain't ashamed to say we begged a little water and maybe a crust of bread along the way as the need arose. We always got the water.

We did finally reach the outskirts of Milledgeville and it weren't long before a familiar face come by in a wagon and was kind enough to deliver us right to our doorstep. We had somehow safely made it back home some 600 miles from the City of New Orleans through the Yankee blockade, but the news we carried with us was not what anyone waitin inside the Tims' home was hopin to hear.

Chapter 18

RUN, SANFORD, RUN

DIARY OF PENIA FITZSIMONS TIMS

My sister and her husband have at long last returned home from New Orleans. They brought news that was most upsettin to me. My Sanford was dead, certain sure, Massa Tims said, and told me and Jesse he saw Sanford's bloodied shirt lyin on the banks of a dark swamp. Now I don't believe it, not for one minute's time. I told Cynthia and Massa Tims that Sanford has been appearin in my dreams of late and he warned me of this very thing. "It's all a trick, Peney, I tells ya, it's all a trick!" he says to me over and over again in my head. When I questioned my sister and her husband bout actually seein Sanford's cold, lifeless body, they say all they see was footprints, a bloody shirt and some of the largest swampgaters they ever laid their eyes on. Said they just put two and two together, that's what they done. I told em they was puttin the wrong two things up alongside one another and their concludin was nothin but nonsense and not real by a longshot.

What if Bienvenu knew in advance they was comin? What if that fella they give the gold coin to, what's his name…William? Why, I bet that boy would sing like a canary iffen someone spotted that coin in his possession. You think all of that had a good chance of happenin? I'll bet it did. That weren't a very good idea for Massa Tims to give him that coin, draw way too much attention, it would. Why information and observation are the stock and trade of niggers in captivity. They would have knowed straightaway bout it and more like as not passed any information along to someone if it might have profited em in some way.

No, we all agreed the news weren't promisin, but I knew in my heart that my man was still alive and I am happy to write here in my memories that I bowed my head in both gratitude and prayer when he did eventually walk right back through our door sometime later. Now this did not happen overnight as a single black man in bondage with a 600 mile journey to travel seemed an impossible task, but I am proud and thankful to say that did not stop my Sanford. He made it home. To me, to us… he surely did, and for that I will always thank the Good Lord for His blessin and great mercy.

Sanford would later tell me that he knew somethin out of the ordinary was a-happenin when Bienvenu's servants rushed him out of the quarters, took him down to the swamp, only to then remove his shirt and spirit him off even deeper into the dark marsh. One of the slaves who was involved in that incident told him later that it was all due to the arrival of a couple, a minister and his lovely wife, who appeared way too curious bout his whereabouts and a plan needed to be hatched to throw em off the trail. Sanford said he knew by the way the couple was described it had to be Massa Tims and Miss Cynthia and chuckled to hisself bout the minister thing. "Dem disguises de always did serb us well," I remember him sayin.

It was early October of '62 when my sister and her husband returned from their unsuccessful trip and that was the very time of year, I discovered later, when the sugar business was startin to bust out at the seams. Sanford would eventually tell us all bout 'sugarin' when he returned home and I would have to say he did not remember the activity fondly.

The cane would be most eight feet high when the cuttin began in mid-October and my husband saw for the first time what to him seemed to be an army of slaves descendin on the cane fields. They all carried wide, sharp knives in hand, some two feet in length. Sanford said he was surprised that slaves were armed in such a formidable manner, but he reckoned it to be the only way the job would ever get done. He did mention that the overseers and guards at this time stood off a bit more or chose to stay up on their horses with shotguns at the ready should any of the workers take a notion to even up the score for the exhaustin demands placed upon em. It weren't bad enough that they had already done the ditchin and drainin, the seedin and the plantin, the maintenance of the levees and the choppin of the wood ("Lordy, Lordy, what a job dat be!" Sanford had said, as four or more cords of wood was needed for each and every hogshead of sugar produced) but that wood would be the very thing that would soon keep the sugar mill fires burnin most continually for the next two months' time. Sanford was assured by others on the plantation that the grindin season he was about to endure was unmatched in brutality and intensity from anythin he had yet experienced in his enslaved condition.

It was durin the swelterin heat of the day when sharp cane knives were brought to bear at the bottom of them green cane stalks and as they fell, another group of black workers trailin behind lifted and placed what was cut into cane wagons for the trip to the sugarhouse. One wagon would follow another in from the fields and each in turn would come to a stop near a long ramp leadin up to a openin near the top of the buidin. That ramp seemed alive, Sanford said, as it was in constant motion thanks to the steam engine that powered the whole affair. The cane was placed on that belted runway and up it would all go, risin almost magically into the air, eventually to disappear inside the buildin itself where it would pass through a series of heavy rollers that would crush the cane as it passed by. The juice would start in drippin beneath the iron rollers and be collected in large flat-bottomed copper pans. This signaled the start of the great conversion…the change from the green plant just cut and collected, into the sweet white crystals folks have come to have such a strong hankerin for.

Now everybody involved along the way knew the need for urgency as the cane had but 24 hours fore it would sour and be of no earthly good. But movin too fast, workers could get caught up in the ramp and rollers, or get badly burned as they moved the liquid with large wooden dippers quickly from one container to another. The sweat would drip from their faces as they tended the fires and tried to balance off the steam for the machinery just right. One mistake, just one mistake and the eighteen-hour workday they had to endure could claim another victim, another bondsman who happened to find hisself condemned to the fiery regions of hell known as the American sugar industry.

Sanford said most of the menfolk on the plantation were considerable taller, blacker and more stout than was generally the case. They also tended to be brighter as they had to manage many complex tasks and tend the machinery. But even more was demanded of the smarter ones, he said, who often knew as much or more than the sugar masters themselves. That made em dangerous in a way, Sanford claimed. Bribes might be offered for increased production, but punishment loomed for any who could not keep up. The clock that hung on the wall ticked right along and a horn would blow signalin the end or start of a new work shift. Time to eat and rest was only but a few hours in length fore the whole thing would start in once more.

Sanford observed that there weren't many women to be found on a sugar cane plantation as he was told they wore out too fast and needed to be replaced quite often. So much was expected that many could not give birth or when they did they lost the baby due to poor nutrition or downright neglect. I guess it was true that some would chew the cotton root or drunk down swallers of turpentine or calomel to avoid the vulnerable condition of pregnancy to begin with and owners often loudly complained that the slave women killed off their babies when they was born in an attempt to deprive the planta-tion of a future workforce. The truth of the matter, Sanford said, was that the work schedule did not allow mothers to tend their babies proper like they should and that, along with poor nutrition and new pregnancies caused many of the young ones to die early on. Those women loved their children as much as they could, and Sanford, he said he even saw a pregnant slave woman one day endure a terrible whippen, but only after she had thoughtfully dug herself a hole in the ground to protect her swollen belly from the ravages of the whip.

Sanford said he had never in his life seen such disrespect for those few womenfolk as overseers on the place were given to pullin up slave womens' dresses just to whip their bare bottoms in front of all present, or took em off deep into the cane or corn fields "fer a little personal brightenin"...all of it done in the most humiliatin manner. There weren't a female slave on the plantation, Sanford was assured, who could honestly claim to have still been innocent in the ways of the flesh after bout the age of thirteen or fourteen years.

Day after day the smoke continued to belch from the chimneys as the cane was fed into the grinnin mouth of the sugar mill monster.

Sanford said "de place wuz like a libin en breedin catawampus or booger dat demanded more en more vittles. We just hoped it would not be us dat would lay at de bottom ob dat greedy kreeture's belly."

Sanford was given the job of tendin one of the many kettles inside the sugarhouse as the black worker who had done that same job previous had recently been horribly burned and was unfit for work. The fire underneath his kettle had to be kept just so and the temperature of the liquid inside made exactly right. He was to add a measured amount of quicklime to the concoction to reduce the acidity of the raw cane juice, then stir it all up with a large wooden paddle. When it reached exactly the right temperature for the exact amount of time, he would then ladle it out into another container. Everythin had to be done in timely fashion as there was more raw cane juice on its way, soon to fill up his empty pot as the recent contents had been passed along to the dog-tired negro standin at his side.

Crystal grains of sugar would eventually start to appear as the process continued on and at long last, them sugar crystals would be separated off from the dark molasses through a series of filters or drains which allowed the molasses to drop from the bottom of the very last container. The white sugar that remained on top was then packed into large wooden hogsheads to be sent off to refineries or stores for purchase. The dark molasses would be turned into brown sugar or rum. Nothin was wasted and sugar masters like Lucian Bienvenu, grew very wealthy as a result of this cruel and punishin process.

Now Massa Tims always did say that my Sanford was "bright as a steel trap," and, even though he learned his job in the sugarhouse right quick and did it more than tolerably well, his resourceful mind began to turn towards a plan of escape.

Sanford recalled for us the followin meetin he had with the plantation master, Lucien Bienvenu.

"Massa Lucien, he tole me ter cum up ter de Big House adder de horn blow six time. I wuz brought into de study by hes hed house nigger, Anthony. Massa, he say dat he dun wanter make a change in my current position."

"Benjamin...you be a most remarkable young man, no? You learn quick and I like what you do in da sugarhouse. You work quick, quick, I tells you...yes, quick like a cat. But you have brains dat be inside dat nappy hed of yurn. As your master I see dees tings. Now...I tink it best you move to a new position, one dat makes better our plantation, yes? I am goin to put you in charge of all da machinery dat powers da mill. What you say on dat?" Bienvenu questioned.

"Massa, don't know nothin bowt no machinery," Sanford offered humbly.

"You learn quick, quick, I say. Don't you worry about no ting. You work with Cicero down dar in da sugarhouse and he teach you to be my machine man, you hear all dat, Nigger Ben?"

"I hears, massa," Sanford replied with eyes lowered and lookin down at the floor as was expected. But enslaved people miss very little even with their heads bent in submission. My husband's eyes would sweep the entire room before he left, takin note of all he saw… the desk, the books on the shelves, the furniture, the rugs on the floor and a certain map that was hung upon the wall. That's right! Sanford said there was a large map of the entire area that Bienvenu had placed there. It was well-detailed and Sanford knew straightaway it could prove very useful to his escape. He did not know at the time that map had been accidently left at the Cyprus Grove Plantation by Reverend Richard and Mrs. Dorothy Granger, known more familiarly to him as Coswell and Cynthia Tims.

"I needs to hab me dat map," Sanford thought quietly to hisself.

ও   ও   ও

Sanford told us he remembered seein somethin very special some time later when he was out cuttin Cyprus trees to stock the mill for the upcomin grindin season.

"Dere it wuz, Peney…en ode rowboat, inside a collapsin boathouse dat all come ter grief. I sees it on de bank ob de brook, off de bayou sum, but I tries ter pay it no nevermind so de uders don't catch me lookin. But I sees it fer sure. I cums back alone lader on when I gets de chance en sees it still pretty good, but it all filled wid wader. Maybe best dat be so fer tightenin. Dare wuz no oars dare, but Sanford he puts eberythin he sees and thinks inter de back of hes head fer sum lader time," he said.

And that later time would come in late November after Sanford had begun his new duties as the sugarhouse machine man. The grindin season was movin along at a dizzyin pace.

Because Sanford had earned a certain amount of trust, he was allowed to move about more freely which allowed him to do some things he might not have been able to do otherwise. It provided him with the opportunity to accidently stumble on a pair of oars that stood in the corner of an old tool shed off the back side of the sugar-house. Also he was able to discover a way to gain entry into the Big House after dark so's he might someday lay his hands on a certain map that he knew hung so invitingly there upon the wall. Sanford figured he would bide his time. The right moment…a moonless night perhaps, when his plan could be put into motion. With the night at its darkest and most of the plantation fast asleep, Sanford in due course figured the time had come. He would pull the map from the wall, gather up those oars and after throwin a sack of necessities over his shoulder, my husband would fearlessly strike out alone and make for the canebrake.

Sanford had to light one of the lucifers he had thrown into the sack, he told me, as he took to studyin the map carefully after reachin the rundown remains of the old boathouse. He said he could see that the City of New Orleans was northeast of his present location which he knew to be near Thibodeaux on Bayou Lafourche, but a quick look also told him the swamps and bayous blockin the way were much too uncertain for him to get there direct. Sanford made the decision to row north towards the town of Donaldson, located where Bayou Lafourche branched off from the great Mississippi. From that point, he figured that maybe with a little luck he just might drift lazily down the great river to his New Orleans destination. He could not have known that town had fallen to Federal forces just a short time earlier.

Sanford rolled the map up one last time and turned his attention to the small rowboat that still lay beneath a partially collapsed roof. He figured the boat must have belonged to Bienvenu's sons, most likely used for catchin crabs, cooters or the many kinds of fish that inhabited the local waterways. Tossin all the loose boathouse boards aside, he was soon able to pull the boat to shore, inchin it up the muddy bank a little at a time. It emptied out as it went. It weren't long fore Captain Sanford Tims and his mighty vessel stood ready to embark on their epic voyage.

Sanford said it took a fair amount of time to navigate his way back to the bayou in the dark, but once he did, he said he began to row for all he was worth so's he could put some considerable distance tween him and his former place of residence. As he grunted and groaned, he noticed before too long a time that his bare feet was beginnin to get wet as water was startin to leak inside the vessel. He told me he just kept rowin, hopin that it weren't as bad as he feared.

It was early mornin when Sanford finally made the decision to lay off the oars and examine the craft more carefully. The water was now ankle deep by this time and he knew somethin had to be done. He brought the boat to the nearby shore and emptied it out. He then began to cut his shirt up into long strips and wedge em with the cane knife he had brought along into the spaces in between the boat's floorboards. That seemed to work right fine and with the boat soon in an improved condition, he launched his vessel once again.

Sanford said he rowed on til mid-mornin of the next day when his voyage was suddenly interrupted, this time by the unexpected sound of gunfire off in the distance. He brought both oars to a complete stop and listened intently, just like he was out on the trail. At first, the only thing he could hear was the drips of water from off his raised oars, but after a spell he said he heard that same gunfire once again. It was comin from upriver, in the very direction he was headed.

Not knowin what he might expect, Sanford made a wise decision and rowed to the bank of the bayou where he could get out of the craft and lift hisself up onto the highest levee for a better view. He said from that position he could see the most amazin thing. "I sees somethin berry large en it be floatin long like a riber monster. It be two flatboats like I seed many time on de Big River, but it hab a wooden bridge sorter connectin de two. De whole thing, it be towed wid ropes by black workers en mules fum each side ub de bayou. Men in de blue uniforms wuz wid dem. De Yankees dey wuz cumin fer sure en de had demselves a catawhapus fer a friend."

Sanford said he only had to ponder this new situation for a minute or two fore he made up his mind to abandon his ship and all earlier plans and throw in his lot with the invaders. Sanford said he observed men in butternut uniforms hidin off in the cane fields and behind the levees and they was shootin their rifles at these Yankees as they advanced. But it seemed that the Yankee army was unstoppable as the southerners they were chasin soon scattered off into the woods and swamps. Sanford decided to greet and maybe offer his services to that rapidly advancin northern horde.

In no time at all Sanford was engaged in deep conversation with several of the black workers that managed the mules and the floatin bridge. He found that the invadin army was under the command of a man named General Weitzel who had been sent from New Orleans by General Butler to clear the bayou area of so-called rebels to insure the safety of that port city. Weitzel had transported his army up the Mississippi in Union gunboats and had destroyed the Town of Donaldson before turnin south down Bayou Lafourche. It was this incredible floatin bridge the general had created that was largely responsible for his success along the way as his soldiers could easily move from one side of the river to the other to engage the enemy where necessary.

Joinin up with this new group was easy, Sanford told us, as the Union army was more than willin to take on former slave labor to aid their cause. He and a few other slaves from the immediate area were soon given a job (and a nice warm shirt) and my Sanford why he now had hisself a new occupation, pullin along a two-piece bayou bridge. Now the job was hard and drivin the mules in the mud of the levees weren't no Sunday picnic, but Sanford's keen mind always remained alert for any new or better opportunities that might happen his way.

The Union camp was all stirred up when reinforcements called the "1st Louisiana Native Guards" arrived at Bayou Lafourche and joined in with General Weitzel's forces. It was a colored unit of all things and had been formed up by General Butler back in New Orleans, enlistin free men of color into the Union cause. Truth be known, Sanford soon learned that the regiment also took in former slaves in many cases to complete their quota. Sanford got to thinkin so much that he said his mind was outrunnin his body at this particular time.

Now them black soldiers had traveled to Bayou Lafourche along the same route taken originally by Massa Tims and Cynthia...by the rail road, but unfortunately for them this time the retreatin southern army had blowed up bridges and tore up track which these Native Guards were obliged to rebuild as they went along. I guess they were generally said to be on "fatigue duty"... the diggin of ditches, choppin wood, buildin earthen works and rebuildin them tore-down bridges. There was some guardin to be done along the way with rifles at the ready, but no one in this colored regiment had yet fired off a shot in battle. Sanford began to ponder on how he might become part of this fine lookin group. It seemed to him it would definitely overtop his present position as riverboat teamster. "How mite dat all be done?" he wondered silently to hisself.

"What are you doing here, boy?" a gruff union sergeant questioned, as Sanford had been seen standin off by himself one evenin silently assessin the situation. "You get your black ass down there with the mules and don't be hanging around all these soldiers."

"Sorry, Massa, Sanford terrible sorry. I'se jus lookin at all de fine folks en de blue uniforms dats gonna free our people. Jus like it say in de Bible, you deliber us from bondage."

"We just may not deliver you out of anything if you don't cooperate with us. Now I'm not going to tell you again to join the rest of your kind down there with the mules and mud."

"Yes, massa," Sanford replied, as he nodded his head and began to walk from the encampment. Not discouraged in the least, he sauntered just a short ways towards the bayou fore he turned and headed back in the direction of the 1st Louisiana. Sanford had already become well aware of the disrespect the Union army had for those negroes who pulled the floatin bridge and those who did other menial tasks around the camp. Perhaps it would be different if he wore the same uniform and carried a rifle and the flag of the invader, he thought to hisself. To fight and die with em had to make a difference in how they would see him in the future. What happened next would make for one of the most lastin and positive impressions Sanford said he ever experienced in his whole lifetime.

Captain Andre Cailloux was standin before a group of his men explainin their upcomin assignment and complimentin the lot of em on the fine job they had done this day. "You are good boys, no?... and we work hard togedder, we gets da job done. We fight soon, yes? Da fact be dat we been called back to New Orleans and will soon be part of da invasion of an important river port. Don't know which one it be yet, but dat be no small ting. We be the first coloreds eber to fight in da war and we will not fail in our duty." Sanford watched as the men around him rose and cheered. Some even had tears in their eyes.

This "Creole of color" was a natural born leader as he stood tall and moved gracefully, his manners and way of speakin showed that he knew exactly who he was. He spoke both French and English comfortably (although Sanford said he sounded much like Lucien Bienvenu, despite the difference in color) and there weren't a soul in his regiment, Sanford said, that did not love and admire the man and would lay down their life for him in an instant. Before volunteerin for duty back in New Orleans, he had been a renowned boxer and an accomplished horseman and as a free negro probably enjoyed the best that his life had to offer. It was true that he had joined the colored regiment early on when it was first assembled by the confederacy, but that had fallen by the wayside with the Yankee victory.

Eager to keep his reputation, his property and do the right thing by his people, Cailloux had joined the Yankee cause and, by golly, they were finally goin to let his people into the frolic.

Sanford stood in the shadows of the tents and found hisself spellbound as he continued to observe Captain Cailloux with his troops. This was a man someone could really believe in, he thought to hisself. "Captain Ki-U, he was magic, I tells ya. I jus knows I needs to join up wid him en whip de fight," Sanford later told us excitedly.

Sanford approached Ki-U cautiously, he said, more out of awe than fear. Ki-U and Sanford hit it off straightaway and Sanford said he felt good about the Captain's comment that he had finally found someone as black as he was. "He tells me he always braggin dat he wuz de blackest man en New Orleans and he figures dat ter be a good thing. When he tells me I be blacker, dat make me feel good bout myself," Sanford confided. He also was interested in Sanford's story, a story Sanford was finally able to share with another person since his abduction by Starlin Finney.

With so much confusion to be had what with the constant brush fightin and all, Cailloux was able to soon give Sanford a uniform from one of the fallen soldiers who had been bitten and killed by some kind of poisonous snake. Sanford shared that he certainly knew exactly what that man had faced. The Captain was glad to learn that Sanford was familiar with firearms and had handled tough situations in the past, certainly many more than most. He also was pleasantly surprised to learn Sanford could both read and write. My husband began his drillin immediately and gettin hisself acquainted with his new life in the federal army. He spent a great deal of time with his new captain, he did, time he would always remember with great joy.

Before they would leave in two days' time, however, the invasion force pushed on farther south and Sanford found hisself on the second day right back in the very place where he had begun his earlier escape. But things had sure changed from what they was. He said he almost felt sorry for Bienvenu when they carried off his sugar which had just been collected and was ready to ship. Union troops burned his mill to the ground for good measure. Sanford said he certainly didn't feel bad about freein the slaves he once worked with. They were all very surprised and most encouraged by Sanford's new appearance. But before the Union soldiers broke open the levees to flood and destroy what was remained of Cyprus Grove Planation, Sanford felt the need to make his way into the Big House for one last meetin with his former master.

Bienvenu was in his library and Sanford saw him sittin with his elbows on his desk, his head in his hands. He knew he was a ruined and beaten man. "Massa Lucien, you knows me?" came a voice from behind the downcast figure. Turnin in his chair, the once successful sugar master could only manage a slight smile when he saw my Sanford standin before him in his fine blue uniform, all the brass buttons and such polished so nice.

"Why if it ain't Benjamin, you sly, old black devil. I always knew you was a quick one. Quick, quick, I always said. I have no ting now and I see you be all dressed up for da occasion and on da winnin side for a change. You win, I lose, no? You gonna kill me today or some odder day?" he asked.

"Massa Lucien. You en your family will be let go iffen you sign de oath, but all yuz own will be destroyed. I would tell yuz dat you weren't de worse massa I eber had, but you weren't de best one neider. My real name be Sanford iffen you wants to know dat en I should have nebber been here in de fust place. If you are not an ebil man, Massa Lucien, den you lib en work wid dem dat is. No good will eber cum ob dat. Good bye, Massa," Sanford said, as he whirled quick and proud like soldiers often do when they change direction. My Sanford's eyes had not been downcast like before and this time they met those of the beaten white man. "Der wuz tears en dem eyes, Peney. Don't know weder de wuz tears ob regret or de wuz just tears ob loss, but I knows I don't feel bad when I leaves de house en helps bust open de levees," Sanford remarked.

The Union army did send gunboats on the third day to transport the colored regiment back to New Orleans in preparation for an upcomin siege. The attack would be upriver at a place called Port Hudson. Now there were two reasons for this, both hidden from Cailloux and his men at the time. One was that Union generals feared the large concentration of armed black men in the difficult bayou area and worried about a possible uprisin of some kind that could not be contained. They could not abide that. The other thing the Union generals knew was that the colored regiment was to be sacrificed in a suicide charge across open ground in an effort to "test the negro question" (as they called it) to see for themselves what kind a fighter a black man would make. That battle would be costly, but would end all doubts of the negro's bravery and their ability to fight.

On the 27th of May, 1863 the signal was given and the 1st

Louisiana Native Guard, led by their beloved leader Andre Cailloux, moved towards the Confederate positions outside the fort. Sanford described the ground as uneven, but outside of a few stumps and fallen trees it was relatively unprotected. The regiment soon began to feel the full fury of the Confederate army as cannons and rifles thundered. Captain Cailloux and his troops began to fall in large numbers. A retreat was finally ordered and it was determined to wait out the southerners with a long siege, maybe somethin that should have been done in the first place. All white bodies by agreement were allowed to be collected for burial, but thirty-five of Cailloux's troops and the great leader himself was left upon the battlefield to rot where they had fallen. Anyone failin to honor this agreement would be shot by Southern sharpshooters. Sanford said he tried a number of times with several of his comrades to retrieve the body of their beloved captain, but it weren't in noways possible. "De let all dem colored soldiers rot en de field fer two months' time fore dey finally surrender de fort. We den bury what left of dose poor soldiers en take our Captain home ter New Orleans fer de proper buryin," Sanford told us.

The bravery of the colored unit that day and particularly that of their leader drew great attention in the north, so much so that many of the major newspapers sent reporters to cover the large military funeral held in the black captain's honor. Thousands attended. Sanford stood proudly in uniform that day to honor Andre Cailloux and was even approached by a New York Times newspaper reporter by the name of Daniel Ames at the end of the service. "We wuz heroes en Mr. Ames he done ask me bout de good Captain en de more we talk, de more he be interested in Sanford en sum ob de things I says on myself. He say maybe Sanford should cum wid him back ter New York so's all could be told in de paper. I say I would do dat, but only if he heps me get back ter my wife en fambly who wuz waitin fer Sanford back home."

PART III

Home Again

"As travelers, all of us must sometimes stop by the wayside to nurse our sick and tend our dead. Sickness and death are a veto on all progress and upon personal plans and schemes, and hopes and ambitions, and fame, and fashion, and folly. There ain't no joy in it."

Bill Arp

Chapter 19

TOTHER FROM WHICH

It caught Barbara Bumgardner by surprise when her husband, Bob, suddenly began to recite a poem from long ago. It was done with great conviction and not without its fair share of theatrics.

"He lay just where he fell,

Soddening in the fervid summer sun.

Guarded by the enemy's hissing shells,

Rotting beneath the sound of rebel guns."

"Where on earth did you hear that, Bob?

"I guess I remember only parts of 'The Black Captain,' but it sure was a great poem. I think a white man by the name of Boker wrote it about Cailloux shortly after all that happened. My dad knew all the verses and I remember him telling me that many of the other black pilots in his Red Tail outfit knew them as well."

"I never even heard of the man, Bob, not before reading about him in the diary."

"I'd have to say he's not the kind of guy who would generally make the history books, now is he? But African Americans know him, I'll tell you *that. He was not only the first black hero of the Civil War, but later on his legacy was very important in the passing of the 13th Amendment and the future civil rights movements. Big deal guy…classy guy and a certified hero of the time. Some called him 'The American Spartacus.'"*

"It was certainly fortunate that Sanford ran into such a man. Also pretty fortunate that Sanford was not killed in the Ft. Hudson battle as so many in that black regiment were. This diary of Peney's sure does bring to light some interesting things," Barbara Bumgardner offered.

"Speaking of that, have you or any of the other cemetery people heard anything more from Mayor Chaney and city hall about the identity of our enigmatic corpse?" Bob asked.

"Not a thing. I know he must be up to something and I'd be willing to bet it's not good."

COSWELL TIM'S DIARY RESUMES

Well, I would have to say there weren't much of a Happy Christmas to be had this year, what with Sanford gone and the ever increasin problems and worries bout the war. Cynthia did give her sister a good-sized piece of fruit, a large orange a friend give her from a trip down south and Peney, why she knitted Cynthia a fine pair of socks. I give my wife a sack of flour which I had to trade a whole pig for. Mrs. Tims baked us all a right fine cake for New Year's Day that delighted us all.

Without any little ones scurryin about the premises, there weren't no need for a Christmas tree what with all the popcorn strands, fruit, wax candles and tins. There really weren't no need for Sandi Claus to stop by our house neither, as no children was there to stand up on their tippy-toes in anticipation of the jolly man's arrival. Children was always somethin Cynthia and me had dreamed on, but none ever consented to come our way. I guess Sanford was about as close as it gets to havin a child of our own and now here he was all full-growed, or at least would be iffen he was still in the land of the livin. Peney still truly believes that to be the case and says that Sanford is alive and tryin to get back home to us, but it seems to Cynthia and me that the woman may just be puttin on horse blinders to keep from heavy grievin and seein the horrible truth of the matter.

One mornin I needed to make a little withdrawal from that small box of ours we had hidden behind three loose bricks in the fireplace.

I found the "bill of sale" for my wife in there, along with the Central Bank deed for our house and about $700.00 in cash money. (Most of that money, thankfully, was in greenbacks from before the war come. The money the Confederacy had to offer was now near worthless and folks was startin more and more to trade one item for another.) There was some reals and picayunes in the bottom of the box as well, foreign coins (but legal) that had refused to fall from my pockets from our journey south. I thought it was downright clever them folks in New Orleans named their most important city newspaper *The Picayune*, after them coins. Even though picayunes was only worth six cents apiece, I reckon the point of it all was that small, seemingly almost worthless pieces of news, like money, do add up to somethin substantial when all gets tallied in together.

Maybe it was a fair thing to say we still had more than many of our neighbors, but the way the war was goin, none of us was gonna get out of this thing without payin a heavy price. We all hoped for the best, but became more acquainted with grief on the home front as time passed. Them boys of ours that excitedly marched off to do battle more than a year ago were now fixin to come home after their enlistment was over so's they could rest up and tend to personal business. That was not about to happen, however. Ol Jeff Davis saw fit to enlist em for another two years, and, to raise the ante up even higher, Richmond begin forcin all healthy male citizens throughout the south tween the ages of 18 – 35 to join up as well. "Conscription," was what it was called.

Jesse and me was both over the legal age limit for such a thing and did have us some important civic duties to perform what with our slave catchin business and all. Miners and important factory workers, mail carriers, newspaper printers, ministers, teachers, telegraph and train operators and others important to the war effort might also find themselves exempt, but the unfairness of the whole thing weren't lost on most.

Politicians, of course, they got theirselves excused straightaway, but what really stuck in most folks' craw was the "20 Negro Law" which allowed wealthy planters with twenty or more slaves to keep a healthy distance from military service. It sure was shapin up to be a "rich man's war and a poor man's fight" as many a man has come to say and believe. Matters run downhill even further when laws was passed allowin rich folks to hire a substitute to fight in their place. It seems like every time me and Cynthia would sit down to look in the newspaper we'd see advertisements for just such people. I would have to say them sorts of things just have a way of doin their level best to trample down any young man who is hard run as it is and most likely scufflin agin both wind and tide. Many are discouraged in the extreme. No sir, 1863 weren't shapin up like a year one would remember fondly around here.

இ   இ   இ

"Coswell, why you just sittin there starin out that window when there's important work to be done," come a voice from behind. I turned my whole chair around without gettin up and saw my lovely wife standin there with her hands full on her hips, hair curled up atop her head, adorned with work dress and apron. Even a few beads of sweat on her brow was added in, all attestin to her early mornin cleanin efforts on behalf of the Tims' family.

"I see you have been very busy gettin all in 'tip-top-shape and apple pie order' as my mamma, Hattie Tims, often used to say. Why you're probably doin twice the work that sister of yours has done and ain't it a fact that she is supposed to be our family servant? Didn't we pay good money for that woman?"

"Now you know that don't hold inside these walls, Coswell. We all work together and as long as no one is peekin in our windows, I reckon we will continue on with those same arrangements. Little Peney is out tendin the animals, by the way. This arrangement seems to work out pretty good for all of us, don't you agree?" Not waitin for an answer Cynthia Tims tossed in another question. "And what do you have planned for this fine mornin, Mr. Tims?"

"Well, I guess you might say at the moment I'm just doin a little early mornin 'puttin,' Darlin. Thinkin bout the war and all. I tell ya, I just can't see how no good can come of it. Why, there was that little set-to we heard bout just a few months back at Sharpsburg up in Maryland. Neither side won a thing, not a damn thing, but it was a cold, hard fact that there was maybe as many as 20,000 boys killed or wounded. They was lyin all over the battlefield, they was, all from that one affair. Now we have to ask ourselves...how many more battles like that do you suppose there's gonna be? You mark my words, Sweetheart, it won't be long fore the railcars will come back full to overflowin with dead bodies and many of our boys will be limpin along behind, half the men they was just a short time back."

"Now there ain't no need to start in cussin, Coswell. It can't come as any surprise to find war's uncertain and unfair what with all the casualties a body can come to expect. But it does seem this war ain't just about the fightin on the battlefield, but now with conscription and the prices of store-boughtin goods out of control, their don't seem to be any end to regular folks sufferin as well," Cynthia added.

"Folks sure like to wave flags and join in with others when they get themselves all lathered up over a cause, but when things start to turn hard, they'll dig in and only take care of their own. Jesse told me just the other day that the Baptist Minister down in State House Square was sellin flour for $300.00 a barrel and cornmeal for $50.00 a bushel and it weren't for any high-minded Christian effort to raise money for the poor or somethin akin to that. The man's got hisself five kids and a wife to feed. I remember Jesse smiled when he added in that he suspected the Right Reverend might soon be chargin a water fee for the Baptismal dippins down in Fishin Creek. Guess I can understand the reasons, even though it ain't doin the rest of us a whole lot of good," I concluded, happy to let the subject drop for a spell. (But it wouldn't be for long as the subject of money and tryin to muddle through this unpleasantness was now all many thought on.)

❧   ❧   ❧

"I know we could use the money, but I ain't takin my dogs and my brother into that den of thieves," I remember sayin to Cynthia after a short argument. Deserters from the Confederate service had become a real problem all over the south as time passed and Central Georgia proved no exception.

"Governor Brown said those deserters over in Pike County had to be rounded up for the public good and he even sent us a personal letter hopin you'd be on board with his recent proposition," Cynthia countered. "He figures to send in all the county Home Guards within 100 miles of the place to root em out. He says the added professional trackers and their bloodhounds would be the very thing to tip the scales and make sure the job gets done all proper-like."

"I do respect our governor and I also understand his thinkin on the matter. It weren't so bad when one or two soldiers would drift home without proper papers, after all, their wives and children were hungry and ragged and most like as not would starve to death if their husbands remained gone for too long a time. Now how many of them kind of fellas do you figure Jesse and me have rounded up already? Six, maybe seven? Broke our hearts to return em to Confederate service, but the law's the law, aint it? As a general rule they're easy to find as most just lay out in the woods at night and work the farm durin the day while their families keep a skinned eye and a keen ear for intruders. Good Lord, what with all the horns, whistles, hog calls, mirrors and other signalin devices them folks have concocted, why me and Jesse figures the whole thing likes to beat a monkey show.

"Now you and your brother have had good luck, ain't ya? I mean the dogs can usually find them caves and hidey-holes in the ground where they spend their time and when you drop by durin the day haven't our hounds been able to do what needs doin?"

"Well, yes, that's all true, Darlin. But what you have to understand is that when you get a bunch of them deserter fellas all joined in together, things change. They don't have the same harmonious feelins towards the townsfolk as they tend to get more swell-headed with increased numbers. They begin to take liberties, that's what they do, and soon become a law unto themselves. They are dangerous in the extreme, I would tell you, specially as ordinary folks are often helpless to offer any resistance with their menfolk away at the war. It is even more dangerous for outsiders if they try to interfere," I added.

"That's why I think it is so important to consider the governor's offer, Coswell. Now I know I often warn you bout the dangers of certain jobs you take on, but this here time it just seems like it's the right thing to do, sides the money won't hurt us none."

"Cynthia, I have heard tell (and I'm sure Jesse will back me up on this) about trackin men who have lost all or most of their dogs to these people, either through poisonin or shootin em straight out. Trackers themselves have been killed or shot up and left for dead. I don't know. It just seems like it ain't worth the risk," I concluded.

All was quiet and serene for a minute or two as both parties paused to think on what might be added to enrich their further arguments, but hoof beats outside changed the nature of the discoursement and sent things off in quite a different direction. Jesse dismounted and come inside with the latest news.

"Did you hear what just happened in town?" he shouted out.

"What could possibly happen on Good Friday that is so all-fired important, Jesse?" Cynthia asked. "I figure most folks in town are over at St. Stephens Church right at this very moment, prayin up a storm."

"Well, we got us a bread riot, sure as hell. Just like what they had over Columbus way. I believe I heard the same thing happened in Atlanta and Macon. Seems as though a hungry mob of our finest female citizens stormed the warehouses and storefronts down on South Wayne, grabbin up all the flour, corn meal and other things that could be carried off. Sheriff Strother didn't know what to do as many were friends and neighbors, so he called out in a detachment of state militia to do the dirty work. My guess is that they have probably arrived by now," Jesse concluded.

"This should come as no surprise. It was bound to happen," I offered. "My guess is that most of the women are wives of soldiers in the field. They recently tried petitionin the government for food relief, but it was a no-go. Folks are desperate, that's what they are. It might be a good idea for the three of us to head to town and help sort things out. No tellin what might happen when tempers get short and toes get stepped on."

We were all in agreement on this. Jesse mounted his horse and Cynthia and me jumped in the family farm wagon and headed to town. When we arrived, we found the offendin womenfolk had indeed been rounded up by the state militia and tossed into Sheriff Strother's jail. Must have been thirty of em all tole up.

The sheriff spotted us as we entered his office and started in straightaway offerin up apologies. "Now I know some of the ladies I have in here are friends of the Tims family. We just didn't know what to do with em, Coswell. They were breakin the law, after all. What we decided to do is to let em go one at a time as folks come in to speak on their behalf. Kinda like requestin an underwriter, you might say. We're just tryin to calm everybody down, that's about the whole of it."

"You do get paid to enforce the law, John" I offered. "Can't blame you for that. Now let's see what sort of dangerous criminals you have behind these walls." With maybe a dozen people agitatin nervously about the premises (many were soldiers and kinfolk) we did finally manage to push our way through to the back room where two large jail cells were located. Cynthia had never seen the like of it, but Jesse and me had been in this place numerous times due to our line of work. But I would have to say that I never saw so many occupants at any one time, specially womenfolk.

Cynthia, she spotted one of our neighbors straightaway who

happened to be sittin on one of the iron benches at the far side of the cell. She was cryin. The woman's name was Thelma Adams and Cynthia had recently taken a strong likin to the poor thing ever since the death of her husband, Charlie. We even sent some vittles over her way just the other day for her and her two young'uns.

"Thelma Louise, I certainly didn't expect a proper lady such as yourself to be in a place like this," Cynthia declared rather loudly.

Thelma got off the cell bench, rushed to the bars and grabbed at my wife's shoulders. "Oh, Cynthia, this has been awful. We're so hungry over our place that it seemed like there weren't no other choice left but to steal."

"Now you know our family would have helped," Cynthia answered back.

"You need that food for yourselves. It's been awful with Charlie dead and gone. It was bad enough when he was in the army. Hardly ever got paid and he was tired of the way he was treated. I never told you this, but my Charlie deserted and tried to get home to us. On the way he fell in with a bad bunch over in Pike County, but when he found out what kind of men they were, he tried to get away as soon as he could. He come back to our farm on his horse with a bullet square in the middle of his back and died in my arms."

"There ain't no shame in that anymore, Thelma," I added in. "Why desertion is breakin out like measles, it is."

"Coswell, that ain't the point here, don't you see? Fact of the matter is that poor Charlie was one more victim of the riff-raff that has collected over near Zebulon. Maybe now you and Jesse might reconsider the governor's request," Cynthia suggested forcefully.

I knew right then and there my wife had come out the topside of our earlier set-to. Jesse threw in his lot with her and I admit to reluctantly doin the same. I still had not turned loose of my earlier reservations, but I guess it was now a fact that the Tims boys and their hound dogs would soon be headed over to Pike County to help clean things up in that neck of the woods. Thelma Louise and her children in the meantime would spend the next few weeks at the Tims' home under the care of two fine and able sisters of mercy.

ॐ   ॐ   ॐ

Thanks to Governor Brown most of our trip would be at government expense. We picked up our free railcar pass for the Georgia

Railroad down at the city hall a day later. At the Milledgeville Depot we would load what was needed for the enterprise and soon travel some seventeen miles to Gordon. From there we would take the Central Georgia Railway about twenty miles distance on to Macon in Bibb County. Turnin northwest, we would then journey thirty more miles on them same rail lines till we reached Forsyth over in Monroe. There would be a brief stop there, we was told, and then our train would continue the last fifteen miles of the journey, finally reachin Pike County at the town of Barnesville. Now that weren't exactly at the foothills of Zebulon where all the devilment was takin place, but it weren't too far from it. The trip in the cars was uneventful, except for one rather humorous and informative occurrence.

When we made our first stop in Macon, two men came aboard and sat down quite near Jesse and me. Both men were dressed poorly and were pretty scruffy lookin, but that weren't the reason folks in the railcar began to scatter. These fellas smelled to the high heavens!

As cranky as Jesse can be sometimes, I guess it really weren't no surprise when he got up and opened the railcar window, givin the two of em quite a look-over in the process. He stared directly at the heavy set one with the thick beard and finally asked him straight out what the hell that awful smell was. I would have to say the man acquitted himself very well with a logical and perfectly understandable answer.

As the man told it, both them boys worked over at the Macon "nitriary," so called. The Confederate government had seen fit to set up shop in that city and had done likewise in twelve other locations in the south. It was all in an effort to produce the main ingredient of gunpowder which is called "saltpeter," he said. He went on to say that could be obtained from decayin and offensive matter which was collected in substantial amounts and placed into festerin nitre beds on the premises. He said their job was to tend them beds on a regular basis and that's why they regrettably smelled so bad.

The man also offered that special soils had been collected from under outhouses, chicken coops, stables, smokehouses, tobacco barns and the like, anywhere where decay might set in. Caves, of course, were an excellent source of this here, "peter dirt," but those had all been commandeered by the government earlier on durin the war. Richmond was leavin no stone or outhouse unturned and the two men even went on to say that women had recently been asked to contribute the contents of their daily chamber pots to the war effort.

A wagon loaded with large barrels would come by each and every mornin, they had been informed, to collect any and all personal donations.

"Good Lord, Jesse," I interrupted. "My Cynthia would never be a party to any such thing. Why she is so private a woman, she'd never consent to liftin her skirts to suit the government's fancy. She would up and die of mortification, she would."

Jesse paid me no nevermind as his interest in the matter by this time had been suitably sparked. He even pressed the two fellas for further information. "I come to figure it's kinda like gardenin," the smaller of the two chimed in. "Exceptin for the smell, that is. All the human, animal and vegetable waste gets throwed into these large pits or beds and then we wet em down with piss, dump water, privy water, or liquid from cesspools and drains. About a dozen of us walk about and tumble that soggy mixture, turnin it over and over with pitchforks to keep it all moist. The smell does get worse as things ripen, but eventually all is readied-up and gets moved to tubs and mixed with clean water and wood ash. After proper boilin in cast iron kettles, that's when them little crystals begin to appear. We gather em up and send em off to the gunpowder mill and eventually it all winds up in Augusta where they do what's necessary to make ammunition for our brave boys up at the front."

After that, Jesse and me give those two a wide and respectable birth and it weren't cause of the smell, mind ya. The reason was they were both doin their patriotic duty to the south and were just headed home to Barnesville to rest up for a day or two fore they would head back to Macon to resume their wartime duties. (We both did hope they could manage a good long bath in the meantime.)

            ❧   ❧   ❧

"All you boys with hound dogs over there, "the man bellowed out as he pointed off in the direction he wanted everyone to go. He was an older fella and by my reckonin most likely had been a military man in his early years, maybe in the Creek or Mexican War. You could tell straight off he liked to give orders and seemed to really enjoy his newfound job as head of the Pike County Home Guards. He was an enthusiastic man, I will give him that.

"Excuse me, Captain," I shouted out, "but I hope you don't intend to put all the dogs and handlers together. Might be a little contentious if that was to be the case."

"That's exactly what I intend to do. All your dogs are goin to drive them deserter sons-of-bitches out of the foothills and ravines around this here mountain. The hounds will drive em hard and we will all be right behind. When we chase them boys into Bull Creek, that's where we'll shoot the lot of em as they cross."

I looked at Jesse and he looked back at me. We both shot glances down at Echo and the Colonel, two fine purebred bloodhounds that had consented to make the trip with us. (They weren't too happy to have been locked up in the baggage car, but there was quite a few dogs on that train and the railroad people decided it would be best if they was kept separate from the passengers.) The Tims brothers both were in silent agreement that this captain's plan was a fool's errand, for sure.

We found ourselves currently standin in the shadows of Buzzard Mountain, not far from where the deserters were reported to be hid out. What this captain was suggetin was an old-fashioned drive like would sometimes be done with game animals. Make a lot of noise, scare hell out of what's in front of you into runnin and then give chase until the quarry is broke down and tired. Short work could be made of em at that point. Now that weren't the proper way of trackin in the Tims' book, but then as we looked around we saw very few purebred bloodhounds or professional trackers in attendance. There was lots of thin scent hounds, nothin but curs really, many with short yellow and brown hair, small ears and long noses. They most likely could track, I ain't sayin otherwise, but if you was to liken em to a bloodhound, why it would be like matchin a broke-down old dromedary to a thoroughbred racehorse. Jesse and me took our two dogs and prepared to leave the field.

I started in conversin with my brother as we walked along. "What the hell's goin on here, Jesse? These Home Guard fellas ain't got a clue and yet they seem to be in charge of everythin. There must have been some real changes goin on round here since Cynthia and me took our little trip down New Orleans way."

"That's a fact," Jesse shot back. "I'm surprised we ain't seen none of the Milledgeville boys yet, but then I heard someone say there was another drive planned just like this one over at Indian Grave Mountain to the southeast. They could be over there, that is, if they come at all."

"Anybody we know in that group?" I asked.

"The Purdy's are card-carryin members, sure."

"I guess I ain't the least bit surprised by that," I answered back. "They're tryin to make fair weather for themselves at others expense, I figure. There's some devilment afoot here, Jesse."

As we walked off the field a man came runnin up from behind. "Now you boys don't need to be leavin, if that's what you're fixin to do."

"Who are you?" Jesse asked.

"My name is Wyeth, boys, Bill Wyeth from over Monroe way. I'm captain of the Home Guard over there and we don't want no part of that fool who's directin the drive, if that's what he wants to call it. I know you fellas and I know your reputations and everyone know the Tims' bloodhounds are the best there is. Now I've got somethin worthy of your talents if you would be willin to stay and hear me out," he offered suggestively.

Now as a general thing Jesse and me are on high alert when any sugar-mouthed individual comes our way, but it somehow happened that after only a short conversation, we consented to join with this man and his Monroe gang, off to see to some folks who he said lived off the beaten path near warm springs close by. Wyeth said great sins had been perpetrated on those individuals and some professional effort on our part was necessary "to balance off the account." Those were his exact words.

Two homesteads had indeed been attacked, we soon learned, both by the same half-dozen men. Family animals had been stolen, food stores emptied and family treasures (modest as they were) had been carted off. One of the deserters had managed to leave his army issue Confederate kepi hat behind…on a nightstand right next to the bed where he had helped hisself to the woman of the house. Unfortunate as that was, it was a good thing for the hound dogs as a good sniff of that hat put us hard on the trail. Wyeth insisted he and his men follow along, but agreed to proper separation so's to not interfere with professional trackin procedures.

We made good time and could soon tell by the way the two dogs began to act that we was gettin mighty close. We went slow and deliberate and were soon rewarded with the sounds of men's voices nearby. We could even smell the tobacco smoke from their pipes. We held the dogs tight to us as we peeked through the bushes to find all the men unclothed and a-settin right there in the warm spring water, relaxin, smokin and enjoyin the fruits of their ill-gotten gains. Their celebration would be short-lived.

We pulled the dogs back with us and started back to where Wyeth and his party were in wait. They took care of business right quick and in ten minutes time, all the deserters had been rounded up. Any earlier smiles had definitely deserted their surprised faces.

Wyeth drove up in a wagon he had commandeered from back at the farm house. It had been kept far to the rear of his twenty or so guardsmen to guard against excessive noise. "Load em in here, boys, and follow me," he commanded.

That fella, Wyeth, seemed to know just where he was headed and when he come to the top of a little hill with the rest of us followin behind, he got out of the wagon and fired a couple of pistol shots up into the air. "Folks should know we are here," was all he had to say.

Some of his men then began to sort through the heaps of rope Wyeth had tossed into the back of the wagon before we left. Jesse and me soon realized they was makin hangin nooses for the recently captured deserters.

"I found us just the right one, Captain," a young guard excitedly yelled as he approached the vehicle, almost completely out of breath. "Just up the road apiece." It took only a few minutes for that same wagon to roll to a stop near a large tree which boasted many stout limbs sproutin from all sides.

"Perfect," the captain commented. "Perfect for the occasion." With that pronouncement the wagon was repositioned and nooses were fastened around each of the captives' necks.

Each rope was tossed over the limb above their heads with the loose end droppin back down. Each in turn was tied off just above the hangin knot. It didn't take but a few minutes time for all six ropes to be made ready.

Wyeth then rose to the occasion. "All of you boys will be hung by the neck until dead. Now that may take a while and I know some of your families are nearby, lurkin off in the bushes and the woods. Any of them will be shot dead if they make any effort to save you. Prepare to meet your Maker, boys."

With no more to say than that, William Wyeth urged his horses forward until all six men were freely suspended in the air. They began to twist and turn, each hangin by his own rope and each dyin on his own time. The wagon did not stop, but continued to roll forwards with the rest of us trailin behind. Backward glances could not be helped. Several shots later heard down the road testified to the fact that some of Wyeth's home guards were not currently among us, but had been left behind to shoot innocent women and children who tried to help their husbands and fathers. Jesse and I were sickened by the sound.

As my brother and I walked along with our hound dogs in hand, I just felt the need to comment on our present situation.

"Jesse, do you remember when we was young boys and Great-Gramma Tims come to live with us? Why, she couldn't tell us one from the other, and for the life of her she just couldn't seem to keep our names straight."

"I do remember that. She was quite an old woman at the time and had a great deal of trouble with her memory."

"Yes, but I remember somethin she said one day when Mamma told her one more time bout our proper names. Great-gramma got so flustered and frustrated she said she 'just couldn't tell tother from which.' I never forgot her sayin that. Now I'm figurin that's just bout what we have here. These are all southern boys and they're killin other southern boys. Shootin children and women, my God, it sure is hard to tell good folks from bad, ain't it, Jesse?"

"I know one thing, little brother, when I get home I'm gonna take me a long, hot bath. From the stink of all this, I may never come clean."

"I don't want a cent of the governor's reward money and I know you feel the same. It's all dirty business, for sure. Why the two of us might just be filthier than them so-called 'nitre monkeys' we had the pleasure of meetin on the train comin over this way."

"One thing sure. I'll bet them boys won't have no trouble sleepin tonight. Wish the two of us could say the same thing," Jesse concluded.

Chapter 20

MIXED BLESSINS, FOR SURE

COSWELL TIM'S DIARY RESUMES

At least this one wore a blue uniform and could be properly identified as an enemy, or so we thought. After what me and Jesse had just witnessed over in Pike County it was becomin quite difficult to tell friend from foe these days. Now this fella's name was Elijah Daniels and he was an officer in the Federal Army, or at least had been before his capture and incarceration at Oglethorpe.

When Jesse and me was headed home on the rail car and passed by Macon, we saw the place for the first time. Ft. Oglethorpe had to be some fifteen to twenty acres in size and had a tall wooden fence around the whole of it. The camp was wedged in between the rail lines and the Ocmulgee River. We was told there were several thousand Yankees imprisoned there, many of em officers, includin Captain Daniels.

Now we did not know this at the time, but this fella would soon take to his heels and escape, unlike his unlucky comrades who had helped build the escape tunnel. Those men would be either shot or captured before they ever reached the safety of the woods. The way Jesse and I heard it told later on, the guards had become aware that an underground shaft that was bein dug right under the stockade fence, but they chose to do nothin bout it. They figured to let construction continue until a little surprise party could be organized for the enterprisin prisoners upon completion. I reckon them guards was figurin to have theirselves a little "turkey shoot" to relieve their boredom and maybe help trim the overcrowded prison population in the process.

Well, when the time come, Daniels he got through the tunnel first and signaled the "all-clear," encouragin the others to do likewise. He did not know that he was wavin them boys on to their death. The guards had all taken up their positions in the woods and when a suitable number of prisoners come pourin from the freedom end of that tunnel, all hell broke loose. It was great sport with many of the guards placin bets on who could shoot the most Yankees in the shortest amount of time.

Now the prison sentries thought this was all fun and games til later on when they had everybody line up for roll call. They had brought all the dead bodies back inside the palisade fence and sent all the prisoners, both livin and dead, down to the far end of the campground. A line was drawn in the dirt and all prisoners had to cross over it one at a time as their name was called. When a dead man's name was shouted out, he would be dragged by a comrade who would announce when he reached the line… "saw fit to forfeit his membership in the Oglethorpe Country Club, sir!" The guards got a great chuckle out of all this til they found their tally come up one man short.

Jesse and I was told Daniels killed two guards who tried to follow him and a couple of dogs as well. He was resourceful, dangerous and worth all of the thirty dollars the Tims boys would get if we could find him and bring him back to the prison camp.

I bid good-bye to the lady of the house without incident and met up with Jesse over at his place. We took the farm wagon down to the livery in town where it could be left whilst the two of us switched over to the iron horse. Somethin I had not counted on happened just at that time.

As we was walkin from the livery stable to the depot, we become aware of some ruckus over on Jefferson. We strolled over and saw a crowd of people gathered round a man most in tears as his wagon and a pair of fine horses had just been impounded by a gang of rough lookin characters.

"How am I gonna explain to my wife and family that we no longer have our wagon and horses?" we overheard the man say pleadingly.

"This piece of paper is all you need, now take it and go," a commandin voice answered. "The government will make good on your claim, now get along with ya."

I knew that voice and so did Jesse and sometime later Wrinkles would know that scent. This voice of authority was none other than the current Milledgeville Home Guard captain, Lem Purdy.

ॐ   ॐ   ॐ

On the train Jesse and me conversed at length on the deplorable state of our southern union. It was bad enough that Richmond had seen fit to pass a tax on income and personal property, but to make matters worse, government pressmen began operatin all over the south in an effort to strengthen southern armies and the southern economy at the expense of the common man at the bottom. Purdy's Home Guards only added to the pain. All agreed that folks was bein sucked dry like spiders do flies. What me and Jesse had witnessed with that poor man losin his horse and wagon, why that was a warnin to us all of what could be expected. Even the Vice President of the Confederate States of America, Georgia's little Alexander Stephens said in the newspaper the other day about our sorry state of affairs... "Georgians, behold your chains!" And all this from our own government, no less! It got us to wonderin how our real enemies would treat us if we ever lost this war.

Jesse was a bit surprised that I thought we didn't need a dog for this here trackin exercise as it was "all a case of advanced plannin," I told him. We weren't even goin to take the train all the way to Macon where this Yankee had begun his escape as we needed to go only part way to Gordon. "I believe we need to let this fugitive come to us," I offered confidently.

Now I had been givin this a lot of thought since the telegram was delivered to our front door early this mornin, offerin us this trackin job. I shared with Jesse my thoughts on the matter.

"This man is runnin and where do you suppose he's runnin to? You know he'll keep to the tracks as it would be sure death for a man not knowin the countryside to attempt the woods and swamps. I'll bet you a half dollar to a half dime Daniels will head towards Savannah because of the Union presence there. Now that's about two hundred miles from Oglethorpe all tole up and I don't figure he wants to walk that far. So what's he gonna do?" I asked.

"That boy's gonna try to get on the train," Jesse responded.

"You're right, but he can't get on that train in a Yankee uniform, can he? Now we're told one of the two Oglethorpe guards he killed was minus some of his clothin, so I figure Daniels will be comin down the line dressed like a genuine Johnny Reb. It's the only way he can get on that railcar," I offered.

"There's only one problem, Coswell. We know that a southern soldier travelin all by his lonesome will be highly suspicioned and questioned by authorities what with all the desertertin there is around here. Daniels will need a written pass, sure."

"And he can get one at the Provost Marshall's office over in Gordon where he's headed and where we're headed as well. Before he gets that pass he will have to walk from Macon to Gordon which is bout twenty miles. For us to get to Gordon from Milledgeville, it's about the same, but then we're goin by railcar, ain't we? He may have started earlier, but we make up for lost time on the train, don't you see? Why I come to figure that we might just be a-settin right there in the Provost Marshal's office at the rail depot when that fella comes in to get his proper papers."

Later that same afternoon all of what I had predicted come to pass. Jesse and me had only been settin quietly on a wooden bench in the Provost Marshall's office for maybe an hour's time, when a lone soldier come in and strolled up to the official's desk. As he started in tellin his tale, Jesse and me got up from our seat, pulled out our revolvers, and walked over in his direction.

"Good afternoon, Captain Daniels," I said with a little smile painted up on my face. "My name is Coswell Tims and this here's my brother, Jesse. We are here to escort you back to your former place of residence." And that's exactly what happened, with me and Jesse collectin a thirty dollar bounty for our strenuous efforts.

ॐ   ॐ   ॐ

A day or two later I had set out with horse and wagon, headin to town with Little Peney on board for company. The two of us soon come upon Butler's General Store, thinkin to buy the few things we could still afford. I was payin off in our few remainin greenbacks when who comes struttin into the place but bare-headed Lem Purdy, just like he was runnin the whole machine. For once he was alone and not surrounded by family or any of his new-found friends. We had not seen each other in quite some time and he sauntered over my way while I was at the counter and starts up a conversation.

"Well, Coswell, I see you finally got back from lookin for that runaway nigger of yours. No luck, huh?"

"No Lem, we come up empty-handed, but it weren't for lack of tryin."

"That's a shame seein's how the boy was so smart and all. Like you always said he was bright as a steel trap, but there just ain't no loyalty anymore what with the Yankees buzzin around…no appreciation on their part for all we done for em. Why I think it's fair to say them darkies think they should be free and we should be the ones workin for them!"

"That ain't so, Lem, leastways not with our Sanford. He was like part of our family."

"You spoiled him, that's what you done. It was your own fault that he run."

I could feel my blood begin to boil inside me. I knew for a fact that my face was startin to reddin and my thermometer was about to burst. I guess I knew I should have held inside what was about to say. I leaned in close to Purdy so's Mr. Butler would not be party to the conversation.

"I'll tell you this, Lem, Sanford did not run away. The boy was stolen. Taken by low-life scoundrels in the dead of night. And I'll tell you somethin else. If I ever find out you was in any way responsible, I will put a bullet right through that bald head of yours. Now you remember I said that, you hear?"

Purdy stepped back maybe out of fear it was, or maybe it was to get a better look at the man who just fired a shot across his bow. "You would do well not to threaten me, Tims. I can make things very unpleasant for you and your family." Not waitin for a response, the man gruffly stormed from the premises.

Mr. Butler looked at me as he finished puttin the few items we had purchased in a sack for Peney to carry out. "I don't know what you said to Purdy, Coswell, but I would not be shakin any red flags in that bull's direction." I knew William Butler was a reasonable man, a long-time man of business, and I certainly would come to realize later on I should have kept my comments on the matter to myself. It ain't always wise to say what you think, particularly in these troubled times.

❧　❧　❧

We all decided at home to go on bout our business the best way we could and try not to let any of the dark changes around us inflict any mortal wounds. We worked the farm together and Jesse and I did do some trackin, although trackin runaway slaves weren't the thrivin business it once was. Gone were the days when a prize runaway who run long and far might command some two or three hundred dollars for their return. What with the Yankee navy full on the coast, many slave owners tried to flee inland. Bondsmen knew their masters were afraid of these recent invaders and that gave many the courage to run off towards the islands and coastal areas that were under Union control. There weren't no bringin em back.

We did get us a few requests to track down more escaped Yankees, specially with added prison camps bein built on Georgia soil as time passed. (There was sixteen all tole up by the end of the war with the most famous bein Andersonville.) We also chased down quite a few southern deserters as desertions continued to rise. We agreed not to track any more deserter gangs that might organize even though our northern mountains and the southern swamps bred quite a few of em. Sheriff Strother was always quick to call on us when someone escaped the penitentiary or the asylum, so our hounds still had a chance to keep their noses oiled and greased for the occasion.

All of us in the family looked forward to simple pleasures like readin the weekly newspapers, despite the often gloomy news. I guess it's true what they say that many papers have gone out of business due to the paper shortage, some even usin wall paper or other sources to try to keep things goin. Some got so small in size there weren't much to em. It was different in Milledgeville, however, with us bein the state capital and all. The latest news was important here and we had us two newspapers that made the heroic attempt to deliver all the latest information in a timely and accurate manner. *"The Federal Union"* changed its name to *"The Confederate Union"* early on in the war for obvious reasons and the other paper, *"The Southern Recorder,"* kept its original name and continued to serve our community well. Without newspapers, we figured folks to be just flyin blind and needin to rely solely on the latest gossip. Both them papers I figure, tried to tell the truth best they could, although early in the war they may have exaggerated the south's victories some to encourage the homefolk. As the war continued on, folks hoped they were exageratin the south's mountin losses, but the number of dead and wounded returnin home seemed to confirm our mountin concerns.

Richmond claimed that many newspapers, including ours, were too honest…givin away valuable information to the enemy in an effort to inform our own people what was happenin around em. *The Southern Recorder* newspaper was our favorite and we spent a great deal of time readin every inch of it, sometimes takin turns readin to each other. Cynthia often declined to do so as she could not read as well as her sister, Jesse or me. (Evidently I was not as good a teacher as Mr. Denison was. He was the man who had run the Milledgeville Academy School many years back where Mamma and Daddy sent Jesse and me as young'uns. We always figured book learnin to have been a great and powerful blessin. Made Jesse and me feel good bout ourselves, it did. Mr. Denison was also the man who first started up the *Southern Recorder* newspaper along with a fella named Orme. Shame a good man like Henry Denison had to find a home in Memory Hill so early in life, even if he was a Yankee from Vermont.)

❧   ❧   ❧

One night in the summer of the year we was all sittin around after a hard day's work and Little Peney had taken center stage in the middle of the room and began readin the paper to her sister and me. She come to a section about the progress of the war down New Orleans way. She read us about the brave defense the south had put up at Vicksburg on the Mississippi and after it fell, the collapse of a place called Fort Hudson.

"Well. I'll be," Peney exclaimed eagerly. "An all-colored outfit that calls itself the "1st Louisiana Native Guard" went into action there. Says they were unsuccessful in their first attempt to take the fort and lost many of their number, but don't that beat all to hear of an all negro regiment, properly armed and fightin, no less."

"That is most interestin," I offered. "It's the first time I believe that has ever happened in this war. There are those on our side who have suggested that very thing for some time, but there has been too much fear of insurrection, I suspect. Now the Federals are doin it and you ladies mark my words here, as soon as our negroes hear bout this, there will be no end of those folks scurryin off in their direction."

"My Sanford would have joined such an outfit if he was able," Peney offered quietly.

"I'm sure he would have," her sister said, as she rested her hand gently upon Little Peney's shoulder.

ê ê ê

The summer of '63 weren't a good one for the south's war efforts. There was that victory in the spring at Chancellorsville which gave some renewed hope. But like so often in life when somethin good happens, folks just push even harder for even more of the good to be squeezed out. Bobby Lee got a little full of hisself as a result and decided to push his advantage by takin his army into the federal state of Pennsylvania. It was a bold move, for sure, but things come tumblin down after three days of intense fightin. General Lee was forced to retreat and brought his army back across the Potomac, headin for home.

It took a while for all the dust to settle and folks to realize what had happened at this place called Gettysburg. We had suffered the loss of another 20,000 soldiers and many fine leaders were also lost in the fracas. Them soldiers and generals could not be replaced and General Lee knew he could only fight defensive battles in the future. The man even offered his resignation which President Davis promptly refused. The papers see-sawed back and forth on the reportin of the event, but it weren't long fore most told the sad truth on the matter. "The clouds are dark over us and we are rattlin downhill with nobody to put on the brakes," it was said in *The Confederate Union* newspaper. It wouldn't be long fore President Davis would set aside a day of prayer to invoke divine aid and strengthen the Confederate cause with hope that the "electricity of Heaven could be enlisted and fall with all its destructive violence upon the infidel from the north... those misguided Yankees who would replace the Gospel of Jesus Christ with the Gospel of the Stars and Stripes," as one fiery Georgia preacher bellowed out in high earnest.

What I found interestin was that our darkies was asked to join in the Confederate cause, but not in any fightin way. They was instructed by those in authority to begin to offer up prayers of support. All plantation masters were told to gather up their black flock and enter into communal prayer for the good of the Southern Nation.

Now I don't know quite what to make of such a thing as those same negroes were never allowed to petition the Good Lord in the past. If they was being punished, for example, such petitions from so lowly a quarter were said to be an insult to God in Heaven above. Negroes were also kept from prayin in their quarters at night. But now, all of a sudden them prayers were thought to have some real value. Was that always the case, I wondered. Had slave owners been afraid that black prayers might actually have been heard and answered in the heavens above? Hard to know the truth of the matter, but it does cause a thinkin man to pause.

> ಲ   ಲ   ಲ

The next day we was all up early and tendin to farm business. I was feedin the dogs out back of the house when Lem Purdy, of all people, rode up with maybe twenty or so men alongside. Cynthia and Peney was first to spot the lot of em out the front porch window and both women come out on to the piazza to find out what they wanted. All the men were heavily armed.

"The first thing I want to do is talk to your husband, Ma' dam," Purdy said as he set himself up a might straighter in his saddle. Little Peney was soon sent to fetch me.

As she come runnin fast round the corner of the pen, the woman was huffin and puffin up a storm and almost run me over in the process. "It's the Purdy's," she said. "And they ain't alone. They got themselves quite a few friends and they's up to no-good, certain sure!"

From the holster at my side I slowly drew the new pistol I had purchase upon our return from Louisiana, just to be sure all was in good workin order. It was a Spiller and Burr and looked much like my old Colt. I just could not abide another of the original after findin aboard the *Defiant* what that man Colt was all about. My new weapon was made right over in Macon, Georgia, it was, and despite the fact that a good portion of it was brass due to the war shortages (they melted down their own church bells), I found it worked tolerably well and would definitely serve my purpose. Why there just might be a lead ball in there for Lem Purdy, I thought to myself as I rotated the cylinder a few times and began to walk slowly back to the front yard, unsure of what might lie ahead.

As soon as they all came into view I realized the odds was

stacked agin me. "What's goin on, neighbor? Why so many friends?" I asked cordially.

"I am here as an officer of the Confederacy," Lem Purdy saw fit to announce. "Your wagon, your horse and one-tenth of your farm crop is needed for the war effort. Are you as a law bidin citizen willin to give your fair share?"

"I am, indeed, Lem, and I'm sure you have given equally over at the Purdy place, too," I answered back.

"Well, some of us serve in different ways," was his response.

"Would that be takin from others and given nothin of yourself?" I replied.

"If you give us trouble, I am empowered to shoot you on the spot. You remember that, Tims!"

"Take what you need, Mr. Purdy, and remember nothin comes without a cost. Not a thing. There is always a price for doin business and you know that to be a fact as well as I do," I concluded, as the group set about their intended purpose. But I can't say I got nothin out of the deal. They were good enough to leave me with a worthless piece of paper promisin future payment.

The group left our place fore much time had passed with our horse and a wagon full of things we had growed up on our farm. There was a couple of pigs and a few sheep thrown in as well, but I was happy to find our milkin cow still remained on the premises.

"Peney. I want you to see if you can reach the hill on the back end of the property so's you can tell me somethin I need to know. You tell me if Lem and the boys go left off to town or head right towards the Purdy place when they reach that fork in the road. Would you do that for me?" I asked.

Peney, she run off eagerly like she was shot out the mouth of a cannon. I had my suspicions, but I wanted to know where Purdy had taken the Tims family contribution.

DIARY OF PENIA FITZSIMONS TIMS

I run to the top of the hill bout as fast as a body could possibly travel in a dress and bare feet. When I was growin up on the plantation in northern Alabama all the young'uns, girls and boys included, would run all over the place in our little cotton dresses. We would race through the fields and play tag and bogeyman. We would play Haley Over and run as fast as we could round the barn after catchin a ball that had been throwed over the roof. If you was a fast runner like I was, you would get there right quick and get to throw that ball at an unsuspecting opponent on the other side. Massa Fitzsimmons children played right along with us and did that until they gets a little older when things began to change. I could never understand why I had to start lookin down with my eyes when around Massa's two sons when I could beat either one of em in a footrace. I was the fastest and they both knew it full well.

I reached the top of the hill in just about the right amount of time as I could see Purdy's group slowly windin their way down the road with our horse, wagon and a few of our farm critters in tow. I figured to be of like mind with Massa Tims that the Purdy's were just featherin their own nest at the expense of others, but when they come to the fork in the road, it looked to me like they was actually headed for town. That still did not make em good people, I thought to myself, but it did make em less the villains than we suspected.

I started walkin back to the farm house, still thinkin back to what life was like on the Fitzsimmons place for Cynthia and me early on. To be honest it weren't all bad, but it was bad enough. As a free man of color once told my mamma…"all the good days of slavery don't begin to hold a candle to the worst days of freedom." Now I reckon that to be true as a general rule. My life here in Milledgeville with my sister and her husband where I was mostly a free woman was sure better than bein whipped and chained even if wartime has been tough on us all and my husband remained missin from my side.

I couldn't help but think bout my Sanford and all the happiness we had durin our short time together and wondered, maybe for the first time, if I would ever see his smilin face again. I knew Cynthia and Massa Tims thought he was dead for sure and that I was just play-actin that he weren't.

For some strange reason I stopped dead in my tracks and turned back around to look one more time down the road. The Purdy's was gone from view with the dust yet to completely settle on the ground. It was at this very time when I spied somethin, small at first, but it soon got bigger and bigger the closer it come. I made it out to be a single wagon, pulled by one light-colored horse. I could see there was three folks all settin together up on the front seat. For some strange reason I supposed these folks to be happy, don't know why that was. Maybe I just wanted to think so or maybe it was the way the horse stepped lively or just the way those three people seemed to enjoy being crowded in close together. I knew I wanted to know more bout this wagon and its occupants. I went up on my tippy-toes as they come closer and closer.

Finally I could see these people more clearly. One distinguished lookin white gentleman was doin the drivin. A well-dressed lady (maybe his wife, I thought) sat one person away. In between the pair was a man, also quite well-dressed, but it appeared as they come even closer, that man was a negro. Now weren't that odd? Not only that whites and blacks would be settin there on the same seat, but also that the black man was not doin the drivin. Very strange, I thought. Very strange, indeed.

But wait! I began to take better notice of the man in the middle, the way he moved his hands and cocked his head when he talked to the other two. I knew those gestures and I knew that man. I could almost see the space between his two pearly white front teeth. Why I never run so fast in all my life as I retraced my footsteps and returned to the Tims homestead well ahead of the new guests who would be much more welcome than the ones who had just departed.

Chapter 21

DEAD MAN WALKIN

DIARY OF PENIA FITZSIMONS TIMS

I thought Massa Tims was just about to have hisself a hissy fit and explode on the spot when Sanford started in tellin the story of his kiddnappin. "It wuz Lem Purdy who done it, Massa Tims, en a fella by de name ob Starlin Finney." With that admission, Massa Tims come up out of his chair and cussed like I never heard him cuss before. "That son-of-a-bitch," he shouted out. "I'll kill that bastard if it's the last thing I ever do on this earth. Fetch me that shotgun over on the wall," he shouted out to no one in particular.

Cynthia reached for her husband's arm in an effort to calm him down. "Coswell, you listen to me. Now just ain't the time. Why don't you sit yourself back down and let's hear the rest of the story from Sanford. We can digest it all and then do some serious 'puttin,' (as you like to say) on the matter when he's finished. Don't that sound like the wise thing to do?" she asked.

Massa Tims stood very still for a brief moment and didn't say nothin, but as Cynthia began to sit back in her chair, only then did he do likewise. "Sanford, why don't you go on and tell us what all happened and how it is we are so fortunate to have you back with us on this fine day," Cynthia said encouragingly.

Sanford took in a deep breath and started in again tellin bout the journey that took him from our home and the world he once knew. He spoke of his time with the Purdys and his frigitenin introduction to slave speculator, Starlin Finney. He told of the long walk south in the coffle and his introduction to Freeman's slave pens down in New Orleans. The sale to Bievenu and another long walk to Bayou Lafourche where the harshness of the sugar industry awaited him and his fellow bondsmen was also told in great detail. Some of what he said about his journey was so brutal and horrible I could not bear to write it down in my memories until a good amount of time had passed.

You could almost see my Sanford's chest swelled with pride though, when he come to the part bout joinin up with the 1st Louisiana Native Guards and the time he spent with Captain Cailloux.

"Captain Ki-U, he wuz de best eber. When he fall, our hearts fall wid em. He be a hero. He had hisself a sword in hes hand en he held it up high en tole us 'keep goin.' When dey shot dat arm ob his en it drop wurthles ter hes side, he use de odder arm en tell us 'come on now, boys...dis be our day!' Den dey shoots him down dead en de leeb his body ter rot on de field ob battle like they done...shameful dats what it wuz....jus shameful!"

But I must remember out of that calamity came my Sanford's deliverance. The funeral in New Orleans and the meetin up with a reporter from a famous northern newspaper was what done it. "A man, he named David Ames, saw me grievin mightily at de funeral en he cum ober ter ask why dat wuz so. When I start in tellin him bout how I luvs Cap't Ki-U en how I comes to be dere in de fust place, dis man say he want ter know more bout poor ol Sanford."

As they conversed, Mr. Ames become more and more interested and suggested Sanford might consider tellin his account in a 'slave narrative,' as it is sometimes called. Mr. Ames said he would arrange for Sanford to journey with him to New York City on a returnin Federal supply ship and once there, his newspaper would see to it that his story would be published for all to see. Sanford agreed, as he thought tellin his story might help someone like him as well as maybe unburnden hisself from much of his past troubles. But Ames, he was shocked to learn my Sanford did not wish to remain free in the north after that time, but desired to return to the slave state of Georgia, deep in the heart of the Confederacy, to Milledgeville, where his home and family awaited his return.

"Very dangerous," I guess this Ames fella said, before he thought long and hard on the matter. He was willin to agree to Sanford's terms, but he said that it would not be easy to "put the 'Underground Railroad' into reverse," he had said.

Sanford did his part up in New York as he told all bout his life as a slave, but purposely changed the name and residence of the Tims family. Also, he keep the name "Benjamin," he said, and was gonna add the last name of "Hudson" in honor of his fallen captain. "Ebreythin else be de truth, so heps me God," Sanford added. The title of the slave narrative *Benjamin Hudson, Struggle for Freedom,* was chosen by the abolitionist editors.

Massa Tims, his brother Jesse, Cynthia, and me listened intently as Sanford came to this next important part of the story. "Mr. Ames, he say dere be somethin dey calls de "Underground Railroad" dat heps slaves escape ter de north, de place he call 'Canada.' He say many slaves escape cause white en black folk long de way offer hidin places fer de fugitives ebery 20 miles or so. Only a few folk, he say, know dat whole line…mos jus know de next stop long de way so's ter keep secret on de madder. Mr. Ames he say dat it be hard ter change it all up backwards, but he say we need ter do dat iffen he wuz ter keep hes word. He sends me alone wid only one place ter go. From dere I'se sleeps in haylofts, hidey-holes, caves, en cellars, secret passageways, en eben under de church floor one time. Ebery place I go dey seems ter know where Sanford go next. De always hab secret lanterns en de windows or certain cloths on de laundry line ter tell de way. I walk, ride en a small wagon, en go en a small rowboat ter get home ter my fambly. En here I is!" Sanford exclaimed with outstretched arms, as he concluded his story. A smile was once more to be found upon his beautiful black face.

"I know those people who brought you in today introduced themselves to us, but I don't remember who they were exactly and why they helped. Do you know, Sanford, what their story was?" Cynthia asked.

"Why dat be de Reverend Ben Tarver en hes Missus frum ober en Jones County. He once worked wid Starlin Finney till he finds out frum de Kellys dat Finney be dishonest. He feel so bad bowt dat en how he treat hes black folk dere dat he gib up on slavery en start settin hes slaves free, pretendin dey all be runnin away. He hep oder niggers get free as well. When he sees me he throw hes arms round Sanford's shoulders en say he members me. He beg me ter forgive him en I say dat I did," Sanford reported.

"I thought slave masters only did that on their death bed," Massa Jesse tossed into the conversation. "Maybe it has more to do with that 'Emancipation Proclamation' that fella Lincoln issued awhile back or could be the fact that Federal troops will most likely be headed in our direction before long that turned the tide."

"Well, in any case, it appears we have a conversion," Massa Tims added. "It don't happen often but we can't say it's impossible, now, can we?"

Sanford's story was a troublin one and would certainly make for interestin readin, but we were just so happy he was finally home safe and sound, that's bout all we thought on at this time. Massa Tims, he have other thoughts on his mind as he began to plan out how Lem Purdy would pay the price for his treachery. I have come to know my sister's husband well and I knew this fella Purdy, despite his high and powerful Home Guard standin, was gonna to be in for a mighty rough time when Massa Tims finally get his hands on him.

COSWELL TIM'S DIARY RESUMES

The Battle of Spotsylvania was fought in early May of '64 and become important to our family for one very special reason. James Rufus Kelly was seriously injured there and would spend time afterwards recoverin at the Tims' homestead. I guess from all we read in the *Southern Recorder* newspaper and what the young Irishman had to tell us when he hobbled back into our lives was that Grant was chasin Lee back towards Richmond and Lee beat him to Spotsylvania, Virginia. There he tried to dig in to halt the Union general's advance. James Rufus was in the 14th Georgia Infantry, Company B, and they had seen some serious fightin over the past couple of years. Our young friend had distinguished hisself as we knew he would, although he still remained a private. As the Yankees poured over the North Anna River, James Rufus was struck with a rifle ball in his lower right leg which would forever change his appearance, but not his fightin Irish spirit.

"Coswell, you been awful quiet. Somethin I can help you with?" Cynthia asked early the next mornin.

"Oh, I reckon it will all get sorted out," I replied. So much goin on these days. Seems like every scratch of newsprint brings with it its own share of problems, don't it." (I said nothin bout my burnin hatred and future plans for Lem Purdy.)

A knock at our door ended any further conversation. It was a young boy from Central Depot down town, givin us a telegraph message that they had just received. An old friend, it said, would be comin in on the next train and "due to situations beyond my control, I may require some assistance to arrive home to see how folks is gettin on." That person closed by sayin he was takin some time off from the war, but "the Yankees ain't seen the last of me yet." The message was unsigned.

Before the boy left on his broke down mouse-colored mule, I asked him what time that particular train was due in the depot and after checkin the watch in his lower vest pocket, he said it was sure to be close to one hour's time. He galloped off with a few more messages in his satchel to be delivered, some, I reckoned, would not be good news for the folks on the receivin end.

"Now who could that be, Coswell? Has to be someone we know real well or that telegram would not have come our way."

"It's James Rufus Kelly, Darlin. I can tell by the way it reads. That little bandy rooster's got hisself shot for sure and needs our help. Maybe a good thing that Jesse left his horse and wagon for us out in the barn. I'll hitch up the wagon while you find Sanford and Little Peney and tell em our plans. You and me will be on our way quicker than it takes a loose woman to hide a strange man's hat."

"Coswell, now that's not a very nice thing to say," she admonished with a smile.

"Why, are you a loose woman?"

"Well, I won't be turnin loose of you anytime soon, if that's what you mean."

I give a little smile over my woman's clever response and grabbed for my hat as we both headed out to the barn.

❧   ❧   ❧

I would be less than honest if I didn't say that our young Mr. Kelly did not look so good when two rail yard attendants took him off the train on a stretcher, but you wouldn't have knowed it if you just listened to what the young soldier had to say.

"Well, it's good to see the both of you," he said. "Been some time and a fair amount of water has passed under the bridge, ain't it? Now please take no offense, Mrs. Tims, iffin I don't get up and make all the proper greetins. As you can see I am temporarily laid out for the occasion."

"Well, we can see that James Rufus," she replied. We're gonna get you up in our wagon and take you to our house for some proper tendin."

"I would never have imposed cept'n I know my mother's ailin down in Gordon and still grievin over the loss of my older brother. You always did sort of feel like family anyways," young Kelly offered.

We got him home and the two women set right to work on the disabled young private. His right leg had been amputated several inches above the knee and it appeared that the wound was somewhat infected as it drained puss steady for what was left of the day and throughout the night. The followin mornin Little Peney suggested that she didn't think it was all the jostlin round in the rail car what cause the problem, but she felt the army surgeon who done the operation may have failed to remove all the splintered bone from the wound. We decided to call in Dr. Samuel White for a little look-see.

Dr. White soon performed a little operation of his own and did find a few fragments of bone that proved to be at the root of the problem. It did seem like no time at all, when James Rufus was feelin pretty good and jokin round like he always done.

"I guess I need to tell y'all bout how this missin lower leg of mine come to be," he started in as we all set around one evenin eager to hear the whole story. "You see we was all dug on in the banks of the North Anna River over Virginia way and the Yankees was comin on like demons. I was firin and loadin my Enfield just as quick as a body possibly could when I was suddenly knocked clear off my feet. Felt like a horse had kicked me in my right shin. I looked down and it was startin to bleed pretty bad, so I cut off the strap of my haversack and wrapped it tight round my upper leg to slow down the bleedin. I began to limp back to camp in search of some proper tendin, now usin my rifle as a crutch. Funny thing, though, this captain, settin up so high and mighty on his horse, sees me goin in the opposite direction of the conflict and thinks I'm runnin scared… thinks I'm runnin away to save life and what's left of my limbs. When he questions me on why I'd taken to my heels runnin, I just tells him it's cuz I was unable at this particular time to 'fly.' He looked a little befuzzled, but I told him if I could fly it would be all the quicker that the doc could give me a little treatment and the sooner I could resume my conversation with the Yankees. He sees my point straightaway and says: "Carry on, Private," and gives me a respectful salute for my efforts."

"When I gets back to camp I go directly to the surgeon's tent and he gives me the bad news. 'Son, that leg gonna have to come off,' he said. He puts me up on a couple of boards that are laid across two rain barrels inside the tent. He puts a rag over my face and tells me to breathe in deep and that's all I knowed till maybe twenty minutes later. When I woke up I look around and soon spots that leg of mine nearby, lyin alongside several others. A man has no trouble recognizing his own, I figure.

They soon carry me over to another tent with soldiers who have had similar operations and all of us are hopin and prayin we will survive another day. Many did not. I do have to say that quite a few were very brave bout the matter and some even took to jokin. One older fella told me he was glad his leg was gone as it had given him so much misfortune his entire life. Said he broke it once as a small boy fallin out of an apple tree, succeeded in breakin the ankle on that same leg later on when he stepped into a ditch and sometime further down the road managed to sprain the knee so bad it laid him up for a goodly amount of time. As a result, he said, the whole thing always did give him a great deal of pain and now as that leg was no more, why, he was gonna get hisself a wooden replacement that the Yankees could shoot at all day long if they were so inclined. I told the man that unlike him, I had become quite attached to mine (or versy-vicey), so much so that I was gonna ask the doctor where all these limbs was to be buried so's my tombstone could someday account for the piece that stood missin from the grave box."

From what a number of soldiers that have returned home have told us, that chloroform was a Godsend for a sufferer. We also learned that amputations were performed quickly, but showed some real skill by the sawbones who done it. Wounds like Kelly's were generally dealt with by cuttin the flesh down to the bone, then pullin everythin back before sawing through the bone itself. That way the flesh could be formed over the end of the bone and sewed up with cotton thread, all nice and tidy. A man who underwent such an operation, we have been told, has bout a 75% chance of survival, which ain't bad, considerin. Those who die from wounds generally die from gangrene or other infections. That is what we worried about until Doc White cleaned things up for our young friend.

James Rufus Kelly showed remarkable progress in the weeks to come. The Tims women were great nurses, with Sanford and I runnin to the apothecary for nitric acid, opium, alcohol, iodine or morphine as the good doctor proscribed. The women cut up his food just so and often served it in a broth so's it would go down all the easier. It didn't take long for us to know our young soldier boy was gonna be just fine.

ờ ờ ờ

The news from the warfront weren't good by any means and most folks knew it was only gonna get worse with time. We even began to prepare for an invasion, maybe by the end of the year. Of course all of that bad news continued to elevate the status the captain of our local home guard, Lem Purdy, who also continued to occupy a prominent position in my mind as well.

Lem knew by this time that Sanford had somehow managed to find his way home so he knew now that I was well aware of his guilt in the matter and he also had to think back to the promise I had made him if I found out he was in any way responsible. I figured Lem would dig in even more and surround hisself with as much protection as possible, but I would find the opposite thing would be the case. Why, it was almost as if he was darin me to come and get him, most like he always dared that old sun throughout his life to try and lay him low.

It was in the middle of the summer, it was, when James Rufus was finally up and about as Sanford had fashioned him a pair of crutches so's he could move around some. The women in the family would take him out in the front yard a little more each day to build up his strength. We all felt he was now ready to return to Gordon to visit that large family of his for the first time. We knew they would be glad to see him as he could now get around fairly well and would not be a family burden. We have noticed with more and more disabled soldiers returnin from the war how different their receptions could be. Some womenfolk would welcome their man back with open arms despite their sometimes hideous wounds, but some seem almost ashamed and felt it only added to their own burden. Hard to know what kind of welcome these boys could come to expect. I reckon it would be more like as not for a high-rankin officer to get better treatment, seein as they did no real manual labor in the first place, so the family burden would be less. The wife might now even be given more responsibility for runnin things and seein as though she was the main person her husband depended on for care, her role could improve in many ways over what it had been before the war when men ruled their families with an iron hand.

Now that generally weren't the case with lower rankin soldiers. Where some wives accepted the added burden and tried to do the best they could, a disabled husband was a poor return on a marriage investment and more like as not would lead to family ruin. I reckon it's no wonder suicide for disabled veterans with "soldier's heart," as they call it, has been on the increase recently. But James Rufus would get a hero's welcome for sure, we figured, and we decided we would make it a celebration of sorts with his upcomin family reunion. His mother (Rebecca), sisters Mary and Elizabeth and younger brothers, Ezekiel and Moses Daniel were all still livin in the Kelly family home and sure would be glad to see ol James Rufus hobble through the door once more after courageously battlin Yankees these past three years.

We packed us a picnic lunch, but had to again use Jesse's beat-up wagon and his old horse as Lem Purdy had seen fit to impound ours for the good of the Confederacy. Even that did not dampen our spirits and enthusiasm for our little adventure.

We left early in the mornin. Jesse stayed at his home and Cynthia, at the very last minute declined to go as she complained she had too much house business to tend to. It was probably just as well, what with Little Peney, her husband, Sanford, myself, and James Rufus with his new crutches and all, fillin the small cart to near bustin.

Gordon was about seventeen miles away and we knew we would be gone most of the day. I guess maybe Lem Purdy thought along them same lines when out on patrol with several others, he spied a slow movin wagon headin down the road in the direction of Gordon. With his field glasses in hand, he saw who was in the wagon and who was not. The Tims family and their young military guest was on the move and it did not take a college educated man to figure what with James Rufus aboard, the boy must be headed for his real home down in Gordon. Lem Purdy gave instructions to his band to follow along after them and then alone, spurred his horse in the direction of the Tims family homestead where my wife had been left all by her lonesome.

When we returned at the end of the day we told Cynthia about the fine time we all had in Gordon and how the Kellys made us feel welcome and thanked us for all we had done. They had fixed us some fine vittles, even though they didn't have much to spare and there was more than enough huggin and such to go around. When we finally took our leave, we was all wore out from their family efforts on our behalf.

Cynthia said she was glad to hear all that, but said the strangest thing happened to her while we was gone. She said she felt like she was bein spied upon, most like it was down New Orleans way when the hair on the back of her arms stood straight at attention. This time I did not laugh or make light of her reaction, instead I asked her what she thought might have been the cause.

"I kept feelin that someone was lookin in the window at me. I even went over to the window a number of times, but didn't see a thing when I looked out. Got to thinkin maybe it was because I had gone to the fireplace to get out a few dollars for our next trip to town. I know how important it is to keep that place secret so maybe that was why I was feelin spied upon and give me the heebie-jeebies."

"Cynthia…did you stay in the house the whole time we was gone?" I inquired.

"No, I had to go to the backhouse one time and I tended the animals while I was out there," she replied.

"Now let me ask you this. When you was in the house gettin all them odd feelins, was there one window in particular that give you the greatest concern?

"The one over there," she said, as she pointed to one of the two windows on the west side of our home.

I grabbed her hand and together we went outside, around the corner of the house. We soon come to the window in question. There on the ground we both could plainly see boot prints that neither of us had ever seen before.

"Oh, My God Coswell… our little wooden box and what little money we had left!" she exclaimed loudly, as we both took to runnin back inside. We needed to check our hidin place, but as we did, both of us could not help but fight a growin concern that perhaps even more valuable things than money might be missin from that small container.

A MOST GRIEVOUS AND SHAMEFUL ACT

COSWELL TIM'S DIARY RESUMES
NOVEMBER OF 1864

Atlanta was burnin and Sherman was on his way south. That much we knew for sure. All else was hearsay. The gates to the Southland had been flung wide open and wild rumors and exaggerated stories abounded. Refugees from Atlanta seemed to be pourin into Milledgeville daily, all with their own tale to tell.

"The Yankees are devils," many agreed. Helpin themselves to people's property and valuables, violatin the sanctity of a woman's bedroom, leavin some families most destitute of food and in some cases even burnin their homes to the ground. This Sherman fella had vowed to "make Georgia howl" and it looked like he was makin good on that promise. The Tims family began to take stock of these stories and plan out our future best way we could.

Now one thing I heard a number of times was that Sherman hated bloodhounds with a fiery hot hate and issued a general order for his soldiers to kill all such critters on sight. Thanks to folks sometimes speakin of bloodhounds as "Nigger Dogs," I reckon Sherman got it in that head of his that these dogs may be close to the heart of the slave institution. As a result many were shot or bayo-netted on his say so up Atlanta way by Federal troops, I was told. I was advised it would be best to hide my dogs if I didn't want em to suffer a similar fate. The fella that give me that information and advice also passed along a story that might be somewhat amusin if it weren't so heartbreakin in nature.

"I know for a fact," the man said, "those blue devils forced their way into the home of a well-to-do family in downtown Atlanta. The husband had vacated the premises as many men did, leavin their wives behind to face the uncertainty of invasion. They robbed her blind, they did, and took whatever they desired, but the woman clung tightly to her little white dog. Well, they grabbed the poor thing from her arms as they got ready to leave, but the woman did put up quite a protest."

"Madam," one of them said. "We have orders to take and kill all bloodhounds on sight."

"That is no bloodhound, you damn Yankee fool. Can't you see it's a just a poodle?" she replied.

"Well, we agree that appears to be the case at this particular moment, but there ain't no tellin what it might become when it's full-growed," was the soldier's response. "Now that kind of stupidity just defies all reason, now, don't it?" this fella asked with me in full agreement. That poor dog was taken out into the street and shot dead. The woman said that despite any and all other depredations leveled against the southern people, she would never forgive the Yankees for what they did to that poor helpless little critter. "Greater injustice was never done," she had said solemnly.

Anna Maria Green was Doc Green's daughter and lived near the asylum. She was a little whisk of a thing, but spunky as all get out. She hated the Yankees and was more than willin to approach her daddy on the subject of hidin my hounds inside the Lunatic Asylum as Sherman got closer to Milledgeville. We all figured that place would breed little interest for the Union army. Doc Green was a little hesitant at first, thinkin the discovery of the hounds would put his institution at risk, but the pleadins of his favorite daughter and the recollections of the many things the Tims Boys had done for him over the years managed to carry the day.

With that settled, we began to think on how we might hide what few valuables we had, along with foodstuffs that were necessary for us to survive. We knew we needed to leave just enough so that the

Yankees wouldn't become too suspicious. Guess this "cat and mouse" game was bein played out all along Sherman's' invasion route with folks hidin things up in trees, out in nearby swamps or buryin em in the ground. Yankees often looked for cart tracks that might indicate family treasures carried from the house. Bayonets were used to probe the ground of any new earth. Even a recently dug grave aroused suspicion. There were stories of successful hidin places, but more times than not, it was reported that the cat won the contest, one of the main reasons bein that the family servants often knew a great deal and were more than willin to share such information with their new "liberators."

We decided we could spend a little time ruminatin on all of this before it came to actually havin to make that decision. In the meantime there was talk of raisin a new army of defenders from the remainin citizenry. Governor Brown unexempted many of the folks who had earlier been excused from service and expanded the ages of those required to serve to now include all males between ages 16 to 60. He sought to enlist 150 convicts from the penitentiary if they was willin to fight in exchange for a governor's pardon. Folks from the hospital were encouraged to get out of bed if they was able and join the noble cause. All of us was told this was the last chance we'd get to resist the foul invaders. I can't believe that Jesse and me would eventually belong to such a rag-tag outfit as this, but sure enough, we soon cast our lot with the Milledgeville Reserve Guards as Sherman and his horde drew near to the city limits.

Now these Milledgeville Reserve Guards were a collection of the very old and the very young and a few sprinkled in between like Sheriff Strother and his deputy, maybe 200 folks all tole up. We had to bring our own weapons to town if we were to be ready for the fight sure to come. One old man, a fella by the name of Jedidiah Williams, had more than a few years on him and told the recruiter fella that he had rumatis so bad that he could barely move. "That's good," his commander reassured him. "We want a man who will stand his ground and not run from danger." Young, old, and in between, we all threw in together and began to drill in preparation for whatever lay ahead.

DIARY OF PENIA FITZSIMONS TIMS

Oh, what an awful day this was! Maybe the worst day of my life. Started out fine what with warm fall weather, but started creepin downhill from there. All the menfolk left early this mornin for more drillin and target practice in town. Massa Tims and his brother went off in Massa Jesse's old wagon, with my Sanford tuggin away at the reigns. Governor Brown had called upon local slave owners to loan some 500 of their bondsman to help defend our homes. Sanford went off willingly, not to fight, but to labor hard as he had once done with the floatin bridge down on Bayou Lafourche. It did seem quite odd in a way as my Sanford once toted a rifle, wore a blue uniform and was free and now here he was a slave, helpin his family and the southern cause. But Sanford he was a smart man and knew that's just the way it needed to be at this particular time.

It was in the middle of the mornin when things darkened considerable. Three men come ridin up to the house, dismounted and walked quickly up to our front door. I yelled to Cynthia that we had us some company and added in that I did not like the looks of it. Neither of us had any weapons to defend ourselves with as those had gone off to town with the menfolk earlier in the day.

Instead of knockin, the door was forcibly pushed open before either of us could make any effort to run or bolt the door to the new visitors. Three of the Purdy boys come inside and spoke not a word. One grabbed me and held my arms close to my sides (I believe his name to be Lucas Purdy) while Lester Purdy grabbed my sister and restrained her in much the same way. Lem Purdy stood in the center of the room with his familiar head bald as a jug and his hands now full on his hips as he declared his intentions.

"Well, Mrs. Tims. It appears that your dishonesty has finally done you in. After all your haughty, high-handed ways and to find out you ain't nothin more than a nigger wench after all's said and done."

"And how would you know such a thing if you had not violated my home and helped yourself to our valuables?" Cynthia shot back, seemingly unafraid despite our helpless situation.

"I am as honest as the day is long. I would not steal from a man less I thought he was unworthy of his money. Notice I did not take even a single picayune from the likes of you and your nigger-lovin husband."

"Don't be a greater fool than you can help, Lem Purdy. You stole somethin more valuable than money and you know it."

"Well, I did uncover the truth now, didn't I? I sort of suspicioned it all along. I'll bet this woman right here (he pointed over to me) might even be your sister…am I right?"

Gettin no answer, the older brother started in givin instructions. "Lucas, I want you to hold on real tight to that little sister of hers so she can watch all that is bout to happen. I want her complete and undivided attention, I do. She's lucky that she knows her proper place in this world or what I am about to do to her sister would happen to her as well."

Lucas Purdy drew me in close with one of his dirty but strong hands and with the other he drew his Bowie knife from his belt and held it next to my throat. The man's breath was horrible and I took to wonderin if the man ever washed his teeth.

"And as for you Mrs. Tims, it's time for you to get a proper dressin down. You get yourself down on the floor on all fours like the barnyard animal you be," he commanded. Purdy then flung his coat down like he was goin off to a fight.

Cynthia looked over at me and the Purdy brother's grip tightened even more. His knife felt cold as it pressed up against the warm flesh of my neck. My sister complied, first with one knee touchin the floor then the other. Her hands would do likewise.

Purdy went over to her and lifted up the backside of her dress and give it a quick toss forward, exposin her naked bottom for all to see. I figured a whippin was what the man had on his mind, but I could also see there weren't no whip or floppin paddle anywheres to be had. When he began to unbutton his trousers I knew then what his intentions were.

With his trousers soon pulled down around his ankles, Lem Purdy moved in slightly and thrust himself deep into the helpless woman before him. She flinched and looked down at the floor, but was quick to return her gaze directly to the wall before her. She looked straight ahead with no expression whatsoever to be seen on her face. I tried to look away, but my head was twisted back to witness the horrors that had seen fit to visit us this day. My sister made no sound and endured the long minutes her tormentor required. When he was done, he pulled up his trousers and buttoned em just as calm as you please. Cynthia continued to remain completely still.

Before pullin her dress back down to cover up her up, Lem

Purdy felt the need to point over her way and announce: "Why this woman here ain't got no more shame that a naked whore on a bed quilt, now does she boys?" Both brothers grinned and laughed some in appreciation of their older brother's wisdom and enterprise.

"Get up off the floor, you filthy piece of trash. Now I want you two women to tell the great 'Master of Hounds,' Mr. Coswell Tims, that he ain't nothin more than a two-bit nigger-lovin bastard and I look forward to the day he gets up the courage to face me and I can finally lay him low. Now you tell him that when he comes home, you hear?"

After our unwelcome visitors left the premises, Cynthia made a trip out to the well where she washed away what she could of the encounter. "We must never speak of this," were the only words she said.

After witnessin what I did, I come to know one thing for certain-sure. When Lem Purdy pushes out his last breath of air on this earth, the man will make one of the fastest trips on record to the low down region of smoke, soot and sorrow than has ever been done before. "Maybe he can find some pride or glory in that," I thought to myself.

COSWELL TIM'S DIARY RESUMES

Jesse and me returned home late in the day. Sanford remained in town to continue diggin ditches and improve the fortifications necessary for our defense. Can't say much was accomplished today. If it's true what they say that 60,000 bluecoats are on their way, it's hard to imagine how we could possible put up any passable resistance, specially with the type of "soldiers" that filled our ranks. Them prisoners ain't worth a cent and don't do what they're told. Some of the sick people from the hospital can barely stand and even manage to topple over on occasion and the old-timers, why, they are almost laughable. It did provide us some amusement when one old gentleman marched right down the back of the fella in front of him and said the reason for it was he was deaf as dog iron and couldn't hear any of the proper drill instructions. On a sadder note, there was a young boy, maybe 14 years of age, who was bein instructed by his grandpappy on the proper use of the family shotgun. Jesse said that boy should be down at the branch with the same old man showin the young lad how to catch fish instead of learnin how to kill one of his own kind. We knew we was all a sorry lot and stood about as much chance as a crippled mud turtle in a horse race if any lively scuffle was to ever come our way.

Cynthia was quieter than usual when I returned home and remained so for a few days' time. I figured she was all anxioused up in the extreme bout the advancin Yankees and what might happen to our home and family. I certainly could not blame her for that, but when I tried to comfort her, she seemed to want no part of it, which was unusual. I could not quite understand that as we have always felt that family is what matters most in this world and we are all in this together, whichever way fortune might see fit to turn. It almost seemed like she had turned her back on the person who had promised to always love her the most.

DIARY OF PENIA FITZSIMONS TIMS

My sister has really withdrawn inside herself. She rarely speaks to her husband and she seldom speaks to me as well. I know the burden she carries is a heavy one, but this whole thing has got a bad feel to it and all just don't seem right. I even think it's gettin worse. I'm now of a mind that I need to look for the proper time to do somethin on the matter and hope I do the right thing when that time comes. I finally got my chance when Massa Tims went off by hisself to feed the hounds out behind the barn.

"Massa Tims," I said to him. "How you gettin on what with all the bad news that's been comin our way?"

"I'll tell ya, Little Peney…I would be gettin on much better if that sister of yours would smile once in a while. Never quite seen the like of it before."

"I needs to tell you somethin," I began. "Your woman, she knows the real meanin of invasion and I don't mean the kind that's comin up the road in blue uniforms." He looked at me kind curious-like as I began to speak on all I had been forced to witness a few days back.

He said nothin when I was done, but asked me if I would finish feedin the hounds. I peeked around the barn and saw him go inside the house.

COSWELL TIM'S DIARY RESUMES

We are on our way! We just received word that 30,000 Union legionnaires had come around Milledgeville, Macon-way, from the southwest. They was comin up fast and almost to Gordon which was only seventeen miles to the rear of our home. Evidently that ol rascal, Sherman, had split his forces into two parts, maybe to better supply em as they lived mainly off the land, or maybe it was to increase the sufferin of any southerners that might happen to be in their path.

About 700 of us met down at the Central Railroad and there was a great deal of excitement as we boarded a train under the command of General Henry Wayne. He figured we would race to Gordon's defense and try to slow them Union boys down a scratch.

We made good time. That train eventually rolled to a stop at the Gordon Depot and we knew we had outraced Sherman's forces to that small, but important town. Many of us thought this the proper time to partake of what little food we had hurriedly packed from home, not knowin when we might have the chance to eat again. As many of us paused to take in a quick bite, off in the distance and throwin up a cloud of dust come a lone rider, hard gallopin for all he was worth in our direction. Jesse always did have eyes keen as a hawk and he turned to me with a quick question after he swallowed the last of his vittles.

"I'll be black-dogged, Coswell!" he said. "Ain't that James Rufus Kelly up there on that horse?"

Chapter 23

HEROES OF DIFFERENT STRIPES

"Oh, that Chaney makes me so mad," Barbara Bumgardner began. "This time he had his lawyer and a couple of council members in with him. I guess he felt the need to gang up on and try to intimidate a couple of middle-aged women who simply happen to have a difference of opinion."

Bob Bumgardner listened sympathetically as his wife recalled the second meeting she had with the mayor since the bodies in Memory Hill had been uncovered. "Maybe seeing the diary the first time gave him some encouragement that he could somehow use it against us. What did he have to say on the matter this time around?" Bob asked.

"He said it was obvious from what had been written there that the body of Cynthia Tims had been put in the cemetery illegally. We really had no way to respond to that… leastways legally, as that was the law back then. But Mattie did something clever and I thought worthy of the best of lawyers if there actually is such a thing. She asked them where the body of Cynthia Tims was currently being kept.

"That body was respectfully handled by the city, I will tell you that," Mayor Chaney responded rather proudly. "Because the grave box was so decayed and the skeletal fragments so brittle, it was all bundled up in a new pine box to await reburial. That box is down at Johnson's Funeral Home as we speak, along with the others that came from the ground. We did them the *same courtesy, I might add."*

"How are you able to tell one box from the others?" Mattie inquired. "I mean, when Cynthia Tims gets reburied, wherever that might be, how will you know if those remains are hers?"

"Well that is easy," the mayor answered. "We wrote her name on the side of the new box." With that the lawyer slightly nudged the mayor in the ribs to get him to terminate the conversation. The door, however, had already been flung open and my friend Mattie was about to step inside.

"Sounds to me like the city with their declaration on the side of the box has officially agreed that the woman was, in fact, Cynthia Tims. Now that woman just happened to be married to Coswell Tims and as such would certainly have had the legal right to be buried next to her husband, wouldn't you agree, gentlemen?" Mattie asked.

With no immediate answer forthcoming, Mattie and I sat back in our comfortable leather chairs as the group at the head table began to converse softly among themselves.

"Good job," I whispered over to Mattie Collins. "I think you've got them on the run."

About ten minutes later the mayor began the conversation anew. "Ladies, we are just mincing words here. It says in the diary that Coswell Tims and this woman were married in Milledgeville, Georgia down at the St. Stephens church on October 23, 1850. Would you agree that is true to the best of your knowledge?"

"I believe that to be factual," I responded, remembering what a big deal Coswell had made out of the ceremony in his own personal diary.

"Are you ladies aware that at the time it was illegal for a white man to marry a black woman, as regrettable as those old laws may have been?" Hearing no response he continued on. "The fact of the matter is, the body of a black woman with a name she came by dishonestly, had no business being buried in the white section of the graveyard in the first place. She was not his legal wife and was only entitled to be buried legally in the colored section of the cemetery which we all know is back where the hill slopes down towards Fishin Creek."

"I notice you said 'is,' not 'was,' Mayor Chaney. Are you one of those racist individuals who believe at this late date that separating people in life or death according to color is the proper thing to do?" I submitted.

"Uh...of course not...I mean, I have stated many times during my political career that all folks are equal when it comes to color. Why half the town is colored and I still keep getting elected, don't I? Besides, we know that black people can be buried anywhere in the cemetery now and that's

been since, oh, I believe… the 1950's," he shot back.

"Well, then what's the problem?" Mattie Collins offered. "Let's rebury Cynthia right next to Coswell and be done with it."

"I wish it was that simple, Mrs. Collins, but as mayor I am supposed to uphold the law even if it is unpleasant to me personally. I would be happy to let the woman rest in peace next to her husband as I don't give a damn about color, but it was the original dishonesty of the thing which has to be heavily weighed, can't you see?"

"Would you also be weighing in the fact that Bill Millar has been banging on your door night and day for the last few months, trying to get Cynthia Tims' body permanently removed so he can bury his old man in that same plot? You and I know that family is very influential and has a lot of money. Would that be heavily weighted in any decision you would be making in the future?" she suggested aggressively.

"Ladies, I am afraid this meeting is going to have to end for now. I have other pressing matters to attend to. You and your group will be informed of our official decision next Monday night right after the city council meets. Good day to you both," the mayor concluded, as he began to rise from his chair along with the others. Our little get-together, it seemed, had suffered an abrupt end.

ଛ ଛ ଛ

Barbara Bumgardner could not help but feel a little sorry for her husband after unloading all this information on him, but that did not stop her from continuing to vent. "What a coward that man is, Bob. We had him on the ropes and he knew it and then he did a little side step. He is a racist, for sure. He knows that there are no remaining lots in Memory Hill to be sold (or at least as far as the city goes) and haven't been since 1910, over one hundred years ago. The only sales have been private ones…one family to another or maybe some unscrupulous goings on where supposed "vacant" lots get claimed by influential people and either used or resold. No, it's true what Chaney said that blacks can now be legally buried anywhere in the cemetery, but it doesn't appear that there is any place to bury them except out in the back lot where they were being buried two hundred years ago. Doesn't quite hardly seem fair, does it, Bob?"

"You're asking a black man that question? Now listen, Barb, this game is not over yet. Most likely next Monday night will produce a decision we won't be very happy with, but even if Cynthia is buried by the city in the "colored" section, that doesn't mean she has to stay there forever. We will

get her home to her slave catching husband, but only if we can come up with the proper strategy to do so. We just can't give up on the promise we made to Rosa Billings," he said encouragingly.

Bob Bumgardner continued on. "And speaking of Rosa Billings let me say that she and I met today over at her house as she called earlier when you were out. She had an old newspaper in hand that she wanted the two of us to take a look at. It's over there on the kitchen table. I just glanced at it quickly, but together maybe we can examine it a little more closely."

An old yellowed newspaper was indeed lying on the table, folded in half with a permanent crease down the middle that both time and tight storage had provided. Barbara picked it up. She noticed that it lay open to a specific article that someone had obviously wished to save. A quick glance told her the story was about some local schoolmaster after the war and she quick wondered about that, but all she had to do was let her eyes drop to the teacher's name in the first line of the story to realize why that article had been singled out and saved.

THE MACON DAILY TELEGRAPH
August 6, 1869
Gordon Schoolteacher Had Heroic Past

James Rufus Kelly brings the same passion to his students down in Gordon that he once did to the battlefield. Mr. Kelly has been teaching at the Turner School there for several years and he said in a recent interview that the loss of his lower right leg does not in any way prevent him from doing his job. "The children know well enough not to challenge me. I told em I can hop faster on one leg that they can run on two and if they come up on the wrong side of Mr. Kelly and mess with the bull, they're sure to get the horns. They all mind their 'P's' and 'Q's' and that's a fact," Mr. Kelly was quoted as saying with a twinkle in his steel blue eyes.

This same dedicated and loving man who now watches over the youngsters of Gordon was once a fierce and determined warrior on the battlefield during the late war. He entered Confederate service along with his brother and many of his neighbors down in Gordon in 1861 and was with the 14th Georgia Infantry where they saw a great deal of action under General Robert E. Lee over Virginia way.

"It was at Jericho Ford on the North Anna River in the spring of '64 when a musket ball caught me square in the lower leg," Kelly reported. "The army surgeon cut it off to save my life. I remain grateful to him to this very day. I thought at the time I was done with the war and went home to recover, but I'll be if that war didn't follow me home and find me once again."

Mr. Kelly went on to tell how that came to be. "I learned of the approach of Sherman's army on its way to Milledgeville the day before I actually met up once again with the Yankees. I was out scouting to see if his forces had come into view when I spotted a negro girl crying alongside the road. Now I have to honestly say before I go any further that I felt kinda sorry for those darkies as they was so enthused about their chances at freedom, only to often find themselves mistreated and humiliated by their Federal "deliverers," so called. Wherever the Yankees had conquered, slave cabins were sometimes burned down along with the plantation homes, negroes were impressed into labor just as they had been before, black women sometimes were seized and carried along as 'whories' for the Union officers and bridges were known to be burned behind the Yankees when large groups of hopeful blacks made the effort to follow."

"In any event, I drew up my horse and listened as she told me she feared for her mistress' life. She was the servant of Dr. Thomas Gibson who, she said, was away at the time. Yankee cavalry had come by the house and Mrs. Gibson was all alone and unprotected. She said the Yankees were up to no good and she feared horrible things would happen. Just then a friend of mine, John Bragg, happened along and I passed this story along to him. Together, we spurred our horses in the direction of Doc Gibson's home."

"When we reached the house, we saw several Federal horses hitched outside and knew we were outnumbered. We also spotted numerous sabers and accoutrements lying off in the grass nearby. We both figured that did not bode well for Mrs. Gibson inside. Just then one of the soldiers come out of the house and when he saw us he drew his sidearm. I shot the man in the stomach and he fell moaning to the ground. Another come running out to see what all the commotion was about and he suffered a similar fate. The third one (turned out to be the last) come out in a cowardly manner, holding Mrs. Gibson in front of him as a human shield. Mrs. Gibson implored us to shoot and not worry at all about her as she declared she hated the man who held her more than she loved her own life. With that, John Bragg took it upon himself to shoot the man directly in the forehead with a dandy Spencer carbine he had just acquired. Mrs. Gibson was safe, or at least for the moment."

"John and I got to talking about that gun when we took that first man who had been severely wounded into Gordon for medical attention. A negro servant drove Doc Gibson's wagon and we pressed two of the cavalry horses into service. (Most of the local horses had been impressed or taken off by the Confederate cavalry before the Yankees ever arrived.) John told me he had recently come in possession of several of these fine rifles, carbines actually, and he said they were the most marvelous thing he had ever laid his eyes on. He told me that it's no wonder the Yankees were winning the war as this firearm had the bullets already made up and they could be loaded into a tube in the butt end of the weapon. All you had to do was tug on the lever, pull back the hammer and fire away. Why a man could shoot seven times without reloading, he said. It was a true wonder of a thing and John was quite proud of the fact that several, along with their wooden ammunition cases, just happened to come his way. (He didn't bother to tell me how.) He did promise to give me one when we got into town. Well, the man in the wagon died before we ever reached Gordon, but John did make good on his promise and outfitted me with a pretty special weapon, one which would better allow me to defend my home, my family and the town I loved."

"Now the next day I was out again on my horse, my crutches flung over the saddle pommel and my new carbine all loaded and strapped to my back. I pronounced myself fit for further service in the Confederacy and was ready to meet the Yankee horde. I knew that General Wayne had been put in charge of the defense forces and also knew his headquarters to be over at the Gordon railroad station. I had it in my mind that if I were to spot Sherman's' forces, I would rush there with the news, which is just what I did."

"There was no mistaking the large contingent of enemy soldiers (I was later told they numbered some 30,000) what with all the dust and clatter and the sea of blue uniforms that were snaking their way into our homeland. It didn't take long for me to arrive at General Wayne's headquarters, but found the man and his staff up in a railcar, making steam and fixing to vacate the premises in short order. He had maybe 700 or so soldiers up in the cars with him."

"I yelled to him that I had spotted the Yankees and said they weren't too far off and asked him what his orders were. General Wayne replied that he had already issued the order to retreat as he felt he could not defend the railroad station area or the town. I remember flying into a rage and may have said some things I would not want my students down at the Turner School to hear. They know when they use profanity they get their mouths washed out with lye soap. Anyway, I held firm to the belief that defending all we love in this world was the proper thing to do and announced I would be defending Gordon all by myself if necessary. I turned and rode off toward the Yankee line with that thought in mind. My friend, John Bragg, joined me on the way and said he was up for the fight."

That day, November 21, 1864, would find James Rufus Kelly riding into history as this one-legged man set out alone to challenge 30,000 of the foe. It was said a man with a Spencer carbine was worth three with a single shot rifle, but any way you slice it, the odds did not look good for Kelly. Kelly and Bragg rode towards the Yankee line and when Union forces came into view, charged ferociously, shooting off their Spencers as they come on. Soon emptying them, they were able to reach back and grab a new tube of bullets and reload while still on horseback. Yankee bullets were snapping in the air like hornets and cannons were soon fired off in their direction in an attempt to strike them down. At the last minute before crashing into the enemy's line, both riders swerved and headed off for the woods on a full gallop back to Gordon. Yankee cavalry took chase with Kelly and Bragg firing back at them when they were able. But Kelly, who did not have the advantage of having both feet planted firmly in the stirrups due to the loss of his lower right leg, fell crashing to the ground after attempting to make yet another evasive turn.

"They took me to Sherman's headquarters where I met the man for the first time. He was not a big fella by any means. He had reddish hair which sprouted all over the place and his uniform looked like it needed some tailorin as well as a good wash. He was smokin a rather large cigar when I was ushered into his presence."

"Well, Mr. Kelly, if that indeed is your name. I have it on good authority a complete description of your damn fool actions today on the field of battle. What do you have to say for yourself now that your singlehanded mission to destroy the Union army is at an end?" he asked, as he took a rather large puff on that cigar of his.

"I would do it again if I had half the chance, General. Home and family are all that matters to any honorable man."

"Well said, Kelly, and I would agree with that sentiment but, you see son, if you wanted to go about such a task, you should lawfully be in uniform."

"I left my uniform up at Jericho Ford as I couldn't get the blood out of it after they cut my leg off. You know what it's like to lose a leg, General?" I asked.

"I don't, but that's not the issue here, is it? Because you are out of uniform and have fired on my men, I have no other choice but to brand you a spy and, as such, condemn you to death by firing squad. Now what do you have to say about that, young fella?" General Sherman inquired.

"I would tell you today I acted honorably and in self-defense. I have no regrets. A man is only going to die once, I figure, and I reckon this is as good a way to go out as any I can imagine."

Kelly said the General eyed him keenly for several minutes time and only slowly did he then turn to the guard and ordered him to "see that the sentence of the court martial be carried out." What Kelly also added was that Sherman issued that order while continuing to stare directly at him with a strange quizzical smile upon his face. Kelly said he felt somewhat heartened by that gesture, but didn't for the life of him know the reason why.

"I was tossed in the back of a field ambulance and told I would be shot at sunrise," Kelly continued. "Their band played the 'Death March' for my benefit most of the night. The next morning nothing happened. That same thing occurred two days in a row and I began to wonder about General Sherman's intentions regarding my fate. I became tired of that death march, tired of waiting to die and tired of being cooped up in that cramped ambulance, so I decided it was time for me to take my fate in hand. I waited until it was full dark and slipped out the back of that vehicle, first falling hard to the ground. I hobbled, crawled, then rolled my way down a small hill until I found myself eventually lyin at the edge of a swamp. I did get wet and it was freezing cold outside. I decided to climb a tree and see if there was any way I could improve my situation. That was not an easy task for a man in my condition, but I managed to do it and spotted a lone fire way off yonder. I made up my mind to reach it, be it friend or foe, as I felt I would certainly freeze to death if I were to stay where I was. Well, the Good Lord saw fit to bless me as I had hobbled over to that fire using a branch I found lying about as a crutch and discovered the welcoming fire of several southern refugees who were trying to stay out of the Union general's way same as I was. I was saved," Kelly concluded, as our interview did likewise.

A most remarkable story about a most remarkable man. A true

lesson in courage, it is. I am sure Mr. Kelly does not fail to pass along his impressive values to his students at the Turner School. We at the *Macon Telegraph* wish him well and hope that the Good Lord will allow him to continue to teach the children for many years to come."

⇛   ⇛   ⇛

"I would have to say that was a story well worth repeating and an article definitely worth saving. And to think the Tims family had such famous friends. Kelly kind of reminds me of that delusional, yet heroic character, Don Quixote, who challenged and dueled with the windmills, thinking them monsters in need of destruction," Barbara Bumgardner suggested.

"Reminds me of the great Spartan King, Leonidas, who once stood fast with 300 of his men blocking the way of a million invading Persians at a small pass in Greece called Thermopylae," her historian husband countered. "He knew he had zero chance of victory, but fought until the end just the same. This story of Kelly's is a story that will also be hard to forget, but there are a number of other things in that accounting that I found quite interesting."

"Like what, Bob?"

"Well, for one thing, do you remember in Coswell's diary, him meeting up with Doc Gibson? Remember it was when Cynthia had been badly hurt by her former master, James Walker?"

"Oh my God, I do recall that in Coswell's journal! Gibson saved Cynthia's life, but also saved the life of their nemesis, James Walker. I never made that connection until you just mentioned it."

"And heres another thing. Doctor Gibson comes to the aid of the Tims family. Then the Tims family tends James Rufus. And then James Rufus goes on to help save Doc Gibson's wife from Yankee invaders. You think thats all coincidence?" Bob asked rhetorically.

"This whole story is truly remarkable, Bob. I wish all the people in Milledgeville felt the same way about it as you and I do. Can't there be a way to have all the people in the city on board with what this story is saying to us?"

"Maybe there's a way we could make that happen," Robert Bumgardner uttered quietly as he found himself currently deep in thought.

"What did you say, Bob?

"Nothing, really. Just muttering to myself, I guess."

Chapter 24

HARVEST OF DEATH

Jesse was right. Sure-God, if that weren't James Rufus astride that horse and the boy looked to be a- rushin like he was headed home for his mamma's hot biscuits and fried chicken. Our young friend drew in his mount and come to a sudden stop right up next to our train. Through a cloud of dust, one of the crutches up on his saddle come tumblin to the ground. Payin it no nevermind, he started in conversin excitedly with General Wayne who was in the rear coach right near where Jesse, me and many of the Milledgeville Reserve Guards had taken up residence. We was close enough to hear, but didn't feel it proper to intrude on the heated conversation that followed.

"General Wayne. I have spotted the Yankees comin up the road not far from where we are this very moment. What are your orders, sir?" he said expectantly.

"Young man, you would be best advised to join with us as we are retreating to the Oconee River Bridge where we can better employ our resistance," the general shouted back through the window.

"We can't be retreatin, general! My God! Our homes and families are here in Gordon. We must make a stand," Kelly yelled back.

"It's a fool's errand, son. Leave your horse and get aboard!" the general commanded.

"Why, why, you ain't nothin but a tuck-tail coward, General Wayne…a white-livered cur for sure. You're a shell of a man who ain't got an ounce of red blood or manhood left inside ya. Damn you and damn all you gutless sons of bitches!" Kelly shouted out, as he raised his fist in defiance and looked up and down the train, seemingly unaware of any friends he might have also included in that assemblage.

As a witness to all this I would have to say that James Rufus' profanity was only matched by his reckless bravery on this day as he took the carbine from offen his back and announced if necessary he alone would defend the women, children and town of Gordon. As he prepared to up and leave, one of the soldiers nearest to James Rufus jumped off the train and handed the courageous horseman his fallen crutch. Cheers come from all the rail cars as Kelly nodded his thanks in the man's direction before beginin his rapid advance towards the enemy line and what appeared to be certain death.

Many people on the train began to mutter about this lone, brave young man, a disabled warrior with one leg, no less (and no more.) Jesse turned to me. "That boy ain't comin back, Coswell, he's a busted institution, that's what he is."

"Well, I would have to say this, Jesse. When you got yourself a rooster, I guess it's just a matter of time fore he's gonna crow," now, ain't that a fact?" I offered in return.

കെ   കെ   കെ

It was over twenty miles and I reckon it took all of two hours for the lot of us to reach the Oconee River Bridge by train. It sure weren't as pleasureful a ride as when Cynthia and me took that same railway on our journey south to find Sanford. (Course we was hold up in the "Ladies Car" at the time as Cynthia has reminded me many times since.) Despite any discomfort from overcrowdin, it did beat the goose feathers out of walkin, I would fully admit.

When we arrived at the trestle bridge, General Wayne and Major Capers had us unload most of equipment and the men started in diggin breastworks and gatherin up firewood for the cold night to come. We noticed several of our cannons was left on the flatbed railcars. General Wayne figured the nearby swamps would slow the Yankees down so's a dug-in enemy and them cannons might just give us a fair chance against their greater number. The night passed by quietly with short watches due to the cold. It even started to snow lightly around midnight, but it was a good thing them rail cars stayed right where they was cause each one had itself a wood stove, providing heat and shelter for any in need.

The next day all efforts to complete the earthen works was redoubled with 150 convicts and several hundred negro slaves that had been impressed from surroundin plantations took on the bulk of the task. We spotted Sanford among em and both me and Jesse tried to get his attention, but he was too busy to take any notice.

As the Tims boys began to take stock of our situation we knew we was well short of a thousand men and many of those were mere boys. But it looked to both of us like the battalion of cadets from the Georgia Military Institute, despite their youth, might prove one of our greatest assets. Major Capers had brought a little over one hundred of these young fellas with him after their school had been overrun by Sherman early on. They had been drillin and livin in tents on the northeast portion of Statehouse Square in Milledgeville since the fall of Atlanta and despite their youth, them boys did have a fair idea what of what military life could be about, or at least as much as any sixteen year old lad with little real experience might imagine.

What give me concern, though, was the presence of the Home Guards in our ranks as I knew their captain had to be somewheres among their number. Jesse did spy Orville Purdy over next to one of the rail cars and we was both on the lookout for his older brother. Jesse knew I had a score to settle with the man, maybe sooner or maybe later, but either way the debt would have to be paid.

On November 23rd the fightin started in earnest with the Yankees comin on the scene and launchin artillery shells at the bridge. The wood trestle began to catch on fire, but it burned slowly and eventually went out due to the inclemency of the weather. There was continued fightin throughout the day with heavy artillery shellin keepin us pinned down in the trenches or huddled back inside the rail cars. We fired off some shots, but at no one in particular as the Yankees were hid up pretty good in the woods and swamps. The four cannons left on the flat cars fired in the Yankees general direction, but it was hard to tell if they did any damage.

Union soldiers began to take up positions nearer the bridge as nighttime commenced to fall. Shootin was sporadic and back and forth. Union sharpshooters started to take aim and did do some damage. Sheriff Strother's deputy was shot through the chest and fell with a thud not far from where Jesse and me was entrenched. We figured them blue-jackets to be hidin up in the trees and numerous branches and limbs soon become casualties of war with our return fire. Hard to tell if any of the enemy fell along with em.

Some Yankee cavalry was targeted and received a deadly volley from our dug in positions on the breastworks. Many of our boys shouted approval as a number of Union horses and men dropped to the ground. For several hours' time the swamp echoed with the loud discharge of cannon fire and the howlin of musket balls, but just as suddenly as it all began, it all come to a sudden stop. An eerie silence fell over the land and although nothin was said, it seemed to be understood that it was time for each side to tend their own. We got reports of many Yankees shot and their ambulances pickin up their dead and wounded behind their lines. Our injured were taken from the field and placed within the safety of the cars and the dead were dragged off and piled up near the woods on the other side of the rail tracks. I saw Sanford and many other negroes engaged in that unpleasant task and for some strange reason, I just got the feelin that it was important for me to hunt up Lem Purdy at this particular time.

My eyes scanned our side of the Oconee where we had chosen to make our stand. I did see two of the Purdys who were in the company of several other Home Guards secured in a forward ditch. I continued to carefully examine the landscape. Nothin in the trenches that I could make out. Nothin over at the raised earthen works. I skinned my eye to scan the long supply train and it didn't take long to find what I was lookin for. There he was, head as bald as a peeled onion, peerin out from an open window in one of the forward cars, one just a few back from where the engine was. Unlike most of the others he still had a rifle in his hands despite the obvious truce that was currently in progress. He also had hisself a pair of field glasses which he kept puttin up to his eyes. What was this man lookin for? I had my suspicions.

I come up on the other side of the train and quietly entered the railcar in question. Lem Purdy was unaware of my presence. Three or four Home Guards was over at the stove huddled in together to keep warm. I stole up behind their captain and reached down for my

Spiller and Burr. Lem had just put his field glasses down and had cocked his rifle. He was just startin to take aim when he heard my pistol cock behind his ear. I pressed it firmly against the back of the man's skull.

"Lookin to finish the job, Lem?" I asked.

He lowered his rifle some and I could feel him drop his gaze from the intended target, a muscular black man by the name of Sanford Tims who had made hisself an easy mark as he walked back and forth draggin the bodies of the dead from the battlefield.

The men round the stove began to stir as one by one they took notice of my presence, but to a man they all sat right back down after I made a little announcement. "It might be a good idea for you fellas to stay out of this fight as it is personal. This man was about to shoot one of our own and I am not gonna take the time to list other things that he is responsible for. If he fired that shot, how many of you might have been killed if the Yankees thought we had dishonored the truce? No, this man don't care a lick bout anyone but hisself. Now I promise all here I will blow his brains out on this spot if you make a single move in our direction," I concluded forcefully.

Lem began to lower his rifle as he turned around to face me. He had a slight smile on his face when he tossed his weapon to the floor. "Why don't you just shoot me, Tims, like the low-life coward I always knowed you to be." He turned slightly in the direction of the men still clustered round the stove. "Boys...this fella is a poltroon and a nigger-lover to boot and he would shoot an unarmed white man for sure, with no reason other than to suit his own vengeful ways. Why don't you pull that trigger, Tims, and show the men here how you would treat a good old southern boy, a neighbor and comrade-in-arms."

I uncocked my revolver and dropped it down to my side. "Not here...not now," I said, lookin Purdy straight in the eye. To be truthful, I was unclear of my next move.

I shot a glance over at the men by the stove who seemed quite content to remain just where they was and then I stole another one, this time out the open coach window. Sheriff John Strother just happened to come into view as he was solemnly draggin the body of his friend and deputy across the tracks near the front of the train. "John!" I yelled out. "It's Coswell. Come up here when you're done."

With that request Purdy went to slowly pick up his Enfield that lay between us on the floor of the car. I waited long enough for him to get his fingers under the thing and when he did, I slowly placed my boot on that same object. This caught his fingers between the rifle and the floor and I pressed down just a little bit harder for good measure. "I'm afraid you are goin to have to face the enemy with a little less firepower, Lem," I told him.

Sheriff Strother soon come aboard and John agreed to have Purdy by his side when the fightin resumed. I knew that offered no guarantees, but it seemed to be about as good as we could make things, given the situation we currently found ourselves in.

All of us knew there was no way we could hold out much longer and some of the men began talkin bout surrender. Stubborn southern pride stifled that possibility and, after what was maybe our last meal (some hardtack, raw bacon and hot coffee which was most likely the last of the supplies General Wayne had stored on board the train) we dug in best we could and awaited the inevitable.

It started with the flash of cannons and a yell, almost deafenin it was, as what seemed to be thousands and thousands of Yankees began to emerge from the swamps. Our boys met the Yankee holler with our own 'rebel yells,' which is said to be somewheres twinx the howl of a hungry wolf and the whoop of a redtail with his savage heart fully set on liftin a scalp. Their cannons, which were raised up on solid ground beyond the tree line, added greatly to the noise.

"This will be the last of it," I thought silently to myself. I saw Reverend James Herkle from Griswoldville offer no prayers, but rise to a standin position above a small group in front of us and shout out "Send em off to Hell, boys!" not somethin a man of the cloth would normally be expected to tell his congregation. He began firin his revolver in the direction of the enemy as the commandment "Thou shalt not kill," had at least temporarily been abandoned. I was witness to a direct hit from a Union cannon just to the left of us. One of our boys was tore to pieces with his insides hangin out for all to see and a man not ten feet away, why he could be found lyin off to the side restin in a tangled heap with a good part of his skull havin gone off in another direction.

Jesse and me was dug in pretty good when my brother asked me what that strange smell was. "That's piss, Jesse." I said. The smell of gunpowder and the smell of piss go hand in hand. I remember back in the Creek War of '35, fellas used to piss their pants fairly regular what with all the horrors of war. After a while you don't even notice it." As I finished sayin that, Jesse pointed over to one of our boys nearby who was doin his level best to hide the ever widenin stain on his butternut trousers.

We set ourselves to the task at hand, but as the Yankeees come on, we soon began to realize that many of em was shootin new Spencer repeatin rifles that's been all the talk round the campfires of late. It just didn't seem fair and looked to many of us like things was headed downhill in general, like a wagon all greased for the occasion.

Suddenly Jesse was hit! He fell right next to where I stood and grabbed at my leg as he went down. He was cluchin his chest. I dropped my rifle and pulled open his coat and tore at the vest and shirt beneath. I breathed a sigh of relief when I saw that my brother had been hit by a spent musket ball which had just bloodied him a scratch, but had definitely managed to knock the air from his chest. Thankful to be temporarily spared, we took to lookin up quickly only to repeatedly duck our heads down again (we musta looked like two drakes a-courtin) as the roar of artillery and musketry and the cries of those around us continued. Curiosity did eventually get the better of me, however, after I heard a cannon shell burst up alongside one of the rail cars behind us. It was the same car that Lem Purdy and Sheriff Strother were held up in. I wondered if there was any casualties and if the situation there had changed as a bullet suddenly passed by my head, the zippin noise as clear as day and as frightenin as a sudden thunder and lightnin storm in the dead of a still summer night.

Well, I do not know how much time passed after that, as fightin time ain't quite the same as normal time. Maybe it was a half hour or so when the first white flag was raised from the earthen works and others soon followed. We all began to come out of our defensive positions with empty hands held high in the air. There had been no other reasonable option left open to us. "It just couldn't of been did, Coswell" my brother thoughtfully reminded me.

What remained of our group was all herded in together by the Federals. Many of us got a real bird's eyed look-see at the place where both sides had met up and howdied for the first time. I would have to say that seein dead friends and comrades who had attempted to do the impossible and failed was a hard tonic to swallow. The good earth had been tore up all around, small fires burned in places and bodies from both sides lay very still and scattered on the ground. The saddest thing and somethin I will never be able to disremember was when my eyes caught sight of the lifeless body of that grandpappy I had noticed earlier now lyin on the ground overtop his also motionless young grandson. The family shotgun lay beneath em both with just the butt end stickin out from the pile. So sad, so truly sad it all was! And to make matters worse, even when the terrifyin noises of battle became a thing of the past, those sounds simply give way to the pitiful moans of soldiers, wounded and dyin, who lay there still. I knew what I had been a part of was just a scuffle as far as battles and wars go, but it sure looked like a harvest of death to me. And what was it all for, any intelligent person would have to ask?

I guess we thought this war was about our freedom...freedom to protect our section of the country and our way of life from outsiders. Maybe we should have thought a little longer bout how that could possibly be done with the other high contractin party feelin so different on the matter. No person or group can always have things their own way as it ain't in the nature of things. Compromises have to be worked out or ruin will be sure to follow. As one southern woman wrote in the paper..."It's queer, it is, that we only want to separate and be off by ourselves, but those folks up north want to risk all they have to keep us cuz they love us so much." Well, it may be true that the north didn't bear us much affection, but maybe we should have weighed the odds of gainin our separation early on and avoided some the misery that I could now see around me. And to think, the war weren't even over yet. What other horrors might there be in store for all concerned after the dust finally comes to settle over this land?

Later in the day the survivors of the Oconee River Bridge skirmish was marched off to a hastily made-up stockade where we was to await some kind of judgment on what was to be done with us. The Yankees did feed us decent and took care of our wounded best they could. Prisoners was sorted out and many quickly released as it was obvious many of the old and very young had been recently conscripted and were not normal fightin men. Jesse and me was among that number and was freed along with em after we all took an oath to fight no more and to respect the Union. A wounded Sheriff Strother would come home to Milledgeville with us. Lem Purdy survived the fight, but was sentenced to die along with several others. All of those particular men was of fightin age and we figured the Yankees couldn't abide any able-bodied individual who had failed to honor their manly call to duty and join the regular army. Even more damnin was the testimony of numerous witnesses who reported that Mr. Purdy was firin at unarmed black civilians who were workin directly behind union lines, "contraband," so called, who had fled slavery and joined their cause. Now Sherman and many of the northern leaders we would later come to find out were not enthusiastic supporters of negro freedom, but to shoot down unarmed and innocent civilians because of their color was more than catbrier crazy and had to be properly dealt with. The punishment would be death by hangin. It appeared that these Northerners just might take care of a certain debt Purdy owed the Tims family.

№ № №

When we returned home all was mirth and merriment or at least for a short time. As I come in the door, Cynthia shouted my name and threw her arms round my neck like she had done so many times in the past. I spun my woman round in a full circle, takin her feet clear off the floor in the process. It took quite some time for the two of us to untangle from the lovin embrace that followed. I guess Sanford and Little Peney must have been bit by the same dog as they took to doin pretty much the same thing. Why the excitement of that moment seemed to fly off in all directions like water runnin off Daddy's grindstone. Unfortunately, Jesse was not able to partake of the festivities in like manner as his wife Becky had come to grief and been dead and lay in the ground for the past thirty years. But he had told me many times over bout how that woman give him all the love he needed to last a whole lifetime, so's that did not stop him from joinin in and bein happy for the rest of us, thankful to be home and among the people he cared for and who cared for him. Some huggin and general gratitude to the heavens above seemed to be in order this day. Life had seen fit to bless this family yet again, but it sure didn't take long for clouds of darkness to gather once more in the skies above.

I would have to say that soon our chances seemed to run pretty even between mirth and mournin after my wife told me all the sad news since our departure. Sherman and his legions had come and gone and did their fair share of damage while they was here. Cynthia said it probably would have been much worse if anyone had put up any real resistance as the only one to do so was Patrick Kane who tried a little too hard to protect the Jarratt place. He was killed for his efforts and the property burned to the ground, she said. Folks in town could hear fightin off in the distance (we found later this was from Griswoldville) on the same day Union soldiers had entered the city. Luckily our little cabin had been spared, but houses of many of the political big bugs had been burned down. Federal forces seemed to know just who to target as a fella by the name of Snelling who had growed up here had defected over to the Union side early in the war, had become a lieutenant in the northern cavalry and pointed out to Sherman the places and people that needed "proper tendin." I got to thinkin it was a good thing that I got on tolerable with David Snelling growin up as that probably saved this slave catcher's house from the torch. The Purdy place weren't so fortunate, however, as Peney and Cynthia told us their house was burned down and all their dogs shot dead.

Governor Brown and all the politicians had fled and the trenches and fortifications built to defend em were abandoned as soon as word come that the Yankees was gettin close. The Governor's Mansion was spared, but homes of prominent secessionist men like John Jones and Judge Harris was burned to the ground. Sherman burned the Central Depot rail station and the bridge that spanned the Oconee. Rail lines were tore apart and bent up and telegraph lines was tore down as well. Also destroyed was the State Arsenal and the Penitentiary. Many houses or buildins containing cotton reportedly was burned on general orders and the cotton destroyed, along with cotton gins and presses.

Cynthia told us the worst of it was that many plantations and homes was pillaged and ransacked and left picked clean. Mrs. Raines, a bed-ridden widow who lived nearby, saw her plantation completely ravaged of all valuables, food and even livestock and like many of our neighbors was now not far from starvation. I guess these "bummers" as they are called, don't really have any military discipline and are havin themselves a grand old time at the expense of the southern people.

Many picket fences, barns, outhouses, and other structures were demolished and used by the Yankees for firewood. What seemed to go beyond general orneriness was when they took to destroyin fodder stacks and hay ricks and slaughterin all the animals they could not take with em, leavin their carcasses to rot right where they was dispatched. Little Peney said she heard tell that St. Stephens church had been used to stable Union horses, the pews turned over for troughs and the organ filled with sticky molasses. Supposedly one Yankee soldier was heard sayin: "Well, That should make their Sunday church music a might sweeter." Now iffen that's true," Little Peney asked, "ain't that just bout as low down ornery and devilish as a body can get?"

But many of the larger homes where federals could be quartered did remain standin as did the State House and the Governor's mansion. The Lunatic Asylum remained untouched as well.

"What have you heard from Doc Greene bout our dogs we left over there?" I asked.

"The dogs are fine, Coswell. It was pretty much like you figured, the Yankees didn't want no part of those loonies locked up in the place and only posted an outside guard to keep watch. Governor Brown figured same as you and hid some important state papers and public records in the basement which might have otherwise been destroyed. Doc Greene sent one of his people over yesterday to tell us to come get the dogs as they are makin quite a mess of things and there ain't much left to feed em," Cynthia reported.

"We'll do that later today," I replied. "We need to settle in a bit and take stock of what remains. Maybe we was luckier than most, but we still have the winter months fore we can begin to plant in the spring and the Tims family could get pretty hungry in the meantime."

Chapter 25

END OF THE LINE

COSWELL TIM'S DIARY RESUMES

The weather took us by surprise as the next day was considerable warmer, a welcome change from the extreme cold of the last several weeks. There was even a light rain fallin when a sudden knock at the door took us by surprise as well. I admit to havin my revolver firmly in hand when I went to open it and as I did, a familiar face greeted me at the doorstep.

"Howdy, John. A little early in the mornin for a visit, aint it?" I inquired.

"Coswell, I've got to tell ya. Purdy got hisself loose from the Yankees and I felt you should know straightaway," Sheriff Strother reported, movin around rather uncomfortably with his left arm all wrapped up in a sling due to his recent mishap down at the Oconee River Bridge. "They hung the others, but I'll be go to hell if Lem didn't manage to fly the coop. Nowheres to be found, I am told. But there was a farmer down that way by the name of McClusky who spotted him runnin through his fields like the devil was fastened on to his coattails. Said for a man of his squatty disposition he appeared to be in high earnest and wasn't sure if he was a Yankee, a southern deserter, an escaped convict, or one of them loonies runnin from the asylum. Said he had no hat upon his bald head and appeared to be goin in a northwesterly direction. Old man McClusky said he thought he should contact me as the man appeared he might be headin towards Milledgeville and I figured what with you bein the only one who's got dogs and seein's though you bear the man a grudge to begin with, I knew I needed to get out here with the news as soon as possible."

"I do thank you for that," I answered. "Too bad the Federals shot all the trackin dogs round these parts or they might have had a better chance of catchin Purdy themselves. It don't make much sense to shoot critters that you just might need sometime in the future, does it, Sheriff?"

"No it don't, but then there ain't too much that does makes sense these days. But I do know that takin care of Purdy after what he and Starlin Finney done to your Sanford does make a lot of sense. Am I right?" Strother inquired.

"Right as the rain on the roof, Sheriff. I guess I knew deep down inside that Sherman and his boys doin my dirty work was a not somethin I could set stock by. This here's my job to finish and I reckon that's the way it should be." (I never did let on bout Cynthia's issues with this same man. I wouldn't tell nobody bout that ceptin my brother, of course.)

"One problem I got, John. I need a fresh horse. The railroad's all tore up and Jesse's mount is so old and beat-up why Sherman didn't even take him along when they come through here."

"That's surprisin, as they generally shoot the horses they don't take so's to keep us from usin em in the war or even usin em to farm with. Ever since those big battles of '63 the general Union policy has been to consider a horse or mule contraband that could possibly be used against em. All horses are ordered destroyed if their army can't find a good use for em…such the pity. I've been told half the horses we once had here in the south are already dead and gone," the Sheriff noted sadly.

"If I am goin back to where Purdy was last seen, I'll need that horse, John. Can you fetch one for me?"

"I believe I can, Coswell, if you don't mind ridin up in a doctor's top buggy. I know both Dr. Massey and Doc White was allowed to keep theirs. Sort of a humanitarian gesture on Sherman's part, I reckon. Why don't you follow me into town in Jesse's wagon so's

you can switch up with Dr. Massey over at the Brown Hospital. I'm
sure he ain't makin no house calls what with all the work he has to
do down there. Aside from shelterin all his patients and the hospital
itself from the Union Army, damn if Sherman didn't leave him twen-
ty-eight more men, Yankees, no less, who were sick or wounded for
the doc to tend. I guess when Massey asked the general what he
should do with em, he said the right thing to do was if they died give
em a proper burial and if they got well, why, send em off to Andersonville. Doc Massey always run strong on the hospital matter and I
reckon that Sherman fella must have caught some of his enthusiasm
as they seemed to get on pretty well despite bein from opposite
persuasions," the sheriff concluded.

I told Sheriff Strother he had to go along without me as I had
a few things to tend to beforehand. He said he would stop by the
Brown Hospital and tell Bob Massey what we had discussed. He
was sure the man would be most obligin. Aside from fetchin Jesse's
horse and wagon and pickin up the dogs down at the asylum, the
most important thing I needed to do before I left was to have a little
sit-down talk with the woman of the house.

DIARY OF PENIA FITZSIMONS TIMS

The Sheriff come by with the news of Lem Purdy's escape. I
could tell by the way Massa Tims acted that his hatred for the man had
not lessened a lick and he is now makin plans to get out on Purdy's
trail. Cynthia sat silent when she heard the news and I don't rightly
know what is goin on in that head of hers. Sanford offered to go, but
he was told that this was "personal" and that Massa Tims would
take care of everythin, all right and proper. He said he would tell
his brother, Jesse, the same thing he told Sanford. I would not want
to be in Lem Purdy's shoes for one single minute as this new-found
freedom of his may soon become a thing of the past.

Sanford and me are tryin to make ourselves scarce as hens'
teeth round the house today as Cynthia and her husband are havin a
real heart-to-heart in the other room. I don't think things have been
worked out all proper-like on their end even though I told Massa
Tims what happened with Purdy. I also told my sister that I had
passed that same information his way. She didn't seem mad, or sad,
or anythin else, far as I could tell. But that sister of mine sure was

quiet after that.

Oh, I can hear Cynthia cryin in the other room and it just breaks my heart. I feel the need to peek my head in. Lordy, I just heard her say how bad this all was for her. "I just don't want to go back and think on it, Coswell. It was horrible. It weren't just what he done but how he done it," were her very words. She went on to tell how others were there to witness the whole thing and how she was treated like the lowest of crawly critters. Treated with hatred and disgust and for no other reason she could see other than the colored blood that ran ever so faintly through her veins.

Massa Tims, I see he puts his arms around her and says some people are inclined to be low down and mean with strange ideas swimmin round inside their heads. He said there ain't much a body can do til they finally act on em like Purdy done here. Now Massa Tims say it ain't no longer just a matter of a man havin his own feelins, but now it's been raised up to where it's a killin offense. And he said it was him who was gonna do the killin. "Your husband is goin to hang that man, Darlin, and you can make book on that," I heard him say in little more than a whisper. It was bone chillin for me to hear. I had no doubt Purdy was about to die and die exactly the way Massa Tims said he would.

COSWELL TIM'S DIARY RESUMES

I admit to knowin Dr. Massey only slightly, but from what I do know, I believe him to be a good and honorable man. He has certainly done a great deal for our town since he come down from Atlanta some time back. He has his head firmly set upon his shoulders and appears to have more than his fair share of skill and wisdom. Reminds me a great deal of ol Doc Fort who we all knew for so many years. This new doc was most accomodatin and his top buggy proved to be a good one with a right fine horse to do the pullin. That horse was a black stallion, well-muscled and maybe ten years younger than Jesse's old nag. He looked to be as slick as a racer and I was so glad the Yankees never got their murderous hands on this fine animal. With Doctor Massey to thank, I soon was on my way with our bloodhound, Wrinkles, settin right up alongside me on the buggy seat.

I suppose I should have named that dog somethin else, but Cynthia give him that name and it just stuck. He was now a magnif-

icent animal, all 135 pounds of pure bloodhound with not an ounce
of fat on him, that is, if you don't count in all the piles of loose skin.
He was a black and tan as some of our finest hounds have been over
the years and I suppose it's possible that his droopy eyes and long
ears might sometimes disguise the great strength and stamina the
dog could lay claim to. He was as tall as a man when he stood on his
hind legs and his teeth were now large and sharp enough to chew
through the toughest bone. It is incredible, however, to note that the
bloodhound is one of the more gentle canine breeds despite their
sometimes intimidatin appearance. I'm sure that Sherman fella never
knew that fact. I only had one bloodhound in my trackin life who
ever bit a man, and thinkin back on it, I believe the dog was right to
have done so and I think I would have bitten the fella myself if the
dog hadn't had the good sense to beat me to it. Yes sir, our Wrinkles
was a good-natured hound, a good tracker with special abilities and
I had no doubt Purdy would soon find the animal sniffin at his heels.

Before me and Wrinkles left, I had flung my leather saddlebags
behind the seat. They contained a number of things needed for this
little "doctor's visit" I had planned out. (I guess I may have looked
the part of a good doctor, but truth to tell here my mission weren't to
save a life but to take one.) I did feel this was the proper thing to do,
to put in the time and effort to eliminate a man who showed hissself
to be possessed of the devil powerfully, someone who, if allowed
to live, might just ruin the neighborhood well past salvation. The
world would be better off without such a man, I reasoned, not just
for me and mine, but for others livin there as well. Just like that fella
the Milledgeville town fathers hired to come round twice a week
with a public cart "to clean all the streets and alleys of filth and other
offensive matter," Coswell Tims would rid Milledgeville of the likes
of Lem Purdy. I was willin to bear the unpleasant burden of takin a
life in an effort to tidy things up.

My Bowie knife and its leather sheath also lay inside them bags,
along with a hangman's rope already knotted up for the occasion.
There was the dog's trackin harness and lead, some iron shackles,
along with some lucifers and a small amount of food and water for
me and my canine friend. I took the blanket Cynthia had folded up
nice and neat and a bedroll which also was tossed into the back of
the buggy.

The trip back to the site of the skirmish was maybe a little less
than forty miles all tole up, so I knew from past experience it would

take a fair amount of time even with a spirited horse. Now if I drove that horse hard, I might have made the trip in maybe five hours' time, but leavin Milledgeville well past the noonday hour, I knew necessitated Wrinkles and me sleepin out on the trail, somethin I was comfortable with and had done many times over the years.

We headed out and soon home was far behind. The buggy handled well and I found the horse had hisself a right fine stride. We made good time. We traveled on for several hours, when, with reigns in hand, I reached down for my pocket watch and hit the little latch to pop open the cover. That timepiece had never failed me since I first come by it when we put Daddy in the ground back in '42. I don't believe it ever failed him neither. It dutifully reported the hour as five o'clock in the late afternoon and I knew we needed to stop soon as it gets dark mighty early this time of year, maybe within an hours' time. We would need to find us a comfortable spot where the horse could get fresh water and graze some. Wrinkles would need his fair share of water too as a dog with a dry nose will not track. As for me, I would get us a good fire goin for supper and to counter the chill of the comin night.

We was most fortunate to find just such a place inside a grove of trees...had a small stream runnin through it and plenty of dead firewood lyin about. I freed Doc Massey's horse from his carriage duties, put that hangman's rope over his neck and led him down to the stream for his fill of cold water. "Don't worry, big fella," I told him. "This rope ain't for the likes of you. It's meant for some ornery two-legged critter who's earned the time he'll spend danglin on the business end."

As I later lay next to the fire with the dog up next to me, I felt the need to check that pocket watch of mine one last time. I took notice that the hour was now seven o'clock and the night had turned dark as a coal cellar. It would be very important, I thought to myself, to learn the exact time Purdy had been spotted runnin through Old Man McClusky's fields yesterday tryin to make good his escape. I would be sure to ask that question when the two of us met in the mornin.

It did not take much time after we awoke to ready ourselves and continue on towards our destination. The McClusky place was only maybe five miles distant and we reached it within the hour. It certainly weren't no grand affair, in fact, it looked more than a little run down. Upon meetin Ol Man McClusky I found he was not by nature real friendly, but he did joke some bout my doctor buggy and said if I come to tend him he felt pretty good for an old fella and, most like as not, could even give me a good run for my money if we were ever to tangle. I told him I was sure that was the case, but I first needed to catch me the man who had run through his fields the day before. The old man sure perked up when I mentioned his name.

"Lem Purdy, why that low-down mean polecat!" were the first words out of his mouth. "I know more than a few people who was robbed blind cause of him and his so-called 'Home Guards.' I'll help you catch him and we can take turns puttin lead in that shadetail."

"No need for that, Mr. McClusky. This is personal, just twinx him and me. There's too much to tell here and you'll just have to take my word on it. I do have to say straight out that I'm goin to hang the man and leave him hangin right where I catch him. You might want to check for buzzards or other critters that are inclined to report such things. I apologize in advance for clutterin up any property you might own if the man is found and hung in this general area."

Maybe it was the way I said it or the look in my eye at the time as the man backed off and took to noddin his head in agreement with my thoughts on the matter. "I'll bury him right where his toes be pointin, Mr. Tims," McClusky offered.

"Now what time of day did you last see him?" I asked.

"It was just past sunset, twilight, I believe. Why, by the time I got back to the house I could barely make out my hands in front of my face."

"Thank you, Mr. McClusky. That tells me more than you know," I responded. "Now if you could show me where you spotted him, I'll get my fetch hound right out on the trail."

It seemed like McClusky and I hit it off pretty tolerable after first firin off a few volleys in each other's direction. He was more than willin to let me leave Doc Massey's buggy at his place and he even loaned me a saddle for the journey ahead. I was unsure of the terrain and knew the buggy would be of no use, but I did need that horse as I wanted to make up for lost time and was also unsure how long we might be out on the trail.

As I saddled up the black stallion, I began to put a few of my thoughts in place. The arrival of the Dark Moon two days back would have stopped Purdy most dead in his tracks when this farmer first laid eyes on him at six o'clock, I figure, and that same fugitive would have been unable to resume his journey until first light around seven o'clock the next mornin. This was important to know for two reasons. One was that I needed to figure how far ahead the man might be as he now had a day and a half head start. What with the Dark Moon a couple days in length, he could only walk durin the daylight hours. With it rainin yesterday, the most walkin time he might claim would likely be only eight hours or so and that under pretty soggy conditions. So, if he was forced to stop the night before, walked maybe eight hours yesterday and maybe two this mornin, the most time he could have been on his feet all tole up would be no more than ten hours. Now a man walkin, Jesse and me always figured, could cover bout three miles in a single hour's time if he walked steady and with purpose. A little cipherin on the matter told me the furthest Purdy could be from us at the present moment would be around thirty miles, but given the weather and his inability to read the sun and continue on his northwest path back home, that thirty miles might shrink to half of that if he wandered around or occasionally doubled back by mistake. "I'll bet he ain't no more than ten or fifteen miles away from where we stand at this very moment," I reassured myself.

The other reason I needed to know the time Purdy had first been spotted was that I knew he would have to bed down for the night close to that spot. Unfortunately we did not have a scent item for our runner that the dog would normally use to start the chase, so we had to rely on another method to track this runner, one we had used before and one that Wrinkles was quite familiar with. Once McClusky showed me the spot he last saw Purdy, I continued northwest a short time just like he might have done. Bein full dark by then with no moon, he would have been forced to stop. Now when a person does that and beds down for the night, in our business that place is it is called a "nest" and if we could find that nest of his it was sure to have enough Purdy scent to officially begin the chase.

After arrivin near the suspected nest site, Wrinkles would be released from the lead and given the command "search!" (Now normally the command would be "find," but that would be only after the dog had been given a scent item which was still missin.) The dog would then begin to crisscross on his own, back and forth over the area in question; till he stumbled upon that nest he sought. It was not even necessary that the fugitive leave somethin behind at this point as the dog would give the whole nest his complete and undivided attention. He would then be put back in harness and instructed to "find" the individual in question. This nest scent would now be stored up the dog's nose and he would be well acquainted with the runner. And that was exactly what happened after McClusky simply pointed his finger off in the general direction Purdy was last seen.

As we moved along in search of the fugitive, the ground give clear evidence of boot marks in the wet soil. Lookin at the depth of the heels and toes, and examinin the length of stride (and also figurin in the man's short legs) I told my four-footed travelin companion from high up atop my horse that our man had settled on walkin, and rather slowly at that. "Why it's as simple as trailin a drunk man totin a leaky jug, ain't it Wrinkles?" I offered up. Now I know my canine friend heard what I had to say, but I also knew he was too busy followin behind his nose to have the time to offer a proper response.

Just as I suspected, the trail did not go northwest for too long a time as we found Purdy unknowingly had swung off to the northeast. Now if he had continued on that first route, he would have run directly into the Oconee River which might have escorted him all the way back home to Milledgeville, but again, by lookin at the tracks, it weren't long fore he had managed to get turned back around once more. That's what happens when the sun don't consent to shine and a person is unfamiliar with new territory.

The dog led me and the horse along, the twenty foot leather lead danglin from off to the side. Wrinkles knew enough not to get too far ahead under this particular type of trackin arrangement. I got to ponderin other things as we traveled which has often been the case in the past. I got to thinkin bout this war and wars in general. When it comes right down to it, war ain't just about the battlefields and heroic soldiers, generals and incredible victories as the books would have you believe. It's really what goes on behind those scenes, much of it bad and unnoticed. Much like a smoke screen, I come to figure.

For example, McClusky hated Purdy and would have shot him dead if he had half the chance. In peacetime that would have been considered "murder," but in wartime it would be just one more casualty to toss in. I thought on how Purdy was about to kill our Sanford down at the bridge if I had not showed up in the nick of time. No one certainly would have questioned a negro's death in the heat of battle. I wondered how many private squabbles were settled violently durin wartime with no one any the wiser. Look how the Purdy family took advantage of the conflict to benefit theirselves, or just like it was with Captain Latham and his blockade-runnin schooner *Defiant*, or that gun maker up north by the name of Samuel Colt. War sure could be a great opportunity for devilment and it all come at the expense of the poor soldiers who, with their pain and dyin, would cover others' misdeeds. Men like our friend James Rufus Kelly would offer their lives so others might enrich themselves. I know I sure will miss that boy as he was only 20 years old and had packed a heap of courage in those few short years before his ill-fated charge towards the Yankee line. (I can't imagine he survived.) Wrinkles, however, must have been thinkin on things of his own, as he suddenly brought our little party up short, endin any further thoughts I might have added to the subject. I saw the dog takin stock of the situation by puttin his long bloodhound nose well up into the air and breathin in long and deep.

Now a bloodhound will often do that. They don't generally just put their nose to the ground and follow along behind. They might do that for a spell, but they'll soon feel the need to rise up and get a good sniff of things overall. Now scent is really just small particles of skin that falls off a person, a very natural thing. Many trackin men believe it to be like a fine mist that rises up when it first leaves with the heat of the body, only to later settle to the ground as it cools. In the process if the breeze is blowin, that scent will travel and fetch high up in nearby bushes and trees. Sometime scent can better be detected by the hounds with their head up and other times, if the scent has made its way to the ground, with their head down. We have found the dog always knows best. Wrinkles nose soon dropped to the ground and with that we continued along on the heels of the Home Guard captain.

Maybe it was a half hour or so later when I noticed some changes in the hound. Wrinkles had momentarily stopped, or at least he had stopped movin forward, and showed signs of both agitation and excitement. Now that generally happens when the scent becomes fresher. His big head began to shake back and forth and he soon took to snortin, blowin out and sniffin in like he just couldn't get enough air into his nostrils. The dog's tail then began to stand and curl, a definite sign that he felt he was close to his prize. Wrinkles even took to liftin up one of his hind legs to relieve hisself, a gesture that often signaled the culmination of all his earlier efforts. Purdy was close by.

I dismounted straightaway as I knew everythin from then on needed to be done with my feet firmly planted on the ground. I threw the saddlebags over my shoulder and the dog most pulled me over as I did so, with his ever-risin excitement. The horse walked slowly behind us on his own account as the dog's head was now full in the air, never to return to the ground this day. That was a sign that the scent of the fugitive had not yet had time to settle. I could feel a slight breeze as I hurried along, but luckily it weren't from the south as we have found over the years a south wind to be the worst thing for trackin. No tracker knows the reason why, but it seems to be true even when the fugitive was upwind of the hound. I suddenly thought I saw somethin up ahead... a blur of movement like somethin or someone had taken to duckin inside a thick stand of catbriers, bushes and trees.

I believe Wrinkles may have been aware of that also, but if he was, there weren't no noticeable difference in his current rate of speed. A bloodhound ain't a fast dog to begin with, they're plodders, but will stay on a trail despite any obstacles faced. "Slow and steady will win the day," might be a good motto for these here critters as they seldom fail to eventually find the party in question.

There he was! It was Purdy, now full in our sights and dead straight ahead! As we had entered that heavily wooded area, Purdy had run out towards an open field. With his short legs and our steady pace we were soon close behind and well within jawin distance. Now I figured Lem would be actin different if he was armed, but I drew my Spiller and Burr just in case. The man ahead of us finally slowed to a walk, maybe reconciled to what he could not help. It was now clear to me that he was unarmed and had nothin in his possession that would allow him to make a successful stand. Strangely enough, Purdy never looked back at us the entire time, not even when he uttered his first words.

"Why don't you stop trackin me with your dog like I was some nappy-headed nigger, Tims," he said, lookin straight ahead and startin to blow like a tired steer.

I shot back. "There ain't no use for you to keep on walkin, Lem. The two of us are prepared to follow along till there's enough frost in hell to kill snap beans."

Purdy did not answer and continued to trudge along, maybe another fifty feet or so before finally stoppin to turn and face his pursuers for the first time. He looked to me to be one used up individual.

The dog and I halted as well, although Wrinkles had his own ideas about continuin the next few feet to officially end the chase. I held the eager manhunter tight to my side just to give Lem a little fresh air and latitude. Lem Purdy looked dirtier than was the general rule, the result of all the mud and muck that nature had recently tossed his way.

"You don't look so good, Lem. Guess bein on the run don't agree with you much," I offered.

"Now why are you on my trail, Coswell? I'm just tryin to shake them blue-bellied bastards. Why don't you try trackin one of them for a change, or maybe a darkey or two in your spare time?"

"I hate to be the one to tell you, Mr. Purdy, but you, sir, have a debt to pay. Seems like them Yankees pronounced just sentence on you and I did as well if you remember back correctly. Do you recall what I once told you would happen if I found out you was in any way responsible for Sanford's disappearance?"

"That boy was seekin to rise above his station, he was. Why, he thought he knew so much more than all the white folks he was workin for and that just weren't right," Purdy answered.

"That's why we made the deal, weren't it, Lem?... so's he could teach you fellas somethin about proper trackin? You're tellin me now that you took away his life here cause he done too good a job for ya?"

"It was him that caused all the problems. It was his damn attitude, don't you see? He was saucy and carried a chip on his black shoulder and we just couldn't tolerate such a thing."

"And my wife, Cynthia, Lem...now what about her?"

"She ain't your wife, Coswell, don't you see that? She's a nigger and niggers can't marry white folks. Now you know that full-well less you've gone back on the way you was raised up."

"What you did to the person I love most in this world will cost you dearly. It will cost you your life, in fact."

"That ain't right and you know it! The two of ya knew what you was doin was wrong. Dodgin around, keepin secrets and hidin slave papers in the fireplace. It weren't like you two was on the up and up. You was the evil ones here, not me," he shouted out. (For some reason all I could think of at this time was the insane pronouncement Benton Wells had issued some time back.)

"Turn around!" I instructed.

Lem complied. I grabbed both his hands and held em together as I reached inside the saddlebags that hung off my shoulder. I drew out the iron shackles, placin em, first one, then the other, around his thick wrists. I turned the key counter-clockwise in each, lockin both firmly in place. With my prisoner now fully secured, I dropped the key into my side trouser pocket.

"Now that you're all dressed for the occasion, let's take us a little stroll back to that thicket you just vacated," I suggested, with a gentle shove off in that direction.

As we walked back the way we come, I kept a skinned eye for a certain object I had conjured up in the back of my mind. The dog had calmed down some and the stallion quietly followed along behind me on his own account like I had sugar in my back pocket. It didn't take us long to enter that stand of trees and find just what I sought. Darn my bristles if there weren't an old log, somewhat rotted it was, but maybe six feet in length and it had come to rest on the ground right next to its former host, a large scaly bark hickory. Maybe it was a little bit thicker than necessary, but I knew it would do the job, specially seein as the bark had taken to fallin off which would make rollin all the easier.

Lem seemed to be more concerned that I was gonna set my dog on him than anythin else at this particular moment, but I assured him he had nothin to fear from that quarter. My guess was that he remembered back to his own dog, Buck, who chewed up more than his share of runaway slaves, that was, til our Sanford give the Purdy's some good business advice to put a harness on that ol boy so that fugitives could be brought back to their masters fit for work and be willin to pay the full price for any slavecatchin services provided.

Lem Purdy was so wary of Wrinkles he didn't even move a single muscle after we stopped, as that big dog just took to settin on his haunches, lookin ol Lem straight in the eye. While they was eyeball to eyeball, I set to work pushin that log from out the underbrush and rolled it onto the flat ground. "You know, Lem, these here scaly bark hickories grow straight and tall as a general rule, but take a look at this one here," I said, pointin skyward. "For some reason the lower limb has gone off in a different direction than the way I figure it was properly intended. See how low down it is…why it ain't no more than a few feet above a tall man's head, is it? Probably the reason this other piece on the ground rotted and fell off, don't you think? I do have to give this remainin limb some credit, though. Looks to be quite sturdy and I figure it could most likely still support the weight of a good-sized individual."

Lem looked somewhat befuzzled over my remarks, but continued to stare upwards as I spoke. "What you fixin to do, Coswell?" he finally asked.

"I think you know exactly what I'm gonna do, Lem," I answered.

"You're gonna hang me like some common horse thief or murderer? That just ain't right, I tells ya."

"Well, there's right and then there's wrong, ain't that a fact? But I guess the point here is that there needs to be someone in charge to sort those kind of things out and seein as though I'm the one holdin the rope, I reckon the responsible falls to me," I responded.

"That's just like you, Coswell. Always settin yourself up on top of the mountain. I've known ya my whole life and you've always been one of them highfalutin people that had all the answers, specially after you went to that school of Denison's. You always thought yourself better than everyone else and were always talkin bout your fancy ideas on this and that. Why, I grew hungry enough to give you a good percussion cap slap right across that smart-Alek face of yours, cep't your big brother was always nearby and nobody wanted to mess with him. But now here we are Coswell...alone, just you and me. Maybe you should take these cuffs off my hands and see after all this time who's really the better man."

I had to admit, Lem's last-minute ramblins here took me quite by surprise. I never did think on it that way. Why that little disclosure might just cause a thinkin man to pause some. I never considered myself uppity or arrogant, but I guess I could see how a fella like Lem might believe that to be the case. I was always proud of what education I had, but why would someone who did not have that see it the same way I did? If the two of us had that in common it might be a different story, but we didn't. Lem never had nothin much in his life to speak of, what with his old man always in the cups and his mother more than slightly daft in the head. I began to see that even if I were to offer such a man an obligin suggestion or two or help him out in some way (as I did) why would he not think I was just tryin to manage things my own way at his expense? I guess I was lost in those new thoughts for several minutes when Lem saw fit to pile on a few more for good measure.

"You know, Tims, I always figured you might just be one of them candy-ankled Nancy boys that struts about piss-proud like a peacock for all to see. A dandy who needs a proper dressin down from a real man fore he gets so full of hisself that he swells up and explodes on the spot."

Now I have to admit that last remark did get under my skin some and I finally spoke up. "O.K. Lem, have it your way. You and me is gonna tangle and the winner will take it all," I announced.

The holster that held my revolver was voluntarily unbuckled and the whole affair folded neatly and placed on the ground next to the tree trunk. I then put the twenty foot dog's lead around the base of that tree to hold the dog and just looped the horse's reigns a couple times round that leather tether. These critters could only bear witness to this contest and I wanted no interference or unfair advantage. As I walked back to Lem, I pulled the key to the iron restraints out of my trouser pocket and instructed him to turn around once again. I began to unlock the cuffs from his wrists, the right one first.

Now I am lucky to have never been the bottom dog in a fight and I've had my fair share of em over the years, too…knife fights, bare-knuckle contests, wrassles, you name it. But one thing I learned and for some reason seemed to forget on this particular day was that you need a plan, but you better not let you mind wander too far off in the process, you have to stay in the moment. A man needs to think on his feet and trust that he will react proper-like to what is happenin right then and there. Well, here I was thinkin bout his remarks and the struggle yet to come instead of what I was doin at that partic- ular moment, which was unlockin Lem's right wrist from the iron manacle. I never counted on him doin what he did, spinnin round quick-like in a circle before I got to unlock the other one, usin that metal chain in a deadly, flailin manner.

The key was still inside when that chain and iron cuff struck me hard up the side of my head just above my right ear. I could feel the blood start in tricklin from that very spot. I was more than a little swimmy-headed and it staggered me for a brief moment. He swung the damn thing around again and caught me once more, this time directly on my forehead. As I fell down to one knee, he began to reign down blow after blow and I tried puttin my arms up to offer some protection. He began to huff and puff like a chargin bull, puttin full energy into this newfound plan.

For the most part all I seemed to be doin was my share of early bleedin and any plan I might have had was well on the downgrade. I did, however, finally manage to catch hold of that swingin object and drew it in towards me and as I did, I lashed out at Purdy for the first time. It weren't much of a clout, but it did give me some time to collect myself and rise up on my feet. Steppin back to gain full footin, I was finally able to send off a smashin lick in his direction. That blow caught him square on his chin and I could feel that bony projection give way to the even harder and faster movin bones of my right hand. I quick come up with that same doubled-up fist, catchin Lem full in the breadbasket and doublin him over in the extreme. It was now his turn to step back a scratch, but sooner than expected he sent a kick my way which caught me full in the groin. I felt sick to my stomach most like it was when Mamma would puke me with ipecac. I knew I had to fight through it, but Lem compounded the agony by hittin me hard several times with his free right hand. I grabbed at him in an attempt to avoid further blows from either his right hand or that danglin contraption that still hung from his left. Grabbin him round the waist, I pushed with all my might and toppled him over backwards. Takin full advantage of the moment, I jumped on top and began to strike downward, tryin to find a way to inflict the most damage. His hands instinctively went to his face and most punches thrown glanced off and did little harm. I could hear the dog growlin and I knew Wrinkles was strainin at his lead, wantin into the fight.

With a mighty heave, Lem finally tossed me off and I could feel he was now makin his way towards the tree where my revolver lay. I grabbed at his legs, but he kicked at me several times in an effort to shake me off. The few kicks to my head hurt, but had little serious consequence. I did have to let go of those legs, however, when he began to use the metal projection on that chained manacle once more, hittin me full on the neck and head several times.

He finally managed to shake completely free and stumbled towards the tree. I knew I would soon be lookin down the business end of a .36 caliber revolver if he was successful, so I give everythin I had one last time, leapin at him and catchin him around the waist. He was a sturdy fella with strong legs and he succeeded in draggin me a short ways, but in desperation I did somethin I admit I had not completely thought out. I grabbed for the free end of the handcuff that he had freely sent my way and snapped it closed over my left wrist, twistin the key in the process. Now we was locked together forever, or for however long this contest might last. There would be no runnin away and no assistance comin from any outside agencies.

We wrassled, kicked, and skull-knuckled each other with our one free hand for more time than I can keep straight in my mind. Both of us was bleedin mightily and our clothes was ripped and covered in blood. There was kickin, scratchin and head-buttin to be sure, both of us tryin our level best to kill the other. We both knew full-well there would be only one survivor as this was clearly a fight to the death. Neither party was about to give up the ghost. We took turns tryin to strangle each other with the chain on the iron fetter, but finally it just all come down to one thing... which of us could endure the most punishment and still continue to take in a breath of air.

We both eventually dropped to our knees in exhaustion. Our left wrists remainin chained together. We continued to beat on each other mercilessly with our one free hand and would continue on with that until finally I sensed his blows were startin to weaken. As tired as I was, that give me encouragement to step up my final efforts. With as much strength as I could muster, I sent off a real sockdologer and hit Purdy square on the bridge of his nose, breakin that smeller of his in the process. Satisfied I might have struck the decisive blow, I give the man several others in the same place for good measure. Each one had a wet thumpin sound to em and I knew if they weren't death blows, they would at least signal the end the fight. My challenger fell at last, face-first to the earth. Lem Purdy had been beaten in a fair and even fight and anyone wonderin bout who the better man might be had to wonder no longer.

But any satisfaction I could take from that lessened some as I looked at the restraints that still bound us together. I was eager to free myself from my now unconscious foe. The key was still in the lock, but I found it was bent over and would not move. I tried several times but it weren't no use. I got to my feet and dragged Lem's heavy body along with me as I headed over to the horse and my canine spectator. But then an idea struck plumb through my head, maybe one of the best ones I ever owned.

I remembered back when our Captain Latham used the capstan (or windlass, as it's sometimes called) to try to remove his ship when it became stuck in the Savannah River. We rowed out an anchor with a rope attached to it and then pulled on the other end with the capstan doin much of the work. I thought I might be able to do much the same here.

I unbuckled the dog's harness from his lead and let Wrinkles loose. He jumped at Purdy, but only to give him a quick sniff before he stepped back and growled some. The horse stood quiet as I took the dog's lead and tied it to his bridle. It was now possible to lead the horse around the tree if I were to tug on it. But this job weren't over by a longshot. There were still a few important things yet to be done.

The horse continued to stand as I took the hangin rope out of the saddlebags that lay on the ground and I fashioned a knot on the other end, loopin that newly knotted end firmly over the saddle horn.

I took the Bowie knife and sheath and stuck the whole of it in my belt. I might have need of that later, I thought to myself. Now I dragged Lem back over to the spot I had selected earlier, directly under that substantial limb. With my one free hand I tossed the business end of the rope over that limb and it obliged by droppin right back down to me. I placed the end that was done up previous around Purdy's neck. With the leather lead now in my one hand, I could now encourage the horse to move away from me slowly around the tree which would then tighten the hangin rope on the saddle horn in the process. Kinda like usin the windlass on Captain Latham's ship.

Feelin pretty confident that this new plan of mine would work, I took to offerin a pronouncement of my own. "The time has come, Mr. Purdy."

I pulled ever so slightly on that leather lead, and the horse consented to move a few steps toward the tree it was looped around. With just those few steps, the hangin rope began to tighten. I encouraged the horse to continue on a little further and as he did, the rope caused the unconscious man to sit up a might straighter. It was important at this point that the horse not move too quick, I reasoned.

When I asked the black stallion to continue on a scratch, Purdy started to come to and began with his one free hand to grab at the noose he now found tightnin round his neck. I could feel the horse get a little skittish at this point as I knew he could now begin to feel the full weight of Purdy's body, but the man was soon stood up almost straight and ready to launch for the heavens. Of course I stood up with him as our left hands had gotten quite attached to one another. Usin my right foot I now pushed that log over in Lem's direction, offerin him a firm place to stand as he desperately continued to claw away at the rope. He eagerly accepted my invitation and took a grateful step forward. With both feet now firmly on the log, he had gained some relief from the ever tightenin noose and again began to work open the knot with his free hand. At this time I did feel the need to tell him in all honesty that the log he now depended on might not be the sanctuary he sought. He looked over at me with a quizzical look as I commenced to pushin that thing out from underneath him with the toe of my boot. In no time at all Lem Purdy found hisself swingin at the end of the line.

Now I will have to say there was some gaspin and sputterin to be had on Lem's part as he made an attempt to grab for my other arm in an effort to remain anchored to the ground, but the horse had inched his way forward just enough, and what with the log now a thing of the past, Purdy's feet could no longer find solid ground. Although he could not speak, his eyes did that for him. I could feel them both borin into me with a fiery, hot hate. His jaw was clenched. His teeth was grindin away first-rate. With a red face and spittle formed up in both corners of his mouth, Lemuel Purdy was defiant and still reluctant to make out any last earthly will and testament.

I could feel my chest tighten and my heart began to race more and more with the effort needed, but as my muscles tensed, I squared away my shoulders to relieve some of the stiffness and as I did, took in a deep breath of air. That cleared my head as I come to realize there was a different kind of contest bein waged here at the end, different than the physical one we had both just endured. This here was a final clash of wills, the last battle for what each of us figured to be the truth. My eyes glared back at his as a picture of my beloved wife, Cynthia, flashed through my head. Just as quick as that passed, another image, this one of a young negro man, lost and in chains, sought to replace it. I would draw strength from those I loved and those who loved me in this last conflict and they would give me what was needed to bring things to a proper close.

I took to settin my feet firmly on the ground with those thoughts in mind, determined to finish what I had started. Lem could now see there weren't an ounce of give in me and with that realization he finally looked away. I saw him glance up, in fact, examinin the tree and the rope that held him tightly in its grip. I saw his lips give way to tremblin, little beads of sweat began to form on his upper lip and forehead. I continued to hold the man's hand, but it weren't out of any Christian charity that it was done.

Lem knew he was doomed, but I had to wonder if there were other thoughts swirlin inside that head of his. Was he gettin ready to explain to his long-dead daddy how he stood tall in life for the things they both believed in, only to be unfortunately "outvoted" or over-matched in the end? Like birds, so many of us seek higher branches than others to roost upon, now, ain't that a fact? Why, imitatin his daddy would give Lem a higher purpose to live for, I come to figure. There weren't no doubt in my mind that Lem had made a promise to that old man, maybe not a fancy affair all drawn up legal-like in some lawyer's office, but a promise nonetheless. Lem lived out his life in the very spit and image of his old man and wasn't it a fact that he had been true to that promise he made him right to the very end? I began to see that maybe Lem weren't possessed of the devil or an evil man by nature, as I may have thought previous, but that his actions had more to do with a simple pledge he had forsworn so many years before. Now undertandin ain't the same thing as forgivin, but it sure does clear a little mud from the puddle after all is said and done.

Lem remained suspended from that low hangin hickory limb and began to sway back and forth, but the iron handcuff we shared did steady him up some. I could see the rope was doin its job as panic had replaced all else. His whole body began to jerk and twist. He fought the rope, but had to know it would be to no good end. His eyeballs appeared larger than before, maybe out of fear or lack of air it was, but they looked about ready to bust from his head. I watched his legs and back straighten in an effort to again gain the ground and relieve the pressure of the noose. As I looked back on all this later on, why it seemed like I watched the whole affair from a far distance. Daddy used to say "never do anythin in the daylight that might keep you awake at night," and I can honestly say that I felt I only did what was necessary that day and any stingin memories that might have crept into my pillowcase at night never come to be, not even for a single minute's time.

I could hear a low moan and a slight gurgle come from Lem Purdy's throat and then his body suddenly went completely limp. I waited for a fashion, thinkin this hangin thing had finally come to an end, but then he seemed to come back to life and started in again, shakin and twistin for all he was worth. But this time it didn't take long for that to stop completely and he went quiet once more. I figured it had to all be over this time, but I still waited, wantin to make sure the condemned man was dead and Coswell Tims' promise to hisself, to his family and to Lem had dutifully been kept.

Figurin it to at last be done with, I took that knife from my belt. (It was all part of the plan I had concocted early on when I figured I might have been in a fine fix with no way to back up the horse and me chained to a dead man with my left hand wavin in the air along with his.) I shook the knife free from its leather holder with a flick of my right hand and with a quick slice through the rope sent Purdy's lifeless body crashin to the ground, me right along with it. We both tumbled over the log and rolled to a stop. I survived the crash, but did sit there for a spell, clearin my head and contemplatin what should be done next.

I still had me a problem as Lem continued to have a pretty good hold on me and I was in desperate need of some proper separation. Now if the key had worked that problem would have been solved right quick, but that weren't the case. I tried it again and again. I come to realize what I needed to now do would not be very pleasant, but would have to be done, nonetheless.

Young James Rufus come to mind. When he was at our house recoverin from his war injury, one evenin we found ourselves engaged on the subject of amputation. James Rufus said he once overheard an army surgeon discussin the removal of a human hand that had gone well beyond savin. There was two bones, not one, that make up the human arm and them two bones come to completion before all the little bones of the hand ever begin to sprout forth, he told us. It was just a matter of findin that place where there was no bone to be sawed through and a man could slice right through the flesh without much fuss and bother.

Now, I figured I would have never done this if Lem was still livin, but it didn't seem to matter much now that he was dead and gone. I took the knife, felt around a bit and then commenced to cut where I thought it proper. The blood from the amputation mixed in with what had been spilt over the two of us durin our grand struggle must have made for a frightful sight, but it didn't take too long a time fore Lem's left hand come clean off and I held it in my own. I slid off the slimy iron cuff, not the least bit concerned bout the part that continued to cling to me as I figured I could take care of that at a later time.

As the night was fast approachin, I had a little tidyin up to do fore I exited the premises and headed back to the McClusky place. I fashioned a new noose to replace the original one I had put around Lem's neck, but had been forced to cut. I run the other end round the tree and pulled tight on it till Lem was fully perpendicular. I stuffed that hand of his inside his trouser pocket as I didn't want it to become food for some nightly critter. I figured it just weren't right for a man to go off and meet his Maker without the full complement of inventory he had originally been issued as that seemed somehow disrespectful. I tugged on the hangin rope till Lemuel Purdy once again was raised up off his feet and tied the whole affair off at the base of the tree. I wiped my blood stained hands and arms on Lem's trouser legs fore puttin my foot up in the stirrup, finally ready to take my leave.

Our little trackin party slowly exited that sorry place. My ears caught the creakin sound of the hangin rope as Lem Purdy's body had taken to swayin ever so slightly back and forth in the gentle early evenin breeze. I heard it sure as I'm alive and he ain't, but I never once felt the need to look back at the individual who had caused me and mine so much earthly pain. What I did notice was how beautiful the sun was as it began to drop lower and lower in the western sky.

DIARY OF PENIA FITZSIMONS TIMS

Massa Tims come home the other day with the news of Massa Purdy's death. All of us was glad of it and he and my Sanford spent the longest time out in the barn, sawin through some iron chains that he had managed to get hisself all tangled up in. Massa Tims never did say exactly how he done it, but it was soon reported that Lem Purdy was found dead, hangin from a tree. It was also revealed that the man had two nooses round his neck, not one, and one of his hands had been cut clean off and stuffed inside his trouser pocket. I guess the fella who found him talked to a neighbor by the name of McClusky and he said it was Coswell Tims who done it and folks would be wise to steer clear of such a man. When Sheriff Strother caught wind of it all, he said that's what happens when a man lies or steals from the Tims family. Maybe in different times there would be an investigation, but not now. Yarns began to sprout up from all over and it is now rumored that Massa Tims is lookin to hang the slave speculator, Starlin Finney, if he ever comes back this way, put three nooses round his neck and cut off both his hands and maybe even his feet as well! Now Massa Tims never said any such a thing, but maybe it's best that folks learn to keep a respectful distance from our family in these, the most troublin of times.

COSWELL TIM'S DIARY RESUMES

Cynthia awoke last night and started tuggin away at my arm. She said she had herself the most delightful dream that allowed her to see clearly into the future. She said the war was over and fully reconciled and all the slaves had been set free. She said the Tims' family had given up the trackin business and had taken to livin in town right next to a fine general store that we now owned. No more muddy boots for ol Coswell out on the trail and no more exhaustin farm chores for our family neither, she had said. "There's gonna be a new day, Coswell," were her exact words to me.

Now I do believe my wife to be in possession of some very special abilities, perhaps even some unknown to the books. She's proved that many times over and again durin our years together, but I don't know bout this one she offered up last night. I do know one thing. Coswell Tims ain't givin up his hound dogs or his firepower anytime soon. Anyone down the road who just might take a notion to step on this family of mine has to know there's more than a good chance they'll get their foot hard bit in the process. Life just ain't as neat and tidy as we'd like, or wish it to be. Now that's a downright shame to have to admit such a thing, but it's a certain-sure fact, nonetheless.

Chapter 26

PROMISE KEPT

The Bumgardners continued their legal battle with the City of Milled-geville, but it was turning out to be a long and drawn-out affair. Lawyers and town fathers were involved, a few social groups as well, but those stalwart women from the cemetery association continued to champion the slave catcher's woman's desire to be respectfully buried next to her husband in the traditionally all-white section of Memory Hill. Despite being few in number, they vowed to fight on.

On a number of occasions Barbara and Robert Bumgardner felt the need to stop by and pay their respects to Cynthia Tims at her current place of residence. Upon Mayor Chaney's insistence, the woman's remains had been forwarded from the Johnson funeral home and buried in the south side of the cemetery where the bank gently slopes downwards towards Fishin Creek, a waterway barely visible through overgrown and untended trees. But even that simple task was not free of complications as workers had stumbled upon an unmarked and highly compromised coffin in the process. Given that this was the more rundown section of an otherwise magnificent burial ground, there was no call for alarm, workers simply covered over the bones and rotted wood and found a new place nearby to inter the problematic Mrs.Tims.

So there Cynthia lay in a recently dug and yet unmarked grave, right alongside other Tims family members and many nondescript black brothers and sisters from ages past. Her sister Little Peney and husband Sanford lay close by, as did their son Jerimiah and his wife Sadie. Mollie Tims and her husband Calvin Billings (parents of Rosa) resided there as well. (It should be noted that Peney and Sanford's other son, Benjamin Hudson Tims, lived up to his famous name and died a Buffalo soldier out west, his gravesite remains a mystery.) Also missing were the bodies of Mollie Tims sister, Georgia, who married Charles Robinson in 1905 only to die in a tragic fire ten years later in Chicago where they had lived for a number of years. Cynthia certainly did have company, but her most fervent burial wish remained ungranted.

Some comfort may have come her way, however, when her 21st century visitors offered that her south-side address may only be temporary after all and a change of scenery could very well be on the horizon. How long that would take was anybody's guess, but time was certainly not an issue for Cynthia Tims. As for the Bumgardner's who stood firmly anchored to the sunny side of the grass, well, the wait seemed interminable.

"Bob, how did things go down at the 'Messenger' today?" Barbara inquired upon her husband's return home from his newspaper job.

"I guess nothing out of the ordinary, Sweetheart. I delivered copies to all the local businesses and I think Ben sent out copies to all the households. You know the drill…every two weeks it's the same old routine."

"How do you like working for Ben Joseph down there?"

"I like it fine. A fella has to do something in retirement, now doesn't he? I still like the few things I do over at the base, but this is right up my alley. Ben told me his family has lived in Milledgeville ever since the end of the Civil War and he said they were never discriminated against even though there were only a handful of other Jewish families living in the area. He's well-liked, a good businessman and people really seem to enjoy his 'Milledgeville Messenger' newspaper and look forward to it coming out every two weeks. What would they do if they couldn't get their hands on the latest social schedules or were unable to cut out the latest advertising specials? But mainly I guess I really appreciate the opportunity he gave me to write my 'History Matters' column. I think Ben just sort of understood my passion for history and I don't think you and I could possibly be in a place that ranks any higher in that regard than our new adopted home here. Now I can't say my history offerings are on a par with Dr. James Bonner or Hugh Harrington, those two gentlemen are certainly the gold standard for Milledgeville history, but I appreciate the chance he has given me to make my contribution," Bob concluded.

"Now that you're home I'll get supper started. For some reason all I did today was read," Barbara acknowledged.

"You go through a couple of books a week and most of them seem to be from the same time period as those diaries the two of us just can't seem to put down. What are you reading now?"

"I guess you're right. I took 'Uncle Tom's Cabin' out of the library yesterday and read about half of it today. I think when Lincoln met the author, Harriet Beecher Stowe; he supposedly said …"So this is the little lady that started this great big war!" Figuring that it would be quite significant to the time period, I thought it would be worth rereading," she concluded.

"Did you know that book was not a book when the public first came to read it?"

"Now, come on, Bob. How could that be?

"No, seriously, it first appeared as a serial in an abolitionist journal over a forty week period. I think the name of the periodical was 'The National Era,' or something like that. I guess the public liked it so much it was only then put into book form and it went on to outsell all books in America except the Bible. I believe it sold almost half a million copies the first year it was published, might have been in 1850 or '51, if I remember correctly."

There was a short pause in the conversation. Neither person in the room spoke a single word until Barbara Bumgardner broke the silence.

"My God, Bob! Are you thinking what I'm thinking?"

"I'm drawing a blank. What would that be?"

"What if Ben Joseph would give you permission to reprint the story of Coswell and Cynthia Tims in 'The Messenger,' one chapter at a time? That would certainly interest people as it did us and it might just increase the support we need for Cynthia's removal and reburial next to her husband."

"I can't believe I didn't think of that. I can just imagine what our old friend, Coswell Tims, might say at a time like this? 'Ain't it true that women see more things, hear more things, and think more things than any man does. Makes a fella wonder why they need men t' all.'" Bob's accent was improving with time, but he admitted he still had his fair share of work to do. "I'll tell you what, Barb... I will talk to Ben first thing in the morning and see what he says about your idea."

☙   ☙   ☙

"Mattie, Eugena and Edie loved my thoughts on the story, Bob, what did Ben Joseph have to say?" Barbara Bumgardner asked her husband as soon as he drove in the driveway and opened the car door.

"'All ahead, full,' he said. He liked both the concept and the possibilities. He had me do a quick intro to it and said Chapter One will be heading for the presses and slated for the next issue. We agreed to call it 'The Promise' because of all the promises made between various parties in the diaries, but I guess that promises us nothing. We'll just have to see how it goes after the first few chapters hit the streets."

☙   ☙   ☙

The meeting at City Hall had been called by Mayor Chaney and was certainly well attended by the cemetery ladies. Of course the "Big Four" (Eugena, Edie, Mattie and Barbara) were right there in the front row, but the mayor noted that their overall numbers had definitely increased since the last time they had met. His intentions were to get them to "call off the dogs" and come to their senses. He also was very much aware of the rising popularity of Bob Bumgardner's column in the local paper.

"Ladies, I called you here today to inform you that the city has graciously consented to provide a rather substantial marble headstone for your Mrs. Tims. We are going to have it specially done up. Now that is not something we normally would do at public expense, it's usually a family matter, but we know how involved you all have become in all this and want to be sensitive and do our part."

"If you want to be sensitive and do your part, Mrs. Tims would be cuddled up right next to Mr. Tims in the white section of the graveyard and not lying over on the south side waiting for some fancy marker to cover her head!" Eugena McBride shouted out above the din of the crowd as the others had immediately begun buzzing after the mayor's announcement.

"Ladies, ladies, please calm down. As I said to Mrs. Bumgardner and Mrs. Collins not long ago, there are certain legal considerations to be taken into account here. Why if it were up to me I'd have the woman moved in a New York minute. No sweat off my back, but you know how these legal things can be. Can we be reasonable, here?" Chaney asked with sleeves rolled up and hands outstretched in a pleading manner.

"We have a petition, Mayor, which has started to go around. We don't have many signatures yet, but we figure we soon will. When we get enough we will be back, you can be well assured," Edie Crandall felt the need to add.

"I wish you all would be more understanding of my position here. I'm sure as longtime citizens of this fair city you all know of the recent tragedy that befell us down on Jefferson Street. Our beloved Confederate Monument down there really took a hit last week when some fella smashed into it with his car going the wrong way. Instead of going around the traffic island he come flying in from Greene on the wrong side of Jefferson. Our soldier was smashed to hell, the marble base he stood on suffered equally and even the large blocks at the bottom of the statue were displaced. It's probably gonna cost all of $30,000.00 to fix the thing and that ain't chicken feed. I've got a lot on my plate right now, things that require a lot of my attention if I'm gonna serve you folks well," the mayor pleaded.

There was a low murmur this time after Chaney spoke and his message did appear to have had a dampening effect on his assembled constituents. Many of the women were lifelong members of the "United Daughters of the Confederacy" and as such held such monuments in the highest regard. After all, it had been the UDC back in 1912 that was responsible for building that monument in the first place. It was their mission at the time to "perpetuate the memory of the daring bravery of the Confederate soldiers" and even the local newspapers encouraged donations to the cause. It was supposed to have been completed for Robert E. Lee's hallowed birthday on January 19th but it was not finished until April 26th of that year. The monument had been moved once since then, but had sat on the Jefferson Street site since 1949, right across from the north gate of Georgia Military College. The sacred statue's future was obviously now in limbo.

Chaney seemed to have found something that had temporarily derailed the rising public emotions over the graveyard issue. The now subdued women began to file out of the city hall, talking quietly among themselves as they left.

Back at the Bumgardner home, the couple discussed the latest setback.

"I just know Chaney is basically a racist and doesn't want to see any change in the way the cemetery operates. He's just using that monument issue to divert attention and appeal to those southern 'lost cause' sympathies,'" Barbara announced angrily.

"No doubt about that, but those sympathies are very real as we have found since we came to live here a few years back. I don't think those sympathies are necessarily racist, however," Bob responded.

"What do you mean? Of course they are racist. The whole Civil War was over race. Just look at the evidence in the diaries on that subject. Come on, Bob...you know better than that."

"Let's be fair on this, Barb. I would be the first to offer that the Confederate government was indeed founded on the issue of continued slavery as you say. It's well known that their Vice President, Alexander Stevens, even gave that famous "cornerstone speech" where he admitted the government had been created to forever embrace the submissive role of the negro in society, but that is different than the war itself."

"How so, Bob?"

"Well for one thing...people fight wars for many different reasons. How many people in history have ever fought for the same reason as their leaders? Not many would be my guess. But ask yourself this. How many were willing to go to war nonetheless, be it out of patriotism, a personal sense of honor or duty, fear of change, fear of cowardice, maybe even holding up a family tradition? No, Barb, the people who fought for the south fought valiantly and courageously and deserve the recognition and respect of the people and place they fought for. Actually, they deserve our respect as well. This legacy has become part of their cherished heritage and you can't take that away from them. That monument down on Jefferson is part of that,

can't you see?"

"Well, isn't the Confederate flag a monument as well? People generally now see that as that as a raciest banner and is coming down on public buildings throughout the south. What about that, Bob?"

"You're right. It is a raciest banner because it symbolizes the Confederacy itself. Any banner that flies above a state capitol or a public building has to represent its people, all of them, and that flag was designed specifically to represent only a select group. That is not true, however, with monuments, tombstones, statues, or celebrating General Lee's or Stonewall's birthday. Those things are about individual sacrifice and that is a 'different bucket of possums altogether,' as our slave taker might have said. There is no reason why those things should not continue to be honored throughout the south and accepted by all Americans. The monuments in particular were so necessary to remind both sides that their sacrifices had real meaning and had not been in vain. Can you imagine all that blood and concluding it was all for nothing?" Bob Bumgardner concluded.

"I never thought of it that way. I guess maybe I just got caught up in these diaries and other things I've read on one side of the issue."

The Bumgardner's decided to contribute $5,000.00 to help with the repair of the Confederate Monument down on Jefferson Street. The interracial couple's reasons were twofold. One was in honest recognition of what it symbolized to the people who had long lived there, but also public acknowledgement of that donation might just endear them to some of the more conservative members of the community, those folks who generally wanted the cemetery to run as it always had in the past. The couple knew that the past simply needed to be outvoted and all that was really required was that all-important "tipping point" be reached. Just like a tree that starts to lean more and more with time... once it achieves that critical angle, the outcome would no longer be in doubt.

℮   ℮   ℮

"Bob, I've got some good news for you. We are printing the 12th chapter of the Cynthia and Coswell Tims story this week and folks seem to have really taken to it," Ben Joseph announced early one morning. "There have been a few responses I've received that are pretty nasty, but I would have to say overall the comments have been more than positive. Now may be the time to get that petition finished and get it on the mayor's desk."

After work that day Bob drove home encouraged by his boss's assessment. He decided to first stop by the home of Rosa Billings to pass along the good news.

"*Rosa, so nice to see you,*" *Bob Bumgardner announced with both arms fully extended. He embraced the elderly woman as one would a beloved grandmother. The latest news was well received and it was returned with an equally warm and thankful smile.*

Rosa Billings was the last of the Tims' family line, the last one standing, so to speak. She was proud of her heritage and could recite any or all of it at a drop of the hat. Despite the fact that neither Coswell nor Jesse Tims left any children of their own, the black side of the family had proved more fruitful. Sanford and Peney's son, Jerimiah did have two daughters and one of them happened to be Rosa's mother, Molly Tims Billings. Pictures of those family members, along with numerous others were constant reminders of that past and continued to adorn the otherwise plain walls of the old lady's home.

Rosa Billings was born on August 6, 1925. She was 92 years old, almost to the day, when she opened that door and heard all the latest news from Bob Bumgardner. She had been assured the petition to rebury her great aunt in the place of her choosing would soon be submitted to Mayor Chaney for official consideration. The diary of her great grandmother which had been in her possession for so many years, now looked to be the key to making this all happen. "My, how times have changed," the old black woman thought to herself.

∾ ∾ ∾

"*Now listen, ladies…I am willing to compromise on this issue. We would give the go-ahead to have Mrs. Tims buried right next to her beloved husband if you would be willing to move the two of them closer to the other Tims family members in the Tims' lot and let the Millar's have the plot they have a deed for,*" *Mayor Chaney announced at an intimate nighttime meeting in his city hall office.*

"*Well, now that the public acknowledges the marriage after all these years and have demonstrated that color no longer plays a part in Milledgeville burials, I don't see why not. What do you think girls?*" *Barbara Bumgardner asked her three cemetery associates who sat nearby. "We'll have to first get Ms. Billings' opinion on the matter, of course."*

It was basically agreed that "racial strife should end" and the proper thing be done, but it was obvious Mayor Chaney's had adopted a fallback position here. The sheer numbers the story of Coswell and Cynthia Tims had generated with the public were definitely not in his favor. It was also fairly obvious that the racial issue may have taken a back seat to the potential loss of support of a wealthy and politically connected family. The reason mattered little in the long run, as plans were soon drafted for a public ceremony where Cynthia's body would be retrieved from its south-side location and Coswell's remains and headstone would be gathered up and moved as well. Together at last, the interracial couple would be moved about eight feet in tandem to their new Memory Hill home, closer this time to the other white members of the Tims family. Problem, at long last, solved.

ɸ   ɸ   ɸ

The Johnson Funeral Home had a good relationship with the city and had often worked closely with them over the years. It was probably fair to say that Mr. Johnson handled the majority of burials with the city doing more of the maintenance and high-profile projects regarding Memory Hill. With one week to go before the Tims expected-to-be –quite-public reburial ceremony, one of Johnson's employees, a man by the name of Thurston Brown, came into his boss's office with an admission. He was afraid that when the city went to dig up the recently deposited body of Mrs.Tims, they would find where he and his partner had dug their first hole and discover what they had...the remains of a body and pieces of an old wooden casket. What with all the sensitivity surrounding the issues, he thought it best to mentioned this in advance.

Johnson was certainly glad his employee had come forward and rushed over to city hall to make an admission of his own. Mayor Chaney wanted no further problems and decided it best to contact Atlanta in an effort to retain the services of the professional archaeologist as had been done earlier. In an effort to be politically transparent on the issue, Rosa Billings and the Bumgardners were also informed.

ɸ   ɸ   ɸ

The small group of people huddled together on the south slope of Memory Hill two days later went relatively unnoticed by the majority of city residents. In the early morning mist city crews had begun to exhume the casket of the nomadic Mrs.Tims. Mayor Chaney, Arthur Johnson (from the funeral home), along with Bob and Barbara Bumgardner and also Rosa Billings, stood silently as the new coffin the city had earlier supplied was lifted from the ground and placed in the back of the same white truck that had transported her there just months before. A state archaeologist also *joined the group and slowly sipped her Starbucks coffee as she stood by, ready to jump in when asked. They all waited patiently as the city workers began to open up the new area of concern, a spot right next to an empty hole where Cynthia Tims had recently been laid to rest, only to then be removed once more.*

With trowel in hand and the coffee cup placed next to her small sifter, the archaeologist from Atlanta soon began work. In no time small shards of wood and bone began to make their appearance and as they did, all were carefully placed in a substantial cardboard box for later review.

Time seemed to pass slowly as the woman methodically went about her business. Most likely all parties involved would have loved to have jumped in to speed up the process. Numerous bones continued to be discovered, some larger than others, many highly compromised. "Definitely a man, and most likely a man of some physical stature," the female archaeologist did eventually announce.

With that last remark she continued to slowly shave away the dirt with the edge of her trowel when something caught her eye. It was a thin piece of what appeared to be human bone with an artificial, man-made hoop encircling it. Without separating the two, the archaeologist placed both carefully in the box.

"Excuse me, Ma'am," interrupted Barbara Bumgardner. "I'd like to have a little look at what you just found if you don't mind."

It was obviously a ring and after Mrs. Bumgardner removed the piece of finger bone from its center and wiped away some of the surface mud, all bore witness to the fact that a gold wedding band had been discovered. As with all gold artifacts, it remained basically free from any major decomposition or discoloration. Except for a little surface dirt, it probably looked no different than it did the day this unknown individual was laid to rest.

All crowded in as the object was freed from any and all last traces of muddy red clay, but Barbara continued to wipe it clean with her fingers. Suddenly she engaged the female archaeologist who was intently probing for new information... "Wait a second. Could I borrow that magnifying glass?"

Tilting the ring slightly and holding it up to the still diminished light of the new day, Barbara Bumgardner was able to finally read the inscription etched inside. "FOREVER," it stated boldly.

A collective gasp arose from the bystanders, followed by incredulous stares. Rosa Billing's old legs suddenly went limp and she began to topple forward. Luckily, Bob was standing at her side and caught the elderly lady just in time. Rosa quickly regained both her footing and her composure and managed a lusty announcement worthy of a much younger woman. "My God," she said, as she grabbed even more tightly on to Bob Bumgardner's right arm. "It's Coswell... it's ol' Coswell Tims sure as I'm born!"

"What the hell is going on here?" John Chaney proclaimed in an even louder voice. "This can't be Tims. That man's over on the other side of the graveyard. Says so right on his damn tombstone. We'll find out what's going on here." The mayor took out his cell phone and called the city garage. "Send that small backhoe over to the Tims' gravesite near the entrance to Memory Hill. I want it there PDQ."

As the archaeologist went back to work, the remainder of the group began their exit, boarding the city truck for a quick jaunt across the 40 acre graveyard. Mrs. Bumgardner and Ms. Billings would ride upfront with the city worker, with the remainder of the group fending for themselves up in the truck bed alongside the casket of Cynthia Tims. But before the driver had a chance to hit second gear, Barbara suddenly had them stop the truck so she could get out and rush back to the gravesite. Reaching inside the cardboard box, she fumbled around some in an attempt to locate that original piece of bone and when she did, she placed it carefully back inside the golden band. "It only seems right," was all she said to the somewhat surprised archaeologist as she quickly turned and ran back to the vehicle.

It took maybe a half hour for the backhoe to arrive, but in the meantime numerous explanations as to what must have happened were discussed. The ring must have been misplaced, Mr. Johnson insisted. The KKK had done something nefarious; maybe brother, Jesse, had a hand in this. All had an opinion, but no one really had a good explanation. But the latest project the mayor had ordered did begin without one. First the removal of the Coswell Tims headstone and then the digging up of his grave. Expertly the backhoe came up just short of any possible human remains, and the two city workers jumped into the pit with their shovels to finish the more delicate part of the job.

"It isn't like we wouldn't have had to do this for the ceremony anyway," Chaney could be heard saying in a barely audible whisper.

"If this is Coswell Tims, we'll see if he has his ring with him won't we?" Barbara asked no one in particular.

All heard the same sound at the same time. It was the sound a shovel makes when it strikes something solid instead of passing effortlessly through the soft ground. They had come upon a not unexpected grave box from the 19th century. It was in poor shape, but certainly recognizable as a coffin (way too fragile to exhume, however). The lid had actually fallen into the casket itself. One of the workers carefully lifted that lid up as the onlookers leaned in, all expecting human bones to lie beneath. Instead, it was unoccupied and only piles of red clay and what remained of old cloth bags greeted their eyes.

The mayor's face turned an indescribable shade of red as he turned his head to the side and tugged at his collar. Earlier news had begun to cast speculation that Tims may, in fact, have been buried elsewhere and now this confirmed that he had never been buried where people believed him to lie. It was all very confusing. Vowing to get to the bottom of the mystery, the mayor strongly suggested that everyone follow him back to the truck.

"Get that damn casket opened," Mayor Chaney barked, as both workers jumped off the back of the vehicle and put out their cigarettes. They pulled the casket from the truck bed, placing it not so gently on the ground. One of them hastily opened the lid.

Barbara tried to hold her rising anger in check when she realized the casket the city had provided for the upcoming internment of Cynthia Tims was not what she had been led to believe. It wasn't wooden as the mayor had previously boasted, but a cheap metal one that would soon rust and leak (the kind generally provided for paupers and indigents.) As it now lay open on the ground, the inside of the casket was even more insulting. Numerous pieces of wood lay scattered along with a plastic container, the kind normally used to bury pets. That housed Cynthia's remains and other important grave goods, including any jewelry that might have been found on site. Mayor Chaney opened the plastic box and immediately grabbed at the ring that easily stood out from a jumble of human bones. It was a gold wedding band just as the archaeologists had initially reported when Ray Richard's early GPR discoveries were the talk of the town.

"Now didn't that diary say both of the Tims people had rings with "FOREVER" engraved on them?" the mayor queried.

Rosa offered an emphatic response. "It most surely did, Mayor!"

"Read the inscription," Barbara Bumgardner encouraged, as the mayor fumbled somewhat in an attempt to grip the small object in his rather large and increasingly nervous hands.

Mayer John Chaney finally brought the ring up to the light as best he could and looked inside. He took out his reading glasses and gave it another try. "Maybe your eyes are better than mine, but I don't see any inscription on it at all." Bob Bumgardner was the next to examine it.

"This woman is not Cynthia Tims!" Bob announced forcefully.

"You have got to be shitting me!" the mayor blurted out in complete frustration.

Barbara Bumgardner tried to take some of the tension out of the moment by offering her thoughts on the matter. "We all know what the journal had to say about this. It has been examined over and over. Rosa knew it and passed it along to us. Mayor, you and your lawyers know it, and, for crying out loud, most of the town knows it now through the diaries we had published in the paper. To refresh our collective memories it said: 'We buried my sister Cynthia today in Memory Hill. A sad day for us, but we made sure her fondest wish was honored. May they both now rest in peace.' Right? So here's my question. If that's really Coswell Tims over in the black section of the graveyard with his FOREVER ring still clinging to his boney finger, where do you suppose that wife of his might be if the journal is to be believed?"

Nobody said a word. Nobody had to. All realized it was obvious the slave catcher's woman was most likely lying right next to her dead husband ("touching if possible," as was stated in the journal). Had the two of them been together all along? A return trip in the truck back across the graveyard hardly seemed necessary, but Cynthia's soon-to-be discovered remains and her "FOREVER" ring found right there on the third finger of her left hand did finally put to rest any and all suspicions. What a day this had been.

❧   ❧   ❧

The Bumgardner's were exhausted and with wine glasses in hand, sat quietly in the semi-darkness of their living room.

"I just can't believe all this," Barbara announced.

"It does make sense when you think about it," her husband responded. "Coswell was the kind of guy who could get things done. He was a good tracking man and wasn't bad at covering up his own trail either. He loved that woman and she loved him. There was never any doubt about that. He knew Cynthia would always have problems being admitted into the white section of the grounds and he was more than willing to sacrifice his loftier view and go wherever the two of them had the best chance to remain together. 'Society be damned,' he must have thought."

"Yes sir, it was the family that must have readied the coffin for the official funeral in the white section," Barbara added. "The pallbearers would have never known the difference with those cloth bags filled with red Georgia clay. Coswell's family must have kept the body hid somewhere during the service and later that night I'll bet rowed up Fishin Creek and snuck it into the black section. More than likely just marked it with a simple rock as that was all that would have been necessary at the time. The family knew the person who lay under that marker and that's where they would bury wife

Cynthia when she died just like it said in the diary. Why those two were together all along, minding their own business and we never had to lift a finger or do a single thing other than to appreciate their story, now did we?"

And what a great story it was, they readily admitted.

ॐ   ॐ   ॐ

As tired as they both were, the couple suddenly felt there was still one last thing that needed to be done. Grabbing a flashlight, a couple of glasses and their just opened bottle of wine, the Bumgardners walked purposely out the front door. Jumping into the car, they would soon arrive at their destination on the south side of Memory Hill, a place where the bank gently slopes down towards Fishin Creek. When they did, they vowed to offer up a friendly toast to an interracial couple from the distant past, a couple in many ways so much like themselves. Their glasses would be raised up high in the moonlight and a simple toast would break the stillness of the hallowed burial ground.

"To love, love for good and always," Bob Bumgardner would ardently announce that night. The couple below would register their approval, adding a long and reverent silence to the already festive occasion.

SLAVETAKER NOTES

The "N" word is certainly an abhorrent reminder of our nation's past. Using this word in this book was discomforting for me personally, but to not have used it would have been even more repugnant. For any historian to ignore uncomfortable pieces of history for personal reasons would be unforgiveable, as that could very well deny a reader a chance to accurately assess the time period in question. Yes, the word was vulgar and it was rough. It was powerful and it was "fully loaded" and meant to insult and discredit. That still remains true today.

It might be interesting to note that the word was seldom used by those in possession of slaves as they generally chose to use the less objectionable term "servant" when referring to their human property. But misbehavior or "uppidiness" could change things in a hurry and the "N" word could promptly be summoned and effected in such a way as to quickly put someone back in their "proper place." Poor whites were especially prone to its use as constant reminders of their superior standing in the social pecking order seemed to often be thought necessary. "Why, if'n I ain't no better than a "n..." well, then what am I...nothin'?" was not an uncommon refrain. I was amazed in my research to discover the depths some would go in an attempt to foster and maintain that illusion. Support for a very destructive national civil war that took its greatest toll on that particular group might be one very good example.

Now a "slavetaker" is one who catches and returns slaves attempting to flee legal bondage. Again, for the sake of historic honesty, we need to be reminded that slavery was a legally sanctioned institution throughout much of America's past. That particular word was a popular slang term for a southern slave catcher who basically operated in bounty-hunter fashion. The main character in this book, Coswell Tims, was such a man. To judge him by the standards of today would be a mistake.

The feedback I received in the wake of the original *Slave Catcher's Woman*, gave me encouragement that such an individual might effectively act as a mouthpiece, accurately describing the "peculiar institution" as it existed around the time of the Civil War. I believed then, as I do now, that a man on the ground, a man actively involved at the contact level of the institution, a man with first-hand knowledge, would be a far better spokesperson than any other. Armed with that conviction, I set out to continue writing the saga of slavetaker, Coswell Elias Tims.

I must confess that writing a sequel was not as easy as I had first imagined. To simply pick up where the other left off and continue the story through the Civil War was simplistic to say the least. This new story had to stand alone. Old characters had to be redeveloped and new ones introduced. Enough background had to be dredged up from the past without retelling all that transpired in the first book. I knew that some readers would have read the first, but some would be meeting Coswell and Cynthia Tims for the first time. Both types of readers needed to be treated with respect and consideration. I knew there was a delicate balancing act to be performed here as I began to write this book.

I was hopeful the addition of another diary, that of a black woman, would add fresh perspective to issues discussed. It was also my hope that a modern side story might expand the readers' understanding of this historic tale by referencing a more familiar time.

My goal in this book, as it was with *The Slave Catcher's Woman*, was to present an honest and balanced accounting of what transpired during this contentious time in America's past. Hopefully Coswell Tims, his family and his friends, along with their beloved bloodhounds, will do their part and lead readers down that intended path.

ACKNOWLEDGMENTS

I am indebted to a number of people for bringing *"Slave-taker: The Promise"* into the light of day. My good friend down in Georgia, historian and writer, Hugh T. Harrington, stood by my side throughout. His guidance and insight in making this all possible is incalculable. Husky Trail Press publisher, Richard LaPorta, again took a dusty manuscript and polished it for public consumption. The incredibly talented, Stephen Marks-Hamilton, did a fabulous job with the illustrations. Great thanks to the artistry of Gabriella Geida for the outstanding cover of the book as she was able to perfectly capture both the characters and the theme of the story with her riveting image. I have Marcus M. Worthington to thank for the final editing. I am deeply saddened by his sudden passing. I know he would have loved to have seen this work in its finished form.

Early readers...Anne McCarthy-Coleman, Kathy Magarian, and Dr. Alan Scott, along with Hugh Harrington were a great help with that part of the process. My wife Georgia Lee ("my Cynthia") continued to provide inspiration. Thanks also to the many people, as well as book clubs, who have shared their hopes with me that they might hear more about the life and times of Coswell Tims. That was certainly a great motivator.

I am indebted to the voice of Bill Arp (Charles Henry Smith) and Sut Lovingood (George Washington Harris) for much of the southern syntax and expressions. Also Georgian, Joel Chandler Harris, offered insight into the Negro dialect of the time.

My library continued to grow as research required. Hugh T. Harrington's *"Civil War Milledgeville"* and *"Remembering Milledgeville"* were a big help. Numerous anecdotes, references and characters used in this book were made possible from the earlier efforts of this fine historian.

The slave narratives of William Wells Brown, Solomon Northup and Georgia slave, John Brown, proved most helpful, as did those of Rose Williams, Robert Shepard, Harriett Robinson, Silas Jackson and Delia Garlic. Information gleaned from those kinds of primary documents is an absolute must if any written work on the subject (historical fiction included) is to have credibility.

The following books provided insight into specific parts of the story. *"But For the Grace of God: The Inside Story of the World's Largest Insane Asylum,"* by Dr. Peter Cranford allowed me to look inside the Milledgeville Lunatic Asylum. Authored by Brian Craig Miller, *"Empty Sleeves: Amputations in the Civil War South,"* gave me some perspective on Civil War amputations and their effects on soldiers and society. Daina Ramey Berry's book *"The Price for Their Pound of Flesh,"* was a real eye-opener with her discovery of slaves' bodies being sold and used for medical dissection. *"Touched By War: Battles Fought in the Lafourche District,"* by Christopher G. Pena gave me an inside look into the area where Sanford would be enslaved.

Lee Kennett's *"Marching Through Georgia: The Story of Soldiers and Civilians During Sherman's Campaign,"* Mark H. Dunkelman's *"Marching With Sherman"* and James C. Bonner's *"Milledgeville: Georgia's Antebellum Capital"* were helpful in allowing me to understand local reaction to the war. *"Desertion During the Civil War,"* by Ella Lonn, brought a new understanding to the magnitude of that issue that I had been unaware of before. *"The Fall of the House of Dixie,"* by Bruce Lavine and *"On the Threshold of Freedom: Masters sand Slaves in Civil War Georgia,"* offered some interesting, but more general information on the dynamics of the time.

I would again like to thank Hugh T. Harrington, along with his wife, Dr. Susan J. Harrington, for giving me a chance to actually walk on Georgia soil. They made it possible for me to stroll the hallowed grounds of Memory Hill, visit plantations and slave quarters, see the asylum up close and personal and visit other places I would later mention in the story. Those first-hand experiences were incredibly powerful. Kneeling at the grave of James Rufus Kelly was a special honor I will never forget. His wartime heroics aside, Mr. Kelly's fifty-one year tenure as a public school teacher in the aftermath of that conflict had great personal meaning for me. If I have any regrets at all it might be that I fell just short of that goal with only forty-eight years of public school service to my credit. My hat is off to Mr. Kelly.

ABOUT THE AUTHOR

Author, Jim Littlefield, was a popular history teacher in his hometown for almost 50 years, but perhaps a more notable commitment was his long-standing relationship with his early childhood sweetheart, Georgia Lee. "I guess it was love at first sight when I spotted her on the school bus back when she was in second grade. She was beautiful and exotic looking. Did she come from some south sea island, I wondered at the time?" At the tender ages of twenty and eighteen, the two would eventually marry in 1965.

Their marriage of fifty-three years has produced two successful children, Maria Elena and Kevin James, along with two loving grandchildren, Jamie Louise and Daniel Littlefield. All have remained close throughout the years. "There is nothing easy about being married young and trying to grow up with another person while you're growing up yourself," both parties agreed. There are many reasons people part ways in a marriage and sometimes all that stands in the way of that happening is honoring a simple pledge both parties once made.

History proved to be a steadying influence in the couple's lives. Jim followed his wife into Civil War re-enacting and also into the care and activities of the local town historical museum where they volunteered almost two decades of their time. The couple's historic image would inspire the design of the cover. The couple would eventually commit to restoring two pre-Civil War homes of their own and Jim would work in the blacksmith shops he built on the premises. Jim belongs to the Connecticut Blacksmithing Guild.

With retirement from teaching the author would begin to write a monthly history column in a local magazine and write two earlier books. *History Matters: Tales of New England that Still Echo Today* would be a compendium of twenty years of archaeological research undertaken while he taught high school anthropology. The other was his first novel, *The Slave Catcher's Woman*. The woman in the book, Cynthia, was beautiful and exotic looking and slave catcher, Coswell Tims, reported that he never forgot seeing her for the first time down in New Orleans walking back and forth on the upper deck of an old steamboat. He could not know at the time that this beautiful woman was enslaved, or that she would soon flee bondage and he would be hired to track her down. Eventually meeting face to face, they would begin to overcome their many differences and together escape to Milledgeville, Georgia where they would attempt to live legally as man and wife. *Slavetaker: The Promise* continues that story through the chaos of the American Civil War.

Jim & Georgia Lee Littlefield

BOOKS BY JAMES N. LITTLEFIELD

The Slave Catcher's Woman
A tale of love, intrigue, death and awakening in the Antebellum South

Georgian bounty hunter Coswell Tims lives with his wife Cynthia and a kennel of well-trained and trusty bloodhounds. A lawman of sorts, he makes an honest, respectable living tracking fugitives. Returning home one day after a chase, he finds his home ransacked, his dogs killed, his loyal house servant brutally beaten and his woman, the true love of his life, is missing—abducted, taken, kidnapped. Coswell must now employ all his skills and experience to track down the perpetrator and rescue Cynthia.

Expertly researched and vividly written this historical novel (with its memorable cast of characters, intriguing twists and turns, and unencumbered portrayals of life during the pre-civil war south) invites the reader to venture upon an unforgettable, enlightening journey into one of the most controversial periods of our history.

History Matters
Tales Of New England That Still Echo Today

Anyone who believes high school students incapable of making a significant contribution to history has not read this book. Exchanging the classroom for a calibrated hole in the ground and textbooks for trowels, students begin a slow and meticulous descent into the past. Share with us a remarkable archaeological journey back in time, with special thanks given to the old timers, who left tantalizing clues behind for later generations to piece together their stories.

The author is available for organizational and school presentations and may also be contacted at his website:

www.JimLittlefield.com

Comments regarding the book are most welcome.